PRA...

CITY OF LIGHT

"A fast-paced blend of fantasy and science fiction that will knock your socks off! Plan to stay up all night."
—*New York Times* bestselling author Faith Hunter

"An intriguing world and a marvelous heroine who speaks to ghosts. . . . Fans of Nalini Singh's Psy-Changeling series will enjoy the similar mix of SF and fantasy."   —*Library Journal*

"Exciting and well-written . . . a remarkable mix of intrigue and action punctuated with sizzling melt-your-mind love scenes. . . . I am waiting on pins and needles for the sequel."
—The Speculative Herald

"Bursting with action, suspense, and the supernatural. If you're looking for a kick-ass heroine with a big heart to match, look no further than Tiger. I suspect big things for her character."   —Under the Covers Book Blog

"Plenty of suspense; a large, fascinating cast of paranormal and genetically engineered characters; and a ruthless but loyal heroine at its heart."   —*RT Book Reviews*

PRAISE FOR KERI ARTHUR

Winner of the *Romantic Times* 2008
Reviewers' Choice Award for Career
Achievement in Urban Fantasy

"Keri Arthur has blown me away again. Her worlds are so complex and 'real.' . . . I highly recommend Arthur's books."
—*USA Today*

continued . . .

WINTER HALO

AN OUTCAST NOVEL

KERI ARTHUR

SIGNET SELECT
New York

SIGNET SELECT
Published by Berkley
An imprint of Penguin Random House LLC
375 Hudson Street, New York, New York 10014

Copyright © 2016 by Keri Arthur
Penguin Random House supports copyright. Copyright fuels creativity, encourages
diverse voices, promotes free speech, and creates a vibrant culture. Thank you for buying
an authorized edition of this book and for complying with copyright laws by not
reproducing, scanning, or distributing any part of it in any form without permission.
You are supporting writers and allowing Penguin Random House to continue to
publish books for every reader.

Signet Select and the Signet Select colophon are trademarks of
Penguin Random House LLC.

ISBN 9780451473516

First Edition: December 2016

Printed in the United States of America
1   3   5   7   9   10   8   6   4   2

Cover art by Tony Mauro

I'd like to once again thank my awesome editor,
Danielle Perez,
for all her work on this novel.
Here's hoping we get to work on many more together.

I'd also like to thank Tony Mauro for the cover art,
and for brilliantly capturing the image I had of Tiger.

And finally, many thanks to agent extraordinaire Miriam;
my crit buddies and best mates—
Robyn, Mel, Chris, Carolyn, and Freya;
and finally, but by no means lastly,
my lovely daughter, Kasey.

Thanks for being there for me, ladies.

CHAPTER 1

There were ghosts in this place.

Most kept their distance, simply watching as I made my way through the broken remnants of their tombstones. One or two of the braver ones brushed my arms with ethereal fingers—a caress that reached past the layers of jacket and shirt to chill my skin. But these ghosts meant me no harm. It was simple curiosity, or maybe even an attempt to feel again the heat and life that had once been theirs. And while I knew from experience that ghosts *could* be dangerous, I was not here to disturb or challenge the dead.

I simply was here to follow—and maybe even kill—the living.

Because the person I was tracking had come from the ruined city of Carleen that lay behind us. It was the very last city destroyed in a war that might have lasted only five years but had altered the very fabric of our world forever. One hundred and three years had passed since the war's end, but Carleen had never been rebuilt. No one lived there. No one dared.

Given that the figure *had* come from that city, it could only mean one of two things: Either he or she was a human or shifter up to no good, or it was one of the two people responsible for kidnapping fourteen children from Central City—the only major city in this region. No one else had any reason to be out here, in the middle of nowhere, at night. Especially when the night was friend to no one but the vampires.

Of course, vampires weren't the only evil to roam the night or the shadows these days. The bombs the shifters had unleashed to end the war against humans had resulted in the rifts—bands of energy and magic that roamed the landscape and mauled the essence of anything and anyone unlucky enough to be caught in their path. But that was not the worst of it, because many rifts were also doorways into this world from another time or dimension. Maybe even from hell itself. And the creatures that came through them—which were collectively called the Others but had been nicknamed demons, wraiths, or death spirits, depending on their form—had all found a new and easy hunting ground.

These rifts were the reason Carleen had never been rebuilt. There were a dozen of them drifting through the city's ruins, and there was no way of predicting their movements. Neither wind nor gravitational pull had any influence on them, and they could just as easily move against a gale-force wind as they could leap upward to consume whatever might be taking flight that day—be it birds, aircraft, or even clouds. Once upon a time I'd believed that being caught in a rift meant death, but I now knew otherwise.

Because the people responsible for kidnapping those children were living proof that rifts were survivable—although by calling them "people" I was granting them a humanity they did not deserve. Anyone who could experiment on young children for any reason was nothing short of a monster. That anyone was doing so in an effort to discover a means by which vampires could become immune to light just made them more abominable.

But it wasn't as if they could actually claim humanity in the first place. I might be a déchet—a lab-designed humanoid created by humans, before the war had begun, as a means to combat the superior strength and speed of the shifters— but every bit of my DNA was of *this* world.

The same could not be said of those responsible for the missing children.

I'd managed to rescue five of the children but I had no idea how they were or if they'd recovered from the horrific injuries inflicted on them. Those who could tell me were no longer my allies; they'd tried to kill me. Twice. They were not getting a third chance.

I continued to slip quietly through the night, following the teasing drift of footsteps. Whoever—whatever—was up ahead certainly wasn't adept at walking quietly. Which suggested it wasn't a vampire, or even a shifter. The former rarely traveled alone, despite the fact that they had very little to fear at night, and the latter were night-blind. Or so Nuri— who was one of my former allies, and a powerful human witch—had said.

I tended to believe her—at least on that point. Even before the war, both shifters and humans had lived in either cities or campsites that were lit by powerful light towers twenty-four/seven. Vampires had always been a problem— the war had just kept them well fed and increased their numbers. It made sense that after generations of living in never-ending daylight, the need for night sight would be filtered out of the DNA of all but a few throwbacks.

No, it was Nuri's promise that no harm would befall the ghosts living in the old military bunker—one of the three in which they'd all been created, trained, and killed more than one hundred years ago—if I helped her group find the remaining children that I wasn't so sure about. While she might not hold any prejudices against déchet, the others were all shifters and, from what they'd said, had all lost kin to déchet soldiers during the war.

While I wasn't by design a soldier, I could fight, and I'd certainly been responsible for more than a few shifter deaths. Only my kills hadn't happened in open fields or battered forests, but rather in the bedroom. I was a lure—a déchet specifically created to infiltrate shifter camps and seduce those in charge. Once I was firmly established in their beds, it had been my duty to gain and pass on all information relating to the war and their plans. And then, when my task was completed, I killed.

I'd been a very successful lure.

And I still was, I thought bleakly. Images of Sal—and the brutal way I'd killed him—rose, but I pushed them away. Sal might have been the only friend and confidant I'd really had during the war, but he'd also been part of the group responsible for kidnapping the children. And when I'd realized that, I'd had little choice but to take action. There were many things in this world I could ignore—many things I had no desire to be a part of—but I could not idly stand by and watch children suffer. Not again. Not if I could help it.

It was thanks to Sal—to the information I'd forced out of him before he died—that those five kids were now free. Six, if you included Penny, the child I'd rescued from the vampires who'd been tracking her in the park beyond the military bunker in which I still lived.

But that meant they still held eight. And while I had no

intention of helping Nuri and her crew, I also had no intention of abandoning those children to their fates.

Which was why I'd been in Carleen tonight.

Sal and his two partners had created what the ghosts there called "false rifts": balls of dirty energy that resembled regular rifts but were—as far as I could tell—nothing more than a means of quick transport from one location to another. I'd gone there tonight to investigate one of them. Cat and Bear—the two little ghosts who normally accompanied me on such journeys—were back home in our bunker. We'd learned the hard way that ghosts could not enter the rifts, and I wasn't about to place them in any sort of danger if I could avoid it. They might be déchet, or they might be ghosts, but they were also only children.

The graveyard gave way to a long slope that was filled with rock debris and the broken, decaying remnants of trees. Halfway down the hill lay a gigantic crater, its rim strewn with rocks, building rubble, and twisted, sick-looking plants. Weirdly, even though I was standing above it, I couldn't see into the crater itself. I frowned, my gaze narrowing. It might be the middle of the night, but the vampire DNA in my body had gifted me with—among other things—a vampire's ability to see as clearly in darkness as I could during the day. But the shadows that clustered just below the crater's rim were thick and impenetrable and emitted an energy that was dark and dirty.

Rift, an inner voice whispered, even as my skin crawled at the thought of getting any closer.

But the figure I was tracking had disappeared, and there was no place he or she could have gone other than the crater. If I wanted to uncover whether that person was one of my targets, then I had to keep following.

I started down the hill. Small stones and fragmented

metal scooted out from underfoot with every step, the latter chiming softly as the pieces hit the larger rocks in my path. The graveyard ghosts danced lightly to the tune, seemingly unconcerned about either leaving the tombs or approaching the rift. Which in itself suggested that whatever that darkness was, it wasn't dangerous. Either that or it was one of the few stationary rifts and, as such, posed no immediate threat to either them or me.

I wished I could talk to them. Maybe they could have told me whether my target came here regularly, or even who he or she might be. But these ghosts, like those in Carleen, were human, and that meant I couldn't converse with them, as I could with shifter or déchet ghosts. Not without help, anyway. The scientists who'd designed us had made damn sure those destined to become lures could not use their seeker skills to read either their thoughts or their emotions. They might have created us to be their frontline soldiers against the shifters, but they'd also feared us. Mind reading wasn't the only restriction placed on us when it came to humans— killing them was also out-of-bounds. Not that I'd ever tested *that* particular restriction—it had never occurred to me to do so during the war, and there'd been no need in the 103 years after it.

Energy began to burn across my skin as I drew closer to the crater. The ghosts finally hesitated, then retreated. Part of me wished I could do the same.

I stopped at the crater's rim and stared down into it. The darkness was thick, almost gelatinous, and lapped at the tips of my boots in gentle waves. It was unlike anything I'd ever come across before. Even the shadows that had covered the other false rifts had not felt this foul, this . . . alien.

This wasn't magic. Or, if it was, it wasn't the sort of magic that had originated from *this* world. It just didn't have the right feel. So did that mean it had come from the Others? From wherever *they'd* come from?

Were they even capable of magic?

I really had no idea. I doubted there was anyone alive who *did* know, simply because anyone who'd ever come across one of them didn't live to tell the tale.

Except, I thought with a chill, Sal and his partners. They'd not only survived, but—thanks to the rift that had hit them just as a wraith was emerging—Sal's partners now had its DNA running through their bodies.

I stared down at my boots, at the oily, glistening substance that stained the tips of them. Revulsion stirred, and the urge to retreat hit so strongly I actually took a step back. But that wouldn't give me the answers I needed. Wouldn't help find the missing children.

And it was *that* desire, more than anything, that got me moving in the *right* direction. One step; two. No stones slid from under my feet this time. Or, if they did, they made no sound. It was still and hushed in this small part of the world—almost as if the night held its breath in expectation. Or horror.

The darkness slid over my feet and ankles, and oddly felt like water. Thick, foul water that was colder than ice. It pressed my combat pants against my skin as it rose up my legs, and the weapons clipped to my thighs gained an odd, frosty sheen. I crossed mental fingers and hoped like hell this stuff didn't damage them. I didn't want to face whatever—whoever—might be waiting at the bottom of this crater without any means of protection.

The farther I moved down the slope—the deeper I got into the darkness—the harder every step became. Sweat trickled down my spine, but its cause wasn't just the effort of moving forward. This stuff, whatever it was, scared me.

I reached back and pulled free one of the two slender machine rifles that were strapped to my back. I'd adapted them ages ago to fire small wooden stakes rather than bullets, simply because wood was deadlier than metal when it came to vampires—at least for shots to the body, which were generally easier. Stakes would poison them if they didn't immediately kill; metal would not. But you had to *hit* them first for either weapon to cause any sort of damage, and that wasn't always easy, given their shadowing ability.

Of course, there was a very big chance none of my weapons would work after this muck touched them, but I still felt better with the rifle's weight in my hand.

The darkness washed up my stomach, over my breasts, then up to my neck. I raised my face in an effort to avoid becoming fully immersed for as long as possible. Which was stupid. It was *just* darkness, not water, no matter how much it felt otherwise. I wouldn't drown in this stuff.

But could I breathe?

I took one final, deep breath, just in case, and then pushed on. The ink washed up my face and then over my head, and it suddenly felt like there was a ton of weight pressing down on me. Every step became an extreme effort; all too soon my leg muscles were quivering and it took every ounce of determination I had to keep upright, to keep moving.

I pressed on, but I really had no idea if I was heading in the right direction. Not only did the darkness envelop me, but it also stole all sense of time and direction. God, what if this was a trap? What if all along they'd intended nothing more than to lure me down here to get rid of me? Sal's partners *had* to be aware of his death by now, just as they had to be aware that I was the one who'd found and rescued the five kids—after all, those kids had been nothing more than bait in an attempt to trap and kill me. That it hadn't gone exactly as they'd hoped was due to good luck on my part rather than bad planning on their part. Or, rather, good luck and a whole lot of help from the adult déchet who haunted my bunker.

And while Sal's partners might have no idea what I truly looked like—and therefore couldn't stop me from entering their businesses in Central, or hunt me down—they were well aware that I lived in the old underground military bunker outside that city. And they'd undoubtedly realized I would not abandon the rest of those children.

I *had* been expecting some sort of retaliatory attack, but against our bunker rather than out here in the middle of nowhere.

If this *was* a trap, then it was one I'd very stupidly walked right into. But there was nothing I could do about that now. I just had to keep moving.

But the deeper I got, the more crushing the weight of the darkness became. My legs were beginning to bow under the pressure, my spine ached, and my shoulders were hunched forward. It felt as if I could topple over at any minute, and it took every ounce of concentration and strength to remain upright. May the goddess Rhea help me if I met anything coming up out of the crater, because I doubted I'd even have the energy to pull the rifle's trigger.

Then, with little warning, the weight lifted and I was catapulted into fresh air and the regular night. I took a deep, shuddering breath and became aware of something else. Or rather, some*one* else.

Because I was no longer alone.

I slowly turned around. At the very bottom of the crater, maybe a dozen or so yards away from where I stood, there was a rift. A real rift, not a false one. It shimmered and sparked against the cover of night, and while the energy it emitted was foul, it nevertheless felt a whole lot cleaner than the thick muck I'd just traversed.

Standing in front of it were four figures—three with their backs to the rift, one standing facing it. The solo person was the dark-cloaked, hooded figure I'd been following. The other three . . .

I shuddered, even as I instinctively raised my weapon and fired. The other three were tall and thin, with pale translucent skin through which you could trace every muscle, bone, and vein. There was no hair on their bodies and they didn't really have faces. Just big amber eyes and squashed noses.

Wraiths.

And they reacted even as I did. Though none of them had anything resembling a mouth, they screamed—it was a high-pitched sound of fury I doubted any human would be capable of hearing, and it made my ears ache. The two front figures—the cowled man and the figure I presumed was the wraith's leader—leapt sideways, out of the firing line. But the other two came straight at me. I kept firing, but the machine rifle's wooden bullets bounced harmlessly off their translucent skin.

I slung the useless rifle back over my shoulder, unclipped the guns from my pants, then turned and fled into the soupy darkness. Just because I *could* fight didn't mean I had to or wanted to—especially *not* when it came to wraiths. And two of them at that.

The darkness enveloped me once more. My pace slowed to a crawl, but my heart rate didn't. I had no idea if this muck would affect them as it did me, and all I could do was pray to Rhea that it did. I didn't want to die. Not here, not in this stuff, and certainly not at the hand of a wraith.

I forged on, hurrying as much as the heaviness would

allow, my breath little more than shallow rasps of fear. While I couldn't hear any sound of pursuit, I knew they were behind me. Ripples of movement washed across my spine, getting stronger and stronger as the wraiths drew closer.

Fresh energy surged into my legs. I ran on, desperate to reach the crater's rim. I might not be any safer there, but I could at least fight a whole lot better out in the open.

The ground slipped from under my feet and I went down on one knee. Just for an instant, I caught a glimpse of starlight, and then a thick wave of movement hit my spine and knocked me sideways. Stones dug into my ribs as the air left my lungs in a huge whoosh. Claws appeared out of the ink— they were thick and blue and razor sharp, and would have severed my spine had the wind of their movement not hit me first. Luck, it seemed, hadn't totally abandoned me.

I fired both weapons in a sweeping arc. I had no idea where the wraiths were, because the darkness had enclosed around those claws and the rippling movement seemed to be coming from several directions now. Something wet splashed across my skin and face—something that stung like acid and smelled like foul egg. I hoped it was blood, but I knew there were Others who could spit poison. With the way things were playing out tonight, it was probably the latter rather than the former.

I scrubbed a sleeve across my face but succeeded only in smearing whatever it was. I cursed softly, then thrust upright and scrambled toward the rim of the crater and that brief glimpse of starlight. If I had to fight, then I at least wanted to see my foe.

The ripples of movement didn't immediately resume, and for an all-too-brief moment I thought maybe I'd killed them. It was a thought that swiftly died as those damn waves started up again.

There was nothing I could do. Nothing except keep running. Wraiths weren't stupid; now that they knew I had weapons that could actually hurt them, they'd be a lot more cautious.

But, cautious or not, they were still moving through this muck a whole lot faster than me. I had one chance, and one chance only—I had to get out and put as much distance between them and me as possible.

The heavy darkness began to slide away from my body. I sucked down big gulps of air, trying to ease the burning in my lungs. It didn't really help. I ran on, my speed increasing as the darkness retreated further, lifting the weight from my shoulders and spine. Then, finally, I was free from its grip and racing over the edge of the crater. I didn't stop. I didn't dare. I needed to gain as much distance as I could . . .

Movement, to my right. Instinct had me leaping left. Claws snagged the edge of my coat's sleeve, ripping it from cuff to shoulder, but not cutting skin. I twisted away, raised the guns, and fired.

At nothing.

The creature was gone. I had no idea whether speed or magic was involved in that disappearance, and no time to contemplate it. I just kept on running. Stones bounced away from my steps, but this time there were no ghosts to dance in time to the sound.

More movement, this time to my left. I fired again. The shots ripped across the night but found no target. The stony hillside appeared empty, even though the foul presence of the wraiths stained the air.

If they were so damn fast—or, indeed, capable of hiding their presence through magic—why weren't they attacking? Had they been ordered not to? Or were they like cats, preferring to play with their prey before closing in for the kill?

If it was the latter, then they were in for a shock, because this little mouse wasn't about to go down without taking at least one of them with me.

The crest of the hill loomed above. Tombs and crosses reached for the stars like broken fingers reaching for help. But there was no safety to be found there, and the tombs themselves were just a reminder of my fate if I wasn't very careful.

Stones clattered to my right; I swung a gun that way but didn't fire. There was nothing there. They were playing with me. Fear pounded through my body, but there was little I could do but ignore it. I'd been in far worse situations than this and survived. I could survive this.

With luck.

I hoped.

The graveyard ghosts gathered near the top of the hill as I drew closer, but their energy was uneasy. Wary. I very much doubted they would have helped even if I could have asked them to. There was none of the anger in them that was so evident within the Carleen ghosts, and that probably meant this graveyard—and these ghosts—were prewar. In which case they'd have no experience or knowledge of wraiths, and no idea just how dangerous they could be.

One of the creatures appeared out of the night to my left—or, rather, his arm appeared. I ducked under his blow and fired both guns, but in the blink of an eye, his limb was gone again. The bullets ricocheted off the nearby rocks, sending sparks flying into the night.

How in Rhea could I fight—kill—these creatures if I couldn't see them?

I guess I had to be grateful that I could at least *hear* them. Sometimes. More than likely when they actually wanted me to.

More sound, this time to my left—claws scrabbling

across stone. If that noise was any indication, it was closing in fast. Perhaps it had decided playtime was over.

I couldn't escape them—not in this form. Maybe it was time to try another . . .

Even as the thought entered my mind, something cannoned into my side and sent me tumbling. I hit the ground with a grunt but kept on rolling, desperate to avoid the attack I could feel coming.

I crunched into a large rock and stopped. The air practically screamed with the force of the creature's approach; I raised the guns once more and ripped off several shots. Then I scrambled upright, only to be sent flying again. This time I hit face-first and skinned my nose and chin as I slid several feet back down the hill.

I had no time to recover. No time to even think. The creature's weight landed in the middle of my back, and for too many seconds I couldn't even breathe, let alone react. Its claws tore at my flesh, splitting the skin along my shoulder and sending bits of flesh splattering across the nearby rocks. It was still playing with me, because those claws could have—should have—severed my spine.

But the blood gushing down my arm and back was warning enough that if I didn't move—didn't get up and get away from this creature—I'd still be as dead as any of those who watched from the safety of their tombstones.

And there was only one way I had any hope of escaping—I had to call forth the vampire within me.

So I ignored the creature's crushing weight, ignored the blood and the pain and the gore that gleamed wetly on the ground all around me, and sucked the energy of the night deep into my lungs. It filtered swiftly through every aching inch of me, until my whole body vibrated with the weight and power of it. The vampire within rose in a rush—undoubtedly fueled by fear and desperation—and swiftly embraced that darkness, becoming one with it, until it stained my whole being and took over. It ripped away flesh, muscle, and bone, until I was nothing more than a cluster of matter. Even my weapons and clothes became part of that energy. In this form, at least, I'd be harder to pin down.

I slipped out from under the wraith and fled upward toward the graveyard once again. But I wasn't out of danger yet. I might now be as invisible to the mortal world as any vampire or, indeed, the wraiths themselves, but that didn't mean they wouldn't sense me. Didn't mean they couldn't kill me. The number of vampire bones I'd seen near active rifts over the years was testament to the fact that *this* particular vampire trick made little difference to a wraith's ability to hunt and kill them.

I finally crested the hill and surged into the cemetery. In this form, I saw the spectral mass that was the gathered ghosts glimmering in the darkness. Their bodies were blurred, barely resembling anything humanoid, which meant I'd been right— these ghosts were very old indeed. Even so, I could taste their fear—of me, not of the things that pursued me. They might not know what wraiths were, but they were familiar with vampires and were now seeing me as one of them.

They wouldn't help me.

Air began to stir around me again, buffeting my particles and sending a fresh spurt of fear through my body. They'd entered the graveyard . . . and in this form, I couldn't use my weapons. I didn't even have a vampire's sharp claws to defend myself with. To use my weapons, I'd have to transform both them and my arms back to solidity, and a partial transformation wasn't something I was particularly adept at.

I raced on, heading for Carleen, hoping against hope that the ghosts there would help me. Because if they didn't . . .

I shoved the thought away. I could do this. I *would* do this. The lives of eight children lay on the line—or so Nuri believed. I very much doubted her statement—that if I didn't find those children, no one would—had been just an attempt to bring me back into the fold. The desperation and fear in her eyes had been all too real.

Though I heard no sound of approach, claws slashed the trailing tendrils of my energy form. Particles spun away into the night, and pain ripped through the rest of me. Panic surged. I really was no safer in this form than the other. In fact, I was probably worse off because I couldn't actually defend myself.

If I was destined to die this night, then, by Rhea, I would go down fighting in *human* form rather than in vampire.

I called to the darkness and reversed the process, becoming flesh from the head down. As my arms found form, I fired both guns over my shoulder, then to the left and the right. A high-pitched scream bit across the night and the rancid, metallic scent of blood washed through the air. I had no idea if I'd killed one of them or not, but at least I'd hit it. And if I could do that, I could kill them. Not that I was about to hang around and attempt it.

I raced on through the broken tombstones and shattered remnants of trees, my gaze on Carleen's distant walls even as every other sense was trained on the night around me.

Air rushed past; a wraith, planning Rhea only knows what. I didn't check my speed. Didn't even fire. While my guns weren't yet giving any indication that ammunition was running low, I couldn't imagine it would be too far off. And while I *was* carrying extra ammo, I had neither the time nor the desire to reload. The minute I stopped, they would be on me—of that I was sure. The only other weapons I had were the machine rifles—which had already proven useless—and the two glass knives strapped to my wrists. They'd been built as a last resort, a weapon designed for hand-to-hand combat with a blade that was harder than steel. But there was no way I was about to get into a last-resort situation. Not when it came to wraiths, anyway.

Up ahead, air began to shimmer and spark. A heartbeat later, one of the wraiths appeared, blocking my path between two crumbling but still-ornate tombs. A thick, bloody wound stretched across its gut, and black blood oozed down its torso and legs. But if the wound was hampering it in any way, it wasn't obvious. It flung its arms wide, its claws gleaming an alien, almost icy green. Sparks began to flicker between the razor-sharp tips, then spun off into the night. But they didn't disappear. Instead, they began to cluster together, each tiny spark sending out tendrils to connect to another, and then another, until a rope began to form. A rope that glowed the same alien green as the creature's claws and pulsated with an energy that made my skin crawl.

The wraiths weren't trying to kill me—they were trying to capture me. I had no desire to know why, and certainly no intention of finding out. I swung left, attempting to outrun the still-forming rope. The wraith appeared in front of me again, the rope longer and beginning to curve toward me.

I switched direction, and again the same thing happened. I slid to a halt, raised the guns, and unleashed hell. The wraith's body shook as the bullets tore through its flesh. Blood and gore splattered the ground all around it, but it neither moved nor stopped creating that leash. The two ends of the rope were close to joining now, and I very much suspected I did *not* want that to happen.

One of the guns began to blink in warning. I cursed and ran straight at the wraith. Firing from a distance seemed to have little effect, so maybe getting closer would be better. I had nothing to lose by trying—nothing but my life, and that was already on the line.

The second gun began to blink, but I didn't let up and I didn't stop. The closer I got, the more damage the guns did, but the creature didn't seem to care. Its body and face was a broken, bloodied mass, and still it stood there, resolutely creating its leash. Did these things feel no pain?

The first gun went silent. I cursed again and did the only thing I could—I launched feetfirst at the creature. I hit it so hard my feet actually went through the mess of its chest, but the sheer force of my momentum knocked it backward and the shimmering around its claws abruptly died as it hit the ground hard. I landed on top of it, caught my balance, and then fired every remaining bullet at its head.

This time, I killed it.

But I didn't rejoice. Didn't feel any sense of elation. As the second creature emitted a scream that was both fury and anguish, I tore the two spare clips free from their holders on my pants, reloaded the guns, and ran on.

The twisted, rusting metal fence that surrounded the grave-yard came into view. I leapt over it, my gaze on Carleen's broken walls. But the wind that battered my back was warning enough that the other wraith was not only on the move, but closing in fast. And I could taste its fury; this one had *no* intention of corralling me, even if that *had* been their orders.

I reached for everything I had left, but my legs refused to go any faster. My body was on fire and my strength seemed to be leaching away as fast as the blood pouring down my arm, back, and face. It was sheer determination keeping me on my feet now, nothing else.

And determination wasn't going to get me much farther. It certainly wouldn't take me to Carleen. The city was simply too far away.

Bear, I wish you could keep your promise to be with me when I die.

But even as that thought crossed my mind, I locked it down. Hard. I might want to die in the arms of my little ones—just as they'd died in mine—but I wasn't about to place either Bear or Cat in the middle of a dangerous situation. There were vampires in this world who could feed off energy—even the ectoplasmic energy of ghosts—and there might well be Others capable of doing the same.

Something smashed into my back and sent me tumbling. I landed faceup, staring at the stars—stars that danced in crazy circles across the wide, dark sky. I could barely even breathe, the pain was so great, but I nevertheless felt the approach of the creature. It was in the air and coming straight at me.

And this time, it *wasn't* invisible.

I raised the guns and fired. It wouldn't stop the creature, I knew that, but I didn't have the energy to get up and there was nothing else I could do.

Everything seemed to slip into slow motion. I watched the ripple of air as the bullets cut through it and the creature's gleaming claws gained length and began to drip with sparks. Saw the creature's flesh shudder and jerk in rhythmic harmony with the bullets that tore into its body. Saw the ever-growing glow of determination and fury in its golden eyes. I might not be able to speak its language, but there were some things that needed no words or explanations. It wanted revenge and it wanted my death, and it didn't care if it had to die as long as it took me with it.

I can't die. There's still too much I need to do.

But I guess someone else would have to do it.

CHAPTER 2

I closed my eyes, not wanting to see any more.

A shot rang out across the night, the sound deeper, harsher, than anything coming from my own guns.

It was just a single shot, then nothing.

I held my breath, wondering where it had come from even as I waited for the creature to crush me. Kill me.

It did neither.

I stopped firing and opened my eyes. Shock rippled through me. The creature hovered above me, but it was encased in a net of silver that was slowly tightening around its body. *An electro-net.* They'd been designed to capture both shifters and vampires, and I was currently using them to protect the main tunnel out of our bunker. But none of the ones I had were capable of holding a captive suspended aboveground and, other than the fact that they were made of pure silver, which made life extremely unpleasant for shifters, certainly wouldn't kill anyone.

The wraith screamed, and this time it was a long, agonized sound of pain rather than fury. As the net began to bite deeper into its flesh, blood and gore began to fall like rain around me; if I didn't want to be covered in the stinking stuff, I needed to move. I tried to roll over, to push up onto hands and knees and crawl out of the way, but there was absolutely nothing left in me and it was all I could do to keep breathing.

Hands grabbed me and pulled me out from under the creature. The familiar scent of cat, wind, and evening rain spun around me, and I didn't know whether to laugh or to cry. My rescuer was none other than Jonas—Nuri's second, a shifter who hated déchet with a passion that bordered on obsession, and one of the rare throwbacks who could see as well at night as he could during the day.

He was also the more sensible of Nuri's two men. The other—Branna, a lion shifter—probably would have let the wraith kill me and then danced on my remains. Especially given that both his efforts to end my life so far had gone astray.

"Don't move." Jonas's voice was low and filled with fury. No surprise there; it seemed to be a regular occurrence whenever he was near me.

And it wasn't like I *could* actually go anywhere, even if I wanted to. My head felt weirdly light, my body was heavy, and my lungs burned even though I was gulping down air as quickly as I could. The wounds that littered my body were becoming life-threatening, and if I wanted to survive the blood loss and shock, I had no option but to fast-track the healing process. I just had to hope that I had the strength to maintain the healing state long enough to make a difference.

I closed my eyes and focused entirely on my breathing,

on slowing every intake of air, on feeling it wash through my nostrils and down into my lungs. After far too many minutes, the fear and pain finally began to slide away and a sense of calm descended. It was in this almost meditative state that my body had been programmed to heal quickly—and it was this same state that sometimes made the process very dangerous. While I might be aware of what was going on around me, I couldn't actually react to it. Not with any sort of speed.

But I doubted Jonas intended any harm, given he'd only just rescued me. Besides, he happened to believe Nuri's edict that the children wouldn't be saved if I didn't do it.

Time passed. Healing could take minutes or it could take hours, depending on the extent and complexity of the wounds. Somewhere along the line, the wraith stopped screaming, and if Jonas moved about, then I certainly couldn't hear it.

But he was watching me.

Even in this meditative state, I could feel it. It was a slow, invisible caress that had heat not only skittering across my skin, but pooling deep inside. And while part of that reaction was undoubtedly because I'd been designed to attract—and be attracted to—those shifters who ruled, this was more than that. How much more I couldn't say; I'd never felt anything this fierce before, not during the war and certainly not in the one hundred and three years that followed it. But it was also a feeling I would never have the chance to pursue. While I had no doubt the attraction was shared, it was one he was unlikely to ever act upon. Because of what I was. Because he believed I was nothing more than an unthinking, unfeeling abomination with no right to life.

The only reason he'd saved me—both now and previously—was the missing children.

Regret stirred, but it was heavily tainted by both

bitterness and anger. I resolutely pushed the emotions down and locked them deep inside—a trick I'd learned a long time ago, when emotions could get a déchet "readjusted." While lures had been designed with the emotional centers of their brains intact—unlike those destined to become soldiers—our creators had believed that we were capable of neither love nor heartache. Whether the former was true I couldn't say, but my heart had certainly ached when I was forced to kill my one and only friend. But the fact was, I *did* kill him. Did that mean any hope of true emotional depth was nothing more than a flight of fancy on my part?

I guess I'd never know.

At least once I rescued the remaining children, Nuri and her people would be out of my life and I could get back to living in solitude, with no one but the ghosts for company. I'd been happy living that way for over a hundred years. I could find that happiness again.

A cool breeze stirred my short hair and crusted the blood on my skin and clothes, and if it weren't for the acidic scent of gore rising from the earth, it would almost be easy to believe that the night held no danger.

But that was a lie. There was still another wraith out there, as well as the cloaked figure I'd been following. Jonas might be a ranger—a formidable class of shifter-soldier who'd once been used to destroy whole déchet divisions, and who now formed the backbone of the fight against the Others—but I doubted he'd come here prepared for *that* sort of battle.

Although given he'd apparently brought an electro-net device with him, maybe I was wrong.

It was a thought that finally forced my eyes open. Jonas squatted near my feet, his arms crossed and the variegated grays of his combat pants and close-fitting shirt almost making him one with the night. He was a lean and powerful man with mottled black hair—the only hint of the panther he could become. The three scars that ran from his right temple to just behind his ear—a signature all rangers wore to this day—stood out starkly against his sun-kissed skin.

"So, the rumors were true." His voice was deep, rich, and oddly melodious, but it nevertheless held echoes of the ice that glinted in his cat-green eyes.

I sat up, but the effort had my head swimming. While my body no longer felt like lead, and blood had at least stopped flowing from most of my wounds, I was a very long way from healed.

"Which particular rumor are we talking about now?" The question came out clipped, and annoyance surged—at myself more than him. Why was emotional control so difficult around this shifter?

"The one that said déchet were capable of self-healing," he said. "It was one of the few rumors I hadn't actually believed until now."

"Shifters heal themselves all the time, so why are you so surprised that we can do the same?" I thrust my guns onto their clips and then resolutely got to my feet.

He rose with me, one hand half-extended, as if to catch me. My legs threatened to buckle, but I determinedly locked my knees. I would *not* fall. I did *not* need his help.

Even if I was only alive because of it.

"Our healing is basically a side benefit of shifting from one form to another—it's more muscle memory than anything else. But déchet don't shift."

"I can." I might not be able take on an animal form— even though I *did* have tiger DNA—but I could alter my body into any other human form I desired. That ability was part of the reason why lures had been so successful during the war. There might have been only a relatively small number of us, but with the ability to totally transform our looks and our scent, huge numbers weren't actually needed.

"Yes, you can." He was still standing close enough to catch me, and his scent filled every breath, rekindling the ashes of desire. "What were you doing out here?"

His abrupt change of direction didn't faze me. Jonas had a habit of doing that; he was always trying to trip me up, to make me whisper secrets.

Not that I had many of those left now.

I took my time to answer and studied him instead, knowing full well it would annoy him even as I acknowledged it was somewhat childish to want that. His face was still slightly gaunt—a result of whatever he'd been infected with when I first rescued both him and his niece, Penny, from the vampires—and it made his sharp nose look even more aristocratic. But even *with* that nose—or maybe because of it—I'd definitely class him as handsome, though not classically so. There was a roughness to his features that made them far more interesting than beautiful.

"*That* is a question I should be asking you," I said eventually.

The smile that briefly flirted with his lips held little in the way of amusement. "Nuri sent me here."

"Why? I told you all several days ago I was finished, Jonas. I meant it."

"Nuri didn't—doesn't—believe you truly mean to walk away from those children. She says it's simply not in your makeup."

"I'm déchet, remember? We don't think, we don't feel, and we certainly don't care."

"The latter has been proven false—at least in your case." His gaze swept me, and just for an instant, pheromones stung the air, his and mine, mixing enticingly. Desire sparked, fierce and bright, but its flame was all too brief and shut down the minute he stepped back. "We need your help, Tiger, and we're not going to leave you alone until we get it."

"Stalk me all you want. It won't make a difference."

Again that cool smile touched his lips. "You might be able to change your form, but that won't stop me from tracking you."

Good luck with that, I wanted to bite back, but somehow held the words inside. The last thing I needed right now was to make him suspect I could change my scent as well as my looks. "Then I believe you're going to get mighty bored."

"Oh, I doubt it." He waved a hand toward the bloody mess of flesh, sinew, and bone—all that remained of the wraith. "Why was it chasing you?"

"Probably because I annoyed it by attempting to kill it."

"Annoyance *does* seem to be a common emotion around you." Amusement glinted in his eyes, but it was gone just as quickly. "Where did you come across it?"

"Not it, *them.*" I motioned to the rear of the graveyard. "I was following a cloaked figure and he led me straight to an active rift."

"Meaning the wraiths killed him?"

I hesitated. While I had no desire to be a part of any investigation involving him, Nuri, or the rest of them, I was also aware that I couldn't chase every lead myself. Practicality had to win over stubbornness in this particular case. "No. He was meeting with them."

"What?" The word exploded from him. "Why in Rhea would anyone want to do *that*?"

"Given I had no chance to ask, I can't really say." My voice was grim. "But as he came from Carleen, I could make a guess or two."

"You think it was one of Sal's partners?"

I nodded. "Who else could it be? No one else has any reason to be in that place, especially at night."

He thrust a hand through his short hair and began to pace. His strides were long, lithe, and full of repressed fury. "But if it *was* one of them, why the hell would they be meeting with a wraith? That doesn't make sense. Unless—"

"Unless," I interrupted, "they're planning to gain sunlight immunity for not only the vampires but also the wraiths— which is exactly what Sal said they were doing."

"Surely not even *they'd* be so stupid as to contemplate that."

"Why not? The three of them were caught in a rift with a wraith, remember, and they now carry those genes in their DNA."

"Yes, but they're still a part of *this* world. Surely they could see that such actions might well destroy the structure of all we hold dear—"

"Which might be the whole *point*," I cut in. "Not everyone likes the current status quo, Jonas. Not everyone is happy that the shifters won the war."

"For Rhea's sake, that was a *hundred* years ago. We've all moved past that now."

"Have we?" I couldn't quite control the bitterness in my voice. "You and Branna still hate déchet as fiercely as ever. Why is it so hard to believe that there'd be some humans who'd feel a similar hatred for the victors?"

He stopped and studied me for several seconds. "Did your déchet friend feel that way?"

My smile held very little in the way of humor. "Oh yes."

And if Sal's loathing of both humans and shifters *had* bled over into the other two, then it wouldn't be beyond the realm of possibility that they'd do whatever they deemed necessary to end the current status quo.

Jonas grunted. "You'd better show me where this meet happened."

"There's at least one other wraith still unaccounted for, plus that stranger—"

"We'll deal with them if we need to." He hesitated, and his gaze swept me again. "Can you move?"

"If that thing attacks, I'll certainly be moving faster than you, Ranger."

He smiled—another all-too-brief flash that bathed me in warmth. "Fair enough." He stepped to one side and waved me on. "After you."

I hobbled more than walked. The cut on my thigh pulled tightly with every step and my knee ached. When or how I'd done *that* I had no idea.

The graveyard ghosts followed us at a distance, still wary, still uncertain, about my presence here in their home, but obviously also curious about what we were up to. I paused once we reached the graveyard's boundary and looked down the hill. The crater was no longer hidden by that foul darkness.

"What?" Jonas immediately asked.

"The rift and the dark veil that was covering it are gone."

He frowned, his gaze scanning the rubble-strewn slope. "It must have shifted when the wraiths were chasing you."

"Real rifts don't come supplied with their own little cloud cover, Jonas." At least all the ones *I'd* come across hadn't. "If they're both gone, then it's because either the wraith or the cloaked figure shifted them."

"The former is a possibility I really *don't* want to contemplate." His expression was dark, and for good reason. If the wraiths were capable of dismantling a rift, then it was very possible they could create them—and *that* would have dire consequences for us all if they ever gained light immunity. "Where was it located?"

"In the crater."

His gaze swept it. "The crater's too deep to see its base, but it's possible the man you were tracking is still there." His gaze met mine. "It's also possible he's set another trap. He's certainly had the time."

Which felt like a rebuke, whether it was meant to or not. "I guess the only way we're going to find out is to go down there."

"You're in no state to traverse—"

I snorted. "Since when have you worried about the state I'm in? If you want answers, Ranger, this is the only way we're going to get them."

He didn't say anything to that. No surprise there. I started down, moving carefully, not wanting to risk the ground sliding out from underneath me. The last thing I needed right now was to split my barely healed wounds open.

The graveyard ghosts remained with us, seemingly intrigued by Jonas even if they kept their distance from me. I wished again I could talk to them, as they were probably the only witnesses to what had gone on in the crater while the wraiths were chasing me. But to do that, I'd have to call in Cat, and that was something I was still reluctant to do. Maybe tomorrow, when the sun was bright and there was no chance of vampires or wraiths jumping out of slimy shadows . . .

I shivered but resisted the urge to rub my arms—if only because the wounds were heavily scabbed over, and I might just open them up again if I touched them. We reached the rim of the crater without mishap and stopped. The darkness that clustered around the base was deep but natural, and filled with nothing more threatening than rocks.

"There was definitely a rift here," Jonas said. "Its energy still lingers."

I raised an eyebrow as I glanced at him. "Meaning you didn't actually believe me?"

His gaze met mine, his expression flat. "Oh, I believed you. I was just hoping you were wrong—that the wraiths *couldn't* produce rifts at will. Wait here while I go down and check."

"Be careful. They might have left a surprise or two behind."

"I'm well aware of that."

He started down the steep slope. The ghosts hesitated, then followed him, their bodies becoming ethereal wisps of fog as they moved into the deeper darkness. That they still accompanied him wasn't really surprising, as they were—for whatever reason—bound to the loneliness of their grave-yard and its surrounds . . . The thought trailed to a halt and I frowned. Why were they suddenly visible? The only time I'd seen them previously was when I was in vampire form.

"Jonas, stop."

He immediately did so. "Why?"

"I can see the ghosts."

He glanced over his shoulder. "And what is so new about that?"

"They're *human* ghosts, like those in Carleen. I should only be able to see them in vampire form or with Cat's help."

"Ah." He drew his gun and slipped the safety off. I wasn't sure how a weapon would protect him against whatever magic might wait below, but maybe he also felt safer with its weight in his hand. "Interesting that I didn't sense anything."

"It's possible that whatever magic it is is aimed at me more than you." After all, he couldn't see the darkness that covered the false rifts in Carleen, nor was he affected by it, despite the fact that he was sensitive to magic. *That* darkness certainly seemed to be designed to prevent someone who had a good percentage of vampire blood in their veins—or maybe even the vampires themselves—from easily entering the false rifts. But if it *were* the same magic, why would it cause the ghosts to suddenly gain substance? As far as I knew, the magic that protected Carleen's false rifts had no effect on the ghosts there—although given that they tended to avoid them, maybe they'd discovered the hard way that it did.

Jonas continued on. The ghosts followed him, but their forms had begun to fade again. Whatever had caused them to briefly appear was obviously situated around the midpoint of the crater.

I started down, carefully picking my way through the debris and loose stones. It was very slow progress, and that was probably the only reason I even felt the magic. It was a subtle caress of foul energy that didn't feel as if it belonged to this world, and one that barely raised the hairs on my arms, let alone any internal warnings. I stopped and reached out with one hand. A jagged whip of light appeared from nowhere and lashed toward me. I yelped and jumped back, losing my footing in the process and ending up on my rump. Pain slithered through me and blood began to trickle down my spine again. I ignored it, jerking my feet closer to my body as the whip reached full length and snapped angrily back and forth inches from my toes—a black snake that intended Rhea only knows what.

"What happened?" Jonas's gaze was on our surrounds rather than me. Maybe he expected the magical attack to be followed by a real one.

Which was certainly possible, though it was more likely that the wraith hadn't risked hanging around any longer than it took to set up this barrier.

"The magic you can't see attacked me." I inched up the hill a little more, even though the whip of energy was beginning to fade.

"They obviously know you survived the wraiths; why else would they protect this crater with magic?"

"Either they're just being cautious or there *is* something down there worth protecting."

"Given the run of luck we've had of late, I wouldn't be pinning many hopes on the latter."

I wasn't, even though he was wrong about our run of luck. We'd saved five children despite the trap designed to kill, and that was a miracle in itself. But I'd also rescued him from the old military bunker that lay deep in the Broken Mountains, one that had been filled to the brim with vampires. If Rhea *wasn't* looking out for us, we'd both be as dead as the ghosts who currently surrounded him.

But how much longer would that luck hold? That was a question I really didn't want to think about—especially *not* after the closeness of death tonight.

I shifted position slightly but didn't climb to my feet. The warmth flowing down my back suggested I'd opened the wounds again; the less I moved right now, the better.

Jonas reached the base of the crater and carefully picked his way through the larger bits of debris that lined this side of it.

"The rift was located on the western edge," I commented.

He walked over and squatted down. "There's been some attempt to hide the footprints."

"Obviously not a good attempt."

"No." His gaze moved to the crater's rim. "Only one of them walked out of here. He left by the western edge."

"That would have to be the person I was tracking."

"Yes. It's certainly not the tracks belonging to a wraith." He rose. "We should follow him."

"You can." I couldn't keep the edge of weariness from my voice. "The only thing I'll be doing for the rest of the night is heading back to the bunker."

His gaze met mine again, his expression unreadable. "Do you need help?"

"No. Not now, not later. But I'm guessing the latter is not an option."

"No, but you could get lucky. The footprints could lead to another trap—this time a successful one."

Annoyance surged and I thrust upright. Something tore across my back and that trickle got stronger. Fair payment for reacting to this man's barbs, I guess. "Do you really think that if I wished you dead, you wouldn't be so by now?"

"It wasn't meant—"

"I don't care how it was meant, Jonas. I'm sick of the mistrust. I've done nothing to deserve it, nothing other than being a product of a war long gone. Either treat me as you find me or live in the past with your rumors and your hatred and leave me *be*."

And with that, I walked away. He didn't follow me, but he did watch me. His gaze was a heat that pressed against my spine long after I'd left the crater behind.

I really wished I'd walked away at the beginning of all this. Neither he nor the vampires nor the damn fools trying to create sunlight immunity for vamps and wraiths would have been a problem if I just *hadn't* rescued Penny and Jonas from the vamps. Our bunker—and all the ghosts who lived within it, be they young or old—would be safe.

And the children you'd rescued would now be dead.

I thrust a hand through my crusted hair and wished I

could ignore that annoying inner voice. But all too often, she was right. I might not be able to love, but Rhea only knew I could do guilt with the best of them. Even after one hundred and three years, my inability to save my little ones was still driving my actions.

I guess I just had to hope it didn't get me killed. Not before I'd rescued the rest of the missing children, anyway.

I slowly walked back through the old graveyard but skirted Carleen itself. The ruined city was an unpleasant place to be at the best of times, and it wasn't just because of the rifts that endlessly roamed the confines of its walls. These days, there was an almost otherworldly feel to the place, which was due in no small part to both the deadly alien moss that now covered much of its ruins and the unnatural darkness that covered the false rifts.

The park that separated Carleen from Central City was still. Nothing moved, not even the leaves on the old trees, despite the wind that gently teased the nape of my neck. Once upon a time this place would have been alive with nighttime creatures, but even birds were a rare find these days. Though cities like Central had been rebuilt with all major services running aboveground to ensure that the vampires had no means of protected access into them, there were still plenty of old service pipes and sewers outside these centers that had never been filled in. This park was near one such outlet, and in the years since the war the vampires had wiped out most of the wildlife in this area. Thankfully, they didn't seem to be out tonight. Given the state I was in, I would have been easy meat for them.

Dawn was beginning to caress the night sky with fingers of pink and gold by the time I finally reached the end of the park. I paused in its shadows, sweeping my gaze over the rail yards that still separated me from my bunker's southern exit. The glowing, caterpillar-like pods that transported Central's many workers to the various production zones that provided the city with the necessities of life were still and quiet, and the city's drawbridge remained closed. It wouldn't open until dawn had well and truly chased the night from the sky.

I slowly headed down into the yards. The vast curtain wall that ran in a D shape around Central towered above me, its rusting silvery surface glinting softly in the wash of the UV lights that topped both the wall and every roof of every building within Central, providing its inhabitants with endless daylight. It was not a place I could have lived comfortably for any length of time. But then, there was vampire in my DNA. I might not crave blood, but I had no fear of darkness.

Only the creatures that ran within it.

I made my way through the platforms and across City Road—the only vehicular access in and out of Central—then headed for the muddy trickle of water that was still known as the Barra River. Like many things in this world of ours, its course and its appearance had been forever altered when the bombs had been unleashed.

As the curtain wall curved away from the road and the river, a ramshackle collection of buildings appeared. Chaos, as it had long been known, was an interconnected mess of metal storage units, old wood, and plastic that clung to the wall's side. It was a place where the broken and the outcast lived, and both gangs and money ruled it—and the higher you lived, the more power, wealth, and protection you had. That particular aspect was replicated in Central, except that it was the city's heart—and the safety that came with being as far away from the walls as was possible—that drew the wealthy and the powerful.

Nuri and her people lived in the midsection of Chaos, in a place called Run Turk Alley, which was basically mercenary central. I'd been there a couple of times now, but had no desire to return. I might not fear darkness, but I had no love of places that made me feel confined and unable to breathe—which was undoubtedly a result of being tossed into a cesspit and left to die during the war.

The thick steel grate that covered the bunker's southern exit came into sight and appeared to be untouched—which was something of a relief given the number of times I'd come back here recently to find it under attack. There *was* a second entrance, but it was located in the museum that had been created out of the area that had once contained the day-to-day operational center of the Humanoid Development Project, and that made it trickier to use on a daily basis. I might have reprogrammed their computers and security systems to ignore my presence, but that didn't mean I dared push my luck too often.

This tunnel, like the tight, circular stairwell that led into the museum, had been designed as an emergency escape route for the humans in charge of the various HDP sections. Neither had been mentioned on any of the base plans that I'd uncovered, which was probably why the shifters, after the mass destruction of all those *within* the bunker, had only flooded the first three levels with concrete. Doing *that* had taken out all known exits as well as the lift shafts and loading bays, leaving the remaining levels and the bodies of all those who had died in this place locked in endless darkness.

Or so they'd thought.

It had been through sheer luck more than actual intent that I'd found the museum tunnel, and it had been several years after *that* before I found this one, but the two of them gave me much-needed access points to the outside world. It might be a world I ventured into only once or twice a month—mostly for food or equipment supplies, but occasionally for company that was real rather than ghostly—but that didn't assuage the desire to know what was going on above me on a regular basis.

I deactivated the electro-nets protecting the tunnel as I approached each one, then reset them once I'd passed. Up ahead, lights came on, the brightness making my eyes water. Then the ghosts surged around me, their energy tingling across my skin as they all endeavored to fill me in on what they'd been doing since I left. Given that there'd been one hundred and five of them who'd found death in the nurseries of this place, that was a whole *lot* of mental noise.

"Guys, calm down. I can't understand a word you're saying when you all talk at once."

Their amusement filled the air as little Cat's energy spun around me to create a light connection. Both she and Bear were the oldest of the little ones, and had always considered me something of a big sister, even though we déchet shouldn't have even understood the concept. Our initial closeness had come from the amount of time I'd spent in the nursery unit in the years leading up to the war. Even during the war, those lures not out on assignment or in a recovery period were put to use in the nurseries, not only to teach the next generation of fighters, but also to protect them. While déchet soldiers had, for the most part, been neutered emotionally in the test tube, there had been a few instances early on when the constant and grueling programming and training had somehow caused a short-out that had resulted in a killing spree. Not against our creators, because they'd made damn sure none of us were capable of harming humans, and not even against other déchet soldiers like themselves. They'd attacked the children. It was after that the lures had been assigned protection detail. While we'd never been designed as soldiers, we *had* been taught to fight and defend.

But the connection between the three of us had deepened when the shifters flooded this place with Draccid—a particularly nasty gas that destroyed the body from the inside out. Not only had both Cat and Bear died in my arms, but some of our DNA had mingled on that dreadful day.

The image of three black-clad figures flashed into my mind—two were men, one a woman—and with it came a wash of trepidation. Neither Cat nor the other little ones liked the feel of those strangers.

"Where are they?" I hesitated and looked around as I realized one of them was missing. "And where's Bear?"

More images flowed into my mind. Bear was upstairs, in the museum, watching the three strangers. They were pointing some sort of handheld device at each portion of the museum's inner wall before moving on to the next section.

It was an image that had all sorts of inner alarms going off. "Did you happen to get close to the scanner, Cat?"

Her energy danced around me excitedly and I couldn't help smiling—she loved anticipating my questions. But my smile faded rapidly when the next image flashed into my mind.

The device was a radar scanner. One designed to uncover people or objects hidden behind the thick walls of concrete.

And *that* could mean these three strangers were trying to find the entrance into the bunker.

I swore and ran, my footsteps echoing sharply in the vast emptiness of this place. Most of the ghosts danced along to the sound, thankfully unaware of the danger these people represented to our home and our solitude, but Cat pressed close, her energy caressing my shoulder and filled with concern. Not just because of the strangers, but because she knew—thanks to our deeper connection—just how fine a line I was walking right now when it came to my strength.

How in Rhea I was going to cope with the three intruders once I got to the museum, I had no idea. But at least I was armed and, from Cat's images, the three strangers weren't. That gave me an advantage—as did the presence of the ghosts. While they might be energy rather than flesh, they could both interact with *and* manipulate the world around them if they so desired. Even though they were little, and therefore restricted in the amount of energy they could expend before it affected them physically, they could certainly toss a human or two about.

It took me ten minutes to reach the fourth level and tunnel D—the first accessible tunnel free from the concrete.

The ghosts followed me into the stairwell, their tiny forms gaining wispy substance in the condensation-laden atmosphere. Most scooted ahead, their whisperings filled with excitement. Only Cat remained close.

I was halfway up the stairwell when there was an odd sort of *whoomp.* For a heartbeat, nothing happened; then the thick concrete walls around me began to shudder. I paused, my grip on the handrail tightening as the noise grew and grew, until it sounded like a troop tanker was roaring toward me.

Then an explosion of heat and dust and debris hit, knocking me off my feet and sending me tumbling back down the stairs. I flung out a hand, scrabbling desperately for something—anything—to halt my fall. My fingers wedged into a crack that was spreading like a canker down the inner wall, and my fall was stopped so suddenly that I damn near tore my shoulder out of its socket. The ghosts spun around me, their confusion and fear filling my mind. I took a deep

breath and tried to reassure them that I was okay, that everything was fine, even if it wasn't.

Another explosion ripped the air apart. Huge chunks of
metal and concrete began to rain all around me as dust and
debris gave the ghosts form.

I swung around, felt for the nearest step with my feet,
then released my hold on the crack and thrust up. Pain
hit, and for an instant, everything spun. The ghosts pressed
close, keeping me upright. I took a deep breath that ended
in a coughing fit thanks to all the dust, then scrambled *up*
the stairs rather than down. Those people had to be stopped,
before they destroyed— The thought died as a third explosion rumbled through the air, this one oddly softer—more
distant—than the previous two. Then the ceiling above me
shattered and everything went dark.

CHAPTER 3

I woke to ghostly hands anxiously patting my face, but for several seconds I could neither move nor react. The air was thick and still, and there seemed to be some sort of weight on my chest, making breathing difficult. But I was alive, and *that* was surely yet more evidence that the goddess Rhea really was looking out for me. Given the strength of those explosions, I should have been dead.

Cat's energy pressed close. *You must get up,* she said. *It's too dangerous here.*

I forced my eyes open. Destruction lay all around me. Huge chunks of concrete and twisted bits of metal filled the dark void, and the curved walls that had withstood everything the shifters had thrown at this base during the war were fissured and looked unstable. No wonder Cat wanted me out.

The section immediately above me had given way, but the twisting nature of the stairs meant I had no idea if the void ran all the way to the museum, or if the explosion had simply reduced the rest of the stairs to rubble. I hoped it was the latter, if only because it would prevent anyone from gaining immediate access.

Below me there was nothing but more rubble and the occasional step remnant. Whatever the three strangers had used had been *very* powerful indeed. I wondered how much damage had been done not only to the museum, but also to the old tower that held all the remaining solar panels. They might be an antiquated curiosity to those alive today, but they continued to power not only the systems that had been preserved on the museum floor for demonstration purposes, but most of mine. If they'd been destroyed, I would be left with only the three hydrogen-fueled generators to power the entire base—and those generators were becoming increasingly unreliable.

The weight on my chest was a concrete boulder large enough to also pin my right arm. I couldn't feel my fingers, so there was, at the very least, nerve damage. There were smaller bits of concrete covering the rest of my body, and a thin sliver of metal had pierced my left calf. Why I wasn't a howling mess of pain, I had no idea; maybe it was shock. Or maybe my pain receptors had simply given up.

"The intruders?" I croaked. "Where are they?"

This time it was Bear who made the connection. *Gone. They left before the two explosions.*

I frowned. Hadn't there been three?

Something cracked in the darkness above us, and debris rained down. The little ones spun around me anxiously, echoing Cat's urgency to move.

"I need the concrete off my chest first—Bear, could you do it please?"

His energy surged, and after a moment the boulder

floated free. He carried it to the end of my body, then dropped it. It bounced loudly down the remains of the stairs, the sound echoing in the dusty stillness.

I drew in a deep, shuddery breath and then carefully sat up. Those supposedly dead pain receptors sprang to life and every part of my body felt as if it were on fire. I hissed, blinking away the sweat and blood that began to trickle into my eyes as I battled not to throw up. Or fall back into unconsciousness.

Cat's energy touched me again. *You need to go to the mediscan beds.*

I did. And fast. But *that* was the least of my problems right now. "Bear, do you want to go upstairs and check that those people haven't come back? And can you also check what damage has been done up there?"

He spun around me excitedly, then zoomed off. I glanced at Cat. "Could you check the rest of the base? See if there's any damage elsewhere?"

There *had* been three explosions—I was certain of it. So if the intruders were responsible for two, where had the third come from? And, more important, what had it been aimed at? I suspected it might have been the south-siding exit, but it didn't hurt to check the rest of the base, just in case the destruction in the museum had set off a chain reaction elsewhere.

Cat hesitated. *Will you need help?*

I smiled and reached out, lightly catching the energy of her hands in mine. "I'll be fine. The little ones can help keep me upright if necessary."

This statement brought a surge of excitement and a sense of importance from the other little ghosts. They might not ever be as adventurous as either Cat or Bear thanks to their age when they'd died, but they still liked helping when they could. Hell, it was thanks to their assistance that Jonas and I had survived the vampires' onslaught the night I saved both him and Penny.

Cat whisked away to check the rest of the base, and the other ghosts pressed closer, the energy of their bodies making my skin tingle. I cradled my arm—an action that had more sweat coursing down my face—then carefully made my way down the stairs. It took an interminably long time, not only because there wasn't much left of the stairs themselves, but because I simply was running far too close to the edge of endurance. The metal stake spearing my calf wasn't helping, either, but I didn't dare remove it until I got to the medical center just in case it had punctured a main artery. I doubted it, but sometimes you couldn't tell.

Once we finally got clear of the stairwell and entered the relatively destruction-free zone of tunnel D, our speed increased. Level four had once housed the main medical and training facilities for the bunker's combatant déchet divisions, and while several of the rooms closest to the main tunnel that led up to level three *had* been flooded by concrete, the rest of this area had survived intact. The medical equipment—although undoubtedly out-of-date by today's standards—still worked. Why the shifters hadn't destroyed the machines along with all the equipment in both the creation labs and the nurseries, I had no idea, but I'd thanked Rhea many a time over the years for that one piece of luck. I might be able to heal myself as well as any shifter, but there were still times when using a machine was infinitely better. Like right now, when my reserves were giving out and I had far too many injuries to heal myself with any sort of speed.

By the time I reached the medical center, my breath was coming in short, sharp gasps and my vision was blurring. I gritted my teeth and forced myself on. As the door swished open, I flicked the knife still strapped to my left wrist into my hand and carefully cut away my right sleeve. A red mist seemed to form before my eyes and I hissed, holding on to the end of the nearest bed as I gulped down air and battled to remain conscious. As the mist retreated, I hastily slashed off the rest of my clothes. I was carrying so many wounds that it was simply better to be naked. Once I'd activated the light panel and set it to do a full body scan and repair, I climbed into the bed and—after gritting my teeth—pulled the stake out. A scream ripped up my throat as blood spurted, and it was all I could do to remain conscious and lie down. But as foam enveloped my body and began to admit a soft but rapid beeping sound—my heartbeat, amplified by the light panel above me—my strength finally gave out and unconsciousness claimed me.

It was the whispering of the ghosts that finally pulled me back to consciousness. There was a mix of anxiety and excitement in their voices, and while neither was exactly unusual, it was the name they kept mentioning that caught my attention.

Jonas.

Apparently, he was a part of the ten-man crew inspecting the damage done to the museum. Four of the other nine were from Central's military corps—their uniforms said they were from the engineering division—and the rest were museum staff.

So what the hell was Jonas doing with them? Not only had he denied any connection with the government, but he was also an outcast. As such, he should not have been included in any official investigation.

Of course, while both he and Nuri had denied government links, they could still have enough pull to have him included. But why would they want it? Nuri was a powerful earth witch—surely she could use a little magic to uncover whether I was alive or not.

I pushed upright. The medibed's monitor told me I'd been unconscious for seven hours and forty-eight minutes, and that it was now nearly three in the afternoon. My leg wound obviously hadn't been as bad as it had looked or felt; otherwise I'd have been out longer. "What's the damage like up in the museum, Bear?"

Images pressed into my mind. The old tower—and its vital solar panels—still stood, even though chunks had been taken out of the sides that faced into the museum. A huge pile of rubble and two twisted remnants of metal that reminded me of fingers stretching toward the domed ceiling were all that remained of the inner section that had held the museum's offices, security people, and the hidden tunnel entrance. Several Acro Props were already in place to hold up the rest of the ceiling, although the dome that arched over the building's remains, shielding it from the elements and further decay, didn't seem to have sustained any damage. The glass was fissured over the old tower, but it had been for quite a while.

"And the stairs? Is there anything left of them?"

The connection between us briefly deepened. *Only a remnant of the third and fourth levels remain. The top two have completely caved in.*

I guess the only surprising thing about *that* was the fact that the force of the explosions hadn't taken out all four levels. I glanced at Cat, who was waiting patiently next to Bear.

"Was there damage anywhere else? Is the south-siding exit intact?"

It wasn't. The third explosion had, as I feared, taken it out. I scrubbed a hand across my eyes. This was going to make getting in and out of our bunker more difficult.

Which was undoubtedly the point.

And while I *had* expected Sal's partners to make a more direct attempt to either stop me or at least stop my use of the bunker, I had to wonder how they'd known about the museum entrance. No one knew about that one—not even Nuri or Jonas.

"Cat, Bear, can you keep an eye on what's going on in the museum? Let me know if they do anything unusual or if Jonas leaves."

They zoomed around me, then raced away, both of them determined to be the first one up there. Their laughter drifted back to me and made me smile. The other little ones followed no less exuberantly. Apparently, the museum goings-on were far more exciting than anything I might be doing. Silence fell, and it was almost unnerving.

I jumped off the mediscan bed and headed down to the sixth floor. Not only had it been the main training area for prepubescent déchet, but it also held the bunk rooms, storerooms, and generators, as well as a secondary medical center and a gun cache—which was now the only cache, given the one I'd set up in the museum tunnel was undoubtedly gone.

The sixth floor was also an area that held one of the unalterable security points. A red light flashed as I approached the main door.

"Name, rank," a gruff metallic voice said. I'd long ago named him Hank, simply because his tone reminded me of the cranky custodian who'd once run the Base Exchange. He was one of the few human ghosts who still lingered here, although he tended to avoid both me and the children.

"Tiger C5, déchet, lure rank."

I pressed my thumb against the blood-work slot. A small needle shot out and took the required sample. While the system usually took an interminably long time to react, it was faster today, thanks to the fact that I was running all three generators twenty-four/seven so I could bring the south-siding exit into the security net. I could probably stop that now, because if the images Cat had shown me were any indication, no one but shadowed vampires was going to use that entrance anytime soon. Presuming, of course, the destruction wasn't so complete that even an energy mass wasn't getting through.

After the scanner had checked my irises, the door beeped and swung open. I made my way down to the generator room first. The backup generator was once again making an alarming amount of noise. I'd run a maintenance check on it only a couple of days ago, but it obviously needed a full-system check—not something I could risk, as it would take me close to a day to pull the thing apart, and probably that again to fix whatever was wrong, then put it back together—*if*, of course, I actually had the parts here to fix it with.

I ordered the computer to do another maintenance run, then coded the south-siding exit out of the system and switched its programming back to running only at night. Thankfully, the other two generators were purring along quite happily, but I included them in the maintenance check anyway. It would take them offline for an hour, but the solar system could cope with running the purifiers and the doors for that short amount of time. And it wasn't as if I needed the full security system running right now anyway, because no one was getting in or out of this place very easily in the near future. Maybe not even me.

With that done, I headed for the hydro pods to clean up. Once I'd dressed, I attached my guns, then grabbed some fresh ammunition as well as a flash stick from the store and headed down to the south-siding exit. The destruction became evident long before I got anywhere near the tunnel. The two nearby nursery units were filled with dust and debris, but the lights were at least working in them. The same could not be said of the third nursery that now acted as a forecourt for the south-siding exit. The force of the explosion had caused a huge portion of the ceiling to collapse, and wires and broken lights hung in long and dangerous lengths. Sparks spun where wires touched, vivid but fleeting motes of brightness in the thick darkness.

I carefully picked my way through the mess and stopped in front of what once had been the tunnel's entrance. Not only had it collapsed, but given the amount of dirt and stone mixed into the debris, it seemed the hill above us had caved in as well. I pulled the flash stick free and hit the switch. Its bright blue-white light pierced the darkness, but all it revealed was a solid wall of dirt, rock, and shattered concrete. I couldn't see any way to get through the mess. The small air pockets and spaces that would normally have existed between the debris of concrete and stones—spaces that would have allowed me to slip through in energy form—simply didn't exist because the soil had filled them.

Whether the whole tunnel was like that or simply this portion of it was impossible to say, but one thing was obvious—I wasn't getting out this way anytime soon, and *that* was going to make things damnably difficult.

I swore, then turned and headed back. Sparks chased my heels, disappearing only once I'd reached the brightness of the next room. I returned to the generator room and shut down the power to the half-destroyed nursery room, then continued on up to the fourth level. If I couldn't get out through the south-siding exit, then my only hope was the museum one, destroyed as it was.

I really *didn't* want to think about what I'd do if it were as impassible as the other.

The little ones spun around me as I neared what remained of the staircase, then ran off laughing again. Apparently, the men had finally left the museum—no surprise, given dusk was coming in and Central's drawbridge would soon be taken up for the night. Even Jonas had left, though he was walking around the museum, heading toward the south-siding exit rather than to either Central or Chaos. Bear and Cat were trailing after him.

I called to the darkness within me and, once I'd become energy rather than flesh, surged upward. The destruction became far more evident past the third level. The outer wall had collapsed inward, as had much of the inner wall. But— unlike the south-siding exit—there were plenty of spaces and gaps in between the huge chunks of concrete and steel, which gave me the room to squeeze through. Dusk had seeped into night by the time I reached the thick metal trap-door that had once separated the staircase from the museum. It had been twisted like tinfoil and was now held in place by a solitary hinge. That it was even here said a lot about the strength of the old cover, given how close to the blast it must have been. I worked my way past both it and the few remaining concrete boulders, and finally entered the museum itself. Once I was absolutely sure no one remained, I regained human form and looked around.

The destruction was every bit as bad as the images the ghosts had shown me. The air was so thick with dust it felt like I was breathing in grit, and there was a vast mound of concrete, office equipment, and furniture sitting in the center of the museum. The whole area was a sea of wires and cabling that hung from what remained of the walls or snaked across the floor. None of them were sparking, which meant the power was probably off. While most of the bunker's old systems were powered by the old solar panels, the museum itself and all the newer additions—including lighting and security systems—were connected to Central's grid. Meaning the laser curtain that usually protected the museum at night would now be inactive.

I walked across to the museum doors, my footsteps echoing lightly in the thick stillness. The security panel on the right side of the doors was dark, so I wedged my fingertips into the joint between the two heavy metal doors and tried to force them open. They refused to budge, so I called in the little ghosts, and after a moment, we'd opened them enough for me to slip through. I didn't bother closing it, though—I just headed for the south-siding exit.

I found Jonas near the remains of the old grate that protected the tunnel's exit. He rose as I approached, and the relief that crossed his features briefly warmed me, even though it undoubtedly stemmed more from Nuri's statement that I was the only one who could rescue the missing kids than any true joy at discovering I was still alive.

I stopped several yards away from the exit's remains and crossed my arms. Cat's energy caressed my shoulder, but Bear was off investigating a section of grate that had been blown at least a hundred yards away from its original position. "I thought you didn't have any government connection."

Jonas frowned. "I don't—"

"Then why were you in the museum inspecting the damage with the engineers? An ex-ranger now living in Chaos wouldn't have been my first choice to call to investigate such an event."

"And normally, that would be true. But the man in charge just happens to be a friend of mine, and we did have a vested interest in knowing whether you lived or died." He paused and scanned me. "I can understand why they blew this tunnel, but what were they trying to achieve by blowing up the museum?"

"There was a secondary entrance situated there. I'm not sure how they knew about it, though. It's certainly not in any of the base plans, and no one has ever seen me use it . . ." My voice trailed off.

Actually, someone *had*.

"What?" Jonas immediately said.

I cleared my throat and looked away. Penny was his niece, and it was unlikely he'd believe she'd do anything to jeopardize the hunt for the other missing children.

"Tiger—" he all but growled.

I grimaced. "The only person who knew there was an entrance in the museum was Penny. We used it the night I saved you both."

"She couldn't—"

"Once that might have been true," I cut in. "But even Nuri has said there's a darkness in Penny's soul now that hadn't been evident before. How do we know that darkness isn't some form of connection back to those who held her?"

"We don't. Which is why she's been placed on sensory lockdown. She can't even contact Nuri telepathically, let alone anyone else. It *can't* be her."

"Then who else could it be?"

"Did Sal know about the entrance?"

"No. He wasn't even in the base when the Draccid was fed into the ventilation system." I paused and briefly closed my eyes, battling the memories that always hit whenever I thought about that day. Cat's energy pressed closer, offering me comfort. In some ways, the little ones were lucky—they might have died a horrible death, but they'd at least died relatively quickly. And because most of them had been so young when it happened, they really hadn't retained much memory of the event. But it was not something I could ever forget. I might have been designed to be immune to all manner of poisons and toxins, but that didn't mean I didn't suffer the effects of them. I'd lain on the cold nursery floor, surrounded by the bloody remnants of the children, as my body first disintegrated and then rebuilt itself. It had taken weeks to regain enough muscle and strength to drag myself into one of the mediscan beds. It was only the presence of the ghosts that had kept me strong and sane during that period.

"Tiger?" Jonas said softly.

I blinked and refocused on him. "If they were trying to stop me exiting the bunker, why didn't they blow the ventilation system?"

"Because vent systems generally aren't strong enough to support human weight."

"Yes, but they know I can become vampire."

"Because of Sal, or because they've seen you do it?"

"I'm not sure if he remembered I could do that, but the vampires have witnessed it." Several times, in fact.

I walked around him and headed up the hill, needing to see how bad the cave-in was from up top.

"But would they have mentioned it to those now working with them?" He fell in step beside me, his shoulder close enough to mine that I could feel the heat radiating off him. "And what if the purpose of the explosions was not to keep you in, but to keep you out?"

I frowned. "Why would they want that? If they had trapped me inside the bunker, they'd have successfully nullified me."

"Yes, but thanks to Sal and the scan Nadel Keller took of your RFID chip, they know what identity you're using in Central and where you're supposedly living."

The RFID chips—or radio frequency identifier, to give it

its full name—were inserted into the wrist of every newborn these days, and held not only your ID papers but work, credit, and medical history. I had one thanks to Nuri and her crew, and the history within it was nothing but fabrication—but it was a fabrication that was fully checkable. According to Nuri, the mercenary network worked on a quid-pro-quo basis, and they backed each other's reinvented histories as and where necessary.

"That's presuming Keller is involved with whatever is going on. I got the impression from Sal he was nothing more than Winter Halo's recruitment officer."

"Even if that's true, your information would now be on their files. It would be easy enough to access."

"Which would only help them if I became one of the new security recruits at Winter Halo. Given that Sal arranged the interview with Keller, I'm thinking we need to find another method of getting in there."

Winter Halo was the company responsible for running the initial drug tests on the families of the missing children. Though the government had cleared the company of any involvement in their disappearance, Nuri still believed there was a connection—but it was one they couldn't directly investigate because they were too well-known within the city. Which was why I'd asked Sal if he could use his influence and get me a job there. Winter Halo apparently had a high turnover rate of night security guards, and getting such a position would have enabled me to investigate without being overly obvious.

"In your current configuration, I agree it wouldn't be wise. But the information on your chip can be changed easily enough." He paused. "Was Sal aware of your ability to body-shift?"

"Yes. And it's a skill he'd also possessed, so it's probable his companions inherited it when the rift mashed their DNA together."

He grunted. "Which won't make it any easier to track them down."

Especially since the names Sal had given me—Samuel Cohern and Ciara Dream—were not the ones they were currently using. And *that* meant they could be absolutely anyone, either in Winter Halo or in the government itself. Because there *was* a government connection somewhere along the line—the crates bearing government IDs being stored in the military bunker I'd rescued Jonas from were evidence enough of that.

The ground above the exit had fully collapsed inward, and the line of destruction snaked all the way up the hill. Thankfully, there was little external evidence that this was anything more than a landslip, or that the ground had actually fallen in on an old military tunnel. I turned and swept my gaze across Central's rusting silvery walls. If I wanted to find those missing kids, then I had to not only get back into the city but find another way to get into Winter Halo. Until we found out more about Sal's partners, it was still our best chance of finding out what was going on.

But until I found a way of doing that, perhaps my next point of attack should be Nadel Keller. He'd be under scrutiny, of that I had no doubt, but he could still be a very useful source of information. I just had to be careful about how I extracted it—perhaps use the portion of my seeker skills that could access information through touch rather than sex. While the latter was undoubtedly easier, Sal had been well aware of what I'd been bred for, and I had no doubt Keller's movements would be under close scrutiny. A suddenly gained new lover would raise alarms in all the wrong places.

"Did you get very far following those tracks last night?" I asked eventually.

"They circled back around to Carleen and went into a rift."

"A false rift?"

"I presume so. I can't actually see them, remember, but given he simply vanished, it was either a false rift or magic." His gaze was a weight I could feel deep inside, but I kept my own securely locked on Central as he added, "What do you plan to do next?"

"I don't know." I actually did, but I really didn't want him tailing me when I went after Keller. His presence would be far too distracting. "But I do need to find another way into Winter Halo."

"Recruitment was our best bet, and that's no longer a viable option. Sal's partners are undoubtedly aware you were trying to access that way."

"Which means we probably need to find someone whose identity I could take over."

"Nuri is already looking into that prospect."

"Good." I finally glanced at him. "And I believe she was also going to find me a former employee to talk to."

Amusement lurked briefly at the corners of his mouth and eyes. "I thought you didn't want our help."

"I don't, but given you're obviously intent on ignoring what I want, I might as well put your presence to use. I'm practical, not stupid."

"Stupidity is not a word I'd ever associate with you. Quite the opposite, in fact."

I snorted softly. "Careful, Ranger, because that almost sounded like a compliment."

"It's not a compliment if it's a simple truth."

And Rhea forbid he actually toss a compliment my way. "Do you know where Keller lives?"

It was said more sharply than it should have been, and the amusement in his expression faded.

"He lives midpoint on Seventh. The Heldan Apartments, I believe."

It wasn't an address I knew, but it was one that would be easy enough to find given Central's street system worked from Twelfth—which was the closest to the curtain wall—to First, the innermost street and one of the few fully circular ones. Victory Street—the only street that ran straight through the heart of the city—intersected each of these streets, which also acted as delineation between the twelve districts within Central. Those near the wall were the poorer sections; the closer you got to Central's heart—where the main business district and government centers were situated, as well as the only green space available within the city—the more exclusive and richer the community. Seventh Street was a step up from the poorer districts but still considered a less desirable area than the Sixth and Fifth, which not only were considered the middle-class sector, but also held the technology district. Winter Halo held a prime spot on Sixth Street.

I had no idea what hours Keller worked, but given it had been evening when he met Sal and me at the restaurant, there was a fair chance he worked late most nights. If I got into the Central fairly quickly, I might be able to meet him coming out of Winter Halo itself.

"Is there a café or some other building nearby from where I can keep an eye on things without raising eyebrows?"

He hesitated. "There's a place called Seven Sins close by."

"Seven Sins?"

He smiled. "It's a patisserie. I'm rather partial to their pistachio and raspberry macarons."

Most shifters had sweet tooths thanks to their higher metabolic rate, but for some reason, I hadn't expected it in

Jonas. Maybe because of all the sour looks he kept throwing my way. "Are there enough credits on my RFID chip for me to buy anything at such a place?"

"Yes."

Then I was definitely going to try one of those macarons. "How long do you think it will take to find someone working at Winter Halo whose position I can take?"

"We should have several possibilities available by midday tomorrow."

"Then I shall meet you at the bunker."

He frowned. "What are you doing tonight?"

"That, Ranger, is none of your business." I sucked in the night and disappeared.

Cat and Bear chased me back to the museum exit, their laughter making me smile. Jonas hadn't been pleased at my sudden disappearance, apparently. Once I'd made my way through the debris to tunnel D, I regained flesh and headed for the bunk rooms. While I'd worn my uniform into Central many times without problems, if I wanted any chance of gaining Keller's attention, then I not only had to wear a different form, but also very different clothes. Thankfully, Nuri had given me a tunic that was more than suitable for seduction purposes. It was full-length, but split to the thigh along one side to allow easier movement, and made of soft gray wool that clung to rather than hid curves. I'd worn the same type of garment many times in the various camps I'd been assigned to during the war, and knew from experience they were not only extremely comfortable, but also sexy. Not that I intended to seduce, but he, at the very least, had to believe *that* was a distinct possibility for my seeking skills to be of any use.

"Cat and Bear, can you keep an eye on things for me here? Come find me if anything happens."

Bear grumbled about being left behind again, even though

he understood my reasons. The little ones had done a mighty job protecting this place against several vampire attacks, but I didn't want to keep relying on them alone. They were young, and sooner or later an attack would come that would overwhelm them. Bear had at least gone through the initial stages of training. He might not be déchet skilled, but he *could* fight. And he was also canny enough to call in the help of the ninety-three fully trained déchet who haunted this place if necessary, whereas the little ones tended to be scared of the older ghosts and generally avoided them.

Once I'd said all my good-byes, I headed back through the mess of the old stairwell and out into the night. I made my way toward Central, aiming for a spot midway between the haphazard walls of Chaos and the drawbridge. Though Central was a city of never-ending daylight, on *this* side of the rusting metal wall, the shadows were deep and heavy. Even in Chaos, it was only the upper reaches that had any sort of continual light protection. Once I neared the wall's massive footings, I surged upward, pressing close to the wall, my gaze on the flood of brightness high above me. But the closer I got to the top of the wall, the more the light of the UVs poured over it, and the more the shadows within me began to unravel. As my flesh form began to reinsert itself, I lunged for the top of the wall. My fingers caught the rough metal edge and for several seconds I just hung there, my heart going a million miles a minute as I sucked in air and tried not to look at the long drop below me. I hated heights, which was daft, considering that not only was there a lot of tiger DNA in me—meaning I generally landed feetfirst—but also that once I was beyond the wash of lights, the shadows in my soul would reassert themselves and halt my fall long before I ever hit the ground. But irrational fears were called that precisely because they didn't actually make sense.

I took a deep breath to steady my nerves, then pulled myself up. Central stretched before me, bright and quiet. While there were guards stationed atop the drawbridge, they only ever did full patrols of the main wall if the vampires were notably active. The UVs had long ago been protected from any sort of weaponry taking them out, and as far as I knew, the last of the bombs had been destroyed at the war's end. None had been made since. No one wanted to take the risk, given the number of rifts already rolling across the landscape.

The guards would, however, come investigating if they happened to spot me walking about the top of the wall, especially when said walls were off-limits to the general population. Which meant I needed to protect myself from casual scrutiny, and that meant wrapping a light shield around myself. It was harder to do at night, when there was no sunshine to draw in, but there was enough light coming from the UVs to make a good second option.

I took a deep breath, then called to the heat and energy radiating off the lights, drawing it deep into my body in much the same manner as I drew in the darkness. Brightness flowed into every muscle, every fiber, until my entire being burned with the force of it. I imagined that force wrapping around me, forming a shield through which none could see. Energy stirred as motes of light began to dance both through and around me, joining and growing, until they'd formed the barrier I was imagining. To the outside world, I no longer existed. The light that now played through me would act like a one-way mirror, reflecting all that was around me while allowing no one to see past it.

I finally looked down, searching for a way off this wall. Old Stan's—the place Nuri had arranged for me to stay while I was here in Central—was only a few buildings away to my left, but it probably wasn't wise to go anywhere near that inn right now. I might be wearing a very different form from any of those I'd used when I was there, but Sal had known I'd been staying there. If his partners weren't cross-checking the identity of everyone who used the place, I'd be very surprised.

I padded along the wall, looking for a building tall enough to provide a dropping-down point. I might have a tiger's sure-footedness, but I also had that stupid fear of heights to contend with.

As I moved farther away from the inn and the ramshackle collection of buildings that represented the market section, the buildings that hugged the wall grew ever taller and I soon found a drop that was only a couple of floors. I took another of those deep breaths that did little to calm the butterflies and irrational fears, and jumped down. I landed safely, my fingers barely brushing the rooftop as I steadied myself, then continued on down, jumping from rooftop to rooftop until I reached a building that provided a one-story drop to street level.

Once I'd checked that no one was watching, I released the shield. As the motes of lights danced around me and faded away, dizziness hit, a warning that while I might be physically healed, my strength still wasn't up to par. I waited until it passed, then quickly altered my appearance. With that done, I made my way along Twelfth Street until I found one of the cross streets that allowed people to walk from one sector to the next. As was the case with most, this one was a three-meter-wide canyon between two high-rise buildings bathed in UV light.

Winter Halo was easy enough to find. It was a glass-fronted

ten-story building situated not far away from Ruby's, the lovely restaurant Sal had taken me to. I paused briefly, studying Winter Halo through its reflection in the windows of the building opposite. Two silver-clad, orange-haired women guarded the front entrance and there were security cameras situated on each corner. Plenty of people were exiting the building, but none was the man I was after. I waited several more seconds, then moved on before I began to attract attention.

How was I going to find out whether Keller had left or not? I could hardly question the guards—that would only raise suspicion. Besides, their rather stern and unhappy expressions were enough to put me off approaching them. My only other option was questioning someone once they'd left the building.

I crossed the street again and waited in the doorway of a place not far away. A random assortment of people continued to go in and out of Winter Halo, but I was looking for someone who had a more authoritative air about him—someone who might have a higher level of knowledge about the company than a mere office worker.

About ten minutes later, a white-suited, rather distinguished-looking gentleman with silvery hair exited the building and began walking toward me. Not only was he talking into the comm on his wrist and paying scant attention to where he was going, but he was also a shifter—a cat of some kind, if the scent I was picking up was anything to go by. It made him the perfect target.

I briefly closed my eyes and began to flood the air with pheromones. While for most this was an automatic attraction response, we lures had been designed to seduce. I could not only release pheromones at will, but also increase or decrease the potency of them, depending on how fiercely I needed my target to be attracted.

Of course, my control wasn't so absolute that I could totally override instinct. My attraction to Jonas was evidence enough of that.

In this particular case, however, I just needed his interest at a level where he wouldn't immediately question my actions, but not so much so that he could think of nothing more than bedding me.

I flexed my fingers in an attempt to ease the gathering tension, and when he was almost level with the doorway in which I stood, I stepped out and cannoned into him. I hit with enough force to send us both tumbling, but his arms automatically went around me, cushioning my fall even as we hit the pavement.

"Oh Rhea, I'm sorry," I said, even as I wrapped my fingers around his arm and opened the floodgates on my seeker skills.

Seeking wasn't telepathy—we couldn't directly read thoughts; we simply picked up a mix of emotion and mental images and made judgments from those. My skills were more honed to bedroom use, but I could still snatch information from something as simple as a touch if I went into the process with one single question that needed answering rather than multiple.

In this case, that question was Nadel Keller—was he still in the building or had he left? Images began to flit through my mind—images that involved the stranger's most recent actions and the people he'd talked to. Seeking answers through touch like this was often hit-and-miss, even if the information I was after was simple.

"It was entirely my fault," he replied. "I was too busy

booking my table for the evening to be watching where I was going."

His voice was husky, his body responding to both my closeness and the pheromones I was outputting.

I rolled to one side but kept a light touch on his arm as he sat upright. His gaze skimmed my length, then settled on my legs—specifically, the amount of thigh the split in my tunic was revealing.

"I guess that means we're both at fault," I said. "As I wasn't watching, either."

The images kept on flowing, diving deeper into the day's actions, continuing to provide glimpses of those he'd interacted with. So far, there was no sign of Keller.

"A gentleman should nevertheless do his utmost to avoid crashing into a lady. And I do apologize."

He climbed to his feet. The abrupt disconnection had my mind reeling.

I made a show of trying to get up, then collapsed with a slight wince of pain and began rubbing my ankle.

Concern immediately touched his expression. "You're hurt? Shall I call medical?"

"No, I'm sure I just landed weirdly. If you could just help me up . . ." I gave him a wide smile and held out my hand.

He gripped it. The minute our hands touched, my seeker skills flashed into overdrive. Images spun through me, but Keller's profile was noticeably absent. Either this man didn't know him or their paths hadn't crossed that day.

And as much as I wanted to, I didn't dare come out and ask. I had no idea how suspicious Sal's partners were, or how close an eye they might be keeping on Winter Halo's top employees, but it wasn't worth the risk.

The stranger pulled me upright and slipped a hand under my elbow in support as I wobbled about on one leg. His grip was firm and warm, and perhaps a touch more intimate than required. Even so, I ramped up the strength of my pheromone output a little. I didn't need him thinking too much right now.

"Are you sure you're okay?" His gaze skimmed me, but it held a whole lot more appreciation than concern. "Because it wouldn't take long—"

"I'm fine." I put some weight on my foot to demonstrate and gave him another warm smile. "Thanks for the concern, though."

"Do you need help to get anywhere?"

I hesitated. "I'm actually supposed to be meeting a friend at Seven Sins, but I don't know this area very well. You wouldn't happen to know where it is, do you?"

"I do, thanks to the fact that the ladies in my office seem to talk about nothing else." His smile flashed, and it lent warmth to his otherwise austere features. "It's two blocks up, but over on Seventh. I can escort you there, if you'd like."

"Thanks, but I've already taken up enough of your time."

"Well, if you do happen to find yourself at a loose end later this evening, I'd love to buy you a drink to apologize for my clumsiness. I've booked a table at Zendigah's on Second at eight." He hesitated and gave me a crooked smile. "I'm Charles Fontaine, by the way."

"Cat." It was the first name that came to my mind, and my using it would undoubtedly amuse my little ghost immensely.

"Short for Catherine?"

"Yes, though no one but my mother ever called me that."

"Then I certainly shan't." He gave me a nod. "I hope to see you tonight."

"And perhaps you will." I caught his arm and leaned forward to brush a kiss against his cheek. There was no suspicion in his thoughts, only a wish to continue the conversation.

With that, I left him. While his regret chased me, he remained where he was and simply watched me walk away. Which meant I'd judged the attraction levels just right, and *that* was somewhat gratifying. I might not have used the skills I'd been designed with much since the end of the war, but at least my control and judgment hadn't lessened any in that time.

Once I'd entered the next walkway and was out of his sight, I ran toward Seventh. Few people paid me much attention; running might be frowned upon in the more genteel areas near Central's heart, but it wasn't so uncommon in the middle-class and poorer areas. I paused when I hit Seventh Street. I didn't immediately spot anyone resembling Keller, so I hurried forward, studying each building as I passed it, looking for the Heldan Apartments.

I found them one block up and, at the same time, saw Keller coming out of a food collective a few doors farther on. He was a tall man with receding blond hair and a thin unpleasant face. As he turned toward his apartment, his gaze swept me, moved past, then snapped back.

Sal had told me Keller liked his women black skinned and big breasted, which was precisely why the form I was now wearing was the complete opposite in almost every way but one—my breasts. I was banking on the fact that a man whose preference ran to ladies with large breasts was always going to look even if said lady did not fit his ideals in other ways. Given Keller's reaction, it would seem I was right. I sashayed toward him. He didn't move; he simply watched.

But as I got close, something strange began to happen. His face lost color, blood began to trickle out of the corners of his eyes, and bubbles appeared at the corners of his mouth.

Then, with little sound or elegance, he fell backward to the pavement.

Dead.

CHAPTER 4

stopped, a curse on my lips, and both surprise and frustration rippling through me. No one else seemed to notice what had happened, and for several seconds people simply walked around his prone form. Then a woman screamed and two men squatted next to fallen Keller, loosening his clothes and attempting to revive him.

But I knew those signs. Keller had been poisoned. There would be no revival.

Which was frustrating, to say the least.

I walked on, around his body and the gathering crowd, and spotted Seven Sins on the opposite side of the street. After waiting for several airscooters to zip past, I walked across and grabbed a table next to the window. A waitress appeared almost immediately, and after I'd ordered a coffee and one of the macarons Jonas had mentioned, I crossed my arms and watched what was happening with Keller's body. The two men were still attempting to bring him back, and there were several people using their wristcoms, calling either medical, the corps, or maybe even the news. Everyone else seemed content to simply watch. I skimmed their faces, looking for anyone who either snagged my instincts or looked familiar. Despite what I'd said to Jonas, I *did* have some idea what one of Sal's partners looked like. The day after I'd used my seeker skills on Sal, I'd asked Cat and Bear to shadow him and report back on everything he did, and everyone he met. While he'd spent most of the day working at Hedone, a high-end brothel he'd owned, he did make one journey outside—to meet a tall, thin-faced man with shadowed skin, dark hair, and magnetic blue eyes, deep in the heart of Winter Halo. My little ghosts hadn't liked the alien feel of that stranger, and I really had no doubt that he was one of the two people who'd been caught in that rift with Sal.

So why had they killed Keller? Was it simply a matter of tying up all loose ends? It wasn't likely to be coincidence that Keller had been murdered not long after several bombs were set off at the bunker. Whether they'd meant to trap me in or out of it really didn't matter; what *did* was the fact that they were covering their tracks and would undoubtedly be extra cautious from this point on—and *that* meant I'd have to do the same.

It was a good thing that the only alterations I'd made to my natural body shape were to erase the black stripes out of my silvery white hair, and increase both my height and breast size. Sal's partners might know I could body-shift, but my short hair and the simple tunic I was wearing were currently very fashionable in Central's expensive heart. Even if they *had* been watching Keller's movements, it was doubtful they'd have picked me out of the crowd. Not when there were so many other tunic-clad, silvery-haired women *and* men on the streets right now.

The waitress brought over my coffee and macaron. Once I'd swiped my RFID chip over the scanner to transfer the appropriate number of credits, I picked up the macaron and cautiously bit into it. I might have ordered it for cover purposes, but, by Rhea, it was *good*—thin and crunchy on the outside, softer than a cloud on the inside, and the absolutely most delicious thing I'd ever tasted. If I'd known exactly how many more credits I had left, I would have ordered a couple more. And probably would have made myself utterly sick in the process, given that sweet things and I weren't always compatible. My taste buds tended to lean more toward the bitter end of the scale—a result, no doubt, of the fact that there'd been nothing like this offered to déchet in the military bunkers, and sweets had certainly been scarce in the shifter camps I'd been sent to during the war.

I licked every tiny crumb off my fingers, then nursed my coffee and continued to watch events across the street. Both the corps and medical turned up, and an exclusion zone was quickly set up around Keller's body. Corps interviewed the two men who'd attempted to save Keller, as well as the people who'd called in the death. There was little else they could do. Keller's body was soon bundled into a bag and whisked away. The two corps officers moved down the street and disappeared into the Heldan Apartments. Obviously, they were going to inspect Keller's residence. I wished I could do the same, but that would be entirely too dangerous. But it was, perhaps, an action Nuri or one of her team could undertake.

Which left me with Charles.

He might not have had anything to do with Keller either today or at any time, but I'd gotten the impression he was a fairly high-level employee within Winter Halo. If that was true, then he could at least provide me with information on either the company—and what they might be up to—or the mysterious man in charge.

I glanced at the clock on the wall. It was already close to eight, but I doubted my being late would make much difference. Not if the evening ended in Charles taking me to bed—which was precisely my aim. My seeker skills were far more intense—and reliable—during sex.

I might have sworn after the war to only ever bed someone because I *wanted* to rather than had to, but there were lives at stake here. Young lives. I didn't care what—or who—I had to do; not if the result was bringing those missing kids out from whatever hell they were currently in.

I finished my coffee and then walked out of the café and headed for Second Street. It took me close to twenty minutes to get there, then another ten to find Zendigah's. It was a small three-story building situated on the corner of Second and a cross street into First, and its interior was as shadowed as any of these places ever got. A large—and very real—hearth dominated the small room. The fire belted out so much heat the air practically shimmered, and there were half a dozen leather sofas scattered about, most occupied by white-clad gentlemen either reading or drinking. Charles wasn't among them.

A waiter made his way through the chairs and gave me a welcoming smile. "How may I help you this evening?" His voice was soft and plummy, and perfectly matched his plush surroundings.

"I believe Charles Fontaine might be expecting me."

"Ah yes, he did mention there might be an additional guest this evening. Please, this way."

I followed him through the small room and up a rather steep set of stairs. The second level held six well-spaced tables, all of which were occupied, but we moved on to the third—and final—level. This floor was almost entirely all glass, and it gave a view directly down the cross street and into Central's one and only park. Charles's table held the prime spot for that view, which had to mean he was not only high-level within Winter Halo, but also rather wealthy. A view like *that* certainly wouldn't come cheap, no matter what the establishment.

He looked up as we approached, and a pleased smile creased his features as he rose.

"I do hope your invitation was sincere," I said as the waiter pulled out the chair opposite. I subtly began releasing phero-mones again. "Otherwise this could get a little awkward."

"No, no, I'm pleased you accepted my invitation." He waited until I was seated, then sat back down. "I've only just ordered—would you like something?"

"Whatever you're having will be fine." And undoubtedly far better than anything I would have had back at the bunker. "How are you feeling after our rather abrupt meeting this evening?"

"I think I've come away with nothing more than a bruised hip. Yourself?"

"Same." I smiled up at the waiter as he poured me a wine, then picked up the glass and raised it. "To new friendships."

Charles clicked his glass against mine, then took a drink, his gaze scanning me appreciatively over the top of the glass. "I have to admit some surprise that a lady as lovely as yourself was unattended."

Which was a very subtle way of asking if there was anyone in my life. I smiled. "I could say the same about a gentleman such as yourself."

"Ah well, I'm afraid I'm rather committed to my work. It makes relationships . . . difficult."

"Just so." I took a drink. "So, what work is it that you're so committed to, if it's not impolite to ask?"

"I'm the financial director at Winter Halo." He grimaced. "It is a somewhat demanding position."

Financial director? Intuition really *had* picked a ripe one when it had settled on this man; if *he* didn't know where the skeletons were buried, few would.

"And one I suspect you do not wish to talk about."

"Well, not really. What about yourself?"

"I'm currently between positions." I shrugged. "And certainly not in a hurry to find anything right now. I'm enjoying the leisure time."

He smiled and started talking about what he did on his days off. I listened attentively, nodding and laughing wherever appropriate. Which isn't to say I wasn't enjoying myself—Charles was a nice if somewhat old-fashioned gentleman, and the food and the view were spectacular.

As the waiter brought us both a coffee, Charles leaned back in the chair, his expression warm but somewhat contemplative. "I've really enjoyed this evening."

"Yes, it's been lovely." Which didn't give him much in the way of a lead-in, but that was deliberate. Going back to his place had to be his idea, not mine.

"Yes." His gaze briefly dropped to my breasts. Desire spun, sharper than before. Keller wasn't the only one who was a breast man, obviously. After a small pause, Charles added, "If it's not too forward of me, would you like to come back to my place for a nightcap?"

"Are we talking cognac?"

"We certainly are."

"Then I would love to."

He immediately called for the waiter and paid the bill. We walked outside in companionable silence, but the night air was crisp. I shivered and rubbed my arms; I needed to get some warmer clothes if this seduction went any further than one night.

Charles took off his coat and swung it around my shoulders. "My apartment isn't too far away, though we'll have to walk, as I don't own a vehicle."

He slid one hand down my spine to a point just above my tailbone. It was a point that would have informed him I was wearing no undergarments. The scent of desire grew sharper.

"A short walk will be pleasant after such a lovely meal." I stepped a little closer so that my shoulder brushed his. His body trembled with expectation, which made me wonder just how long it had been since he'd lain with a woman.

His apartment was situated two blocks down from Zendigah's, right behind the area on First Street that held most governmental buildings. Regulations restricted construction height to a maximum of twenty levels on both First and Second, and his building was one of the tallest. He scanned us in, then escorted me to the elevator. It, like the building itself, was glass fronted and, as we got higher, offered amazing views over the parkland. His apartment was situated on the twentieth level—a top position that was not only the most prestigious but also the most expensive.

The elevator opened into a foyer that was spacious, bright, and white. There were only two doors—one on the left, the other on the right. Charles touched my back and guided me right. The sensor beeped as we approached and then the door opened. Obviously, it had been programmed to respond to his RFID chip.

The room beyond was one vast white space, with walls of glass on two sides that provided spectacular views over

Government House or the park. The furniture was either white leather or glass, and even the air smelled different; cleaner.

"This place is beautiful," I said.

"The building is family owned. I inherited this apartment from my grandmother." He took the coat from my shoulders. After hanging it up, he walked across the room and pulled out a beautifully ornate bottle from a drinks cabinet, pouring a generous amount of alcohol into two large balloon glasses.

"And I would think you'd thank your grandmother every day for gifting you with such a gorgeous view."

I went over to the window, knowing the bright lights of the nearby UVs would make my tunic translucent.

"I was rather lucky. But then, I was also her only grandson."

He moved toward me. Though I wasn't actually watching him, the strengthening scent of desire told me he was enjoying the view.

"Then why do you work?" I asked. "It sounds as if you don't need to."

He handed me a glass. "Because I want to. And because my other option is not one I wish just yet."

I didn't ask what that option was, simply because a note in his voice suggested he didn't want to talk about it. Silence fell as we sipped our drinks. After five or so minutes had passed, I leaned back against him. His free hand slid around my waist, his fingers briefly skimming the underside of my breasts. Desire stirred; it wasn't a fierce thing, wasn't a rush, but I nevertheless welcomed it. Seduction was always easier when I felt at least *some* connection, and that hadn't always been the case during the war, despite my natural affinity to shifters. But then, I'd never found brutal men appealing, in bed or out, and many of the generals during that time had been little more than the beasts they accused déchet of being.

Once I'd finished, he plucked my glass from my hand, then turned me around and kissed me. It was at first almost too polite, but it deepened—became more ardent—once he realized I was willing.

I wrapped my arms around his neck and pressed closer. His kisses became fiercer, his tongue tasting and exploring my mouth. Then he pulled away, caught the end of my tunic, and tugged it over my head. He tossed it onto the nearby sofa and stood back.

"Magnificent," he murmured as his gaze did a long, slow journey down my body. "Just magnificent."

Then he stepped close again and with hands and mouth tasted, teased, and explored. I undid his shirt and slipped it from his shoulders, but as I loosened his trousers to caress the heat of his erection, he caught my hand, stopping me.

"This will be over far too fast if you do that." Amusement warred with desire in his expression. "I also believe we have provided the neighbors with enough entertainment."

He tugged me away from the window and led me into one of two rooms at the rear of the apartment. It was a bedroom complete with a huge glass bath—something I'd never seen before. The bed itself was equally impressive—a huge round thing covered in white silk and furs.

Sensation rippled through me as I lay down, and memories of times past when I'd lain on coverings such as this stirred. At least this time I was doing so of my own free will.

"Before we continue," he murmured, tracing a circle around my belly button, "I need to inform you that while I might be in my twilight years, I am still fully fertile."

"Your scent told me that. But it's not a problem." But not,

as he would undoubtedly presume, because I was protected from impregnation, but because I'd been created sterile.

He smiled and continued his seduction, until sweat sheened his body and desire was evident in mine. Only then did he let me touch him, caress him. Only then did he let me climb on top of him and drive him deep inside.

That was the moment I unleashed my seeker skills.

My energy and my aura merged with his, entwining as intimately as our bodies were now entwined. Emotions and thought became something I could see and taste, memories something I could raid. I ran swiftly through the surface images, sensing in them utter delight and monstrous need. It really *had* been a long time since he was with a woman.

I plunged deeper, seeking hidden recesses and pockets of memories. Saw, in rapid succession, fragmented images of the past week—his actions, the projects he was working on, the financial problems he was dealing with, as well as those who worked under him. I dove deeper still, looking for information on the man who ran Winter Halo, and caught a name—Rath Winter. An image rose, one that matched what the ghosts had already given me. And with it came a sense of frustration; whatever Rath Winter had Charles doing right now, Charles wasn't happy with it.

I wanted to chase those emotions down and try to find out why, but I refrained. Cats tended to be a little more sensitive to such intrusions than other shifters, so it was always better to access information over a period of sessions than to attempt to gather it all at one time.

I slowly—carefully—withdrew. As awareness of the here and now resurfaced, I reimmersed myself into the sensations flooding my body. Became aware of his hands on my hips, holding me down, and his teeth as he alternately grazed and then suckled my breasts. Became aware of his groans as his body became more demanding and desperate.

I rode him harder and harder, until his roar of completeness echoed in the stillness as his seed pumped deep inside me.

For several seconds neither of us moved. Then I leaned forward and kissed him gently. "*That* was very pleasant indeed."

He chuckled softly and touched a hand to my cheek, running a thumb across my lips. "And *that* was most definitely an understatement."

"Perhaps." I slid to one side and ran a finger down his chest. "So, are you the type of gentleman who hustles a lady out the door once he's had his wicked way with her, or are you the sort who provides breakfast?"

"Definitely the latter if the lady is willing."

"The lady is most definitely willing." I let my fingers trail across his flaccid cock. It jumped lightly in response. Charles might be a centenarian with an unadventurous bent when it came to lovemaking, but he certainly *wasn't* lacking in sexual stamina. "Especially since I'd really love to try out that bath of yours."

He laughed and immediately got off the bed. In very little time, we were ensconced in hot, bubbly water and drinking cognac.

I'd certainly had worse assignments in the past.

Charles was as good as his word and made breakfast while I took a shower. I left with a promise to meet him again tomorrow night. While I would have preferred to attempt a second reading of him tonight, I needed to get a new identity in place—one that matched the name I'd given him.

Unfortunately, the only person who could provide that

was Nuri. I might have wanted to avoid getting involved with them again, but if it meant getting the information I needed to free those children, then I would.

I walked along Second Street until I found a walkway leading to Victory Street, the only street that ran in a direct line between Central's two gates. The walkway was empty, so I quickly wrapped a light shield around my body. The last thing I needed was anyone spotting me moving toward Chaos in *this* form. It probably would have been better to simply change back to my natural body, but it would also be a waste of energy. I'd have to change back again for Nuri to readjust the information in my newly acquired RFID chip, so it was better to stay as I was.

I headed north down Victory and eventually reached the huge gatehouse. The ends of the silver curtain that Central used in place of the more conventional portcullis had been drawn up for the day's exodus, and the drawbridge was almost lowered. I held back, waiting until the bridge was down and most of the crowd had flowed across, then followed them out. The sensors fitted into the thick metal walls didn't react to my presence, though they would have had there been more vampire in my DNA. It had taken ten years to completely rebuild Central, and by then not only had all the HDP bases been well and truly destroyed, but the déchet population and all those who had created and looked after us had been decimated. It had never occurred to anyone that someone might have survived such destruction, so they never built that possibility into their security systems—an oversight I was extremely grateful for. Feeding myself would have been far more problematic had I not been able to make regular raids into Central.

Once I was beyond the rail yards and out of sight, I released the shield and silently called for Cat and Bear. I might have to go into Chaos to get what I needed, but I had no desire to go in alone.

As I walked up the hill toward the ramshackle community, my two ghosts zipped around me, excitedly filling me in on the morning's events. Apparently, the engineers were back, trying to decide whether the museum was worth salvaging or not. The other little ones were having great fun moving their equipment around.

The metal containers that made up most of Chaos's ground level soon came into view. They were garishly decorated and basically supported the weight of the ten levels above them. They were used as shops, factories, and trading posts, and were only now finding life thanks to the fact that the sun had fully risen. The inhabitants of Chaos might show little concern about the vampires, but they didn't invite trouble, either. When dusk returned, all those who worked here would retreat upward, and all ladders and stairs would be either drawn up or locked down. It didn't often help, but the illusion of safety was better than nothing, I suppose. As I walked through the six-foot gap that was the designated entrance into this side of Chaos, the shadows closed in and the fear of being caged—of having no room and no air— swiftly followed. I swallowed heavily and forced my feet on, hitching up the ends of my tunic as I splashed through water that was thick and oily while trying to avoid the muck that dripped steadily from above. Rubbish lay in gathering drifts, emitting a stench that was a putrid mix of rotting fish and human waste. Central did provide a degree of medical, water, and sanitation support to Chaos, but just about everything else was acquired via theft or trading. Only those who lived in the upper portions of Chaos had the money to purchase anything.

I climbed the first staircase and moved on swiftly through

the next couple of levels. As usual, Cat kept close, but Bear scouted ahead, checking everyone out. Just as those people we could see—and undoubtedly the ones we couldn't—were checking me out. My fingers itched with the need for a gun, but it was probably just as well I didn't have one. Nuri lived in the middle of the mercenary district, and mercenaries tended to be trigger-happy at the best of times. While I had no doubt she'd have sent out word to let me pass unhindered, I wasn't about to trust everyone in the district to obey her. She might be a powerful witch, and she might be someone most of them respected, but they were still mercenaries— and that made them untrustworthy in my book.

I eventually made it to Run Turk Alley and once again had to weave my way through the maze of extended legs and dark gazes of the men who lounged there. Nuri's building was a construction of wood and metal coated with years of grime, graffiti, and advertising posters. It was also three times the size of the other buildings in the alley, and even had several windows along its frontage—all of which were barred.

I opened the door and stepped inside. The ghosts zipped ahead of me to check the room, their energy a mix of excitement and tension. The first time we'd walked into this place I'd been darted with Iruakandji—a drug that had been developed in the latter part of war by the HDP, but one that had only been used on a couple of occasions. While it *did* kill shifters with great alacrity, it had proven extremely unviable as a weapon thanks to the discovery that it was also deadly to déchet, no matter how little shifter blood they had in them. The fact that I'd survived the darting was due in no small part to my immunity to all known toxins and poisons.

The main room was all but empty. Two sturdy-looking men stood at an old wooden bar to my right, nursing drinks that looked too dark to be regular beer. There was no one sitting at the odd selection of tables directly in front, and booths to my left were also empty. The bartender was a woman I didn't recognize.

Her gaze scanned me critically. Deciding whether I was a potential threat, I suspected. Eventually, she said, "Can I help you?"

"I'm here to see Nuri."

"She expecting you?"

I couldn't help smiling. "More than likely."

The woman raised an eyebrow, then motioned with her chin to the rear of the building. "She's out back."

"Thanks."

I followed Cat and Bear through the main room and into the next. This room was smaller and held a ramshackle collection of chairs as well as a solitary table that had seen better days. Nuri stood next to an old electric stove near the center of the room; she was a rotund woman with rosy cheeks and wiry hair that ballooned around her head like a sea of steely snakes. Though she didn't, in any way, look dangerous, she was undoubtedly the most formidable woman in this section of Chaos—if not the entire city. The force of her energy—a force that came from the fact that she was an earth witch as well as a seeker of some power— electrified the air. To someone like me—someone who was sensitive to such energy and a seeker besides—she appeared surrounded by a halo of flickering, fiery blue.

"Tiger," she said, glancing around. "This *is* a surprise."

I doubted it, given her expression and the amusement lurking around the corners of her sharp brown eyes. "I need help."

"Indeed?" She turned back to the stove and continued stirring whatever she was cooking—which smelled delicious enough to have my mouth watering. "I was under the impression you wanted nothing to do with us."

"Yeah, well, as I said to Jonas yesterday, you're apparently intent on ignoring what I want, so I might as well make use of you."

"Indeed," she repeated, the amusement stretching to her lips. "And what is it that you want?"

I asked my two little ghosts to keep an eye on the exits, then walked across to the stove. "Some of that stew would be a good start."

She chuckled. "There's bowls under that bench over there. Grab three—Jonas will be here soon enough."

I did as she bade and watched as she generously filled them. Jonas appeared as I was carrying two of the bowls across the table and stopped somewhat abruptly, his nostrils flaring when he saw me.

Which made me *damn* glad I'd taken the time to shower.

"Impressive." His tone was neutral, but amusement teased the corners of his mouth and eyes. "I'm gathering that particular body alteration is *not* for the benefit of anyone here."

"You gather right, Ranger." I sat down, grabbed a spoon from the cutlery holder in the center of the table, and tucked in.

He sat down opposite me and pulled the second bowl closer to himself. "Then can I ask just who it *was* meant for?"

"Nadel Keller, initially. Sal told me his preference ran to dark-skinned ladies with large breasts, but I figured he would never ignore an impressive rack regardless of skin color."

"Few men would."

"Yourself included?"

The amusement in those sharp green eyes was deeper. "I would never ignore such an attraction if they came my way, though I am of the firm belief that more than a handful is something of a waste."

Just for an instant, there was something in his smile that made me wonder yet again whether he was actually attracted to me, or if it was simply some sort of game he was playing.

Nuri joined us at the table, placing a round of bread between us and breaking the moment. Whatever the moment actually had been.

"So," she said, tearing off a chunk of bread before pushing it my way, "what do you need?"

"Three things, the first being a new identity. One whose name is Cat—which will need to be short for Catherine." Little Cat clapped her hands in delight at this bit of news, and a smile tugged my lips.

"That is simple enough to do," Nuri commented. "But I'm thinking the rest of your requests will not be."

"No." I munched on the bread and contemplated her for several seconds. "I need the identity to be based on Third Street—at the very least—and I need enough credits to go with such an identity."

She leaned back in the chair. "As I suspected, a tall order. Why?"

"Because Nadel Keller is dead, and I've found a new target."

"Did you kill Keller?" Jonas asked.

I glanced at him. "No. He was poisoned. He dropped dead on Seventh before I got anywhere near him."

"Meaning Sal's partners are tying up loose ends."

"So it would seem."

"Who is your new target?" Nuri asked.

"Charles Fontaine. He's the—"

"Financial director at Winter Halo," Nuri finished for me. "And the perfect subject for information gathering."

I frowned a little at the odd emphasis she seemed to place on information—it was almost as if Charles had more information to give than just about Winter Halo. And maybe he did—it wasn't like I knew all that much about him at the moment. "My selecting him was more good luck than good judgment."

Nuri smiled. "Perhaps. And perhaps the goddess is favoring our quest."

"Maybe. None of us are dead yet, after all."

Her smile grew. "What did you tell Fontaine about yourself?"

"Not a lot. I'm currently between jobs and enjoying the free time." I hesitated. "I'm also going to need more clothes. I cannot keep meeting him in the same tunic."

"Especially given that the seams on the current one would appear ready to give way," Jonas commented.

"Nice of you to be worried about such an event happening, Ranger."

His smile flashed. "Oh, I'm not. Trust me on that."

An answering smile tugged at my lips, though I didn't reply.

"Everything you've asked for we can achieve," Nuri said. "Even if it will take some time to do so. It does create another problem, however."

"Just the one?" I said, amused. I tore off some more bread and dunked it into my stew. "And what might that be?"

"The Winter Halo security position. While they might not question Fontaine gaining a new lover, they most certainly will if said lover also applied for a position at Winter Halo."

"I couldn't apply as Cat—wrong hair color for a start."

"Which isn't a problem, given you can change it at will," Jonas said.

"Yes, but then my looks won't match my RFID chip, and that *is* a problem."

"That it is," Nuri said. "Perhaps what we need is not only someone already working at Winter Halo with the same blood group as you, but someone who happens to be left-handed."

I frowned at her. "How is *that* going to help the situation?"

"RFID chips are always inserted into the dominant hand," Jonas said.

"Meaning I could wear two separate chips, and no one would be the wiser?"

"As long as you kept aware of which hand you were using in each identity, then no, they shouldn't," Nuri said.

"How much more difficult will it be to find a left-hander?"

She shrugged. "We have some access to their personnel profiles."

I refrained from asking how. Right now I really *didn't* want to know just how close their links with the government were—and I just hoped Nuri meant it when she said both my ghosts and I would be left alone when all this was over. "And these profiles list whether you're right- and left-handed?"

"RFID chips do. Even sexual preferences are listed on the things."

"Is nothing sacred?" I asked, somewhat bemused by this news.

"Not since the war. What blood group are you?"

"O-positive."

"Good. Having the most common blood group makes our task a little easier." Nuri pushed upright and walked over to the old bench. When she returned, she handed me a small piece of paper. On it was a name—Kendra James. "She's a former employee of Winter Halo who is willing to talk. I've set up a meeting with her for ten this morning."

I glanced at the old timepiece on the wall. It was now

after nine, so she wasn't giving me a whole lot of time to get back into Central. "Where? And what does she look like?"

"Place called Farmers on Twelfth, about a block up from the market. And aside from the orange hair, she has a nose ring."

Which was unusual, as most shifters tended to avoid piercings. "And there's enough credits on the current chip to at least buy her a drink?"

Nuri nodded. "We put five hundred on it, so more than enough."

Meaning I *could* have had more of those macarons. I finished my stew, then pushed the bowl away and rose. "How long will it take to set up the new ID?"

"When is your next meeting with Fontaine?" Nuri countered.

"Tomorrow night."

"Good. We should have it mostly set up by then." She hesitated. "Be wary if you head into Carleen over the next couple of days—there have been some very bad vibrations coming from that place recently."

I frowned. "Bad in what way?"

"There is a dark magic growing in there now—a magic far blacker than the stuff that guards the false rifts. It stains the earth and fouls the air; I can feel the force of it from here."

"That's probably the huge wall that has been raised around the main plaza. It protects the false rift that was shifted there recently." I grimaced. "The ghosts were complaining that it blights their bones with its malevolence."

She frowned. "Can you describe it?"

I hesitated. "There's no sign or indication that it exists when you approach it. There's not even any sort of energy overflow. But it is, according to little Cat, two trees high, and when you get within arm's reach, a thin strap of green light snaps up from the ground and attempts to snare you. Its feel is foul, and it's unlike anything I've come across before."

"That sounds like the energy of the earth itself has been corrupted," Nuri murmured. "And if that *is* the case, we are truly dealing with a witch of some power."

Of that I had no doubt. "Can you counter such a barrier?"

She hesitated. "It takes time to dismantle spells from unknown origins, and I fear *that* is something we do not have enough of."

My frowned deepened. "Meaning time is running out for those kids?"

"Yes." She rubbed a hand across her eyes, and for the first since I'd met her, I sensed fear. "But my main worry is what these people intend. If they're anywhere near finding a form of immunity for either the vampires or the wraiths, we are all in deep trouble."

A chill ran through me—a chill caused not so much by her statement, but rather by a sinking feeling that the vampires *would* attack en masse sometime in the very near future.

I shivered and rubbed my arms. "When I asked Sal why he and his partners had separated the five children we rescued from the others, he said it was because they had outlasted their usefulness."

Jonas frowned. "Did you ask why?"

I nodded. "Yes, but he didn't really say. He just said that all the children in the program were either survivors of the rift doorways or the children of said survivors."

I hadn't actually been aware that there were two types of rifts at the time, but, according to Sal, while most *did* kill, the small minority that were doorways bled not only magic into this world, but also the matter—the very atoms of creation—from the other side. And this meant that those who survived such doorways were neither of this world nor of the other, but a creation of both.

Nuri and Jonas shared a long glance. In that moment, I remembered all the times I'd not only glimpsed the darkness in Penny's eyes, but also seen it in theirs.

It was a darkness I'd also glimpsed in Sal's eyes, and one I now knew to be the darkness of a rift.

Both Jonas and Nuri were rift survivors.

CHAPTER 5

Nuri must have seen the realization dawn in my eyes, because she smiled grimly and said, "We were caught in a rift with Penny five weeks after the war had ended, when few were even aware of their existence."

"Which is why you all have a strong telepathic bond." Then I blinked as the rest of her words impacted. "Five weeks *after* the *war*?"

Jonas's smile held very little in the way of humor. "You once asked why I hated déchet with such passion. It's because I fought in that war. Because I witnessed the atrocities of your people."

It certainly explained the rage I'd seen when he told me about the gas chambers in the old Broken Mountains military base. He'd *been* there. He'd watched those deaths. It *wasn't* history and rumors to him, but something he'd actually survived.

Rhea help me . . .

I cleared my throat and said, "My people weren't the only ones who committed atrocities, Jonas. And most déchet had no will; they were only doing what they were ordered to."

He snorted. "Even the humans were not so debase as to order some of the things your kind did—"

"I would not be so sure of that." I hesitated, then added, "It was not my people who gassed yours in that base, remember. And it was a gas your people subsequently used, on us, and all of those who looked after us, even knowing what it did."

"Because there was no surer way to wipe the stain of déchet from this world."

"There were better drugs that could have been used," I snapped. "There were children down there, for Rhea's sake."

"Something only those in charge knew. And it wasn't as if the rangers had any say over how those bases—and everyone left within them—were dealt with."

"But if you did, you still would have killed us."

"Yes." He met me glare for glare, his expression cold. "Just because *I* survived does not mean everyone I loved did."

"Enough," Nuri intervened. "The past is something we cannot change. We need to move forward."

I snorted. "Has Branna moved forward? I'm gathering he's another war and rift survivor." He had to be, given the sheer depth of his hate.

"Yes," Nuri said. "But he was caught in a completely different rift."

I took a deep breath and tried to ignore the anger flitting through me. Anger wouldn't help; in that, Nuri was right. "So if you're all actually older than even I am, how is it you show no signs of aging?"

"The rifts stop the aging process. We can die, but we cannot and do not age."

Which explained why Penny had often seemed so much older than she looked—she was, in real-life terms, as old as I was.

"And is that why you said you're outcast? Because you're rift survivors rather than simply Central's unwanted like most who live here?"

Nuri nodded. "In the early years, when not much was understood about the rifts, it was erroneously believed that survivors had a connection to them and that having us in the city would somehow cause them to appear."

"Which is wrong, of course," Jonas said. "We are simply sensitive to their presence. We cannot draw or control them."

"But a law was passed that forced survivors to places such as this," Nuri continued, "and that law has never been repealed, even if we understand much more about the rifts these days."

"So why were all those people who got involved with Winter Halo's initial testing program living in Central?"

"Because most of them were undeclared rift survivors. As I said, the law is antiquated, and it is not often enforced."

"Which is why you're able to move around Central without reprisal?"

Jonas's smile once again held little humor. "We may be outcast, but we are not without use. There are many operations that the government—for various reasons—does not wish to openly support."

So I'd been right—they *did* have government connections, even if covert ones. "Well, I hope one of those black ops is not focused on either me or my bunker. And I would hope that none of you would take the job if it was offered."

"I have promised on the goddess that I would not," Nuri said. "You obviously know enough of witchcraft and magic to understand what would happen if I did, in any way, condone any action that would harm you."

"*That* does not apply to Branna."

"We will do our best to control Branna; more than that, we cannot promise." Jonas's gaze met mine, his face expressionless. "But he is only one man, and you have proven yourself more than capable of self-defense."

Yes, but even the mightiest warrior could be brought down by long-distance weapons. I glanced at the timepiece again. "I suggest you keep a very close eye on Penny. The raids on my bunker suggest she is still of value to them."

"She is well guarded in this place. No one is getting to her." And no one would want to, if Jonas's expression was anything to go by.

"I'd also suggest you get her DNA-tested."

Nuri frowned. "Why?"

"Because you said yourself, Penny is not what she once was. Given what they're trying to achieve, I wouldn't be surprised if she now has vampire and even wraith in her."

Nuri shared a concerned glance with Jonas. "I wouldn't think that possible to achieve outside the force of the rifts."

"These people can create rifts."

Her expression became even grimmer. "I'll have her tested immediately."

I glanced at Jonas as I pushed away from the table. "I'll see you tonight."

The two ghosts spun around me, excited to be leaving again. While neither of them had my fear of enclosed spaces, they nevertheless disliked this place. They loved the noise, the space, and the color of Central, but Chaos was simply too shadowed and colorless for them.

Once we were free of it, I sucked deep breaths to clean

the foulness from my lungs, then stopped close to Central's curtain wall. While I doubted anyone would be keeping an eye on former employees, Kendra was expecting someone who was going for a job at Winter Halo, and that meant someone with tiger orange hair. And while I had tiger DNA, it had come from the rare white tiger. No one had ever told me why they'd chosen to use those genes over that of the more common orange tiger, but I'd always figured it had something to do with aesthetics. White tigers might be a genetic mutation, but it was one that was considered very desirable by most cat clans—especially if, like me, they also had blue eyes.

I closed them and imagined a face that was rounded, with dimples and amber eyes as well as the requisite orange hair. I also reduced both my height and my breasts back to normal; I didn't mind this rather well-endowed version, but it certainly wasn't a form I had any desire to remain in for too long.

After I'd frozen the image of my new shape in my mind, I reached for the magic. It swept through me like a gale, making my muscles tremble and causing the image I desired to waver. I frowned and concentrated harder. The energy pulsed as the change began. My skin rippled, bones restructured, and my hair color changed. The pain that came with the shift was incredible and I gritted my teeth against the scream that tore up my throat, my breath little more than sharp hisses as pinpricks of sweat broke out over altering flesh.

When the magic finally faded, I collapsed back against the wall and sucked in air until the burning had eased. Shifting was never a pleasant thing, but sometimes it was more painful than others. No one had ever been able to explain why.

With that done, I resolutely made my way back to Central. Once I was through the gatehouse, I swung left onto

Twelfth. The curtain wall stretched high above me, a rusting silver monolith that under normal conditions would have cast this whole area into deep shadow. But the UVs burned night and day, and there were never any true shadows in this place.

I caught the sound of stall holders promoting their prices and goods long before I ever neared the market. As I got closer, I drew in another deep breath, letting the riot of delicious scents filter through my body and make my mouth water. The market was a sea of tents and temporary stalls that stretched across the entire street, forcing all those needing to get farther down Twelfth through the many higgledy-piggledy rows. Cat and Bear's excitement stung the air as they raced through the textile section, making the clothing flutter even though there was no wind in this place. As we moved into the fruit and veg section, they continued the chase, eventually managing to upset a cart of oranges.

Careful, I said, even as I snagged some of the fruit for later.

They raced on, their giggles of enjoyment making me smile. Thankfully, nothing else was sent tumbling. Once we were free of the market, I began looking for Farmers. It was, as Nuri had said, one block up, and was little more than a hole-in-the-wall place that served hot drinks and the hard, vegetable-laden flatbreads shifters had once used as trail food. I hadn't actually had the stuff since the war, and I'd certainly never seen it in Central before. This place had to be new.

I scanned the small crowd gathered at the front of the building, but couldn't see Kendra, so I joined the line and eventually got inside. An orange-haired woman with a large circular ring hanging off her left nostril was sitting at the small counter to the left of the door.

"Kendra?" I said.

A sliver of energy ran around me as her gaze met mine. It didn't feel like magic and it wasn't seeking as such, but it was certainly something similar. As it faded, she seemed to relax. "Yes. You're Zin?"

I presumed I was, if Zin was short for Zindella, the current surname on my RFID chip. "Would you like a coffee or something to eat?"

"Just a coffee, thanks. Black, four sugars."

I couldn't help my shudder. While I didn't mind some sweets, I'd never been able to face my coffee with the syrup-like consistency most shifters preferred.

Jonas, it seemed, was rare in that he liked his coffee with only one sugar—which, while still too sweet for my taste buds, was at least drinkable.

When I finally made it to the counter, I ordered two coffees and several of the flatbreads to add to my stash of oranges for later. Both would be better than the beef jerky I was currently living on.

And maybe, given how many credits I had on the RFID, I should take the opportunity to stock up at the market. It'd make a nice change from stealing.

Once I had our order, I returned to the small counter and perched on the stool next to Kendra's.

"So, what do you want to know?" She pulled the lid off the container and blew on the thick black liquid.

"What was it like to work for Winter Halo, and why did you leave?"

She snorted. "Simple questions, but the answers are somewhat more complicated."

I took a sip of my coffee. It was smoky and rich in flavor—the sort of coffee they'd often made in the camps during the war. Maybe that was why this place was so popular—it harked back to a time when shifters were considered a nomadic people. Few of them were these days. The forests had mostly recovered from the destruction, but the rifts made it far too dangerous to live within them. Though in reality, the metal curtain walls should not have provided any sort of protection from the rifts, but it was an odd fact that no cities had ever been hit by one. Maybe it had something to do with the silver most walls were coated with, which was not only a deterrent to vamps, but often used against magic.

"Complicated how?" I asked. "You can take your time to explain, because I'm in no particular hurry right now."

"Well, bully for you. *I*, however, start work in fifteen minutes and the boss doesn't like me being late."

"Then talk."

She drank some coffee. "Halo was, at first, a good place to work. The money is above set salary rates, and being a security officer isn't an overly taxing position either physically or mentally—not with all the electronic shit they have installed."

"What did you have to do?"

"Watch monitors and do hourly patrols. There's two guards per floor, but which one you're assigned varies night to night." She shrugged. "Even so, it can get monotonous."

"Is that why you left?"

"No. I left because the fucking place is haunted."

I blinked. *That* certainly wasn't an answer I'd expected. "Haunted as in ghosts? Dead-people-type ghosts?"

"What other fucking kind is there?"

Her tone was sarcastic and I couldn't help smiling. "What did these ghosts do?"

She grimaced. "Nothing at first. I mean, I heard some of the other guards saying they'd been accosted and the like, but I put it down to nerves. Many of them really aren't made of stern stuff; they're hiring on looks rather than suitability if you ask me." She paused and looked me up and down. "You certainly fit the profile, and at least you've got some muscle tone on you."

"Years of working in shitty positions," I said, voice dry. "Did the women report the assaults when they happened? Or go to corps?"

"It was reported internally, but nothing ever happened. I mean, they're ghosts. What can be done to stop them?"

"A witch could have been brought in to banish them." But I was betting it was an option that had *never* been considered, even if we *were* talking about ghosts and not something a whole lot darker in origin. Or, in this case, brighter, given we already knew at least one of Sal's partners was capable of using a sun shield. If there were *actual* ghosts in Winter Halo, I'd be very surprised.

"Yeah, well, one wasn't," Kendra said. "And even if it weren't ghosts, they make you sign a contract when you're employed that basically states anything that happens inside that building stays in that building. Anyone caught discussing or complaining outside—even to family—has to repay all credits and face the possibility of prosecution."

"I wouldn't have thought a contract like that would be legal."

"It is. Had it checked before I signed the thing."

"I would have thought even *that* would be frowned upon."

"You'd think so, wouldn't you?" She shrugged. "But they said they had nothing to hide."

On the surface, at least, it would appear so. "When did you become a victim of the ghosts? And what happened when they attacked you?"

"It happened when I was finally assigned to the tenth

level." She paused. "It's the top level any of us regular guards get to. You have to be one of the *favori* to go any higher."

"And how do you become one of those?"

"You're promoted. Don't ask me how, because I never got there." She drank some more coffee, then continued. "The first time I was attacked, I was slammed against the wall and touched up."

"Breasts and butt, or further?"

"Oh, the lot. Ghostly bastard even dry-humped me."

"So you think it was a male?"

"Yeah, felt his cock pressing against me." She laughed, the sound sharp. "But it wasn't really erect. The old boy wasn't enjoying himself much, it seemed."

"And the second time it happened?"

"It wasn't sexual. The bastard bit me."

I raised my eyebrows. "He *bit* you."

"Yeah." She swept the hair away from the right side of her neck. "You can still see the scar."

You could, but it wasn't teeth marks; wasn't a vampire bite. They were far too precise for either of those. They'd been created by either a very small blade or a large syringe.

"Do you remember much about the attack?"

She frowned. "Oddly, no. I felt this sharp sting on the back of my neck and then everything sort of went hazy. I could feel him biting, but that's about it."

Meaning it was possible a very short-term drug had been used. But why would anyone want to steal blood if they weren't actually a vampire? Did this have something to do with the attempt to gain light immunity for the vamps and the wraiths? Or was something weirder going on?

"How long were you hazy?"

She wrinkled her nose. "Ten, maybe fifteen minutes at the most." She shrugged again. "What was weird, though, was the fact that my fellow guard claimed she saw nothing. I played back the vid, and she was right. Nothing showed up."

"Had it been erased?"

She shook her head. "No, it simply showed me walking through the foyer as usual. No assault, no nothing, despite the evidence on my neck. Weird, as I said."

Meaning someone, somewhere, had tampered with it—and had done so pretty much at the same time as the attack. "What did you do after that?"

"I went down to personnel and quit on the spot. No job is worth putting up with that shit."

"So why did you, given you were aware it was happening to others?"

"Because it wasn't a fucking problem until it happened to me, was it? And as I said, the pay was good. It was worth gambling on it *not* happening."

"Are all guards assigned to that floor attacked?"

"All of them are attacked, yes, but not everyone gets bit. I was hoping to be in the latter group. Guess I got unlucky." She shrugged again. "That's why there's such a high turnover of security guards. Some are scared to go up there again, and some simply don't want to risk it being worse on the upper levels."

And I had no doubt it *would* be worse if they were taking blood samples. It was unlikely they'd be looking for something as simple as guards with a specific blood group—especially given that information had already been scanned in from their RFID chips when they were first employed.

Kendra glanced at the time. "You've got a couple of minutes left."

"Did you ever talk to the *favori*? Or talk to anyone who knew what was going on in the upper levels?"

"No. But I can say that everyone who was bitten was

moved up. You could probably talk to personnel and get a list from them."

Nuri probably could. I wasn't about to risk either of my current identities being outed to Sal's partners by accessing yet another employee.

Kendra took a gulp of her coffee. "You know, if there's one good thing about working in a brothel, it's that I'm at least getting paid to be touched up and bitten."

Intuition stirred. "What brothel?"

"Deseo."

Which just happened to be the brothel Sal had not only owned, but one that had a false rift sitting in its basement. Thank goodness I'd taken the time to alter my appearance—though I daresay if anyone *did* question Kendra, then an orange-haired woman asking questions about the company would still raise alarms.

And if I was going to raise alarms, I might as well do it properly. "Who runs that place now? I thought I heard something about the owner dying recently."

She raised an eyebrow. "That's news to me. The manager certainly hasn't mentioned anything along those lines, and the place is running as usual."

Sal had said he was a silent partner, so were the two people he'd been caught in the rift with now running Deseo? Or was it someone completely unrelated to either Sal or the immunity plot? And did he or she know about the false rift sitting in the basement?

Maybe *that* was a question Nuri and her crew needed to ask.

I shrugged. "Maybe it was another brothel and not Deseo."

"Maybe." She glanced at the time again, then drained her remaining coffee and rose. "I won't wish you good luck, because a woman with your looks won't have any trouble getting the job. But I do hope you manage to avoid them damn ghosts."

"Most of the ghosts I've come across have always been the friendly, if somewhat mischievous, type." Laughter ran around me at this statement, tugging a smile to my lips.

Kendra's expression suggested she wasn't sure whether to take me seriously or not. "Yeah, well, let's hope for your sake you don't discover otherwise."

And with that, she left.

I finished my coffee, then made my way back out to the market, stocking up on meat and fruit before walking back to the bunker—only to discover it was filled with not only more engineers and museum staff, but also bright lights. While I *could* shadow in light, it took a whole lot of strength— strength I wasn't about to waste, given I had no idea what I might be facing tonight when I headed back into Carleen.

So instead I walked deep into the park and found a nice tree to sit under. The meat had been cryovacced and placed in cool bags and the day wasn't hot, so both it and the fruit would be okay until this evening. After asking Cat and Bear to keep watch, I closed my eyes and got some much-needed sleep.

I woke with dusk and made my way back to the bunker. The horde of people had gone and the museum was quiet again. Once I'd slipped through the doors, the rest of the ghosts greeted us, excitedly filling us in on everything that had happened over the day. Cat and Bear returned the favor as I hugged the food containers close, then took on vampire form and slipped through the staircase remains.

By the time I'd stored the food, then showered and dressed, the ghosts informed me that Jonas was outside, waiting. I headed to the ammunition store and grabbed my automatics, attaching them to the thigh hooks on my combat pants as I walked across the store to get a couple of the slender machine rifles I'd adapted to fire small sharpened stakes rather than bullets.

On the way out, I remembered the reason Jonas had come here, and tracked back to the bunk room to grab my tunic as well as the trail bread to munch on the way to Carleen. I hesitated again as intuition flared, and grabbed a medipac even as I hoped intuition was wrong and I *wouldn't* need it.

Jonas was waiting to the right of the main doors, leaning against the glass dome that protected the old walls of the tower and the various other bits of the operations center—a position that normally would have resulted in him being fried by the laser curtain that protected the museum at night. But the power still hadn't been restored to the museum, and the curtain wasn't working. It was a point that made me nervous; if I could get in and out of my bunker by shadowing, then the vampires certainly could. I guess the only thing I had in my favor was the ghosts and the fact that I knew where the stair entrance had been located and the vampires—and those who were working with them—did not. Even so, I silently asked Bear to go back and boot up the lights in the bunker's main corridors. If the vamps *did* get down that far, then at least the bastards would fry long before they got anywhere important.

Jonas rose as I walked toward him, his gaze briefly scanning me. "Back to normal proportions, I see."

"Yes. Did you bring the scanner with you?"

"I did." He motioned to the backpack at his feet. "Nuri managed to get you an apartment on Third Street—it's small and near the gatehouse end rather than the more prized area closer to the park, but it'll do for your purpose."

Any apartment on Third would do. Even the so-called less preferable ends were worth more than most of the people on Twelfth could ever hope to make. "Is it rented? Because that might be a problem if anyone checks—"

"It belongs to a friend of hers," he cut in. "Access logs have been altered to show you've been staying there for three weeks."

"And the friend?"

"Left this afternoon to visit relatives in Brighten Bay. She'll be gone for two weeks."

Brighten Bay was an upper-class holiday port on the other side of the Broken Mountains. It was one of the few rebuilt cities that wasn't fully surrounded by a curtain wall. Instead, both the wall and the buildings it protected stretched out over the water for about half a kilometer and then simply stopped. Despite this, it had never been attacked—not on that open side, anyway. Theories were numerous and varied, but most seemed to think the wraiths couldn't swim and the vampires simply didn't like or didn't trust the sea. There *were* UVs, of course, meaning the sea was never dark, and that in itself provided an additional barrier for any wraiths or vamps that *did* get that far.

"Is two weeks going to be long enough?"

"According to Nuri, it has to be. If we do not rescue the kids by then, they're dead."

"No pressure, then," I muttered.

"None at all. You want to change appearance so I can scan in your details?"

"You want to turn around?"

He raised an eyebrow. "You're shy? Really?"

"There are some things I really prefer not to share, and the shifting experience is one of them. It's . . . unpleasant viewing."

"I am a war survivor, remember. There aren't many things

that could or would disturb me." Even so, he crossed his arms and turned around.

I stripped, changed to the appropriate shape, then put on the tunic. As before, my breasts tested the strength of the seams. I really needed to get more clothes.

"Right, let's do this." I lightly plucked the soft material away from my belly in a vague attempt to cool the sweat still dotting my body after the shift.

Jonas grabbed the scanner from the backpack, then hit a button. Blue light swept me, running my length several times to store all measurements—even my iris details. Once it had beeped to indicate completion, I held out my right hand, the underside of my wrist facing upward. His fingers wrapped around mine, his grip light and warm as he held me steady. I tried to ignore the flick of desire it caused and watched as he pressed the scanner against my skin. This time there was no sting of an RFID chip being inserted under my flesh. Instead, there was an odd, warm tingle as the information on my existing chip was altered.

When the scanner beeped to indicate it was done, Jonas released my hand and stepped back. "Nuri has sent a new tunic, but said there will be more clothing in the apartment by the time you get there. Here are the address and security details, as well as the details of the new ID."

He handed me a piece of paper and a tunic in the softest pink. I scanned the note quickly, then tore it up. The ghosts chased the pieces as they fluttered away on the breeze.

"You can now turn around again while I resume my regular shape."

"Seriously, have you ever seen a shifter shift? It's not pretty—"

"I have, but I'd still like you to turn around."

"You can't have been in many camps during the war," he commented, turning. "Because nakedness was common-place."

"I'm aware of that. But being naked in front of someone I'm—" I cut the rest of the sentence off. It might be stupid to refuse to admit to the attraction, given the pheromones that often stung the air whenever we got too close, but by voicing it, I gave it power. Made it something we had to confront rather than ignore.

He didn't say anything, even though there was something in his expression that said he was well aware of how I'd intended to finish that sentence. He turned around. I repeated the shifting process, then redressed in my combat gear. Once that was done, I leaned against the wall and sucked in air.

"You okay?" Jonas asked.

"Yeah. It's just that multishifting in such a short time period always takes it out of me."

"A problem all shifters face," he said. "It is not something we ever do lightly, no matter what human history might have you believe."

Which was an echo of a statement I'd made and one that had a somewhat bitter smile twisting my lips. The shifters had come out relatively sparkly under the prewar human version of history compared to the hatchet job the shifters had done on us after the war.

I folded the two tunics up and placed them near the door; they'd be safe enough there until I got back. The vamps and Sal's partners were the only ones likely to come out at night, and two nondescript tunics weren't going to help them much.

"I don't know what your plans are this evening, Ranger, but I'm heading back to Carleen."

"Then so am I." He dropped the scanner back into the pack, then slung it over his shoulder. "Do you hope to find that stranger again? Because it's unlikely he'd risk a second meeting so soon after being discovered."

"*He* could be a she, remember." I made my way across City Road and headed for the park.

Jonas shook his head. "The scent track I followed from the false rift site had male overtones, not female."

I glanced at him. "But we're talking about people who now share DNA and can shift form."

"Which does not mean they can alter their basic physiology. They can't become male if they are female—you can't, can you?"

"No." Though Rhea only knows our creators had certainly tried to make that happen. The in-tube death rate of the lure program had been high enough, but that rate became one hundred percent every time they tried to create a multisex body shifter. "But just because I can't doesn't mean that rule will hold when two males and a female were fused by a rift."

"I think it does, if only because, psychologically, they'll identify as one or the other." He shrugged. "How did your meeting with Kendra go?"

"It was interesting." I dug the trail bread out of my pocket and offered him a piece as we moved into the park. "She claimed the place was haunted."

He shook his head. "By ghosts? Or something else?"

"She said ghosts. I believe it might be someone using a sun shield." I broke off a bit of the bread and munched on it.

"That's a rare talent—"

"And one Sal was not only capable of, but also his partners. Remember, I was tracked to Old Stan's by someone who neither of us could see."

"Someone whose scent was feminine." He was silent for a minute, his gaze sweeping the shadows. "Did these so-called ghosts do anything?"

I quickly repeated everything Kendra had said, then added, "But the wounds she showed me were made by either a knife or a needle. I believe they were taking a blood sample."

He frowned. "Is that going to create a problem for you when we get you in there?"

"Given that we're not sure what they're actually testing for, I can't say. They'll find both vampire and tiger shifter DNA, but it might be something of an advantage in this case."

"Except that they'll know you're a déchet."

"Yes, but for all they know, the person I'm replacing might be one of the rare survivors of a vampire attack and therefore a dhampir. I'd imagine their DNA would be similar to that of a déchet, given survivors undergo a physical change."

"Yes, but the vampire factor will undoubtedly cause alarm. The next logical step would be to check that person's history, as all survivors by law have to be listed." He paused, his expression thoughtful. "It could be possible, of course, to alter said history and add a line or two about surviving an attack."

I snorted. "And how are you going to do that? With the government connections you swear you don't have?"

"We are *not* connected. As I said, we just undertake certain operations on a per-mission basis."

"*That* is a connection in my books." I finished the portion of trail bread and brushed the crumbs off my fingers. "Whatever is going on at Winter Halo is happening in the upper levels. Until I can get in there, Fontaine is our best source of information."

"*If* he knows anything. He may not."

"If the financial director doesn't know where the bodies are buried, I'm not sure who would."

Jonas half smiled. "Stranger things have happened."

Yeah, like a ranger being attracted to a déchet despite his experiences in the war and the hatred that ran river deep within him—not that he'd verbalize the attraction any more than I intended to.

It took us just under an hour to get to Carleen. I paused on the wide, empty verge that separated the park from the city's broken walls and scanned the area. As usual, Carleen was still and silent. Something had changed, though—the pall of darkness that hung over this place whether it was night or day had deepened. But it wasn't just the darkness that came from the suffering and the death of all those who'd been in this city when the last bombs of the war razed it, nor was it the darkness that came with the presence of so many rifts. This darkness held not only a deep and alien sense of power but also hate. The sort of hate that had started a war and almost destroyed a world.

And it was coming from the center of Carleen, where the wall of unseen energy surrounded the city square and the few building remnants that still stood there.

Nuri was right. The magic was growing in power. What that meant for not only Carleen and its ghosts, but also those of us who lived beyond its broken walls, I couldn't say. But I had a bad feeling we needed to find some way to either stop it or destroy it before it gained too much of a foothold in this world.

"There are no rifts nearby," Jonas said.

"I wish the same could be said about that magic."

He glanced at me sharply. "It's moved?"

"It's more that it's bleeding into the surrounding areas rather than moving." I hesitated, then forced my feet forward. "I think you'd better tell Nuri to get her ass up here as soon as the sun is up tomorrow. I think it's a threat that needs to be dealt with promptly."

He didn't say anything, meaning he was more than likely passing my comments on to Nuri. I jumped onto a low section of wall and once again paused, taking in the ruptured remnants of buildings and—to my left—the remains of what had once been a main road through the city. It was littered with building rubble, weeds, and trees that had been twisted into odd shapes thanks to the eddying magic of the rifts. Plastic of various shapes and sizes—rubbish that had survived the destruction far better than Carleen itself—provided spots of color against the gray of this place, as did the alien moss that continued to claim a growing portion of the city, and which glowed with an unworldly luminescence.

"Nuri is on the way."

I glanced at him. "She's risking coming out at night? When she's night-blind?"

"Yes. There are such things as night-vision goggles, you know." He stopped beside me. "She asked us to wait for her."

"You wait. I need to go investigate the rift this magic protects."

"But—"

"No," I cut in. "It'll take Nuri at least an hour to get here, and that is time we cannot spare if indeed it is running out for those kids."

"If the magic has grown, then you may not get past it. Nuri can at least tell us where its boundaries now lie."

"My ghosts can tell me that." I met his gaze evenly. "And let's not pretend you are, in any way, concerned for my personal safety. Just that of the mission to rescue the children and the part I still have to play in it."

"Meaning you have yet again misjudged me." He waved a hand, as if in dismissal of the disbelief that instantly sprang to my lips. "Go. I'll wait here for Nuri."

I hesitated, then simply nodded and leapt off the wall.

But that didn't stop the questions that crowded my mind. How the hell had I misjudged him? He'd done nothing but snipe and mistrust from the moment we officially met in that cell lit by vampire lights. Had done nothing but question both my motives and my actions, attempting to trip me up and reveal secrets. While his overall demeanor *had* lightened somewhat since he peeled away the last of those, the hatred of my race still ran deep. I could feel it, even if I could no longer see it.

I reached the road and headed up the long slope toward the central plaza, taking care to avoid the long strips of moss that now covered a good third of the broken asphalt. I knew from experience the moss leaked a substance that acted like acid on the skin; to say it was an unpleasant and painful experience would be something of an understatement.

Both my little ghosts kept close as we moved farther up the hill, but the Carleen ghosts were noticeably absent. Whether they'd been banished, or whether they'd simply fled the encroaching magic, I couldn't say, but it left an uneasy feeling in the pit of my stomach. Anything that frightened ghosts sure as hell was worthy of fear.

"Bear, do you want to warn me the minute we near that barrier?"

His reassurance swept through me, though both of them were uneasy about getting too much closer. But it had to be done, just as the rift it was protecting had to be explored; there was no other way we were going to uncover where it went.

The farther we moved up the hill, the closer we got to the plaza, the more the dark magic grew, until its foulness burned every breath and my skin itched with the sting of a thousand fire ants.

This might have originated in a dark witch's corruption of the earth's power, but it was now being fueled by magic that wasn't of *this* world—the same magic I'd felt in the shield that protected the false rifts, but deeper, more dangerous. Maybe that was why I was aware of it tonight when I hadn't felt it previously.

We were still a good twenty meters away from the top of the hill when Bear's energy slapped against me, warning me to stop.

I'd been right—the dark magic *was* on the move, even if at a slower pace than I'd first feared. But there was still no sign of its presence on the ground or in the air; if not for the foul corruption staining my lungs and burning my skin, it would have been easy to believe nothing had changed since I was last here.

I glanced up. Again, nothing. "Cat, can you check how far up this thing now goes? Bear, do you want to check the circumference? But be careful, both of you."

As they spun off to investigate, I crossed my arms and studied the city square above me, even though I couldn't see much of it from where I stood. But I *could* see the top of the false rift. The first time I was here, it had hovered at the base of the bomb crater, above the remnants of the shelters that now housed little more than the bones of all those who had died there. I shouldn't have been able to see the rift from where I stood, which meant either the rift had grown or it had been moved again.

If what I was seeing was real, that is.

Given the strength and bite of the magic, it was totally possible that it was fouling not only the earth and the bones of the ghosts, but what I was seeing as well.

I shivered and rubbed my arms. I really didn't want to either breach it or go into that rift. I had a bad feeling doing either would be inviting trouble. But I wasn't about to turn around, as much as instinct was telling me to.

I couldn't.

Cat returned with the news that the height was now three trees. Which meant, working on the average size of the trees in the park, somewhere between forty-five and sixty meters.

"Is it open at the top?"

Her energy touched me lightly. *Yes.*

I wasn't sure whether that was good news or bad. It certainly made it easier for me to get in there, but that might well have been the whole point.

Bear's news also wasn't great—the barrier had leached much farther down the other side of the hill and the force of it was destroying whatever building remnants had survived the war.

"Did you see the Carleen ghosts?"

Bear made a brief connection. *They have gathered near the old cemetery.*

I frowned. "The one outside the walls?" The one I'd battled the wraiths in?

Yes, though they gather inside the walls, not beyond them.

I hesitated and then said, "Cat, could you go down there and ask them why they moved?"

You don't want us with you? Bear asked.

I caught their hands lightly. "I'd love for you both to accompany me, but I'm going into the false rift and we already know you can't. Once you've talked to the ghosts, go back to Nuri and Jonas. Keep an eye on what they're doing. I'll be back as soon as I can."

I released them. Once they'd left, I took a deep breath, drawing in the night, letting it filter through me, change me, until I was once again little more than shadowed energy. I surged upward, being mindful of both the distance I was traveling and the shield I couldn't see but could still feel.

Once I was well over sixty meters in the air, I moved toward the square, making sure I took a curving path rather than a more direct flat one. The foul energy briefly grew more intense about three meters in and then disappeared. Its abrupt absence made me feel a whole lot lighter—and a whole lot cleaner.

When I reached the center of the old city square, I paused and studied the ground below me. I'd half expected vampires or wraiths or some other force waiting for me, but the square was empty and quiet. The only thing stirring was the occasional dust devil caused by the wind drifting through. The false rift still hovered above the bones of Carleen's people, meaning what I'd seen on the other side of the wall had been nothing more than an illusion.

Unless, of course, what I was seeing now was the illusion.

I took a deep breath to calm the nerves, but just as I started down again, movement caught my eye. The rift had begun to spin gently on its axis, its dark surface alive with shimmering, sparkling energy.

A heartbeat later, a fist-sized hole appeared in the shield I'd only been able to feel up until now. Light began to peel away from this point, until what had formed was a doorway.

Through this stepped a woman.

She was tall, thickset, with dark hair and skin, but even as I watched, her form began to ripple—change—until what stalked toward the rift was tall and thin, with pale skin, close-cropped blond hair, and an odd mark at the nape of her neck.

And the power that radiated from her was every bit as powerful as that I sensed in Nuri—only its feel was corrupted, alien.

This was our earth witch, and the third of Sal's partners.

I arrowed down as fast as I could, but the woman disappeared inside the rift before I could get close enough to grab her. I cursed and shifted shape, landing feetfirst and in my true form. Lightning lashed out from the rift's dark surface; it wrapped around my wrists and ankles, then unceremoniously dragged me toward the fast-rotating dark orb. Air spun around me, thick and foul and filled with dust, growing stronger and stronger, until it felt like I was being pulled into the heart of a gale—and one that might very well lead to a trap. Just because there'd been nothing waiting for me on *this* side of the unseen shield didn't mean there wouldn't be anything on the other.

The darkness of the rift encased me. Energy burned around me, through me, tearing me apart, atom by atom, until there was nothing left but an echo and a thought. Then, piece by tiny piece, it put me back together again.

I had no idea how long I hung in that darkness, silently screaming, but eventually the energy died, the whips holding me disintegrated, and I was jettisoned out onto a surface that was hard and cold.

All I wanted to do was collapse in a bleeding heap and let my body repair itself, but I had no idea where I was or who might be near. And the witch I'd followed surely couldn't be too far away.

I forced my head up, sucking air into my burning lungs as I scanned the immediate area. The room wasn't locked in darkness, as I'd half expected, but instead washed by a clean blue-white light. I couldn't sense my quarry's presence—or anyone else's, for that matter—but the room itself wasn't empty. Rows and rows of high metal shelving stretched before me, each one filled with an assortment of boxes or old bits of office equipment. Dust swirled through the air, the only indication someone had been through here recently.

I took a deep, shuddering breath, then crawled over to the wall and called to the healing magic. I might want to give chase, but doing so when my strength was low wasn't a good option right now.

Once the lash marks on my body and limbs had healed and my energy levels were somewhat replenished, I changed the color of my hair and eyes as well as my scent, then pushed myself upright.

The dust had settled, but it had left enough of a trail to follow. I wove my way through the metal canyons and couldn't help noticing that many items on the shelves bore government bar codes. Had I landed in some sort of dumping space for unwanted items? It might explain the government-marked crates I'd discovered in the Broken Mountains base—though all of those had seemed far newer than anything here.

I continued on, but the room was vast, and it seemed to take forever before I finally reached anything resembling a door.

But it was one hell of a door.

It was ten feet high and at least that in width, and made of a sturdy metal that rivaled anything I had in my bunker. It not only had blood and iris scanners on board but almost medieval-looking dead bolts. While these had been slammed home, they weren't actually padlocked, but they didn't need to be, thanks to the attached electronics.

I wasn't getting through *this* door with anything short of a cannon. Certainly, none of my weapons would make even the smallest dent in it. And I doubted I could shoot the panels out of action—as I had done in the basement of

Deseo—simply because these appeared to be a more modern version of the ones I had in the bunker. Shooting *them* sure as hell hadn't gotten me anywhere.

Which meant I had two choices—either I went back through that damn false rift, or I made some noise and got some attention.

After a moment's hesitation, I stepped up to the door, raised a fist, and hit it as hard as I could.

CHAPTER 6

The metal rang like a bell and the sound echoed loudly in the silence. I moved back and away, keeping to the left of the door as I hastily wrapped a light shield around myself. I wasn't sure how strong it was or how long it would hold, given the low-grade level of the lights in this place, but it was all I had. The corridors and rooms beyond this one would undoubtedly be brighter, so taking on energy form would be pretty pointless—especially given my reserves weren't great.

For several seconds, nothing happened. But as the echoes began to subside, the panel on this side of the door sprang to life, quickly running through its various checks before it cleared whoever was on the other side.

I unclipped a gun, flicked the silencer into place, and held it at the ready. The bolts slid back and then the panel flashed green and the door silently opened. No one entered, nor could I see anyone. Not from where I stood, anyway.

But I could hear them breathing. Could sense their tension, expectation, and alert readiness. Whoever these people were, they were well trained.

After a moment, one man in a mottled blue uniform slipped through the door, his movements quiet and fluid.

I closed my eyes and silently swore. *Corps.* Rhea help me, they were corps.

The first man stopped to the right of the door and silently scanned the room, his rifle raised and ready to fire. After a moment, he motioned to those behind him. Three more slipped in, blue ghosts who quickly and silently moved toward the shelving.

Tension ran through me, but I didn't move and I kept my gun raised and ready.

The three disappeared into the long metal canyons. The fourth remained near the door and didn't move. It left me with little choice but to risk slipping past him.

I silently—carefully—pulled off my boots and attached them to the spare hooks on my pants, then padded forward lightly. The stone floor was cold, but better that than the guard hearing my combat-heavy footsteps. Both the corps and the rangers might have learned the art of walking with little sound, but it wasn't something I'd ever needed.

As I neared the guard, his gaze narrowed and his gun swung toward me. I held still, not daring to breathe. His nostrils flared as he drew in a deeper breath and I knew in that instant he'd sensed me.

I fired. There was nothing else I could do—not when his finger was curling around the trigger. As the bullet tore through his brain, I darted forward, grabbing his rifle first, then a fistful of shirt to ease him gently to the floor.

I had a couple of minutes, if that, before his men realized something was wrong and returned.

I slipped through the open doorway and into the next room. The light here was sun-bright and I quickly drew it around me to strengthen the shield. The room held little more than a series of light panels and a couple of chairs. Two heavily armed guards stood near the barred exit; there was a security panel next to the guy on the right—one that was both a fingerprint and an iris scanner. The two guards had their weapons drawn, though neither showed any awareness of my presence or the fact that someone now lay dead in the room beyond.

My gaze went back to the scanner. My only way out of here was to get past both it and the guards. And finesse wasn't an option—not when every instinct I had was warning that time was fast running out. I flipped the rifle so that I was holding it by the barrel rather than the butt, then stepped closer and swung it as hard as I could. As the first guard went down I spun and kicked the other in the nuts. He doubled over instantly, clutching himself. I swung the rifle again, and he went down like a sack of potatoes.

I hooked the weapon around my shoulders, then grabbed the smaller of the two men and hauled him toward the scanner. I slapped his right hand against the screen and then, once it had registered, shoved his face against the iris scanner and forced a lid open. The scanner did its work and the gate opened.

But I didn't go through it. Instead, I wrapped my fingers around the guard's wrist and opened the floodgates on my seeking skills. The question that needed answering was simple—how the hell did I get out of this place?

Images flooded my mind and one thing quickly became apparent—leaving wasn't going to be easy. The whole place was locked down with scanners. Short of cutting off the guard's hand and stealing his eyeball, I was stuck. I frowned and dug deeper; learned that there were two emergency exits—one on this side of the building, and one on the other. Thankfully, both were ordinary exits, unfettered by security apparatus.

Sound whispered across the stillness. I glanced at the other room. I couldn't see anyone, but they were close, so very close.

I rose and ran through the gate. But as I did, blue light flashed and an alarm went off, the sound strident. The damn thing had been equipped with a body mass scanner, and because I hadn't matched the guard's registered details, the alarm had gone off.

There was nothing I could do now but run. I pounded down the bright hall, heading for the stairs I'd seen in the guard's mind, the slap of my feet against the flooring echoing softly. There was little point in being quiet now—the corps knew I was out here.

More guards appeared at the far end of the corridor. Between them and me was the exit I was looking for. I increased my pace, giving it everything I had. The guards stopped and raised their weapons. They might not be able to see me, but they could hear me.

I swore and lunged for the door. There was a sharp blast of noise, and a heartbeat later bullets rained all around me, pinging off the floors, the walls, and into my skin. I thrust the door open and all but dove through it. But I wasn't safe yet—far from it. I rolled to my feet and ran up the stairs. There was no other choice; I was already at basement level. But I wasn't aiming for the ground floor, as I had no doubt there'd now be a whole lot more than body scanners awaiting in the main exits out of this place now. My only hope of escape was the roof.

Blood began dripping from the wounds on my arms and

legs—wounds I couldn't even feel thanks to the adrenaline coursing through my body—leaving a trail behind me that would be too easy to follow. It didn't matter; nothing did but getting to the very top of this building.

I raced up the steps, my gaze on the levels high above me. One level down, then two, then three; at least five more to go . . .

Down at the basement, the exit door crashed back against the wall and men flowed into the stairwell. Time was rapidly running out.

I reached for everything I had and raced on. The stairwell became a blur of concrete and light, the level indicators unreadable.

Two more floors down, then three, four, and finally five . . . the exit door was locked. I slid to a stop, skinning my feet on the hard concrete, and pulled the rifle free. Two shots took the lock out. I raised a bloody foot and kicked the door open. UV light flooded into the stairwell, its touch warm, welcoming.

But I had no time to enjoy it. The guards were only a few floors below me now.

I raced out. The rooftop was filled with lights and photovoltaic cells, a metal forest that wouldn't do much to hide me in my current condition. I swung left, heading for the building's parapet, and saw the green of trees beyond it. And knew, without a doubt, where I was.

Government House.

The place where the ruling council met and where most of them had offices.

And Sal's partners had a direct line into it.

That was information Nuri wasn't going to be pleased to hear—not that she *would* hear it if I didn't get off this building and lose both the corps and the guards.

I wove through the forest of equipment, taking an indirect route to the edge of the building in the vague hope that such a path would at least gain me some time. But I didn't leap over the edge—even I couldn't survive an eight-level drop. Not in this form and there was no way I could change to the other. Not when my strength was draining as fast as the blood down my limbs.

I stopped, yanked my boots free, and slapped them on. The only chance I had was *not* leaving a bloody trail for everyone to follow.

My pursuers had reached the roof; even now they were fanning across it, some following the bloody trail, others ensuring that I could not slip past them.

It was tempting to immediately run—every part of me was quivering to do *just* that—but it would be pointless given the amount of blood I was losing. I tore open the medipac, pulled out the sealant, and sprayed the worst of the wounds—the ones responsible for leaving the trail. It hurt like a bitch and the nerve endings that had been dormant until now sprang joyously to life. I gritted my teeth against the pain, slapped a bloody hand against the parapet to ensure I left a print, then tossed the empty sealant container over the side. As it tumbled toward the pavement, I walked on, following the parapet around to the left edge. While I wasn't overly familiar with this part of Central, I knew the buildings along this section of Victory had even tougher height restrictions than those enforced on Second Street. Which meant both Government House and the long white buildings on either side of it were all the same height.

There was a walkway between the next roof and me—a canyon that might be only three meters wide but one that seemed a whole lot more right now in my weakened state. I edged back a couple of steps, then took a deep breath and ran. My leap was high but not quite long enough, and I barely caught the edge of the other building. For several seconds I simply hung there by my fingertips, my body screaming in pain, my lungs burning, and a red mist beginning to form in front of my eyes.

A whisper of sound—a soft footstep—from the other building got me moving again. I somehow hauled myself over the edge and rolled onto the other side, where I wasted several more minutes sucking in air and trying to ignore the pain.

"See anything?" a somewhat metallic voice said.

"No, Captain," a woman replied. "No indication of blood on this side, either."

"You and Vince stay there, but watch your back. Whatever magic this woman is using to disappear can't last much longer. Especially given the blood loss."

"Righto."

So they thought I was using magic rather than a light shield to remain invisible, which was at least something, though it was unlikely Sal's partners would be fooled. And *that* would undoubtedly mean they'd intensify the security both here and at Winter Halo.

I released the shield, then rolled onto my hands and knees and crawled away. The parapet was giving me cover and I needed to conserve every scrap of energy I could. This roof, like the rest of them in the city, was a metal forest of equipment. The heat and electricity rolling off them quickly dried the blood on my skin and clothes, but even so, there was no way I could enter either Victory or First Street as broken and bloody as I was. I had to find somewhere safe to heal as well as clothes to steal, and I wasn't going to achieve either of those aims here.

I followed the edge of the building around until I reached the next one. A huge sat dish now prevented the two guards who'd been stationed on this side of Government House from sighting me, and a quick glance over at the next roof told me it was empty.

I gathered the ragged ends of my strength together and formed another sun shield. This time the motes of light were slower in responding, but they did at least respond. I slid over the dividing wall and ran—hobbled—toward the stair entrance. It was locked. I cursed and moved on to the next building—the stairwell door there was also locked.

But the next one wasn't.

I entered it gratefully and limped down the stairs as carefully as I was able. I had no idea where I was, but if I didn't find somewhere to recover soon I'd be in trouble. Two flights down I found an entrance into the building. I wrapped my fingers around the doorknob and twisted it. Relief flooded through me when the damn thing opened.

The corridor beyond was filled with a harsh white light and people moving back and forth. There were far too many to risk entering; the sun shield might stop them seeing me, but it wouldn't stop them feeling me if they ran into me—and with so many people about, that was a distinct possibility.

I carefully closed the door and continued down, but the story was the same on the following three floors. The next one was the lobby level according to the sign. Hoping like hell Rhea gave me a break, I cracked open the door and looked out. There were plenty of people in the foyer beyond, but it was also a vast space, leaving me lots of room to move. Unfortunately, the exits were monitored not only by guards, but by body scanners—not surprising given this place, whatever it was, was still close to Government House.

But I had no choice now. It was either go out there or risk repairing myself in this stairwell—and even if I *did*, I'd still be left with the problem of getting out.

I sucked the sun shield as close to my body as I dared, then slipped out and tucked in behind a silver-suited, dark-skinned gentleman striding toward the exit scanners. The guards nodded as he approached, suggesting he was well-known to them. He stopped, placed his briefcase in a tub, and then stepped through the scanner. I was one step behind him. The scanners—predictably—went off.

The guard stepped forward and politely wrapped a hand around the stranger's arm. "Sorry about this, my lord, but I'm going to have to ask you to step this way so I can do a personal scan."

My lord? Even in this part of Central, there were very few people who could claim such a title. Both the royal family and most of the ruling families had been wiped out during the war. As far as I knew, there were only three families left who could still use the lord moniker, though I couldn't actually name them. This man had to belong to one of them, though, even if he was a shifter rather than human.

I hesitated, glancing at the door, knowing I had to escape while I still could. But the part of me that was a seeker stirred, and the need to see his face rose. I moved around. His hair was close cropped, his eyes as dark as his skin, and his nose rather reminded me of a bird's beak. It certainly dominated his otherwise unremarkable features. He wasn't someone I knew, but that wasn't surprising. Nuri probably would, though.

I spun and followed a cluster of people out the door. No more alarms went off. I was free.

The relief that swept me was so intense my knees threatened to buckle. But while I was free of the building, I wasn't entirely out of trouble. I needed to find fresh clothes and I needed to heal myself, and I had to do both before my energy ran out and the shield dissipated.

Up the street, the blue-suited corps officers were running toward the buildings on either side of Government House. They'd obviously figured out what I'd done.

I spun and headed left, but the sudden movement left me feeling light-headed. It was a warning I dared not ignore. I limped down Victory Street, heading toward the curtain wall. While I didn't know much about this section of the city, I knew there'd more than likely be upmarket clothing stores near where First and Second Streets intersected Victory. I might not have enough money to purchase items in such places, but I could certainly steal them.

Which was exactly what I did in the first place I came across.

With that done, I paused and once again looked around. Several doors down was a small, rather ornate-looking apartment building. The gentry were moving in and out of it at a dignified pace, making it easy for me to tuck in behind one of them. Although there were both hand and iris scanners, the doors themselves weren't equipped with sensors, so no alarms went off. I hesitated again inside the foyer but soon found the perfect target—a young man who seemed to have had a few too many drinks. I followed his stumbling steps into the lift and then into his apartment, and watched as he stripped and all but fell to bed. He was out of it in minutes flat.

I heaved a sigh of relief and released the light shield. The combination of fatigue, pain, and blood loss had reached a point where my body was ready to give out. But I couldn't let go yet. I staggered through the combined living and bedroom area to what appeared to be the only separate room in the place—the bathroom. By the time I'd stripped off what remained of my clothes and tossed them down the laundry chute, I was on the point of collapse. I stepped into the shower pod and let the combination of hot air and water wash the blood and dirt from my body. It didn't make me feel any better, but at least I was cleaner. I peeked out the door to check on my unknowing host; his snores were deep and loud, giving every indication he wouldn't wake up for several hours, at least.

I settled onto the warm tiles and began the deep-breathing exercises that would sink me into the healing state. Thanks to my sheer exhaustion, it took a while, but it eventually happened.

I have no idea how long it took, but when I eventually climbed back to full consciousness, there was still a cacophony of noise coming from the other room. I stood and scanned my body in the mirror opposite. My skin was free of wounds; only the one on my wrist—an old wound caused by the vampires ripping through my body when I'd been shadowed—remained. Obviously, the atoms that had been torn away couldn't fully be replaced. I guessed I had to be thankful they hadn't hit somewhere more obvious.

I hadn't really taken much notice of the clothes I'd stolen—size and shape hardly mattered when I could change either at will—and they turned out to be a larger fit than my natural size. I shifted shape so it matched what was on my RFID chip, changed my scent to a softer, sweeter one, then slipped on the silvery blue, corsetlike top and the soft, swirly skirt. Charles, I thought, with an amused glance at the mirror, would certainly approve—especially the corset portion of the outfit, given it revealed an impressive amount of breast.

I slipped on the sandals, then carefully opened the door again. My host was still sleeping, but the snores had eased off—probably because he was now sleeping on his side rather than his back. I padded across the room and hit the button to open the door. He stirred, but I was out in the corridor and heading for the lift long before he woke. If he *was* waking, that is.

I strode back out into the street and then hesitated. High above, the night skies were giving way to flags of pink and gold, which meant the drawbridge would still be locked down for the night. There was an inordinate number of people about given the early hour, and many of the shops were open. The corps and the guards were also still out, and they appeared to be checking everyone's IDs.

It was tempting to swing right and head down the nearest cross street, but that might not be the best move right now. I had no doubt the corps were active throughout the city, and while it was unlikely they'd check the ID of every single person living in this place, they really didn't have to. Not when they had hound shifters within the corps.

I scanned the street a final time, spotted an open café a few doors down, and walked over. A silver-clad, silver-haired woman greeted me serenely and showed me to a table near the window, then handed me a menu once I was seated. The prices, I noted wryly, were a tad higher than those on Twelfth Street. But then, I was undoubtedly paying for location as much as for the plush and comfortable surrounds.

I ordered bacon and eggs on toast, as well as black coffee, then leaned on my arms and watched the proceedings up the street. The corps had reached the retail sector and were moving from building to building; in each case, two men remained outside while two others went in. It didn't take them long to reach the café. Tension wound through me as they stepped inside, but I forced myself to ignore them and relax, and smiled up at the hostess as she brought my meal over.

The two corps officers moved to the back of the café, one of them stepping into the kitchen, the other remaining outside. His gaze swept the room and his nostrils flared. *Hound,* I thought, momentarily meeting his gaze and giving him a brief smile. He didn't return it.

I tucked in to my meal but could barely even taste it. Every sense I had was locked on to the two men who were now moving from table to table, checking everyone's RFID chips. Thank Rhea I'd taken the time to change my looks and my scent, both in the basement and up in the apartment.

They eventually reached my table. I glanced up and flashed them a warm smile. "Morning, Officers. How can I help you?"

"We're conducting an RFID check," one said, his voice gruff, no-nonsense. "Please present."

I raised my right wrist. The second man no longer watched me; I'd obviously passed the scent test. The scanner was held over my wrist for several seconds and then the guard checked the screen and grunted.

"All good," he said. "Enjoy the rest of your breakfast, ma'am."

"Thank you."

The two guards checked the remaining patrons, then moved out and on to the next building. I released a long, slow breath and leaned back in my chair. I'd done it. I'd escaped. Rhea was obviously as desperate as the rest of us to rescue those children; it was the only way to explain my near-miraculous escapes of late.

"Everything all right?" the hostess asked, pausing briefly at my table. "Would you like more coffee? Or perhaps some additional toast?"

"Both would be great, thanks."

I might have healed myself, but I needed to top up the reserves, and the best way of doing that was with food.

It was a good hour later by the time I stepped out of the

café. The sun had well and truly risen and there were even more people out on the street, all moving with a serene grace I wished I could echo. I headed for the nearest cross street and walked down to Third. I was in the area, so I might as well familiarize myself with the apartment Nuri had found me.

It was, as she'd said, close to the wall end of Second, not far away from the drawbridge. Like most of the apartment buildings on this street, it was twenty floors high, but extremely thin, and sandwiched by the two buildings on either side of it. The door was print-coded. I hesitated, crossed mental fingers, and then placed my fingers on the scanner. Blue light ran across my hand length, and then the screen beeped and flipped over, revealing a keypad. I typed in the security code Nuri had given me, and after a heartbeat a green light flashed and the door opened.

The foyer beyond, like the building itself, was tiny but plushly decorated in gold and plum tones. There was no guard—a good thing, given I'd supposedly been staying here for weeks. The lift doors opened as I walked toward it and a metallic voice asked for my floor number.

"Seven, please."

The doors closed and the lift zoomed me up to my destination. I stepped into the carpeted corridor and paused, looking right and left. There were only two apartments here, which I guessed wasn't surprising, given the width of the place. The one I was after was at the front of the building.

I once again pressed my fingers against the scanner, then punched in the security code. The door slid open, revealing a room that was a combination living and kitchen area. Despite the narrowness of the building, the entire place was bright and spacious—a feeling undoubtedly helped by the mezzanine level stopping well short of the double-height windows, enabling them to flood the room with light. Once again white was the dominant theme in the room, but there were at least splashes of bright color in both the cushions that lined the L-shaped sofa and the sunset pictures that lined the wall.

A circular chrome-and-glass stair was tucked into the corner to my right. I went up and discovered two bedrooms and a bathroom. Neither of them was huge—in fact, there was very little in the way of maneuvering room either side of the bed. I slid open one of the wardrobe doors and discovered an assortment of neatly stacked clothes, all of them silver. I tugged out one of the tunics; it was far too small to fit my new identity, so this room obviously wasn't mine. I put the tunic back and headed into the other bedroom. It was basically a mirror image of the first, but the silk sheets were a rose rather than silver color, and the clothes in the wardrobe were a range of soft pastels as well as the requisite silver. It made me wonder if Charles preferred his women in items that bore a slight blush of color.

The bathroom was small but perfectly formed, containing not only a shower and a glass sink, but also a hip bath. Water obviously wasn't so much a concern in this part of Central— or maybe it was simply a matter of the people here being willing to pay the exorbitant prices for a little bit of luxury. I walked back down the stairs, then across to the windows. The view was nowhere near as dramatic as Charles's, but I did at least have a reasonable view down Third to the draw- bridge. It was open, but there was little point of heading back home if the museum was once again filled with people.

I called Cat and Bear, then crossed my arms and leaned a shoulder against the window, enjoying the early-morning warmth. When my two ghosts arrived, they were bursting with news and excitement. Nuri had apparently managed to disengage the wall—not the entire thing, but enough that she, Jonas, and the ghosts could get inside. And while Nuri hadn't been able to destroy the false rift, she *had* moved it into the center of the square, away from the resting place of the Carleen ghosts.

Which was a surprising move. While it meant the ghosts would no longer suffer the agony of having their bones stained by the evil that resided within the false rift, there was still the evil of the wall to contend with, and I suspected its unhealthy darkness would do far more damage to the ghosts' bones than the rift it protected.

"Do you know why she moved it?" Because by doing so, she'd basically informed Sal's partners there was a witch of some power working in opposition—if they didn't already know it, that is.

Bear's energy touched my arm lightly. *She said the ghosts had suffered enough. That while she could no longer offer them the choice of moving on, she could at least stop the suffering the rift was causing.*

I frowned. Why couldn't she help the ghosts move on? She'd forced the déchet ghosts in the Broken Mountains bunker to move on, so why not those in Carleen? Why could she move déchet spirits on, and not human? "What are they doing now?"

This time it was Cat who answered. *Nuri returns to Chaos to replenish herself. Jonas has gone to the bunker. There are men there again.*

"Doing what?"

Deciding whether it is worth the effort of restoring the museum.

Which could be either good or bad news, depending on whether closure meant simply abandoning it or going to the trouble of bulldozing it and then reverting the area to more parkland. Not that they needed more parkland outside the walls. Few people used the current parks, especially these days when the vamps had all but wiped out the wildlife.

"I gather our little ones are keeping an eye on them?"

Amusement spun around me. I had a feeling the engineers were suffering an inordinate number of misplaced tools.

And while Cat and Bear might be oldest of all the children, it was still something of a favorite trick of theirs. Even I wasn't immune to it, especially when they had nothing else to catch their interest.

I pushed away from the window. Going back to the bunker was now out of the question, so I might as well rest here. It wasn't like I was going to get a lot of sleep when I met Charles tonight. He might be in his sunset years, he might not have had many lovers of late, but there was certainly nothing wrong with his stamina. "Can you both keep an eye on what is happening on the street? If any corps or guards look set to enter the building, wake me."

Bear's energy touched mine briefly. *Can we explore the building?*

I smiled. "Just don't forget to keep an eye on the street."

They spun around me happily, then zoomed off, leaving me wondering if the residents here were also about to suffer an inexplicable number of missing or moved items.

I headed upstairs. My head had barely touched the softer-than-a-cloud pillows when sleep hit. I woke at sunset—not that it was evident, given the never-ending brightness that was flooding the room. Central's people feared darkness so much that they didn't even sleep in it. There'd been no light controls in any of the apartments I'd been in; the lights were simply on twenty-four/seven.

I dressed and headed downstairs. Cat and Bear happily filled me in on everything that had happened over the day.

They'd explored the entire building—in between checking the street, they added somewhat hastily—and approved the place as a temporary residence.

"I'm afraid it's not one you can stay in," I said. "I need you both at the bunker tonight, just in case another attack comes. But return once the sun is up tomorrow."

I gave them a hug and sent them on their way. Then I headed out to meet Charles. He gave me a smile when he saw me approaching, but there was little warmth in it, and the kiss he placed on my cheek was also rather functional.

"Is there a problem?" I asked, when he didn't immediately do anything else.

He started, then scrubbed a hand across his eyes. "Yes. I mean no." He grimaced. "Sorry, it's work. And I shouldn't be letting it get in the way of my time with you."

"If you'd prefer to simply go home, we can do this another—"

"No, no," he cut in hastily. "The prospect of your company is the only thing that got me through the day."

"Then perhaps we should retreat somewhere where you can relax rather than continuing on to the restaurant. My place is just down the street. Or we could go back to yours." I hesitated and touched his arm. Despite the fact that it wasn't skin-on-skin contact, one word nevertheless leapt into my mind—Daybreaker. Whatever it was, he sure as hell was worried about it if my seeking skills were picking it up on such a fleeting contact through cloth. "And I have been trained as a sexual masseuse."

"Ah well, that is an invitation I cannot refuse."

I smiled and tucked my arm into his. "I also have a very well-stocked autocook and a lovely selection of wines. And as a bonus, I have the place to myself for the next two weeks."

"You share?" He sounded somewhat horrified at the thought.

"Yes." I shrugged. "Until I decide what I want to do, it is for the best."

He grunted and lapsed into silence again. I didn't mind, because my seeking skills were picking up random bits of information. Whatever Daybreaker was, it was sucking up huge amounts of money—too much, in Charles's opinion. There were also staff troubles, but the images I was receiving on that were rather random and fleeting. To know more, I'd have to wait until he was deep inside.

Once we reached the apartment, I pulled free and stepped toward the kitchen. "Would you like something to drink before we start?"

He caught my hand, tugged me back into his arms, then kissed me soundly.

"I would rather partake in the promised massage," he said eventually. "Otherwise I fear I might be poor company tonight."

I smiled and led him up the stairs. "I'm afraid the bedroom is rather small compared to yours."

"I've slept in smaller," he said, amusement evident in his tone as he glanced around. "I may be from a wealthy family, but I did my required stint in the corps when younger."

Surprise rippled through me, though I checked it before it got anywhere near my expression. But it was a reminder of just how little I knew about life in Central—and how careful I would have to be both when I was with Charles and once I got into Winter Halo.

Once we were in the bedroom, I told him to remain still, then slowly began to strip off his clothes. I took my time, exploring his body by taste and touch. By the time his shirt fell to the floor, his chest was heaving and his body was quivering with desire. I kept going, kept teasing, my fingers playing around the waist of his pants but not undoing them. Not releasing him.

When I finally did, his groan was one of sheer relief. His cock jumped free, thick and hard and quivering with expectation. I ran my tongue over its tip and he groaned again, the sound almost desperate.

"God," he said with a shudder. "If you treat all your clients this well, I can imagine you'd be in high demand."

"I did start training in the therapeutic area, but the demand for sexual massage was so high I soon switched."

He grinned. "I'm betting most of your clients pretended to have problems simply to enjoy sessions with you."

"It would be cheaper and easier to go to one of the approved brothels than come to me." I rose, brushed my lips across his, then stepped back and motioned to the bed. "Lie on your stomach. I'll go get the oil."

His gaze skated down my length. "I do so hope you intend to get naked somewhere along the line." He paused and ran a finger across the top of my breasts. "Although I am rather liking the corset."

"Then perhaps I shall leave it on."

He nodded thoughtfully, though amusement teased the corners of his lips. "I would quite enjoy releasing your bounty later, I think."

I didn't comment, just motioned to the bed again. He took a deep, somewhat shaky breath, then climbed onto it. I retrieved the oil from the bathroom, then quickly slipped out of my skirt and sat astride him. His skin quivered where our flesh touched.

When the heat of my hands had warmed the oil enough, I undid the top and dribbled it onto his skin, starting at the base of the spine, then moving upward to his shoulders.

Once the bottle was recapped and dumped onto the floor, I moved back to his butt and began to work the oil into his flesh, alternating long sweeping strokes with more circular ones. I kept my hands on his skin, increasing sensations for him as much as snagging information for me. The pieces were fleeting, somewhat insubstantial, but I could examine and connect them all later. I slowly worked my way up his spine, across his shoulders and down each arm, and then repeated the process back down his body. After dribbling more oil onto my hands, I continued on, over rump and down his sinewy legs, concentrating on his feet and toes for a while before moving back up his legs. When my thumbs slipped between his thighs and brushed his balls, he jumped slightly and groaned.

I smiled and did it again. This time his groan was more a growl. "God, this has to be the sweetest form of torture I have ever experienced."

"And it's a long way from over yet." I slid to one side. "Roll over."

He did. His cock glistened with precum, visible evidence of the desire that rode the air heavily. I sat astride him and repeated the process until his need was so thick and heavy it caressed my skin with its heat and filled every breath. It was more his than mine, but that was okay. I wasn't here for pleasure. I was here for information.

I leaned forward and said, "How badly do you want me?"

"Very."

I raised an eyebrow. "I'm not really convinced. Perhaps I should continue—"

With a low growl, he wrapped his arms around my body and quickly flipped our positions. With very little finesse, he thrust inside me, driving deep and then holding still, his body quivering with the effort of restraint and his expression one of utter pleasure. Then he began to move, and as he did, I unleashed my seeker skills. I didn't have time to sort through the images and try to understand the information—I'd worked him into such a state that he wouldn't last too long this first time. But that had also been very deliberate. Not only were cat shifters more sensitive to this sort of intrusion, but they also tended to compartmentalize the various bits of their lives—meaning that when it came to sex, that was all they focused on. Everything else—their day, their plans, and often even their emotions—were locked away into neat little boxes that could only be accessed when need was all-consuming.

I became aware of the increasing tempo of his thrusts and carefully withdrew from his energy and aura. As I re-immersed in the sensations flooding my body, I wrapped my legs around him and raised my hips to meet his movements. It was his undoing. He came with a roar, his face twisted in sweet ecstasy as his body shuddered and shook. For several seconds after, he didn't move; then he rolled to one side and gathered me close.

"That," he said, kissing my forehead lightly, "was a most excellent massage. I did notice, however, that your enjoyment was not as great as mine."

"We have the rest of the night for that." I pushed away from him and sat up. "Right now I think some food and wine might be in order."

"Followed by dessert," he murmured, one finger lightly tugging at the corset's drawstring, "which is, of course, the unwrapping of your glorious breasts."

"Perhaps." I bounced off the bed.

He followed me down the stairs, and for the rest of the night we shared food, alcohol, small talk, and sex. Each time I gained a little more information about Winter Halo, its financial and staff problems, but there was never much on the project that had him so worried. It was frustrating, but it couldn't be helped. I'd obviously done my job too well; he was totally and utterly relaxed, and that project was now the last thing on his mind.

Maybe I needed to catch him in the middle of the day, when he had no choice but to go back to work . . .

As dawn began to stir the shadows from the skies—something I felt rather than actually saw in this place of eternal brightness—he reluctantly showered and got dressed.

"So," he said, catching my hand and tugging me into his embrace. "When will I see you again?"

"What about lunch tomorrow?"

"What about dinner tonight?" His lips moved down my neck.

I smiled. "I'm seeing a friend tonight."

"Competition?" he said, with a nip on my earlobe.

There was no concern in his voice, just the stirrings of determination. While many shifters were monogamous, the cats weren't. Like the animal variety that had once roamed this world, female shifters had the final say on who could and couldn't court them, and it was the males who had to strive for their attention and favor. In the camps, at least during the war, it wasn't unusual for women to have had many children with different fathers, although those who were not nomadic did tend to stick to the same mate. It was a trait that had, at times, made my task difficult.

"Maybe," I murmured. "So, are we on for lunch?"

"Indeed. My place or yours?"

I smiled. "Mine is closer."

"I shall be here at one thirty, then." He kissed me a final time and then headed out the door.

I took a deep breath and slowly released it. It had been a

long night, and my body and muscles ached with fatigue. It had, I thought wryly, been a long, *long* time since I was this active. Unfortunately, the only way to improve sexual stamina was to keep doing it, and while Charles was a considerate enough lover, he wasn't . . .

A wry smile touched my lips. The end of *that* sentence was pretty pointless, given I had no idea what Jonas was like in bed. He might be a selfish lover—I somehow doubted it, but sometimes you could never tell.

Once I'd shifted back to my normal self, I walked back up the stairs and took a long hot shower to wash the scent of sex and Charles from my skin, and to ease the ache in long-disused muscles. All the clothes in the wardrobe had been designed to fit my alter ego, so I increased my bust size just enough that the tunic didn't fit like a tent all over, then grabbed a scarf to belt in the waist. I also lengthened my hair and changed the structure of my face. The building might not have either cameras or guards, but I couldn't risk the wrong person spotting the real me coming and going. As I headed back downstairs, I called to Cat and Bear and then set about making breakfast.

I was on to my second cup of strong black coffee by the time they appeared. They zipped around me as usual, but this time their energy was filled with a mix of uncertainty and trepidation.

"What's happened?" I said, immediately fearing the worst.

Images began to flow through my mind—men and women taking down the steels that had been supporting what remained of the old roof, others moving what equipment had survived the blast into the carryall ATVs that lined the road outside it. Weirdly, there were also other people moving equipment and random bits of furniture in.

I frowned. "Did anyone say why they were doing all this?"

Bear touched me lightly. *No, but Jonas is there, supervising.*

Then I needed to get over there to see what he was up to—even if I had a bad feeling I wasn't going to like the answer.

I grabbed a cloak to ward off the chill of the morning air, then headed outside. Bear led the way, but Cat kept closer, her energy playing through the long strands of my hair. Guilt flickered through me. She'd missed me.

Finding the children is what matters now, she said. *We have plenty of time; they do not.*

I smiled. She might have been only seven in human years when she died, but she'd always been far wiser than most adults. Even if at times she was as playful and silly as any child.

Her energy slapped me lightly even as her giggles spun around me. My smile became a grin as I headed through the gates and into the warmth of real sunlight. The rail platforms were filled with people, all of them patiently waiting for the next lot of pods to arrive. I wove my way through them, then headed across the road toward the museum. There were only two ATVs stationed outside the museum now. Both vehicles were still being loaded, and two of the museum's security guards watched proceedings from either side of the door.

One of them stepped forward and held out a hand as I drew near. "I'm sorry, miss, but the museum has been closed down for the immediate future."

Which might be good news depending on whether the temporary closure simply meant they hadn't yet decided what to do with it, or if it was a first step toward demolishing it.

But if it was the latter, why were they taking stuff into it?

"Are you refurbishing it?" I motioned toward what looked like movement monitors two men were carrying inside.

The guard snorted. "No, we are not. I'm afraid you'll have to go back—"

"It's okay," Jonas said as he came out the door. "She's with me."

Something close to amusement lurked around the guard's lips as he rather grandly motioned me forward. "Might have volunteered for the job myself if I'd known there was going to be such lovely company."

I frowned and glanced at Jonas for an explanation, but, as usual, his expression gave little away.

I followed him inside. The ghosts immediately swamped me, just about frying my mind with their uncertainty and concern. And no wonder—the huge room was all but cleaned out. Nothing remained, not even the hanging electrical cables. I glanced at the old tower and was relieved to see the tops of the solar panels glinting in the sunshine that streamed through the fissured section of the dome. At least I wasn't reduced to relying solely on the generators—if, of course, they hadn't also ripped out the old cabling that ran from the tower to the storage cells.

I calmed the ghosts down as best I could and watched the two men deposit the monitoring units next to an odd assortment of other furniture and equipment. Including, I saw with more than a little trepidation, a generator and vampire lights.

"What in Rhea is—"

"Not yet," Jonas murmured, motioning me to remain where I was as he walked over to the two men.

One of them pressed a button on his wrist cell and produced a small light screen. Jonas raised his arm and ran his RFID chip across it.

"Right," the stranger said, when the screen flashed green. "That's all logged and accounted for. Good luck."

They gave me a nod and left. Once the ATVs' engines had started up, I said, my voice holding an edge I couldn't quite control, "It very much looks to me like you're moving in."

"That," Jonas said heavily, "is because I am."

CHAPTER 7

This news was greeted by a swell of excitement from the ghosts, but while they might be delighted at the prospect of having someone new to follow around, I sure as hell wasn't. I might be attracted to the damn man, but that didn't mean I wanted him around twenty-four/seven.

"And why would you want to be doing that?"

Jonas grabbed one of the lights and walked across to the museum's entrance. "I don't."

"Then why in Rhea are you here, doing just that?"

He looked at me, his expression edged with anger. Though it wasn't really aimed at me, I still felt the wash of it. "Because I cannot stay in Chaos, as much as I might want to."

I frowned. "Why?"

"Because Nuri has foreseen there will be problems if you continue to move in and out of Chaos. And corps now has it under watch. We cannot afford to jeopardize anyone's safety by allowing the suspicion of our connection to you to become a certainty."

"Meaning she's seen the possibility of Chaos being attacked?" I hesitated, and remembered where his allegiance lay. It certainly *wasn't* Chaos. "Or will my presence there endanger Penny?"

"The latter. I didn't rescue her from the vampire hordes just to risk her falling back into their hands."

"Technically, I was the one who rescued you *both* from the horde." I crossed my arms, my frown deepening. "Sal's partners already know about the connection between me and Nuri, given that she returned the five children we rescued to Central."

"No, because another mercenary group unconnected with either us or Chaos did that."

I raised my eyebrows. "And where, exactly, did they say they'd found them?"

"They were on their way into Chaos when they discovered them wandering in the park. It holds enough kernels of truth to be believable."

"To everyone except those kids and Sal's partners."

"To everyone but Sal's partners," he corrected. "The children's memories have been adjusted."

Adjusted. What a quaint term for altering or erasing someone's memories. Unfortunately, it was one I'd heard more than once during the war, when lures didn't perform their tasks as expected. Thankfully, it wasn't something I'd ever gone through. Not just because my performance had been considered satisfactory, but because I was very careful about revealing any sort of emotion in front of either my handler or those who controlled us.

"How? Nuri's not capable of something like that."

"No, but Ela is."

Ela was the fourth member of Nuri's crew, and the one shifter I'd yet to officially meet. Her being telepathic did at least explain why Nuri had sent her into Deseo to keep an eye on events there.

"That still doesn't explain what you're doing setting up camp here," I said.

He grabbed a second light and walked it across to the nearer side of the door, then hit the activate switch on both and moved back to the generator, remotely connecting the two lights. Technology, I thought, as the lights flared to life, had certainly improved since the war.

"I'm here simply because I provide a direct line to Nuri. I can relay any information and requests, and bring back anything you need."

"Sensible, but won't that just shift the corps' attention to the bunker?"

"No, because the engineers have advised the council to run a series of stability tests on the area before deciding on the viability of the museum. They're worried the landslip over the South Tunnel is just the beginning."

"That landslip was caused by the explosion."

"Something they're *not* aware of. They believe the grate is part of an old sewer network that once ran under this area, and are now concerned that further collapses could endanger the whole hillside."

Hence the monitoring equipment. "That still doesn't explain how *you* got to be here."

He began setting up another string of lights in front of the old tower. "Can you imagine anyone in Central willingly taking such a position? Especially when they want it physically monitored twenty-four/seven?"

I frowned. "Why wouldn't they just set the equipment to automatically relay results across to the engineering department?"

"Because the explosion damaged the data-relay terminals and they're not going to replace them until they decide what they're doing with the museum."

He connected the string of lights to the generator and they came to life, surrounding the old tower in a fierce ring of light.

"And before you ask," he continued, "Nuri was commissioned to find someone willing to take on the position. I, naturally, volunteered."

I blinked. "So Nuri is basically an agent, brokering services and assignments Central cannot or will not fill or complete?"

He nodded. "It is an ideal situation for everyone involved."

It wasn't ideal for me. Not if whoever they were dealing with got wind of my presence—and *that* was a possibility growing stronger with every day I passed in their company.

I tried to ignore the sense of inevitability that washed through me and walked through the lights. Their heat danced across my skin, but didn't burn me as they would a full-blood vampire. After righting the nearest chair, I sat down at the small table that had definitely seen better days. "But why would the government deal with someone who—under their own rules—is outcast?"

He moved the autocook onto a second table. One thing was certain; he wasn't intending to go without some comforts. Or eat my food.

"Because she is *not* just anyone. She's an Albright."

"And this is important because . . . ?"

He raised an eyebrow. "Because the Albrights emigrated

here from the Eastern Provinces and to this day remain the most powerful ruling family still active in Central City."

I frowned. "Why is the fact that her family comes from the Eastern Provinces so important?"

"Because the Eastern Provinces have a history of cultivating magic and its use. Apparently, the ruling houses there habitually tracked down—and bred with—those strongest in both earth and personal magic. The Albrights were one of the most successful—and therefore powerful—of them all."

"So why did they come here to Central if they had it so good in the Eastern Provinces?"

He shrugged. "Nuri's never said, but I've heard it had something to do with the desire to keep the magic pure."

My frown grew. "Meaning what?"

"I don't know. And we've had no contact with the Eastern Province since the war's end."

"Meaning its cities were destroyed like Carleen?"

"No one knows. All contact was lost with that region after the war."

"So why has no one bothered to reestablish contact?"

He shrugged again. "In the aftermath of the war, people were too busy both surviving and rebuilding. It was nigh on twenty years before any sort of communication and trade resumed with the other three provinces. But the deep desert lies between here and Valora, and it makes the monumental task of fixing shattered communication lines and equipment too expensive for one city to take on alone."

I raised an eyebrow. "The deep desert surely isn't so large that a long-haul solar vehicle couldn't traverse it."

He smiled. "No, but the fact that the Eastern Provinces have raised some sort of magical barrier to keep everyone out *is.*"

"Meaning whoever *is* alive in that place wants no contact with anyone here." And really, who could blame them? While the war had very quickly encompassed all provinces, it had started here, in Central, thanks to the endless land grab by humanity and the rage of a people pushed to the edge of existence—a people who had the skill and the madness to create and then unleash the bombs. "I still think it's odd Nuri's family remains in contact with her, given that those in the House of Lords tend to be sticklers for following the rules and holding themselves above any hint of taint."

"Outcast or not, she is still considered a spiritual leader by many." Jonas shrugged. "And sometimes blood is all that matters. Would you like a coffee?"

"Since it has to be better than anything I have in the bunker, most definitely."

"*That* is the truest statement you've ever made."

The amusement in his tone had me biting back my instinctive reply. If I wanted Jonas to treat me as he found me, then I really had to start doing the same. He might hate what I was, but he was at least trying to treat me with both civility and respect. It was a definite step up from Branna, who saw nothing but an abomination that needed to die.

Once the autocook had been hooked up and the coffee made, he picked up the two cups and walked over to the table, handing me one before moving over to the second chair. His scent spun around me, wild and alluring. I frowned down at my coffee and wished there was some way I could control this constant pull toward him. Maybe it was just as well I'd be spending so much time in Central over the next couple of days—it meant less time to do something stupid. Like acting on an attraction that might be mutual, but one he certainly wasn't likely to explore. Or even want.

He took a sip of coffee, his expression thoughtful, leaving

me wondering if he knew what I was thinking. Which was stupid. Nuri was the seeker, not he.

Except that he and Nuri now shared DNA, so *anything* was possible.

"What happened when you went to explore the wall and the rift it protected?" he asked eventually.

I quickly filled him in. "I escaped through luck alone."

Jonas scrubbed a hand across his jaw and swore. "Nuri feared they might have government contacts, given the boxes in the Broken Mountains base and the ATV they used to move the remaining kids from Carleen, but this . . ." He shook his head. "I doubt if even her family will be able to get us into that place to investigate."

Suggesting it was her family—and their connections— that had been helping us so far. "Would they be able to get me on the employment roster there?"

He shook his head. "A false identity might hold up against casual scrutiny, but anyone being considered for employment at Government House undergoes deep and rigorous checks. The fact that we use New Port as the place of birth in all our refits will raise red flags."

I frowned. "I thought you used New Port because the records were destroyed and there was no way to check whether an ID was legit or not."

"Yes, but the government is well aware that false IDs are coming from that place. They just don't do anything about it unless the security of Central and the government is at risk."

Which was fair enough, I guess. "Then it might be better to simply find someone I can replace."

After all, that was exactly what we were planning to do at Winter Halo.

"That's possible, but Government House is not Winter

Halo. For a start, the bioscanners there are programmed for both external *and* internal markers. You might pass the former, but you wouldn't the latter."

I swore and took a drink. "When I made it out of that final building, I did so at the back of a man the guards called 'my lord.'" I gave Jonas a brief description. "Any idea who he is?"

Jonas shook his head. "But given the nose, I would say he'd be from the ruling house of Valkarie."

"But he wasn't human."

"The Valkarie aren't—they're one of the shifter clans who were selected to fill the empty positions in the House of Lords after the war. Why does it matter?"

I shrugged. "Intuition stirred, that's all."

"I'll ask Nuri to look up his history." He paused, and briefly contemplated me over the rim of his mug. "How did the evening with Charles go?"

I gave him a brief rundown of everything I'd caught, then added, "Whatever the Daybreaker project is, it's sucking up huge amounts of money and is in danger of making Winter Halo broke."

"If it *is* the project behind the kidnappings, I doubt Sal's partners would care overly much—not if they achieved their aims." He took a drink. "Did you get anything else on it? Any mention of links to the missing children?"

"Nothing I picked up from Charles indicated he had any knowledge of the project beyond its finances. Although funding did begin around the same time the children started going missing." I shrugged. "Seeking isn't an exact science, you know, even for someone like me."

"Someone who was specifically created to seduce and steal, you mean?"

"Yes." I returned his gaze evenly. "You surely can't have

a problem with that, especially when it's being used to help save those children."

"I have a problem with the *concept*—"

"And yet you're using Ela and her telepathic skills in the exact same way."

"—of creating life with specific skill sets in mind," he continued, ignoring my remark. "Life is sacred. It should be a creation of two people rather than one of science."

"Being created in a tube doesn't make me any less of a being, Jonas."

A smile ghosted his lips. "Most would disagree with you."

"I can't change what I am."

"And I cannot help the prejudices of my past. You, however, are something of an outlier."

I frowned. "Meaning what?"

"Meaning," he said, draining his cup, "that I *have* been unfair in treating you with suspicion and distrust—even *if* it was initially deserved—and I'm endeavoring to rectify that. But you need to stop treating every statement I make as an attack."

I half smiled. "I know."

He stared at me for several heartbeats, his expression unreadable, then nodded, once. A deal had been struck. Now we just had to both keep it.

He pushed upright. "Another coffee?"

I shook my head and watched him walk across to the autocook. Like most cats, he moved with a predator's grace.

"When do you meet Charles again?" he asked.

"Tomorrow for lunch. I'll try to pin down more information about both Daybreaker and his boss."

Jonas crossed his arms and leaned against the tower's wall as he waited for his coffee to be made. "Has there been any evidence of contact between him and Rath Winter so far?"

I shook my head. "But as senior financial director for the company, he surely must have." I paused. "Have you had any luck finding someone for me to replace?"

"Nuri's pinned down two possibilities. She's going to read them today and see if one is a fit. If she's successful, they'll be here tonight."

I frowned. "I hope she's careful. Both the corps and Sal's partners are obviously suspicious of her."

A smiled touched his lips again. "They won't even know she's in the city. She may not be a body shifter, but magic has many uses."

"Including disguises, obviously." A huge yawn broke free and I waved a hand. "Sorry, it's not the company. It's just been a long night and I can't get downstairs to my bunk until tonight."

"You can't shadow in light?"

"I can, but it's physically draining." Mainly because it involved creating a light shield that blocked all light, providing me with a capsule of darkness in which to shadow. "It's something I do only in extreme emergencies."

"Then sleep here. The air bed is basic but comfortable enough."

I frowned somewhat dubiously at the pack near the tower's door. It wasn't so much the thought of sleeping rough after all these years, but rather sleeping knowing he was here, watching me.

The amusement lurking at the corners of his eyes suggested he was well aware of the reason behind my hesitation. "You're safe enough here. They've issued an out-of-bounds alert, so the public won't come near, and the vampires can't during the day."

Being safe wasn't the problem. Being too aware was. And

he knew it, damn him. But I walked over to grab the pack. "Do you mind if I head up to the top of the tower? I'd rather sleep under sunlight than false light."

And well away from you, that inner voice added.

The amusement increased. No surprise there, given the pheromones stinging the air. But he didn't say anything and neither did I. He simply shrugged and motioned me on.

I pushed the heavy metal door open, and then unlatched the silver curtain behind it. There was enough shifter in my blood that my skin tingled, but—like the vampire lights—it didn't burn me as it would a full-blood like Jonas. I slung the pack over my shoulder and ran up the old concrete stairs, breathing air that was still thick with dust from the explosion. The ghosts dashed ahead of me, their tiny figures briefly finding shape. When we reached the metal exit plate at the top of the stairs, I drew back the bolts and pushed the plate open. Though it was also silver, it was so scarred with heat and blast damage it barely had any effect on my skin.

The children threw themselves into the bright sunshine, but I followed more cautiously, keeping low so that the building parapet hid me. The museum might have been declared out-of-bounds, but there was still the possibility that someone in Central was keeping an eye on us. The glass dome certainly didn't offer much in the way of protection when it came to visibility. Not during the day, anyway. When I'd reached the shade of the building's edge, I rolled out the pack and waited for the mattress to inflate. Then I stripped and climbed in. With the music of the ghosts' murmurings streaming through my mind, I quickly fell asleep.

Dusk was rolling in on fingers of pink and gold by the time I woke. Cat and Bear were nearby, but—if the excited chatter drifting up the stairwell was anything to go by—the other ghosts were all downstairs.

I yawned and stretched, trying to get some of the kinks out of my body. The air bed was comfortable enough, but two nights of vigorous lovemaking had taken their toll—and *that* was a sad state of affairs. I might have made numerous incursions into Central over the last hundred years to satisfy base need, but I'd certainly never risk staying more than a couple of hours with my partner.

"What's happening downstairs, Cat?" I flipped off the cover and began getting dressed.

Two images immediately flowed into my mind—Nuri and a stranger with orange hair and a pinched, worried face. Both were downstairs with Jonas.

Meaning, I hoped, that Nuri had found someone in Winter Halo whose position I could take. I shoved on my sandals, then deflated the mattress and rolled it up. I doubted Jonas would want to sleep up here, given that he was being employed to monitor the equipment.

I snuck across to the hatch, keeping low again even if it was probably unnecessary with night closing in so fast. Once the bolts had been shoved home, I clattered down the stairs, making just enough noise to warn those below. Jonas would have heard me stirring, but I didn't want to do anything to frighten the other woman. If the images the ghosts had shown me were anything to go by, she was the flighty type. Which was odd, considering she was a guard—I'd have thought they'd at least make some effort to employ people who weren't likely to run at the slightest threat.

Of course, given the attacks on the guards, maybe it wasn't just a specific look they were after, but also a specific blood type. They were experimenting on the children because they were either rift survivors or the children of survivors, so anything was possible.

Jonas handed me a coffee as I stepped out of the tower,

then took the pack from me. I gave him a smile of thanks, but my attention was on the woman sitting close to Nuri at the table. She was about the same size as me—the real me—but her eyes were yellow-brown, her nose broad, and her orange hair long and pulled back in a ponytail. Worry and fear oozed from her, and her body seemed to hum with the effort of remaining still. I suspected it was only the fact that it was almost dark outside that prevented her from fleeing.

"Ah, Tig," Nuri said, giving me a broad but decidedly false smile of greeting. "This is Sharran Westar. She has kindly taken up our substitution offer for the next couple of days."

Sharran looked me up and down, and the worry ratcheted up several notches. "Are you sure she's going to pull this off? I don't want to lose my job, even after last night."

I sat on the opposite side of the table and nursed my coffee in both hands. "What happened last night?"

She tapped her fingers on the table—nerves, not impatience. "The ghost got me, didn't it? Felt me up good and proper."

"Did you report it?"

She snorted. "There's no point, is there? No one ever does anything about it."

I wondered if Charles knew anything about the attacks—and whether they were the source of the staff problems he was having—or if it was something else. We knew about the high turnover of guards, but it would be interesting if there were something else going on as well.

"And this is the first time you've been attacked?" I asked.

She nodded. "I've been assigned to that floor before and never attacked. I guess my luck just ran out."

"So everyone assigned to that floor is attacked?" Kendra had certainly implied that they were, but it was odd it took longer to happen to some than others.

Sharran hesitated. "It seems to happen to the newer recruits more often than those of us who have been there longer. But we're not immune. Not now."

Intuition stirred. "Was there any specific time you noticed it happening more to those of you who've been there awhile?"

"Well, it's definitely gotten worse in the last week or so."

A time frame that meshed with Penny's escape and my emergence. I glanced at Nuri.

"Hence the *lack* of time we now have," she said. "We have them worried."

"Which might just result in them shutting down the projects and erasing the evidence," I said.

"I doubt it. They have too much invested in all this now."

I hoped she was right, for the sake of the kids still missing. And if her expression was anything to go by, she was hoping the very same thing.

Sharran's gaze was moving between us, her expression confused. "Look, what else do you need to know? Because I start work soon, and if this is going to happen—"

"It's okay." Nuri's voice was soft, unthreatening. Yet her energy fell like a cloak around the other woman, the feel of it soothing, calming. Sharran relaxed almost immediately. "Just tell us everything you think we'll need to know about Winter Halo and your position within it."

"But first, give me your hand," I said, holding out mine.

"It's okay," Nuri repeated, again in those soothing tones. "She's a seeker, like me. She'll get images of the places and people you know in Winter Halo as you tell us about them. That way, no one will suspect she isn't you."

Sharran grunted and somewhat tentatively placed her hand in mine. Images and emotions instantly began to flow, thicker and stronger than such a touch usually allowed. She was, I thought, either a latent seeker or an untrained, unregistered psychic.

She took a deep, somewhat shuddering breath, then began. As she spoke, images flowed into my mind, crisp and clear. I saw the people she liked and those she didn't, the places she could go and those she couldn't, the various codes she needed to know—everything. It took about twenty minutes and by the end of it, my body was trembling and my head booming with both the intensity of the connection and everything I'd learned.

When she finally stopped, I pulled my hand free and leaned back in the chair. For several minutes I didn't speak; couldn't speak. Every part of me felt drained and weak. Fighting vampires, I thought, wasn't half as exhausting as reading this woman.

Of course, fighting vampires *was* a whole lot more dangerous.

"We really appreciate you doing this, Sharran," Nuri said into the silence. "Hopefully, by the time you return, we'll have sorted out the source of the attacks and eliminated them."

"You can really get rid of ghosts?" Sharran said, doubt in her voice.

"Yes." Nuri once again sent out those reassuring vibes. "Ah, here's Ela now. She'll take you down to Crow's Point, where we've arranged accommodation for you."

I forced my eyes open and watched Ela striding toward us. She was a strong-looking woman with brown skin, brown hair, and the most intense blue eyes I'd ever seen. She met my gaze evenly and gave me a polite nod, which was more than Branna had ever done. Maybe he was the only sourpuss in the bunch.

"Is it safe to leave now?" Sharran's jittering returned full force. "It's dark and all, and the vampires—"

"Have no hope against a fully armed ATV," Ela cut in, her tone warm and rich. "And if the bastards *do* get too close, we'll just run them over. They crunch rather delightfully, let me tell you."

Sharran's expression suggested she wasn't a fan of macabre humor. "But we have to get out of here first—"

"The ATV is parked right outside the door," Ela said, and unslung the rifle sitting at her back. "And I have Boomer with me, just in case."

Nuri reached out and clasped Sharran's hand. As she did, energy surged, fierce enough that my breath momentarily caught in my throat.

"It'll be all right," Nuri murmured. "Just relax and enjoy your time in Crow's Point. You won't remember your problems or any of this when you return, that I promise you."

Sharran opened her mouth, as if to protest, and then the cloak of energy settled around her and she froze, her expression briefly blanking. Then she smiled and nodded. "Thank you," she said, rising. "I appreciate everything you've done."

"No problem, my dear girl," Nuri said.

Ela caught the other woman's arm and escorted her out. Jonas closed the doors, then walked over to the autocook, collecting several waiting plates. One he gave to Nuri, and the other he handed to me. Hers was rice and stew; mine was not.

"You have steak in the autocook?" I said, surprised he'd take creature comfort that far. The portable units tended not to have a lot of refrigeration space and meat was generally reconstituted rather than fresh. And this was definitely fresh.

"Only a couple," he said as he walked away. "But you looked as if you needed decent sustenance."

"I did. I do." I plucked some cutlery from the container

in the middle of the table and tucked in. "Is Sharran really being taken to Crow's Point?"

Nuri's smile was wry. "What do you think?"

"Then where is she going?"

"Up to my kin in the Broken Mountains." Jonas deposited another plate of stew and rice as well as a loaf of bread on the table, then sat down. "They'll keep her sedated and under watch for however long we need."

"It would have been too risky to send her anywhere else," Nuri commented. "Especially as we don't know who else might be involved in this crime."

I pushed the cutlery container toward Jonas. "What hours is she supposed to be working tonight?"

"From ten to six." Nuri hesitated. "Did you pick up much information from her?"

Surprise rippled through me. "You didn't?"

"No, but I've always found it more difficult to read those who are psychically gifted, even if those skills were latent."

"And yet you can read me." Both my ability to see the ghosts and to create a shield out of sunshine were psychic abilities, even if the latter had been enhanced in the lab.

She smiled. "Not as well as I would like."

And probably a whole lot more than *I'd* like. "Whatever her psi skills are, they made the connection stronger than anything I've experienced via that sort of touch. As long as you managed to download her RFID information, we should be set."

"We did. And the bioscanners in the foyer shouldn't be a problem—they check the external digital markers that are scanned in when everyone is first employed. The guards will only pull someone up if there's a marked difference from what is on record."

Meaning I'd better be *very* precise when I took on

Sharran's shape. "And will there be a problem if I am pulled up?"

"Probably." Nuri reached for the bread and broke off a chunk. "If what Kendra told you holds true, you'll be attacked tonight."

Meaning she didn't want to elaborate any further on what might happen if the bioscanner did raise the alarms. Or maybe she simply didn't know. Even a witch and a seeker of extreme power couldn't see every thread of the future. "Did you manage to track down any of the *favori*?"

Nuri shook her head. "We have a list of names, of course, but none of them remain in their homes."

I frowned. "Then where are they now living?"

"In Winter Halo."

"Why would they do that?"

"That I don't know. But their families are being well compensated for their absence and aren't complaining."

I snorted. "Because money always compensates for absence, doesn't it?"

"It's all very well to be critical of such a decision," Jonas murmured. "But you do not live in Central, and you have no experience of trying to exist in a city that basically worships the almighty dollar."

"But I *do* have experience of living without it."

"You are able to conceal or alter your appearance, which means theft is not such a problem for you," Jonas said. "Those in Central don't have those sorts of skills to fall back on. And it's not like they can choose to live elsewhere, because there are few who could cope with life beyond the walls these days."

Because of the vampires. And because most of them could no longer see in the dark, thanks to their cities of endless light.

"It does mean," Nuri said, "that if you do become one of the *favori*, we may lose contact."

"Only if I can't find a way to get out unseen." I hesitated, remembering my initial impressions of Kendra. "Could latent psychic skills be one of the things they're after? Maybe the first attack is nothing more than an investigation, and if the target passes that, they're then blood-tested."

It would also explain why some guards weren't attacked a second time.

Nuri frowned. "You can't confirm the existence of psychic skills through blood."

"No, but maybe once they confirm the existence of psychic skills, they're testing for something else in the blood work."

Nuri's frown deepened. "It's possible, but I can't see what benefit it would be to them. It's not as if you can inject psychic skills as you would a virus."

"No, but the cells responsible for their existence *can* be grown and enhanced in a tube. I'm evidence enough of that." I pushed my empty plate away and leaned back in the chair. "What if they're doing what the humans did during the war? What if they're creating not just a means of providing a sunlight immunity for vampires and wraiths, but a whole new race—one whose DNA is not only psi-enhanced but is a combination of wraith, vampire, and shifter?"

"Impossible," Jonas said automatically.

"Why? Again, I'm living proof that the impossible is very possible."

"Yes, but it took years of research and experimentation to successfully produce déchet. And *that* was all destroyed at the end of the war."

"Are you sure? Because there were shiny new intrauterine beds up in the Broken Mountains base."

"Which in itself doesn't mean anything," Nuri said. But her expression was troubled.

"Sal and I survived the war. What if someone else did? Someone like a scientist well versed in the means and methods of creating and enhancing life in a tube?"

And *that* was possible, given Sal *had* been caught in a rift with two humans, even though he'd professed a hatred of them. He'd had no reason to be anywhere near them after the war—unless, of course, he'd had no *choice*.

What if his two companions weren't randoms? What if they were instead fellow military survivors—ones who happened to be a scientist and maybe even a handler?

The latter would certainly explain why Sal had followed orders he didn't agree with—not if the anger I'd witnessed after one phone call was anything to go by. Not only had déchet been rendered incapable of killing humans, but we also could not go against orders issued by our military handlers. If Sal's handler was one of his two partners, then there would always be that innate pressure to obey, even if the rift had muddied their DNA and basically made them separate parts of a whole.

"I guess it's possible," Jonas said. "But that only makes it more imperative we get inside Winter Halo."

"If they are creating such creatures," Nuri said, voice heavy, "it is doubtful they'd be doing so within Winter Halo itself. *Any* form of gene manipulation carries the penalty of death. They can't possibly control everyone who works within that place, and would not take such a risk."

"Which goes back to the intrauterine pods we discovered in the Broken Mountains base."

"And," Jonas said, expression grim, "raises the scary prospect that they've already succeeded in creating a wraith capable of withstanding sunlight."

"Even if that *is* true, we have time to stop them," I said. "This program hasn't been running all that long, and any new being to come from it would still be young. If there's one thing the déchet program revealed, it's that growth can only be manipulated so far."

Nuri frowned. "Everything I've read suggests accelerant was used on déchet."

"It was. But development could only be increased to a certain point before death or madness stepped in—especially given that the mind doesn't always grow at the same speed as the body."

"They might not care about that." Jonas's voice was grim. "Not if all they want is the eradication of life on this world."

"If they wanted total annihilation, why wouldn't they just develop the rifts as a weapon? We still don't understand them, even one hundred years down the track." And we really had no protection against them, even if the huge metal curtain walls that protected all major cities from vampires also seemed to provide some sort of barrier against the rifts. "And the false rifts prove their existence here may not be as random as we first thought."

"The initial rifts *were* a consequence of the war and the bombs," Nuri said. "Doorways were opened that never should have been, and the Others quickly took advantage of a whole new killing field."

"Then I guess we should just be thankful it has taken as long as it has to bring their plans to some sort of fruition." I hesitated and scrubbed my hands through my hair. The steak had stopped the trembling weakness, but a dull ache remained behind the backs of my eyes. "I need to get moving if I'm to take Sharran's place tonight."

Jonas rose. "I'll get the scanner."

Nuri took a piece of paper from her pocket and pushed

it toward me. "Here's some basic background details you might not have gotten from Sharran's mind."

I quickly scanned the list. It was indeed basic stuff, like where she'd been born, who her parents were, where her siblings where living and what they did, as well as where she currently lived and who her neighbors were. Everyday stuff that I *hadn't* gotten from her mind, and which might well trip me up if I wasn't very careful.

Once I'd committed the information to memory, I crumpled the paper and tossed it lightly in the air. The ghosts caught it and began playing with it, their giggles of delight filling the air and making me smile.

Once Jonas had returned and the new RFID chip inserted into my left wrist, I said, "How am I going to get information to you? Come here?"

Jonas hesitated. "It's probably the best option. If they're watching Chaos, then they're also probably keeping an eye on anyone we deal with on a regular basis—"

"Won't that put Ela's position at Deseo in jeopardy?" I cut in.

"She's not actually in there as herself," Nuri said. "It's not too hard to alter someone's appearance with a little bit of makeup and contacts."

A little bit of magic didn't hurt matters, either, I'd wager. I pushed up from the table. "I'd better get into Central and get ready for tonight."

"Turn off the lights near the door," Nuri said, with a glance at Jonas. "We can't risk someone seeing the light spill when it opens."

Jonas nodded and walked over to the door. Nuri grabbed my hand, preventing me from following. Energy surged, running up my arm like an electric charge. But it didn't feel like she was attempting to read me, nor did it appear she was using magic on me, as she had done with Sharran. It was more an injection, one that made my body hum with renewed vigor. And one that, if the sudden pallor of her skin was anything to go by, left her feeling a whole lot poorer.

"Do not waste time if you get into Winter Halo's inner sanctum." Her voice was soft. Distant. "Your time there will be short."

A chill ran through me, but before I could say anything, she blinked and released me. "But time is short all round when it comes to saving those children. Go."

I hesitated, then left. Jonas switched off the lights as I neared the door and then forced it open just enough for me to squeeze through.

"Be careful," he said. "And watch your back. Especially around Charles."

I paused and glanced back at him. "Why?"

"Because his allegiances, like most of the gentry, lie with the government, and he will report any suspicions he might have about you to those in charge."

"If he had any suspicions, I would have sensed them."

"Perhaps, but as you said yourself, seeking isn't an exact science, even for one such as you."

A smile tugged my lips. "There's nothing quite like having your own words used against you. But I'll be careful." I hesitated, then added, "Thanks."

He nodded and closed the door. I turned and hurried toward Central. I still had two hours before I needed to report to Winter Halo, but I wanted to get to Sharran's place on Twelfth and familiarize myself with her surroundings first.

Cat and Bear came with me. While I was generally reluctant to put them in the way of danger, they could go places in Winter Halo that I could not. And if Nuri was right—if my time there *was* going to be fleeting, for whatever reason—then maybe my two little ghosts could uncover the truth about the place. And *that* just might be the difference between rescuing the missing children and not.

Once I reached the wall, I shifted shape to take on Sharran's appearance and scent, then reclaimed my vampire form and surged up the wall. When the light spilling over the wall from the nearby towers began to chase the shadows away, Bear grabbed me and boosted me up the final few meters. I landed on the wall in a half crouch and quickly concealed my presence with a light shield.

This time I headed right, closer to the drawbridge rather than away from it. Sharran's place was a small, three-story concrete structure that would have sat in the deep shadows of the gate if this place had such things. I jumped down to its rooftop, then lowered myself over the edge and—after a deep breath to calm the irrational fears that immediately resurfaced at the thought of a three-story drop—let go. I landed in the small walkway between Sharran's building and the next, my fingers brushing the pavement to steady myself. I quickly checked for cameras—although it was unlikely anyone would place them in a back alley like this; hell, I'd never even seen them in the main street in all the years I'd been coming to Twelfth.

There were a couple of windows on the building to my right, but Cat and Bear—anticipating my needs—checked them. No one was watching, in either of the nearby buildings or the one directly across the street.

I released the sun shield and strode toward Twelfth Street. Though there were plenty of people still out on the street, no one paid any attention to me. I ran up the three steps to Sharran's apartment building, swiped my left wrist across the scanner, and then pushed the door open. The foyer inside was basic, and smelled faintly of age and mold. The flooring was some sort of plastic that squeaked underfoot and the walls a grimy gray. There was an old-fashioned tenant directory directly opposite the entrance, a metal staircase that had definitely seen better days, and two doors. Sharran's apartment—1B—was the one on the left.

I repeated the scanner process and entered the room—and there was only one. It held little more than a single bed, the oldest autocook I'd seen in Central so far, and a curtained-off area that turned out to be the bathroom. Above the air shower was a smallish window; I slid it open, peered out, and saw the walkway I'd just left. Which meant I had a second exit, and didn't have to risk leaving this place via the front door in any identity other than Sharran's.

Her tunics and coats were hanging from a rail that had been attached to the wall to the right of her bed, and the rest of her clothes were neatly folded into the small shelf unit underneath it. I walked over and lightly sniffed some of them, double-checking that the scent I was now using did indeed match the one lingering on the material.

Bear's energy lightly brushed my arm. *Can we explore the rest of the building?*

"Yes, but no trouble-causing."

Their amusement spun around me as they headed back out. I stripped, donned one of Sharran's tunics, then reached for a matching pair of brown boots. The material in both was scratchy and somewhat unpleasant, and made me realize just how lucky I'd been to have a store filled with old uniforms in the bunker.

Cat and Bear returned, and were decidedly unimpressed by our new abode. I grinned. "We won't be staying here much, never fear."

I grabbed Sharran's pack from the end of her bed, shoved in a coat, and then headed out again. High above me the stars were out, but I couldn't see them thanks to the glare of the UV lights.

I slung the pack over one shoulder and wound my way through the various walkways, heading for Sixth Street and Winter Halo. Bear scouted ahead, but Cat once again kept fairly close. Despite the excitement of new adventures, she really didn't like Central any more than I did.

As we approached Winter Halo, my gaze slid up its glass front and my steps slowed as trepidation surged.

It wasn't fear. Or, at least, it wasn't fear for my own safety, but rather that of the missing children. Nuri had already warned that the children's time was short. One misstep within this place, however minor, might well spell the end for them.

And yet if I didn't take that risk, we might never find them. Might never rescue them.

You are not alone, Cat said. *Not this time.*

No, I wasn't. I took a deep breath, pushed away the trepidation and the glimmers of intuition that said trouble would come a-hunting, and strode toward Winter Halo.

CHAPTER 8

One of the guards stepped forward and held up a hand. "Present for ID confirmation immediately."

The second guard produced a scanner. I stopped, pulled up my left sleeve, and ran the RFID chip across it. She studied the screen for several seconds, then nodded and stepped out of my way.

One barrier down. A ton to go.

I continued on. The doors swished and light swept my length as I stepped through them. No alarms went off, so I obviously passed the bioscan.

The foyer was a vast space that was all metal, glass, and polished concrete. There were another half a dozen guards in here, and all of them armed. Despite the current penchant for recruiting orange-haired cat shifters to be guards, four of the six here were male and, from the scents I was picking up, human. Maybe on the ground floor, they actually deferred to experience and capability rather than looks.

I threw my pack into one of the plastic tubs, then stepped through a second scanner. This one, I knew from Sharran's memories, checked for any sort of weapons, be they metal or glass. Once my pack had been scanned, I slung it over my shoulder and headed for the elevators. I didn't look anyone in the eye; didn't even glance around, as much as I wanted to. I had to keep in character, and Sharran was, unfortunately, a bit of a loner.

"Floor," a metallic voice said as I stepped into the elevator.

"Three."

The doors closed and within seconds I was on the third floor. I paused in the bright hallway, looking right and left. This level held the changing rooms, the security monitoring section, and the personnel department. The entire floor, aside from the changing rooms that were situated in the right corner of the building, was a maze of glass partitions. There was no privacy here; not only could everyone see you, but there were security cams mounted with movement sensors on every glass corner.

I spun on my heel and made my way through the glass corridors to the changing room. No one appeared to pay me any attention, but the cameras tracked my progress—I could hear the electronic buzz of their movements.

No one here looks happy, Bear commented.

No, they didn't. But then, if the bits and pieces I'd been getting from Charles were any indication, early starts and late nights were the norm in this place. I had no idea if it was the same elsewhere in Central, but it would certainly explain the general air of malaise so evident on this floor. Long hours were not only tiring, but meant fewer chances of seeing your lover, or family, or even of having a life. It made me wonder yet again how Sal had stood living in this city. He and I might have been bred to obey, but we'd also been given the luxury of thought and emotion, as well as a love of life, even if the latter had been unintentional by our creators. The longer I spent in Central, the more it seemed to me that its people had forsaken freedom in exchange for security. And while I could understand both humans and shifters making that choice, given the triple threats of vampires, Others, and rifts, Sal had been an assassin with salamander in his blood—a creature of forest and shadows. He had no need for any of this.

But again, the choice might not have been his to make. And while I certainly had no regrets about killing him, a glimmer of sadness resurfaced. Maybe being forced to live in a city of endless light and little freedom had changed him as much as that rift.

There were three others in the women's changing room. Two ignored me, and the third—a tall, thin woman with a mane of black and orange hair—looked decidedly unhappy to see me.

"You just lost me five credits." Her voice was as tart as her expression. "I was betting you wouldn't be back."

I half shrugged as I frantically searched Sharran's memories for her name. *Rae . . . no, Raedella.* She and Sharran had worked together on numerous occasions, but weren't exactly friends. The taller woman was something of a prankster . . . and Sharran's nervous nature tended to make her the ideal target.

I let my gaze skitter away from hers and mumbled, "Can't afford to lose the job."

Raedella snorted. "That's not what you were saying last night."

I had no idea what Sharran had said last night; it wasn't in any of the memories I'd plucked from her. So I simply shrugged again and walked over to Sharran's locker. It was a couple down from the other two women, but they didn't even look around. And I was fine with that. The fewer people I interacted with, the less chance there was of someone sensing something out of kilter.

I stripped, then grabbed a guard's uniform hanging from the hook inside the locker. Not only did the almost overpowering scent of flowery musk cling to the material, but the undertones of sweat and fear did as well. Sharran had obviously changed and run last night, and had forgotten to dump the uniform in the laundry chute. My nose wrinkled in distaste at the thought of wearing it, but I had no other choice. Fresh uniforms were only provided if one was returned.

Once I was dressed, I grabbed the weapon—some sort of Taser by the look of it—and strapped it on, then closed the locker and walked across to the allocations board to see where Sharran had been positioned for the night. Not unexpectedly, she was back on the tenth floor.

"Well, well," Raedella said, stopping so close behind me her breath stirred the ends of my hair. Had I been myself rather than Sharran, I would have elbowed her. Hard. "Looks like you got lucky again."

I grunted and ducked away from her. She laughed, a quick sound that held a hint of callousness. "But perhaps the ghost will decide you're really not worth the effort of biting."

And perhaps she needs a little ghostly interaction herself, Cat mused. *Shall we cause a little mischief?*

I barely managed to contain my smile. *Oh, most definitely.*

I walked out and left them to it. I'd almost reached the elevators when there was a high-pitched screech that was both fury and fear. People looked up from their glass boxes, but the only ones who went to investigate were two women from the security center.

Cat and Bear joined me in the elevator, their laughter filling the air and making me smile again. They didn't exactly provide full details of what they'd done, but it involved various items in the changing rooms suddenly gaining flight and a lot of white talc.

"Floor," a metallic voice demanded as the doors closed.

"Ten."

The elevator zoomed up. The first thing that struck me when the doors opened again was the hush. Not that the third floor had, in any way, been rowdy, but there'd at least been the murmur of conversations, the whir of cameras, and the electric buzz of the various other machines on the floor.

None of that was here; even the air con was silent, though a light breeze played with the ends of my hair, so it was obviously on.

I headed left. The lights were harsher—brighter—up here, but that was no surprise if there *was* someone using a light screen to hide him- or herself. Lights with this sort of output would definitely make shielding easier. It was also a whole lot colder up here, but given this floor supposedly had a lot of laboratories, it once again wasn't all that surprising. The temperature in all the military labs I'd been into had always been set several degrees lower than what I would have called comfortable, though no one had ever explained why. Maybe they'd simply wanted to ensure that no one fell asleep on the job.

Cat, Bear, do you want to have a look around the floor? See if there's anyone else here?

They raced off. I continued walking down the hall, heading for the security office at the north end of the building. Which was an odd place for it in my opinion. Surely it would have been better positioned closer to both the elevators and the emergency exits, so that they could get to either faster if there was a problem?

A woman looked around as I entered the small office; she was short, round, with spiky orange hair and long, sharp nails. There was nothing in Sharran's memories to give me any idea who she was.

"Sharran," she said, voice neutral, flat. Not the friendliest of souls, obviously. "I'm surprised to see you after the fuss you raised last night."

"Need the job." I sat down at the spare console and scanned myself in. Light screens flared to life in front of me, a checkerboard pattern of various-sized laboratories that were as empty as the halls. If they were doing any ongoing testing within those rooms, then it certainly wasn't evident. "Besides, it might be your turn tonight; let's see how calm you are when some bastard dry-humps you."

Surprise flitted across her features. I cursed inwardly. Sharran the mouse wouldn't have bitten back like that.

"I'm thinking the ghosts have no taste for me," she said. "Been on this floor many a time, and have never been attacked."

"Until last night, I was saying the same thing," I muttered, and ducked my gaze away from hers.

She continued to study me, her stare a weight I could feel. But after a few seconds, she returned her attention to the screens in front of her. I did the same. Not that there was anything to see; Kendra had been right. This *was* a cushy job.

Cat and Bear returned; the floor was as empty as it appeared on the screen. I frowned, wondering why when everyone else who worked at Winter Halo seemed to be doing long, *long* hours. It wasn't as if the labs were old or in need of refurbishing—not if the equipment I was seeing on the screens was anything to go by.

Time drifted by with agonizing slowness. My spiky-haired companion did the first hourly check, and I did the second. My body practically hummed with tension as I walked through the various corridors, checking that doors were locked and the labs still empty. Nothing happened. Not then, and not for the next six hours.

Maybe Sharran hadn't passed the psychic "sniff" test—if that was indeed what the first assault was all about.

One of the movement sensors on a subscreen flashed red. I leaned and switched the screen to full-size. The alarm had come from the lobby area, but there was no one there. No one the cameras could pick up, anyway.

"Problem?" My companion leaned sideways on her chair and studied my screen.

"Probably nothing," I said, even as intuition was whispering that this was it. This was when the attack would happen. "But I'd better go check."

"Yeah. You might as well do the rest of the floor while you're at it. I'll take the final one."

I nodded and rose. Cat and Bear danced around me, excited by the prospect of action—only that wasn't on our agenda right now. None of us could react in any way, simply because Sharran wouldn't have done so.

Bear's energy touched mine. *But if there is a light shield in use, Cat and I will be able to see past it. That will help, won't it?*

Yes. If nothing else, it would confirm whether the person behind these attacks was the same person Sal had reported to—and argued with—the time both Cat and Bear followed him into this place.

I strode down the hall, one hand on the butt of the Taser, even though I didn't expect to get the chance to use it. As I neared the lobby entrance, energy and awareness trailed across my skin. It wasn't the ghosts; the energy was too sharp, too bright. Behind it was the scent of deep forests, dark satin, and something else. Something unexpected and icy. Sal's scent, but also the scent of the person who'd watched us when we went to the restaurant to meet Keller.

Remember, I said to my two little companions, *no reaction, no matter what happens.*

Cat's energy touched mine. *But if he hurts you?*

I'll be okay. They need me. This is all about them getting blood and me getting into the upper levels. Nothing else matters right now.

She wasn't happy, but both she and Bear promised to behave. I drew in a breath, tasting that familiar and yet alien scent once again, then brushed my left wrist across the scanner and entered the foyer. As I did, something sharp pricked the back of my neck. Dart, I thought, even as I instinctively brushed a hand upward. Only there was no dart. I frowned; then dizziness hit and I stumbled, my knees buckling slightly as an odd warmth began to flood down my spine.

Whatever I'd been hit with, it was fast-acting. But what scared me was the fact that I was *reacting* to it. I was a lure, designed to be immune to all known drugs and poisons. Even those that *did* affect me did so long after the drug would have killed anyone else—it gave me time to do my job, escape, and then take the cure. But I'd been created a long time ago, and this drug, whatever it was, had obviously been developed in the years *after* the war. I had no immunity to it. None at all.

I stumbled to the wall and tried to remain upright. But my legs gave way and I found myself on my knees. Everything was spinning, and an odd buzzing seemed to fill my ears—I couldn't hear, could barely see, and my breath was short, sharp pants of air. No wonder Kendra had quit; I'd been expecting this attack, but it nevertheless scared the hell out of me.

Bear, connect, I said silently. *I need to see.*

His energy instantly whipped through me, connecting us on a level far deeper than mere speech, because when he pulled free, the connection lingered, allowing me to see and hear through his eyes and ears. It was a connection that wasn't without some danger, because if we held it too long, it could drain us both.

But I needed to see who was behind all this for myself.

The door behind us opened and a tall, thin-faced man with shadowed skin, dark hair, and magnetic blue eyes stepped through. Both Bear and Cat stirred uneasily. This was the man Sal had met, and one they didn't like the feel of. I couldn't say I blamed them. Even in my disconnected state, there was something very cold—and very alien—about him.

There was a slight shimmer around his body, which was the only indication that there was a light shield in play. Which meant neither the cameras nor my spiky-haired companion would see him. They'd only see me, collapsed against the wall.

Even so, why didn't my fellow guard come running to help? Or at least raise the alarm? She had to at least see I was in trouble.

Bear drifted backward as the stranger approached, not only wanting to keep his distance, but also not willing to risk the stranger sensing him. We knew one of Sal's partners was an earth witch, so it was more than possible that the merging of their DNA could have passed on the ability to sense the dead. Just because Sal apparently hadn't been able to didn't mean this man wouldn't.

He pulled a small medikit out of his pocket and undid the zip as he knelt beside me. He chose a syringe, then grabbed my arm and quickly—but professionally—found a vein and filled several blood collection tubes. He briefly put pressure on the site and then sprayed the area with something that stung like blazes. Within seconds there was little evidence of needle entry on my arm.

He carefully placed the blood samples in another kit, then took a small knife out of the first. After spraying it with sterilizer, he pushed my head to one side to reveal my neck. With little flourish, he made two small cuts near my throat. As blood began to ooze down my neck, he replaced the knife, zipped up both kits, and walked away. It was all very quick and efficient, which I guess was to be expected, given he'd been doing this for at least a couple of years now.

Bear, break the contact. I need you and Cat to follow him. I hesitated as Bear's energy whipped back through me and broke our connection. The dizzy confusion hit full force again and it was all I could do to add, *But be careful. Don't take any risks.*

They raced off after the stranger. As much as I wanted to do nothing more than drop into the healing state and chase the drug from my system, I couldn't. Not just because I had to react as Sharran would react, but because I could barely concentrate. All I could do was wait for whatever I'd been injected with to wear off. It took another five minutes for my limbs to start obeying my orders, and even then I still felt very shaky. I leaned back against the wall and slid the rest of the way to the floor. My head was still pounding and the brightness of the lights was making my eyes water, but my heart had stopped racing and my mind was at least a little clearer. I closed my eyes and concentrated on healing myself.

It didn't take all that long to erase whatever the hell it was they'd used on me, but I didn't immediately get up. The cameras were still on me and my companion might be watching, so when I did finally rise, I made a show of rising shakily and then stumbling back to the security office.

And discovered my companion was out of it.

I stepped closer, swept her hair away from the back of her neck, and saw a small needle mark. Which was odd, given they'd gone to the trouble of hiding any needle evidence from my arm. But this was obviously why there were no collaborating reports; they just knocked *both* guards out. It did, however, still leave the question of why any of the secondary guards didn't at least report the loss of consciousness.

I moved across to my station and hit the rewind button on the foyer screen. Just as Kendra said, the playback showed little more than me entering the foyer, checking the surrounds, and then moving on. Maybe this was why the attack hadn't happened earlier in the night; maybe they needed to record the material that would later be spliced into the live recording.

The other guard began showing signs of recovery. I moved back to the door, being careful to keep out of the line of sight of the cams in the hall.

"What on earth . . . ?" she muttered.

"Did you see it?" I said, forcing fear into my voice as I stepped forward and gripped her arm tightly. "It happened again. The bastard attacked me!"

She shook my grip from her arm and scooted her chair away from me. "I didn't see a damn thing. And why are you even here? Go downstairs and report it, and get a grip, for God's sake."

"You didn't see it?" I all but wailed. I had no idea if I was overdoing it, but Sharran did seem the type to wail.

"I didn't see it last night, and nothing has changed tonight." She glanced at the time. "Go report it. I'll finish up here."

"But it happened in the lobby and it might come back!"

She growled low in her throat, then thrust upright. "I'll fucking escort you. But I better not get into trouble for leaving my station, or there'll be hell to pay."

She pushed past roughly and I scampered after her. Of course, nothing else happened. When the elevator arrived, I thanked her profusely and stepped inside. Once the doors had shut, I closed my eyes and released a breath. Playing someone close to neurotic wasn't exactly easy.

"Floor," the metallic voice said.

"Um, three."

Once I was there, I stumbled across to the main security office to report what had happened. Interestingly, few of those who remained in the glass maze even bothered looking at me. These attacks had obviously become so regular they were no longer of any interest.

A stern-faced woman in her mid-fifties looked up as I pushed the door open, and her expression switched to one of frustration. She slammed her palms against the desk and pushed upright. "I wish the bastards upstairs would actually *do* something about these damn attacks. This is getting ridiculous." She walked over and placed a comforting arm around my shoulders. "You okay, love?"

I nodded. "Just shaken."

"As you would be." She stepped back and eyed the wound. "Report to medical and get that attended to. Then you can go home."

I glanced at her, unable to hide my surprise. "Really? My shift hasn't officially finished yet."

"It will be by the time you go to medical and fill in the required report." She hesitated. "Are you planning to stay on in the job, or leave like some of the others? Because I'll need to pass that decision on to personnel."

"Staying," I said. "I need the job."

"Good lass." She patted my shoulder lightly. "Rest up, and I'll see you back here on Friday."

"But I need the money—" *And* time was tight.

"It's full pay," the woman said. "So just rest up and relax."

I couldn't exactly fight the decision given Sharran wouldn't have, so I thanked her profusely and then headed down to medical. It turned out she was right about the amount of time it would take—it was nearly an hour and a half later by the time I'd been patched up, done the incident report, and left the building.

I sent a silent message to Cat and Bear, then headed back to Sharran's place. I stripped and chucked the tunic in the laundry chute, then stepped into the shower to wash away the odorous scents that clung to my skin. Once I'd redressed in my own clothes, I checked the autocook to see what was available, finding a surprising range of breads and proteins. It might be the oldest machine I'd ever seen, but at least it was well stocked. I ordered a stew and toast, and the rich smell of meat and cooking bread soon filled the room, making my mouth water in anticipation. It had been a long night, and the only break guards were allowed was the occasional bathroom stop.

Cat and Bear still hadn't returned by the time I finished, so I sent them another message telling them to wake me on their return, and settled down to get some sleep.

The sting of their excitement woke me a few hours later. They swirled around me, both of them talking at the same time, creating a whirlpool of sound, color, and trepidation.

They might have liked the assignment, but they hadn't actually liked what they'd seen in Winter Halo.

I waited until they'd calmed down, then said, "Where did that stranger go?"

Images flashed into my mind. The stranger had disposed of the light shield in the elevator and gone up to the twenty-seventh floor. It was another floor of laboratories, but this time all of them were filled with people. He walked into one labeled SCREENING and handed the medikit containing the blood samples to the technician, then left and made his way to the thirtieth—and top—floor. Here he walked down another of those solid corridors with only the one exit. This led into an office that dominated one-half of the entire floor—and one in which he was the only occupant.

"What else was on that floor, then?" I asked, surprised.

Coming to that, Cat said.

More images rolled. The stranger pulled up a light screen and made a call. The woman on the other end had broad features, dark hair and skin, and eyes that were the green of a newly unfurled leaf. It was a startling combination, and one I'd seen before. Not just because this was the woman I'd followed into the false rift that had led me into Government House, but somewhere else. Somewhere deep in the past.

I frowned, but the information of where remained elusive.

"What did they talk about?"

He was asking about the break-in at Government House, and whether the rift should be dismantled and moved, Bear said.

"And are they planning to do either?"

No, Cat said. *The woman said security had been tightened and that she'd retune the rift to only allow both of them to use it for the time being.*

Which meant any possibility of doing a search of that building via the rift was now out of the question. Not that I actually thought the children were being kept at Government House, despite the fact that the Carleen ghosts had said the government ATV that had collected them from Carleen had been headed toward Central.

"Did they talk about anything else?"

She asked about the dissections.

I blinked, even as a sick feeling began to churn my gut. "What dissections?"

Neither spoke. They simply showed me. On the twenty-ninth floor, there was a room that held six gleaming metal tables. On each of these lay an orange-haired woman. They were all hooked up to mediscan units that were now acting as their hearts and their lungs. Each woman had had her skull removed and a series of electrodes and probes attached directly to her brain. They were all dead; it was only the machines keeping their bodies alive.

I closed my eyes and took a deep, shuddering breath. I knew well enough just how the déchet had been created; knew because I'd witnessed scenes not unlike this in the lead-up to the war, as human scientists extracted and then refined the cells and neurons responsible for both shifting and psychic skills.

But that had been well over a hundred years ago, and it was a sight I'd hoped had been relegated to pages of history and long forgotten.

If it was happening *here*, in Central, then it all but confirmed that at least one of Sal's partners had been a scientist working on the déchet program. There was no other way they could have gotten to the extraction point so quickly.

"Were there only six of them?"

On the tables, yes, Cat said. *There were five others in holding cells.*

"Alive?"

Yes, but they looked drugged. And there was one empty cell.

Which meant those five were probably awaiting their turn for dissection. It also explained the somewhat random pattern of attacks. They obviously only went after a fresh subject when there was space freed either in the cells or on the tables.

"What about the rest of that floor? Any more horrors?"

More laboratories, but none of the machines that helped make us, either on that floor or others.

Meaning no in vitro equipment or incubators. And *that* meant if they *were* creating new beings, they were doing it off-site. Which was damn frustrating, but not unexpected. Nuri had already theorized as much.

"So, what was on the rest of the top floor?"

Once again, they didn't reply; they just showed me.

The rest of the floor was empty, except for the existence of two not-so-minor items.

The biggest false rifts I'd seen yet.

CHAPTER 9

I suppose it wasn't really surprising that there were other false rifts in Winter Halo, especially when they had one inside the bowels of Government House.

But the sheer size of these two was terrifying; you could, literally, drive a truck through them.

And maybe *that* was the whole idea.

"Did you notice a freight elevator on that floor anywhere?" I asked.

It was a somewhat random question. While it wasn't unusual for military bases to have industrial truck elevators, I wouldn't have thought them necessary in cities such as Central. Not given that the VTOLs—short-hop vertical take-off and landing vehicles—meant goods could basically be delivered closer to the required floor rather than to a catchall basement. Their size also meant landing bays could be much, much smaller. There were often three or four in most of the taller nonresidential buildings.

Yes, Bear said. *There are exit points on the fifteenth and thirtieth floors. It appears there were also access points on the lower floors, but they have been sealed.*

Which was understandable if what they were mostly transporting in and out of the building were stolen kids and vampires. It could also be the reason why Sal and his partners had chosen to infiltrate Winter Halo rather than the many other pharmaceutical companies that worked out of Central. Bringing in cargo they didn't want anyone else to see would definitely be easier in a freight elevator capable of holding a sealed truck rather than a smaller, catchall VTOL bay.

I scrubbed a hand across my eyes. If things went according to plan, then I'd be promoted upstairs when I returned to work in two days. The only problem with *that* was the fact that I now knew I could be as affected by modern drugs as anyone else. Which meant I had today and tomorrow to get into Winter Halo and investigate those rifts. They surely couldn't retune those two—not if they were using them to transport the children and Rhea only knows what else.

There is another problem, Cat said.

As if we didn't already have enough. "What?"

Once again, she simply showed me. And what I saw was Sal. On a table, attached to machines that were pumping his blood and keeping his flesh alive, even as other machines dissected his body and his brain.

I didn't know what to feel or how to react. The Humanoid Development Project—the project which all déchet had come from—had had a waste not, want not philosophy in place; those embryos that failed to develop into mature life were dissected and studied in an effort to understand what had gone wrong.

But I hadn't expected Sal to fall foul of the same philosophy—which was stupid on my part, if only because

Sal was a rare survivor. The in-tube death rate in the grays program had been even higher than that of the lures—only five had ever made it to full maturity. If one of his partners *had* been an HDP scientist, then it would be natural for him to want to understand why Sal had survived when so many others had died.

And while part of me believed Sal had gotten exactly what he'd deserved—in both the manner of his death and what was now happening to his body—the part that had mourned the passing of a friend wanted to stop it.

But there was also a practical reason for doing the latter— none of us could afford these people unlocking the secrets of Sal's success in reaching maturity and apply them to their own creations.

I glanced at the time and swore. It was already close to eleven. Given that I was supposed to meet Charles at one thirty, that didn't give me a whole lot of time to report back to Jonas and get things organized. "Could you two go back into Winter Halo and see if you can uncover the entry point into the freight elevator? But for Rhea's sake, be careful."

You keep saying that, Bear mused. *Even though we always are on missions such as this.*

"That's because I don't trust the people we're dealing with, so just humor me with a 'Yes, we'll be careful.'"

Yes, we'll be careful, they both intoned solemnly, and promptly shattered the illusion by giggling merrily as they left to investigate.

I walked over to the bed to put on my boots, and then quickly altered my form, becoming myself once again. And Rhea, it felt *good.*

I took a deep breath, let it filter through every part of me to sweep out the remnants of those other identities, then wrapped a light shield around myself and clambered out the window. No one was in the small walkway, and there were no faces peering out the windows of the nearby apartments that I could see. I relaxed a little but didn't release the shield. The museum was officially out-of-bounds, so I couldn't risk being spotted walking to the place.

It didn't take me long to get there. I rapped on the metal door as hard as I dared and then waited.

Footsteps echoed as Jonas approached. "Who is it?"

"Me."

He didn't reply, but a heartbeat later the door was pushed open. I swept inside and released the shield with a sigh of relief. The little ones buzzed around me excitedly, some of them dropping tingly kisses on my cheeks and others patting my arms. Relief that I'd returned was uppermost in their energy, even though they'd had fun following Jonas about as he investigated both the tower and the pile of rubble. It made me feel guilty about having to return to Central so soon.

"Tough night?" Jonas left the doors open and walked over to the autocook, ordering two coffees.

"Yeah, but only because I was bored out of my brain." I followed him across, then leaned a shoulder against the museum's outer wall and watched the autocook fill two mugs. "Sharran was attacked, just as we'd thought."

His gaze briefly scanned my length, then rose and lingered on my neck. I hadn't bothered healing the wound, so it was still red and puffy looking. And while my attacker might have had access to a spray that had healed the needle's entry point, the medical center doc had declared it was a waste of resources to use it on the neck wound and that it'd heal just fine. Obviously, the financial problems Charles had mentioned were hitting *all* departments.

"Were you able to see who it was?" He handed me a mug and motioned me toward the table.

I took a sip, then gave him a brief description. "It was Rath Winter. Or, rather, the imposter who has usurped his life."

"I'm a little surprised he's doing his own dirty work. In an organization that large, he'd surely have people he could completely trust."

"Obviously, given the dissections they're doing upstairs."

He just about choked on his coffee. "They're *what*?"

I updated him on everything my ghosts had seen, then grimaced and added, "The fact that they're drugging the women in the holding cells creates a major problem, however."

"One that means we might have to get you in there tonight rather than wait for Sharran to be promoted upstairs." He began to pace instead of sitting at the table with me, his strides long, powerful, and filled with frustration. "Our only obvious chance of doing *that* is via the freight elevator, which is *another* problem, given we had no idea it existed until now. And I'm not sure Nuri's family can risk pulling up any information about it without raising alarms in the wrong quarters."

"They don't need to. I've got Cat and Bear trying to find the entry point at the moment."

Amusement momentarily broke the tension radiating from him. "They're very handy allies, these ghosts of yours."

"They're not my allies. They're my friends."

He paused, his gaze on mine and his expression . . . odd. Odd in a way that had the hairs at the back of my neck rising and my pulse racing. But it wasn't fear. It was something far baser than that.

"What sort of life did you have here?" he asked.

I took another sip of coffee, pretending to consider the question as I tried to get my reactions under some semblance of control. Which, as usual, seemed damn near impossible in the presence of this man. "You've read the texts, haven't you? Surely you can guess."

He came back to the table and sat opposite me. "I've guessed many things about you, and all but one have been wrong."

A smile touched my lips. "That one thing being the fact that I'm déchet?"

"Yes. And I killed my fair share of you during the war and never once did I see the spark that I see in you."

I raised an eyebrow and tried to ignore the internal havoc his comment caused. "And what spark might that be?"

"Life," he said. "Humanity."

I couldn't help the contemptuous snort that escaped, even though I'd promised to curtail such reactions. "As I've said before, being born in a tube doesn't make me any less human than those who created us or those who destroyed us."

"Perhaps that is true of you and the little ghosts you've gathered around you, but can you honestly look me in the eye and say the same about those who were frontline fighters?"

"We're *all* a product of our upbringing, Jonas. Those who were bred to be fighters were only doing as they were taught, and were both chemically *and* emotionally castrated. They didn't *know* any different. If you want to blame anyone for what they did in the war, blame those who created and trained them."

"You were trained to kill, weren't you?"

"To seduce and then kill, yes, but as a lure, I had to be able to understand and respond to emotional cues. They couldn't do to us what they did to the fighters." I hesitated. "Why all the sudden interest?"

"I'm just trying to figure you out."

How could I respond to a statement like *that*? No one,

not in all the years I'd been alive, had ever made any attempt at knowing the person inside—the real me. Those who'd created us had never thought it necessary, and even Sal, who'd been my friend and the only adult I'd really been close to, had never truly known me. If he had, he wouldn't have underestimated me the way he did in our final meeting.

I drank some coffee; it didn't help ease either the sudden dryness in my throat or the erratic pounding of my pulse. "Why? We both know you're only here because you need me to help rescue those kids."

A somewhat wry smile touched his lips. "While that is totally true, it has nothing to do with my reasons for trying to unravel the conundrum you present."

"And why would you even want to do that? Once those kids are rescued, we go our separate ways." Either that or I'd be dead.

"Perhaps," he agreed. "But in understanding you, I might also understand the reason why I am so attracted to someone I should logically hate with every inch of my being."

So there it was: confirmation that I wasn't reading him wrong. That he was indeed as attracted to me as I was to him. And I didn't know whether to dance with joy or run as far and fast as I could from the man.

Because mutual attraction didn't make him any less dangerous, even if that danger was now more emotional than physical.

Presuming, of course, I was capable of a deeper emotional connection. Having never been in the state of love, I really couldn't say. But this thing between Jonas and me was already far different from anything I'd felt before, and we'd only just stopped snarling at each other.

"Attraction is a given, I'm afraid. I'm a lure, bred to be

nigh on irresistible to cat shifters." Once I would have added "when I chose to be," but Jonas's presence in my life had certainly knocked *that* notion on the head.

Amusement danced in the rich depths of his green eyes, even if little of it showed in his somewhat serious expression. "So lures capture attention by doing their utmost to avoid any admittance of attraction as well as all physical contact, however slight?"

"Well, no, but—"

"I am—was—a ranger," he cut in. "We're trained to read people—not just through what is said and done, but in the giveaway signs few are aware of. You have been fighting this every bit as much as I have."

"And we both know why."

He nodded. "Because neither of us trusted the other."

"And still don't, to some extent."

"Given that you were bred to kill my kind, and I was trained to erase yours, *that's* to be expected."

"So what's the point of bringing all this up, Jonas? It's not going to change anything anytime soon, is it?"

His smile held an edge I didn't quite understand. "Maybe not. But I learned the hard way that avoiding issues is never a good idea when you're working closely with someone. Confronting them, and talking through them as a team, is always the most efficient method of problem-solving."

"So is that what this is?" What I was? "A problem you need to solve?"

"Oh, I think this thing between us is probably a whole lot more than just a problem. But that is neither here nor there, given it is the female of our species who decides which males can or can't court her."

I couldn't help my sudden grin. "You'll have to excuse

my amusement, but it's hard to imagine you actually *courting* anyone."

He raised an eyebrow again and leaned back in his chair. "I'll have you know that it was a rare day when I *didn't* win a female's favor."

Which almost sounded like a warning. Shame my hormones weren't actually listening—*not* that they were going to get satisfaction anytime soon. Not with Jonas, anyway.

"Meaning there's a tribe of little Jonases running around in the Broken Mountains right now?"

"They're not exactly little, given I lost fertility when the rift altered my nature and most of them are now well into their twilight years. But yes, I have children and grandchildren."

My smile faded. "At least you had the chance to have offspring, even if it has subsequently been taken from you. I never even had the choice."

The little ones crowded around me at that, all of them hugging me, kissing me, making my skin twitch with their tingly energy. Reminding me that while I was not by birth their mother, I was the only one who'd cared, the only one who'd shown them laughter and happiness. The only one who'd tried to save them when the gas came. If that was what being a mom meant, then I was theirs.

I blinked back tears and gave them all a mental hug. They laughed in pleasure and danced around me, their energy so bright the air sparkled.

Cat and Bear chose that moment to return. They happily joined in the dance for several seconds, then asked the younger ones to quiet down so that they could make their report. Silence didn't exactly fall, but they did at least tone it down a little.

Images began to scroll through my mind. The first bit of

bad news was the fact that the elevator shaft was filled with lights that had been set into concrete at regular levels. The second was that there were sensors along the entire length of the shaft. Any movement beyond that of the elevator would undoubtedly set them off.

And was the exit at ground level or deeper? I asked.

Ground, but it wasn't in that building, Cat said. *It was in the parking area of a Seventh Street building that backs hard up against it. It is hidden from the public who use the area, but a truck arrived when we were there and we saw where the sensor was.*

"I'm guessing Cat and Bear just returned?" Jonas said, the sudden question making me jump a little.

I glanced at him and nodded, even as I silently asked, *Did you get a chance to look inside the truck?*

We did, Bear said, sounding a little smug. *We thought you might ask that.*

We also stole the sensor thing from the truck, Cat added, dropping the small device into my hand. *They didn't need it to get out. We checked.*

I rolled the device around in my hand. It didn't look any different from the sensors they'd placed in military vehicles during the war. *And the truck's cargo?*

Their amusement died. *It was two children. They were drugged and they did not look well. Something had been done to their mouths.*

The image of the sewn mouths on the five we'd already rescued rose, and my stomach churned. If they were doing *that* to these two, then maybe they'd outlived their usefulness. Maybe they, like Sal and the guards, were destined for the gleaming dissection tables. But why bring them to Winter Halo in a truck? Why not use either of the false rifts? It would certainly be safer.

Unless, of course, my use of the rifts had forced them to move the children to a more secure position *away* from the things. I swore and rubbed a hand across my eyes.

"What?" Jonas leaned forward, his expression intent. The warmth and amusement had fled, leaving only the dispassion of a soldier.

I gave him a quick rundown, then said, "I really do have to get in there tonight."

"Yes." His expression was slightly distracted. Updating Nuri, no doubt. "You can't do this alone."

"We have no other choice, Jonas. Ela has brothel duties, Branna would kill me, and if you show your face in Central after having taken this job, questions will be asked in the wrong quarters."

"I'm aware of all that. It doesn't change what I said." He scrubbed a hand across his jaw. The rough sound echoed lightly in the hush that surrounded us. The younger ghosts had finally fallen silent—perhaps even they realized the gravity of the situation. "Are there cameras in either the parking area or on the thirtieth floor?"

"The kids won't be on the thirtieth. They'll be on the twenty-ninth, where the holding cells are."

If they'd gone there for dissection, that is. It was always possible the scientist working to develop immunity for the wraiths and vamps had another serum ready to test, and had requested the two children brought in to enable that. Though why they'd risk that rather than take the serum to them, I had no idea.

"I'm aware of that," Jonas said. "Just ask the question."

No, Bear said. *But there's everything imaginable on the remaining floors.*

I repeated what he'd said. "Getting onto the thirtieth is going to be useless if we can't get onto the other floors."

"Let Nuri and me worry about that." He frowned suddenly. "Don't you have a lunchtime meeting with Charles?"

I looked over at the autocook clock and saw it was just past one. I had less than half an hour to get back into Central and make myself presentable for seduction.

"This sensor is from the truck that delivered the children; we'll need it to get into the elevator." I dropped it onto the table, then drew in the power of the lights that flooded this entire area, using it to wrap a shield around my body. "I'll come back here as soon as I can. Keep the door open for me."

"The ability to shield like that," he said as he rose, "is one I'm damnably glad the soldier déchet didn't have in the war."

"It's hard to give someone a psychic gift when you've all but gutted their mind." I rose and followed him across to the door. *Bear, Cat, I need you to remain here this afternoon.*

If you need help, call, Cat said.

I will. I stepped through the door, then hesitated and looked back at Jonas. He might not be able to see through the light shield, but his gaze nevertheless met mine unerringly.

"What would you do if I did decide to pursue this attraction?" I asked.

"Until it actually happens, I honestly can't say." A smile twitched the corner of his mouth. "But it's an event unlikely to occur anytime soon, is it?"

"That is a question *I* honestly can't answer."

I turned and walked away. He didn't immediately move back inside. He just stood there, watching me, his gaze a caress I could feel against my spine and one that had my whole body tingling.

Having Jonas stay in such close proximity really *wasn't* a good idea—either for my hormones or my determination to keep them all at arm's length.

I made it back into Central. Given that it was lunchtime and the cross streets would undoubtedly be filled with people, I instead made my way to the nearest public convenience. Once I'd shifted back to my Cat identity, I hurried across to Third Street and my apartment there. Thankfully, Charles hadn't arrived yet. I stripped, tossed my clothes into the laundry chute, and had a quick shower, just in case any scent of dust or even Jonas lingered on my skin.

The door alarm went just as I stepped out. The nearby monitor came to life, revealing Charles standing outside the building. I buzzed him in and then walked into the bedroom to grab a sheer gown before heading downstairs. By the time I'd opened and poured two glasses of whiskey, he was at my doorway.

"Enter," I murmured, pushing a husky note into my tone.

The door slid open and he strode in. His expression was initially thunderous, but that gave way to delight and desire when he saw me.

"I'm gathering it's been a hard morning," I said, sashaying toward him.

His gaze swept me, and lust burned the air. He accepted the drink with a nod of thanks and downed it in one quick mouthful.

I laughed and handed him mine. "Seems you need this more than me." The second drink disappeared as fast as the first. I raised an eyebrow and added, "Would you like another?"

He took a deep breath and released it slowly. "Yes, please."

I plucked the second glass from his hand and walked across to the kitchen. He followed and, when I stopped to pour the alcohol, wrapped his hands around my waist.

"What I need more than a drink, however," he murmured, dropping a kiss on the side of my neck, "is to lose myself in the glory of your body and simply forget my problems for a short while."

Given that I certainly wanted the former so that I could read the latter, I stoppered the whiskey and pressed my butt back against him.

He groaned and moved his grip to my hips, pressing me harder against his erection. "I'm really not in the mood for self-control. Not this first time."

"Self-control is sometimes overrated." Fast wouldn't gain me much information, but Charles was a man of amazing stamina. The first session would not be the last, even if our time this afternoon was limited.

He dropped another kiss against my neck, then undid the gown's ties and slid it to the floor between us. I tried to turn and face him, but his grip tightened, preventing me.

"I need control," he murmured.

Because he doesn't have it at work, intuition whispered.

He stepped back and stripped. The fact that he tossed his clothes onto the nearest chair rather than neatly place them said a lot about his urgency and his desire to forget.

He began to caress and tease my body, and for a man in a hurry he did a damnably good job of making sure I was ready for him. But as his breathing got faster and the lust stinging the air felt liquid, he kicked my legs farther apart and thrust into me. There was nothing gentle, nothing civilized about this mating; it was all heat and need and desperation, and the images that filtered through my mind were fractured and all over the place. But I saw enough to know he'd been called up to the thirtieth floor to face Rath Winter. He came before I could glimpse the outcome of that meeting.

"That," he said, resting his forehead momentarily against my spine, "definitely chased a few demons away. Thank you."

"You're most welcome." I turned around and wrapped

my arms loosely around his neck. "I'm thinking said demons aren't entirely banished, though?"

"You could say that." He traced a line around my lips, his expression edging toward dark. Furious. "I was given an ultimatum."

"Whom by?"

He leaned forward and kissed me for several minutes. It tasted of anger and hate—the former aimed at his boss, the latter for the situation he'd been forced into.

"My boss," he said eventually.

I raised a hand and cupped his cheek, my expression one of concern. "What sort of ultimatum? Or aren't you allowed to talk about it?"

He snorted, a sound that was rough and wrong on his lips. "The latter, but it's not like they can sack me when I've already given notice."

"Why?" The shock in my voice was real enough. *Why, why, why?*

"Because he's asking the impossible and as much as I love working there, I do have other options. I don't need the stress of impossible targets."

I resisted the urge to ask what those targets were or what his options might be. Now was not the time, even if the latter would certainly play a part in what happened next between him and me. "I'm so sorry, Charles."

"So am I."

I rose on my toes and kissed him. After what seemed like ages, he pulled back, then caught my hand and tugged me toward the stairs. "Let's take this somewhere more comfortable."

We moved into my bedroom. This time, he took his time; even when he entered me, there was no rush, just a gradual buildup of heat. It gave me time to go deeper into his mind, catch more than fleeting glimpses. What Rath had demanded was the cessation of financial support to all projects on the lower level, with funds being diverted to those on the upper levels. He hadn't specified which projects, but it wasn't hard to guess the ones he meant. Charles had refused and then quit. Rath Winter had immediately ordered guards to escort him out of the building. No good-byes, no here's your stuff, now leave, nothing.

I dove deeper into his memories, trying to discover how many people had access to the thirtieth floor. It seemed most departmental heads from the lower floors did, which meant around six people. I couldn't find any information about the upper levels, but it probably ran along similar lines.

I became aware of heated movements and carefully withdrew from his memories. My body had been primed for completeness by then, and I came at the same time as he did. He kissed me, then rolled to one side and gathered me in his arms. Neither of us spoke for a while, but eventually I said, "So, what are you going to do now? Go back there until they find a replacement?"

"No." His breath was warm against my cheek. "They marched me out; my personal stuff and severance pay will be forwarded, apparently."

"Oh, that's dreadful!"

"But not unexpected. He's done it before with departmental heads who refused to play his games." He sighed and rubbed a hand across his eyes. "As to what I'll do, well, the family has been after me for a while to take up my position in the House of Lords."

Which explained the odd emphasis Nuri had placed on information gathering when I mentioned Charles to her. As a member of the House of Lords, he had full access to

Government House and everything that went on there. And it was yet another example of Rhea favoring our quest.

"And is that something you really want?"

He grimaced. "It's something I've been avoiding, but I am my father's only son, so it is both my duty and my place."

"And here I was, believing that sort of thinking went out with the Dark Ages."

He smiled. "There are some traditions that never go away, I'm afraid."

And I couldn't help being glad of that, because if Charles did take his seat there, it would certainly work to my advantage. As his lover, I might not get access to Government House itself, but I sure as hell had access to his thoughts and memories.

He threw one leg over mine and dragged me a little closer. "As I appear to have the rest of the afternoon and the evening free, I would very much like to spend it with you."

I sighed. "I'd love to spend more time with you, but I'm afraid I have a dinner appointment."

"Ah." He idly played with my nipples. "Is this another rival for you affections, or the same one?"

"The same."

"Should I have cause to worry?"

"He is the most annoying and opinionated man I have ever had the displeasure of meeting." *Not to mention strong, thoughtful, and caring,* that inner voice unhelpfully whispered.

Charles chuckled. "In other words, I *should* be concerned."

"Perhaps." I slid my hand between us and began to caress his erection.

"Then perhaps . . ." He paused as the door alarm chimed, then added, "Ignore it."

I started to agree, then stopped as I felt the energy of the ghosts. They didn't come into the room—while they were both aware of what I'd been bred to do, they also knew I didn't like them witnessing it.

"And what if it is my other suitor?" I began to untangle myself from him. "It would be terribly awkward if he decided to break in and discovered us midcoitus."

"Indeed," Charles agreed. "But perhaps him realizing there is another in the mix would improve his behavior."

I laughed. "That I doubt."

I jumped free of the bed and ran down the stairs. My two ghosts spun around me and a note fluttered free. I caught it, then continued on to open the door, even though I knew there was no one on the other side. I proceeded to softly converse with that nonperson even as I unfolded the note.

Tonight not ideal. Better if you stay where you are, it read. *Meet for breakfast in the usual spot.*

I glanced up at the ghosts. *Do you know why there's a delay?*

Bear's energy touched mine. *Lack of time to organize an assault. Plus, they can't get the children out at night.*

But why would they want to do that? Most of the children had lived in Central with their families before they were kidnapped, so why go elsewhere?

It has something to do with the five we rescued, Cat replied.

Are they okay? By Rhea, don't tell me we'd gone to all the trouble of rescuing them only to have them fall foul of these people again.

Physically, yes, Bear assured me. *But there are other problems.*

Which wasn't surprising, given everything they'd gone through. I closed the door and walked across to the kitchen, quietly opening drawers until I found an old pen. *Take this note back.* I quickly scrawled both my agreement and my uncertainty that delay was the right course of action, as well as the information about the departmental heads all having access to the thirtieth. *But when you've done that, go back into Winter Halo and keep track of the two children. One of you let me know the minute there's any sign of them being moved.*

And be careful, they both intoned, before I could.

I chuckled softly and told them to scoot. Then I grabbed the whiskey and two glasses and headed back upstairs.

"I realize it's never a good idea to drink on an empty stomach," I said as I climbed onto the bed and handed him a glass. "But given the situation you have found yourself in, I think it's entirely appropriate."

"So the rival has been given his marching orders?"

"Until tomorrow morning, yes." I unstoppered the whiskey and poured him a generous amount. "I *did* have to promise him breakfast before he'd leave, however, so I'm afraid you'll have to depart at the rather unseemly hour of seven."

"Which still gives me plenty of time to indulge in both the alcohol *and* you." He tossed the whiskey back. "And perhaps I will even combine the two pleasures."

I raised my glass and let the whiskey dribble down my torso. "Perhaps? That doesn't sound ideal to me."

He laughed, grabbed my arm, and tugged me downward. From that moment on, there was little conversation and few other sounds except those of pleasure.

"It might be a couple of days before I can see you again," Charles said as we walked toward the front door. "I may be the only son, but claiming my seat in the House of Lords is a somewhat lengthy process."

I stopped. "Which saddens me, but I'm sure I'll be able to find something to do to fill my time."

"Which is a none-too-subtle reminder that I am not the only tom in *this* particular cathouse." He wrapped an arm around my waist and dragged me closer. "I am, however, a tom who expects to win."

He kissed me hard, then released me with a curse and added, "I had best go, before I do something ungentlemanly, like throw you over my shoulder and cart you upstairs."

I laughed. "We can do the caveman thing when you are next free. I do own silk restraints; perhaps we can put them to use?"

His gaze darkened. "I look forward to it."

And with that, he left. I watched until he'd entered the elevator and the doors had closed, then shut my door and leaned my forehead wearily against it. What a night. It might have been an enjoyable one, but it was nevertheless one in which there'd been no sleep. That, ultimately, was what I now needed—and the one thing I wouldn't get anytime soon. I pushed away from the door and headed upstairs. By the time I'd showered and put the bedroom back into some semblance of order, an hour had past. Even so, I took the time to sit down and boost my energy levels. It might not erase all the tiredness, but hopefully it would help get me through the day.

Outside, it was cool and crisp, and the bitter wind that swept down Third Street made me glad I'd thrown on a coat. I hitched the bag holding my change of clothes a little higher on my shoulder and headed for the nearest cross street. I slowed my pace once I'd entered, waiting for the couple at the other end to exit, then glanced over my shoulder to check that no one else was approaching. Once I was in the clear, I quickly drew a light shield around my body and then changed both form and clothes. Doing all that while holding on to the shield was not something I'd attempted too often, and it left me shaking with fatigue. So much for boosting my reserves earlier.

And while it would undoubtedly have been easier to simply find another public convenience in which to shift, I couldn't risk using them too often. Cameras still monitored the entrances to most of them, thanks to the attacks that used to happen in the early, somewhat turbulent years after the war. Going in as someone who didn't come out would attract attention; if it happened too often, it might also attract the attention of the very people I was trying to avoid.

I repacked my bag, then headed for the drawbridge. By the time I reached the bunker, my head was pounding and the shield was beginning to pulse, a sure sign that I was close to losing it.

Thankfully, the museum's doors were already open. I all but dove through them, falling to my knees as the shield disintegrated around me.

"For God's sake," Nuri said. "Are you all right?"

I nodded slowly, and even *that* was hard.

"Well, you look like fucking shit," Nuri said. "Jonas, rustle up that remaining steak and pile it high with eggs and potatoes. This girl needs some starch and protein in her."

"Must have been one hell of a night," was Jonas's only comment.

"It's more the fact that I've gone almost thirty-six hours without much sleep; the final straw was holding the light shield in place while I shifted shape."

Nuri clucked. "No wonder." I didn't hear any footsteps, but suddenly she was beside me. "Up you get, my girl."

She grabbed my arm and gently hauled me upright, then helped me over to the table. Once I'd sat, her grip slipped to my hand; electricity immediately bit into my skin and dove deep into my body. Recharging me with her own strength.

"Don't." I uselessly tried to pull my hand from hers. "You'll need all the strength you can get if we're to pull this rescue off."

"I don't need my strength, because I'm not the one going in," Nuri replied evenly. "You and Jonas are."

"But Jonas can't—"

"Jonas *can*, with the aid of a little witchery," Nuri cut in. "You can't drive the truck *and* rescue those kids. It's a two-person job."

"So you've figured out a way to get us in?"

She nodded. "Took a bit of a risk and put the relatives to work again. There's a truck delivering supplies to the fifteenth floor. You two are now the drivers."

I frowned. "That won't help us any. If this place follows general protocols, it will be programmed only to that floor."

"Which is why we'll be replacing its current sensor with the one your ghosts stole."

"I'm not sure I can rewire—"

"You won't have to." Jonas returned with a large plate of food and a cup of hot green muck that was actually an herbal drink favored by shifters for its energy-boosting properties. I'd had it on occasion during the war, and was not a fan. "I'll switch the two sensors while you drive us in."

"Which doesn't answer the question as to how you plan to get to the children when they're on the twenty-ninth and we'll be on the thirtieth."

"Thanks to the information you sent, we have acquired the cooperation of one Nevel Williams," Nuri said. "He's a divisional head and is willing to help on the proviso we immediately relocate him and his family—which we already have done."

Making me wonder if they'd snatched his family before or *after* he'd agreed to help. I snagged some cutlery from the center container and began to tuck in. "So, where and when do we pick up this truck?"

"It's coming in from Harston."

Which was, as far as I knew, a mining town. I frowned. "Why would a pharmaceutical company be bringing in minerals?"

Nuri shrugged. "Industrial minerals have long been used in both pharmaceuticals and cosmetics."

"Not that what they're carrying really matters." Jonas handed Nuri a mug of coffee, then pulled out the chair beside mine and sat down. I might be weary and totally loved out, but his wild, stormy scent still stirred something deep inside me. "It's just the excuse to get in there."

"So, when are we intercepting this truck?" I asked.

Nuri smiled. "The trucks from Harston regularly stop at the refuel center past the greenbelt farmlands to grab lunch. The exchange will happen then."

"And the guards?"

"Will know very little about it."

Meaning they'd be dead? Or simply drugged? And did it really matter if it meant rescuing those children? *No,* my inner voice whispered, *definitely not.*

I picked up the mug of grassy liquid and drank some of it. A shudder went through me. The taste had not improved a century down the track. "So, who is staying here while Jonas and I are out?" My gaze returned to Nuri. "You?"

She nodded. "I'm well able to deal with anyone who gets too curious."

Of that I had no doubt. "If we do manage to grab the children, where are we taking them? The note you sent with the ghosts implied it wasn't Central."

"No." Nuri paused and glanced at Jonas, her expression concerned. "There have been problems with all of them."

"Penny included?"

She nodded. "It would appear that whatever they have done to her has disrupted both her physiology and psychology. She is not the child she was."

"But still my niece, regardless of whatever else is going on." Jonas's voice held a note that suggested this was an argument they'd had before.

"I did tell you there was a darkness in her," I cut in, before that argument got rolling again.

"This is more than the taint of a rift," Nuri said. "The only thing she can keep down is raw meat. She drinks little, not even water, and her canines show signs of lengthening."

Becoming a vampire, one that had been neither bitten nor born. "Has she shown any signs of being affected by lights?"

"None at all."

No wonder Sal's partners were desperate to get her back—if they'd created a pathogen capable of altering someone's base biology to make them a vampire, they surely couldn't be too far off being able to reverse that process, and make a vampire human. Or, at the very least, someone immune to sunlight.

But if that *were* the case, why were they still testing on the remaining children? Had Penny escaped before they'd been able to test the success of the latest batch of whatever they'd given her, and they were therefore unaware of how close they were?

I scooped up some food, then said, "I gather you've had her tested?"

Nuri nodded. "There is now vampire sequencing within her DNA as well as something else we can't identity."

"I'd bet wraith." I glanced at Jonas. "What are you going to do?"

"Everything we can." It was grimly said. "She is *family*. I will *not* allow her to be placed in a medical facility to be poked and prodded like some new life-form."

"Jonas, she is not *safe* in Chaos." And Chaos wasn't safe from her. Nuri didn't add that, but it nevertheless hung in the air.

"Then we send her somewhere else. But *not* a medical or military center."

"We *cannot* take her to the Broken Mountains. Her presence would jeopardize your kin there just as much as it does Chaos."

"I know, but there must be other options." His expression was glacial. "Options that do not involve locking her away from all that she knows and loves. Our presence is all that's holding her together. Take that away, and Rhea only knows what might happen."

Nuri sighed and leaned back. "I'm still looking for options, Jonas, but there are difficulties—"

"Guys," I cut in gently. "This needs to be a conversation for another day, when there's more time."

"That," Nuri murmured, "is something I doubt any of us have enough of."

Unease slithered through me, but before I could say anything, Jonas said, "I've placed security on high alert. No one is getting in or out of Chaos without us knowing about it."

"Knowing about it may not fucking help," Nuri bit back, then sighed again and leaned forward. Her gaze was on me rather than him. "If you succeed in getting these children out of Winter Halo, you are to head back to the truck stop. Our people will meet you there and transfer them to a waiting vehicle."

"Where are they taking them?"

"A military research center." Her voice was flat, but the glance she threw at Jonas simmered with annoyance. "Until we know precisely what has been done to them, it's our only option."

"What about the other five we rescued? Cat and Bear implied there were problems with them, too."

She nodded. "There are severe behavioral problems with all of them, which is unsurprising, given what they've gone through. I cannot sense darkness in them, but they have been injected with God knows what, and we have no idea yet what the result might be."

"Sal said they were rejected because they'd outlived their usefulness—"

"For what his aims were, yes," Nuri cut in. "But that does not mean we can simply release them. Both they and their families—if they have kin alive, and some don't—have also been transferred to a military center."

To keep Central safe more than monitor them, I suspected. It was a step that was totally logical, and one I was surprised Jonas was fighting. "How are we going to get to the refuel center?"

"Via the rail pods, of course." Nuri handed me an image screen. On it was a somewhat blurred picture of a brown-haired, muscular-looking woman. "That's who you're replacing, Tiger. You'd better take her form before you leave here."

I frowned. "Won't that raise alarms, given we're supposed to be driving a truck into Central rather than catching a train out of it?"

"Only if someone is paying attention, and really, why would they be?" She handed me a pair of coveralls and made a hurry-up motion with her hand. "And don't give me that shy crap you gave to Jonas. We've both seen far worse than a déchet shifting."

I opened my mouth to argue, then shut it again at her steely look. I pulled the coveralls on over my clothes and then studied the image on the screen for a minute to fix it in my mind. Altering my body was a far quicker process this time—I guessed like any skill, it got easier with time and use, and I'd certainly done enough of it of late. But even so, my head swam and weakness stirred. I grabbed the green swill and quickly downed it. It might taste like a swamp, but I needed the boost.

"Your turn, Jonas." Nuri handed him what looked like a random selection of strings platted together to form a bracelet and a small silver disk.

He immediately pocketed the disk, then slipped the bracelet over his wrist. Power surged, its caress sharp, biting; it shimmered up his arm and across his body, transferring his form to that of a blond-haired, craggy-faced, weedy-looking man in his mid-fifties.

"Now, *that's* an attractive image," I said, voice dry.

He raised an eyebrow, creating a myriad of wrinkles across his forehead. "So I should wear it more often?"

"Yes, because it would definitely solve all sorts of dilemmas." I reached out to test the strength of the transformation. The invisible net of power that surrounded him wavered and then retreated from my touch, and what met my fingertips were steely arm muscles rather than weedy ones. This was more a glamour than an actual transformation: one that could fool from either a distance or close up, but didn't stand up to physical human contact. I glanced at Nuri. "Will the image hold when he's in contact with inanimate objects? When we're seated in the truck, for instance?"

She nodded. "It's fed by the power of the earth, so it won't falter unless contact with the ground is lost for more than half an hour."

I frowned. "We'll be in the truck longer than that."

"And the truck tires provide enough of a connection to feed the spell. The freight elevator, however, does not have a direct link to the ground, so you cannot linger in Winter Halo."

If everything went according to plan, we wouldn't. *And if everything didn't?* I shoved the thought from my mind and hastily finished the rest of my meal.

"We'd better get moving." Jonas rose.

"If there's too many people on the platforms," Nuri said, "head into the park before you release the concealer shield."

"I will." He glanced at me. "You'd better disappear, too."

As he spoke, he pressed the disk Nuri had given him. An almost static buzz caressed the air, and a heartbeat later he'd disappeared from sight. It seemed Nuri had more than magical tricks up her sleeve.

I pulled in the energy of the lights around me and headed for the door. Jonas gave Nuri a hand to close it—something I knew only by the location of his scent—then followed me across to the rail yards and into the fringes of the park opposite.

Once both shields had been dispensed with, we made our way onto the platform and joined the many others already waiting there. A string of pods soon slid silently into the station. The doors opened and its passengers exited—a mix of farm and factory workers, from the look of them. Jonas pressed his fingers against my spine and lightly guided me toward a pod near the front of the string.

I stepped inside and glanced around. There were only half a dozen people in this one, and all of them were clustered near the door. I walked past them and claimed the seats at the very front of the pod.

Jonas sat next to me, keeping just enough distance

between us to ensure the shield remained unaffected. Unfortunately, that also meant his scent was entirely *too* close. I suspected it was a very deliberate ploy on his part. He might be trying to figure me out in order to understand why he was so attracted, but that didn't negate the fact that he *was*. By his own admission, he was used to getting what he wanted—a fact borne out by Penny's continuing presence in Chaos, despite Nuri's misgivings. And while he did appear willing to wait until I decided whether I wanted to explore the attraction between us, he obviously wasn't above putting a little sensory pressure on.

A bell chimed and then the pod door closed. Within seconds we were leaving the station, and the countryside began to blur as the train picked up speed. After a moment, I asked, "Why don't you want"—I hesitated, suddenly aware of the silence and the fact that the others could possibly hear us—"your niece moving? We both know it's for the best."

"Because I promised her mother I'd look after her." His voice was flat, growly. It wasn't his voice, but it wasn't far from it, either. "I can't do that if she's not near me."

"So why does she live in Central and you elsewhere?"

"Practicalities. But one of us is always near enough to help if there's trouble."

Meaning Nuri as much as him. The telepathic connection that had come from the rift they'd all been caught in undoubtedly helped them counter—or at least deal with—said trouble.

And I couldn't help wondering whether the "practicalities" he mentioned were simply the fact that she didn't age thanks to the rift, or something else. Because in reality, Penny was almost as old as me, and having the mind and probably the desires of an older woman while being stuck in the body of a child had to be hell. "And your sister?"

"Died not long after Penny's birth."

Meaning she'd died in the war. I looked out the window. There were so many reasons why he and I were a bad idea. So damn many.

Silence fell. There was little point in saying any more; if Nuri couldn't convince him it was dangerous to leave Penny in Chaos, there was little chance I could. But I had to wonder if he was prepared for the consequences, because the second Sal's partners realized she was in Chaos, the vampires *would* attack en masse. And that might very well end in a bloodbath.

It took just under an hour to get to the greenbelt rail station. We stepped out of the pod once the string had come to a halt, and followed the crowd to the exit. But instead of heading across to the processing station to register for work like the rest of them, we waited until the train had left, then walked across the track and followed the road down to the refuel station.

Without a word, Jonas led the way to the café adjoining the refuel center. Once inside, he walked through the many occupied tables until we reached one near the back of the room, where a man with dark hair and green eyes almost identical to Jonas's waited. In front of him were three steaming mugs of coffee.

"Didn't know what you wanted," he said, briefly glancing my way. "So I ordered black with milk on the side."

I smiled. "Perfect. Thanks."

He nodded, but his attention had already returned to Jonas. "There's a backpack under the table. In it is everything you need."

"And the drivers?"

"Will be found with the truck in a few days' time." He glanced at me. "Drugged but alive."

I raised an eyebrow and wondered if he'd read my thoughts. Telepathy wasn't a common talent found among shifters, but it did exist.

"Thanks," Jonas said. "Say hello to your mom for me."

A smile broke the seriousness of the stranger's face. "Like that won't cause more problems than it's worth."

"I know." Jonas's expression was amused.

The stranger's grin grew, but he didn't reply. He simply picked up his coffee, gave me a nod, and walked out.

I picked up my cup and took a drink. "Am I allowed to ask who that was?"

"One of my six grandchildren." He kept his voice low. Though there was a lot of noise in this place, he obviously wasn't about to chance anyone overhearing him. "His mother—Demi—does not approve of his decision to follow my steps into the business."

Meaning the mercenary business, no doubt. "He works with you?"

"On occasion." He picked up the pack from under the table and slung it over his shoulder. "Let's go."

I gathered my coffee and followed him outside. The truck we'd appropriated wasn't one of the hulking haulers that often carted goods between Central and other major cities, and I guessed that was no surprise, given the truck needed to fit inside a freight elevator. It was still larger than any I'd ever driven, and nerves briefly ran through me. I shoved them aside and climbed into the cabin. It wasn't like I hadn't been trained to drive all sorts of vehicles, be they ground-bound or flighted. The vehicles and onboard instruments might have changed over the many years since then, but surely the basic principles hadn't.

Jonas had already climbed into the passenger side and was in the process of scanning a notebook. Whether it had come from the backpack or the truck, I had no idea. I studied the truck's console for several minutes, familiarizing myself with the layout, then found and pressed the start button. Nothing happened.

"You'll need one of these before this beast will go anywhere." He put the notebook aside and plucked two clear containers from the pack. Inside each was a small electronic chip.

"What are they? RFID chips?"

"No. They're basically day passes. They're inserted into the nondominant hand of everyone working for the freight companies, and reprogrammed daily to confirm access into whatever company the truck's freight has been allocated to. The truck won't start unless you're wearing the correct chip."

"So I take it these two were removed from the hands of the driver and his partner?"

Jonas nodded. "It's the only way we'll have any hope of getting in and out of Winter Halo without raising suspicion."

If we managed to do that, I'd be surprised. Rhea might be smiling on our quest, but there were so many variables I couldn't help thinking something was bound to go wrong.

"I'm gathering there's also something to insert them into our hands in that bag of yours?"

"No, because it's not necessary thanks to the recent production of artificial skin. Those in charge believe mercenaries haven't been able to get their hands on it. They're wrong."

"But I thought the RFID chips only worked when inserted inside your flesh?"

"The original ones did. The newer versions are still powered by the heat emanating from your body, but it doesn't really matter whether they're in your flesh or simply touching it—something we discovered by chance." He motioned toward my arm. "Hold out your hand, palm up."

I did so. He placed one of the chips in the middle, then

pulled out a small can and sprayed a clear liquid over both my palm and my fingers. Within seconds, the chip had disappeared under a layer of what looked like real skin. I prodded it gently. It even felt like real skin. "How long will this stuff last?"

He placed the second chip on his palm then repeated the process. "Until we physically remove it."

"Which will be when we get back here?"

He nodded, placed the bag at his feet, and then said, "Let's go. We have children to rescue."

I pressed the starter key again, and this time the engine roared to life. I carefully backed the truck out of its spot and headed for the highway into Central.

And crossed mental fingers that the inner whispers stating something would go awry were wrong.

Even if they often weren't.

CHAPTER 10

We made it into Central without mishap. There were only a couple of cross streets big enough to give trucks this size passage, so it took a bit of time to reach Seventh Street and the building that hid Winter Halo's freight elevator.

I turned the truck into the parking area, and sent several pedestrians scattering.

"Easy," Jonas murmured. "The last thing we need is to attract attention by mowing down innocent citizens."

"If said citizens are too stupid to get out of the way of a truck *this* size, they deserve to be mowed down."

I could feel his gaze on me, but kept mine strictly front and center. The entrance was tight; there were only a couple of inches between the sides of the truck and that of the building. If I so much as twitched the steering the wrong way, we'd be wedged. And *that* would be just as inconvenient as running someone over.

"This is the first time I've felt any tension emanating from you," he said eventually.

"Then you haven't been around me enough."

"I've been around enough to know this is different." He continued to study me. "Is intuition hitting you?"

"Like a bitch."

He reached into the backpack and drew out a couple of guns, tucking one beside his seat and the other beside mine. "Just in case the bitch is right."

A smile tugged my lips. Guns might not help if everything went to hell, but it was nevertheless comforting to have one within reach. I guided the truck into the gloom of the parking area—*not* that it was anywhere near dark. It just wasn't quite as bright as the street.

A guard appeared out of a booth to Jonas's left and motioned us to stop. I did so.

Jonas wound down the window and flashed the guard a smile. "Frankie," he said cheerfully, "that wife of yours had her kid yet?"

"Could happen any time now." He glanced past Jonas and gave me a nod. "I'm sure as hell hoping it's a boy this time. Manifest?"

Jonas handed him the electronic list. "The scans didn't reveal anything?"

The guard snorted as he flicked through the various screens. "If it did, the wife isn't telling me."

"Meaning it might be another girl?"

"Possibly." He handed the list back to Jonas. "These no-inspection clauses are going to come back and bite them in the ass one of these days. Hand?"

Jonas pressed his hand against the scanner the guard produced. "Hopefully, not on my damn shift, they won't."

"Amen to that, brother." Blue light flashed the screen's length; then the guard stepped back. "Righto, you're clear."

"Thanks, Frank." Jonas wound up the window.

I threw the truck into gear and continued on to the rear wall. "How did you know all that stuff about him? The notebook?"

He nodded. "Not only did we arrange a basic background check on the guards here, but Jarren scanned the thoughts of the two drivers so we knew what sort of interaction was expected."

Meaning it was possible his grandson *had* read my thoughts. It was a good thing I hadn't been thinking about Jonas in any way, shape, or form, or that could have been embarrassing.

Up ahead, the solid-looking wall began to slide to one side, revealing the metal doors of a freight elevator. Once they'd also opened, I carefully drove inside, then stopped and pulled on the hand brake.

"And this," Jonas said softly, "is where we both cross our fingers and pray to Rhea I've installed the sensor right."

He'd barely finished speaking when the sensor beeped; behind us, the doors closed and then the elevator began to move slowly upward. Five floors, ten, then fifteen. My breath caught as the elevator seemed to slow, but it didn't stop and the floors continued to roll by. Neither of us spoke; there wasn't much to say now and certainly nothing either of us could do. Not until we reached the top floor anyway. Besides, it was possible that the sensors inside the elevator shaft would pick up any conversation.

We finally came to a somewhat bouncy stop. For several seconds, nothing happened, and then the elevator doors at the rear of the truck began to open.

A stout, ruddy-faced man with a receding hairline hustled

over to my door. I wound down my window and glanced at his name badge. Nevel Williams himself.

"Manifest?"

Though his voice was curt, sweat was beginning to bead his forehead. I hoped like hell he could hold it together.

Jonas handed me the manifest and I gave it to Williams. He grunted, then glanced at the two men waiting near the end of the truck. "Get those crates out stat, and take them to lab 29-5." As the men obeyed, the stout man handed me back the manifest. "The return cargo is ready. Please turn off all external cameras and remain in the truck."

I obeyed. This was obviously a routine process, but it was one that made me nervous simply because we couldn't see what was being loaded. I doubted Williams would betray us, given Nuri had his family, but I also wasn't about to trust someone who could even contemplate using children as guinea pigs. Williams scurried away—something I heard rather than saw. I glanced at Jonas. If he was in any way tense, it wasn't showing.

"It shouldn't be too long. They're usually pretty efficient here."

I didn't reply. I couldn't, really, given I had no idea what the woman whose image I was wearing sounded like. I tapped my fingers against the steering wheel as the minutes began to tick by. The cargo was soon emptied, but for altogether too long, nothing else happened. Then footsteps approached; three sets were heavy, the other two light. Hope ran through me. The latter *had* to be the children. Those steps definitely weren't those of an adult.

Williams reappeared at my door. "Right," he said, holding up a scanner. "You'll need to confirm receipt."

I pressed my left hand against it. Light swept my palm and the light on top of the screen flashed from red to green.

Williams grunted, then glanced back at his two companions. "Those doors secured?"

"And locked."

"Unusual code?"

"Yes, sir."

"Right, then, see you in twenty." Williams opened the truck's rear cabin door and climbed in. The sting of his sweat was so strong and sour I couldn't help wrinkling my nose. "You can drop me off at the gates as usual."

I glanced at Jonas. This wasn't in the plan as far as I was aware, and Jonas's grim expression suggested he hadn't been expecting this development, either. The doors behind us closed and the elevator began its slow descent. With every floor we dropped, Williams's fear got stronger.

We finally made it to ground level. As the elevator doors opened, the guard once again came out. Williams opened the window and handed Frank another manifest. The guard checked it, nodded, then stepped back and waved us on.

I shoved the truck into gear and resisted the temptation to flatten my foot. Once we were on the street and heading for Central's gatehouse, Jonas turned to Williams and said, "What in Rhea is going on? Why are you in the damn truck?"

"Because I'm not taking a fucking chance of being stranded," Williams bit back. "So suck it up and get us out of here."

"Your absence will be noticed, and *that* is going to cause problems."

"I won't be missed immediately," Williams said. "It's not unusual for divisional heads to accompany cargo past the main gate, just in case anyone decides to do a full inspection."

"They could provide a regular guard with the correct paperwork to prevent that." I stopped at a cross street and waited for several airbikes to scoot past.

"Regular guards don't have the authority to override random goods inspections. I do. Now shut your fucking trap and get us out of here."

"Say anything like that to her again," Jonas said, voice mild, "and I will knock you out, tie you up, and dump you somewhere nice and convenient for the vampires."

The scent of Williams's fear got stronger, and I hadn't thought *that* possible. But the threat achieved the desired result—he shut up. I flashed Jonas a smile and concentrated on getting the hell out of Central without drawing any attention to either the truck or us.

Williams relaxed once we got through the gate, but I wasn't sure why. We weren't exactly out of the woods yet.

"You'd better get off the main road," Jonas said, voice flat and annoyed. "Alarms will be raised once our passenger is missed."

"Going off-road won't exactly help," I said, even as I swung the truck onto a track that would eventually join what had once been a secondary arterial road into old Central. "A truck this size will be easy enough to spot, especially if they send out aerial."

"Yes, but we won't be staying in this. In about twenty kilometers we'll hit a crossroad. Turn right, and after another ten you'll see a series of abandoned factories. Head into building ten."

"Seriously," Williams said, "you're going to extreme lengths for very little reason. They're not going to miss me until I fail to show up for the meeting at three. That gives us plenty of time to get away."

"You overestimate the speed of this truck and underestimate the determination of those behind the experiments," Jonas growled. "You should have followed the plan you were given. By joining us, you've endangered everyone."

Williams snorted. "I've worked too fucking long for Winter Halo to trust *anyone*. Which is why I came equipped with a backup plan."

Something inside me went cold. "What sort of backup plan?"

"Each kid has a pellet containing a variation of VX inserted into him. Get me to my family, and ensure that we're safe, or I'll kill them." Williams's voice was smug. "And don't think you can wrench the control from my grip before I have a chance of setting it off, either."

VX was an old-school, man-made poison, and one of the deadliest to ever have been developed. All stocks had supposedly been destroyed long before the war, which meant the only way Williams—and Winter Halo—could have gotten hold of it was if they were now making it. And that, alongside whatever else they were trying to achieve in that place, was a scary development.

The urge to reach back and throttle the smug bastard was so strong my body shook. It took every ounce of control I had to keep my hands on the wheel and the truck headed in the right direction.

"How much of that stuff has Winter got stored?" Jonas's voice remained flat, but his fury was so strong the force of it filled every breath.

"Enough to wipe out Central," Williams said. "But it's not stored or even created on-site. They wouldn't risk that sort of exposure."

"Then where *is* it created?" Jonas said. "And how did you get your hands on it?"

"That information," Williams said, again in that smug tone, "can wait until I'm safe."

I didn't look at Jonas. I didn't need to. Williams was a dead man walking. He just didn't know it yet.

I reached the crossroad and swung right. A series of scarred, broken buildings soon began to dot the horizon. At first it was hard to distinguish their size and shape thanks to the vegetation that had begun to reclaim this area, but after another couple of kilometers, the green growth gave way to reveal a series of interconnected metal and concrete buildings. This area had been one of the first hit in the war, as it had been a main manufacturing hub for old Central. That so many of the buildings remained relatively intact despite the ravages of time was no doubt due to the fact that this entire area had been hit by more conventional weapons rather than the bombs that had ended the war and brought the rifts and the Others to our world.

I spotted building 10 and swung the truck toward it. Part of the structure had collapsed, and the exposed roof struts looked like rusting metal fingers reaching for the sky. There were a number of open loading bays along the still-standing portion of the building, but only one was free of debris. I dropped the truck's speed and carefully drove inside.

Despite the brightness of the day, it was surprisingly shadowed in this portion of the building. There were no windows, and while there were skylights, time and bird shit had opaqued their surface. Odd bits of metal machines dotted the floor, all of them covered by rust and grime, but there was little else to be seen . . . I frowned, my gaze narrowing as I spotted an odd lump in the far corner. That, I suspected, was our next mode of transport.

I stopped the truck and glanced at Jonas. "What now?"

"Now we change vehicles." He dug into the pack and tossed me a starting disk. "You'll find an ATV under camouflage netting over in the corner. Williams, you get the children. I'll let the others know we're switching to plan B."

I didn't ask him what that was. I had a feeling he didn't

want to give Williams too much information. I glanced back at him. He didn't look happy at this turn of events, even though the change of plans was entirely due to his refusal to follow orders.

I grabbed the gun, tucked it onto one of the coverall's clips, then got out of the truck and strode across to the other side of the building. The air held the taint of grease and oil, even though the machine remnants hadn't been in use for a very long time. An odd rustling noise caught my attention, and I looked up to see a couple of black-and-white magpies watching me from the safety of the rafters. I couldn't help smiling. The birdlife in the parks and forests around Central and Carleen had basically been wiped out thanks to hunting by both the vampires and those in Chaos, but it was nice to know they still existed elsewhere. And magpies were a favorite of mine; their calls always seemed so joyous.

Once I found the ATV—the same ATV that Jonas and I had used to escape the Broken Mountains vampires, if the repairs and patches to its bodywork and roof were anything to go by—I pulled off and stored the camouflage net, then climbed in and started it up.

Williams had the two kids out of the truck by the time I pulled up. Though Cat and Bear had warned me about what had been done to them, seeing their tiny mouths so roughly sewn shut made me want to grab the gun and fire every last bullet into the smug little bastard holding them. He might not be directly responsible for this atrocity, but it didn't matter; he was here, and he didn't seem to see anything wrong in what they were doing. How that was even possible given that he had children of his own I had no idea. Maybe he really did see these kids as guinea pigs—or perhaps even a more evolved form of lab rats. Those who'd been responsible for the déchet program had certainly held that sort of mentality when it came to any life created in a tube.

But these kids were a product of two people, not of a lab, so how could he be so . . . blasé and uncaring? It was almost as if the part of his brain that controlled such emotions had been castrated, but by self-control and scientific desire rather than by chemicals or design.

Both children were wearing what looked like hospital gowns, and the bits of their bodies not covered by these garments revealed emaciated frames and scarred limbs. The latter didn't surprise me, given Sal's partners obviously used the false rifts to move the kids from one point to another where possible, but the former shocked me. Penny had been thin, but not like this. And it wasn't starvation, because I'd seen this look before, on the bodies of almost every vampire I'd come across.

Did that mean these kids were further along the path of becoming vampires than the five we'd already rescued? Was that why their mouths had been sewn shut? To null the risk of the scientists being bitten?

And, like Penny, neither of them showed any sign of fear. In fact, there was no emotion at all on their faces, and their eyes . . . I might as well have been staring into a vacuum. There was simply nothing there.

My gaze met Jonas's through the windshield and caught a brief glimpse of rage before he mastered it. He helped Williams and the two children get into the ATV, then slammed the door shut and climbed into the front passenger seat.

"Right," he said, voice tight. "Get back to the old highway and head toward the Broken Mountains."

"What the fuck is up there?" Williams said.

Jonas's hands clenched so tightly his knuckles went white,

but his voice remained even. "Nothing, because we're not actually going up there. We're meeting a truck halfway; you and the children will be transferred to separate vehicles, and you'll be taken to your family."

"Ah, good."

Williams leaned back, obviously mollified by the answer. Which made me wonder just how much he'd actually learned about trusting people during his time in Winter Halo, because the slight but oh-so-cold smile that touched Jonas's lips suggested that what was going to happen next to the scientist was anything but good.

We made it back to the old highway without incident and I increased our speed, pushing the ATV to its limits. Williams might be certain we had until three before he was missed, but I still couldn't escape the feeling that time was running out.

The countryside grew wilder and the road rougher. The ATV's treads skimmed across most of the potholes, but one or two of the deeper ones caught an edge and pitched the vehicle sideways.

"You'd better slow . . ." Jonas hesitated, and frowned.

"What?" I asked immediately.

He held up a finger and continued listening. After a second or two, I heard it—a low but continuous buzzing, and one that was approaching at speed.

Jonas swore and twisted around. "Kids, hunker down in the foot wells. Williams, grab the blanket and throw it over the three of you."

The two children didn't obey; they just stared at Jonas blankly. Then Williams repeated the order, his tone harsh, and the two of them scrambled to obey. That sick feeling inside me intensified. If Jonas didn't kill this bastard, I would.

I slowed the ATV's speed, despite the desire to do the exact opposite, then moved my side mirror so that I could see the skies. A small black dot jumped into the middle of the screen, but it was still too far away to see what it was.

"What are we going to do?" I glanced at Jonas. "This thing might outrun vampires, but it hasn't much hope against airborne vehicles."

"No." Jonas checked the passenger's-side mirror. "But I think that thing might be a drone. If it is, we still have time to get to the meeting point."

I hoped he was right. I kept one eye on the road and the other on that black dot in the mirror as it drew ever closer. It soon became apparent that it was, indeed, a drone. The multispoke circular object zipped past us, then did a wide turn and came back, its body rotating so that the camera faced us. They might not be able to see either Williams or the kids, but they'd certainly see two people who weren't supposed to be at the helm of an ATV.

I glanced at Jonas. "How long do you think we have?"

He shrugged. "It depends who they send after us. If it's the ranger airborne division, then maybe fifteen or twenty minutes."

"And will that be long enough?"

"It'll be tight." He wound down the window and fired several quick shots at the drone. Three missed; the fourth didn't. As the drone went down in a blaze of smoke and sparks, I swerved the vehicle and ran over its remains. We had no time for finesse now; the only thing that mattered was getting the kids to the meeting point.

Everything became a blur, even time. I kept my attention on the road, on keeping the ATV going no matter what got in the way. We crashed through potholes and over rubble, and the distance between Central and us quickly grew. It didn't ease the tension; if anything, it only increased it, because we were so damn close to safety now, and yet still so very far.

"Swing right at the next turn." The sudden command made me jump. Jonas leaned across and squeezed my arm. "It's okay. We'll be okay."

"Says the man who has no seeking skills to tell him otherwise."

I swung right but didn't slow, and the ATV pitched to one side and threatened to topple. Several lights on the driving panel flashed red as the electronic stability control kicked into gear. The ATV quickly righted itself and I continued on without losing much speed.

"In one kilometer take the gravel road to your left—but this time, slow down or you'll have us in the forest."

I flashed him a somewhat tense grin. "You say that like it would be a bad thing."

"If we want to remain alive, then yeah, it possibly is."

I spotted the road and slowed down as ordered. Dust flew up behind us, a trail that would be easy to follow if it didn't settle quickly enough. But Jonas didn't seem to be overly worried, so I tried not to be. After a few more kilometers, an old farm and a couple of barns came into view. The barns were in reasonable condition, but the house was a weird conglomeration of tree, stone, and metal. I very much suspected it hadn't been built that way—that it had, in fact, been rebuilt. Not by anything human, but rather a rift. It had the same twisted, not-quite-of-this-world feel that I'd seen in other organic materials hit by the rifts. I shivered and prayed to Rhea that the one that had caused this destruction had left the area. The last thing we needed, on top of everything else, was to be chased by one of the things.

In front of one of the barns were three long-distance solar vehicles. I stopped beside them but didn't kill the engine.

Jonas tugged Nuri's bracelet from his wrist and shoved it into a pocket. The blond-haired, craggy-faced image thankfully disappeared. "Remove the RFID from your palm."

I picked the edge of the false skin layer free, carefully peeled it away, and then handed him the chip. He placed the two of them back in their plastic containers and opened the door.

"Wait here, both of you."

"Where are we?" Williams asked.

"I have no idea." I watched Jonas disappear into the darkness of the barn and tried to keep a lid on the ever-spiraling tide of tension. "And keep your damn head under that blanket until I tell you otherwise."

"Lady, enough with the tone. Remember, I can kill these kids with the simple press of a button."

"Kill them," I snapped back, "and you'll erase the only reason I'm not filling you with lead right now."

The stink of fear jumped into the cabin again. *Good.* The bastard deserved to be afraid, just as those kids had undoubtedly been afraid, before their emotions had been curtailed.

I reached for the shifting magic and changed to my own form, then tugged my way out of the coverall and dumped it on the passenger seat. And immediately felt better simply because I wasn't expending energy on a form that wasn't mine. I might have had a decent enough meal at the museum, but that hadn't been enough to fully recover my strength. Only time and rest, or using the healing state, would do that.

Jonas reappeared, accompanied by two men I didn't

recognize. He opened the rear passenger door and the two strangers each picked up a kid and walked across to the solar vehicle.

"Hey," Williams said, throwing off the blanket and sitting upright. "What about me?"

"You," Jonas said, "can get you own ass out of the vehicle."

Something in the way he said that had the hairs along the back of my neck rising. His gaze met mine and that small, cold smile touched his lips again. The ranger was not only back, but on the warpath.

Williams hastily climbed out, but I remained where I was. Jonas strolled around the front of the ATV and, as Williams hustled past, threw a punch so hard that I heard the crack of Williams's jaw from inside the vehicle. He dropped like a ton of concrete to the ground and didn't move.

Jonas straddled him, then pulled a cable tie from a coverall pocket and tied Williams's wrists together. Then he went through the scientist's pockets, eventually pulling out a small black control disk.

Relief spun through me and I closed my eyes for a minute. The kids might not be out of danger, and a very long way from ever being healed, but at least the immediate threat of being poisoned had now eased.

Unless, of course, Sal's partners had a similar disk and remotely triggered the pellets.

Two of the solar vehicles hummed to life, and a heartbeat later they'd risen from the ground and disappeared into the shadows of the forest. They wouldn't be able to stay there long, as it would drain the batteries far too quickly, but it would at least make it more difficult to immediately trace their whereabouts, given that there was little indication on the gravel as to where they'd gone. I crossed mental fingers that they'd arrive safe and in one piece wherever it was that they were headed and climbed out of the ATV.

"It's kind of hard to interrogate someone when they're unconscious." I stopped on the other side of Williams's prone form from Jonas. "Or is that not what you intend right now?"

"Oh, I intend it all right." He grabbed Williams by the scruff of the neck and dragged him over to the ATV, where he produced a longer cable tie and threaded it through one of the ATV's treads, then looped it around the tie binding Williams.

"And what about the hunting party from Central? Or have you forgotten about them?"

"I forget nothing. There's a well over there." He motioned to the house with his chin. "You want to get a bucket of water while I set up our escape?"

I did as he bade. By the time I'd come back with two buckets of water, the third solar vehicle was off the ground and ready for a quick getaway.

Jonas grabbed one of the buckets from me and pitched the water over Williams's head. The second bucket got the result we wanted—Williams woke, making sounds that rather sounded like a cat mewling in fear.

Jonas squatted in front of him, shoved a hand around his neck, and thrust him back against the ATV's tracks. "You have one chance, and one chance only, to tell me where they're making the VX."

Williams's mouth flapped, but for several seconds no sound came out. When it finally did, his words were slurred and barely understandable. Not surprising, given that the man had a broken jaw. "Base, Crow's Point," was all I caught.

Crow's Point had been the location of the third déchet base—the other two being my bunker and the Broken

Mountains. I doubted it was a coincidence that these people were using them—not only had Sal been familiar with all three, but if his two partners *had* worked for the HDP, then they would also be.

"And are they keeping the children there as well?" Jonas said.

Williams shook his head. "Dangerous," he ground out.

"Then where *are* they keeping them?"

Williams shrugged. "Moved them. Not sure."

Jonas glanced at me. "You believe him?"

I crossed my arms and studied Williams. His teeth were bloody, his mouth was swelling, and he was sweating heavily—a mix of fear and pain, I suspected. But I didn't have an ounce of sympathy for the man; he deserved a whole lot more than this. "No."

"Truth," Williams said, his voice little more than a squeak of fright. "They're west, that's all I know."

"West of Central?" Jonas asked.

Williams nodded. "Honest, that's all I know."

Jonas grunted and glanced at me. I shrugged. It was doubtful Williams knew anything more than what he'd said. Sal's partners were obviously playing their cards very close to their chests, and it was unlikely they'd trust *anyone* with that sort of information, let alone someone like Williams, who was so full of bluster and self-importance.

Jonas obviously agreed with me, because his next question took a different tack. "How are the children getting into the trucks if no one knows where they're being kept?"

"Drivers met."

A soft but distant buzzing caught my attention. I glanced skyward, but there was nothing to see; not yet, anyway. "Jonas—"

"I know," he said, but didn't move. "What have you been doing to the children?"

"Testing drugs. Splicing."

"Splicing what? DNA?"

Williams nodded. "Not part of splicing program. Reynolds is in charge of that."

"Joseph Reynolds?" Jonas asked.

Williams nodded again. The sweat pouring down his face was becoming a river and his skin was ashen.

"What about the drugs you've given the children? Are they reversible?"

Williams's gaze flicked away. "Maybe. With time. Can help with that, though."

Jonas tightened his grip on Williams's throat; for an instant I thought he was intending to strangle the man, but as Williams's face began to turn an interesting shade and his breaths became shuddering gasps, he released him and thrust upright. "We'll keep your family free and safe, as we promised," he said. "But you? You won't be helping anyone. You can reap what you've sewn and rot in hell."

With that, he spun and strode toward the waiting vehicle. I followed. Williams alternated between screaming in fury and begging us to keep our promise *and* keep him safe, but neither of us acknowledged him or turned around. Once we were both seated, Jonas closed the doors, spun the vehicle around, and headed in the opposite direction to the vehicles that held the kids.

"It might have been a better move to keep him with us than hand him back to Central and Winter Halo," I said, once we'd cleared the vegetation and were scooting along some sort of track.

Jonas snorted. "If Williams lives any longer than the time

it takes to get him back to Central and debrief him, I'll be very surprised."

"Hence my statement. He could have helped us understand—and maybe even reverse—whatever has been done to the children we've rescued."

"There is no reversal. Williams was lying when he said that." His gaze met mine. "He was in charge of the program but had no direct input. He wasn't involved in the actual creation of the drugs being used."

"Yes, but he'd know—"

"Undoubtedly. But sometimes to take an enemy down, you have to make a sacrifice. In this case, it's whatever help Williams might have given us."

I raised an eyebrow. Obviously, there was a lot more to this rescue plan than I'd been told. "What did you do?"

"I wasn't actually throttling him, as tempting as it was. I was injecting a microtransmitter under his skin. We'll have people close enough to listen in when he's questioned, and hopefully we'll gain some information about who else might be working with Sal's partners." His expression was grim as he glanced at me. "Because you can bet they'll be involved in the debrief."

"Great plan, but one that presumes he'll be taken back to Central. What if he's not?"

"Then we're in trouble. But he will be. The rangers would balk at sending him anywhere else."

"But if they're ordered—"

"Such orders would risk questions being raised, and I doubt Sal's partners would chance outing themselves that way."

Not until they were ready to take over, anyway, and it didn't appear they were near that point yet. "Then we're heading back to the bunker?"

"Yeah, though it'll be via a long and rather circular route

to avoid any possibility of detection. Nuri needs to get back into Chaos before sunset."

And I needed to get back into Central just in case Charles decided to take a break from the paperwork and legalities, and visit the woman he knew as Cat. I shifted in the seat to study Jonas. In the bright afternoon light, his profile was sharp and strong. "Any particular reason?"

He shrugged. "Just a general uneasiness. You know how it is, being a seeker yourself."

"She's a whole lot more than just a seeker."

"That she is." He glanced at me and raised an eyebrow. "Whatever the question is, just ask it."

I couldn't help smiling. "Why were you and Nuri caught in that rift together? The tensions between humans and shifters were very high for *months* after—"

"Not just months, but years," he cut in. "Even now there are pockets of resistance within both societies, despite everyone knowing we can only defeat the Others by offering a united front."

"So why were you both together?"

"Because Nuri is, as I said, an Albright."

"And this is important because . . . ?"

"Because the Albrights were instrumental in paving the way for peace after the bombs were dropped. The other surviving houses wanted to fight until the bitter end, but the Albrights convinced them that peace was the only way our world was going to survive what was to come."

"So she and her family foresaw the rifts and the coming of the Others?"

He hesitated. "She's never really said, but I get the impression they saw the latter if not the former."

"All of which is interesting, but doesn't do much to answer the initial question."

"No." A smile made a brief appearance, then fell away. "She was sent as an envoy to broker a deal with my kin in the mountains. Central wanted to use the lands at the foot of the mountains for farming purposes, but were well aware those lands were traditionally ours. Given that forced acquisition of shifter land by humans was the cause of the war, the ruling families in Central—new and old—sent Nuri out as an envoy to seek permission and broker a deal. I was assigned to accompany her."

"Why did the shifters allow humans to remain in positions of power after the war?"

"It was a way of appeasing the human masses—a means of showing them that while the shifters had won the war, they intended to treat all survivors equally." A somewhat cynical smile touched his lips. "And it wasn't like they could overrule the decisions of the five shifter clans who stepped into the remaining seats."

How very true. "And Penny?"

He blew out a breath. "Shouldn't have been there. I was on an official assignment and broke all sorts of rules, but the couple looking after her could no longer do so. I was taking her up to kin, as I've already said."

I frowned. "So she wasn't living with you at the time?"

He shook his head. "I was still a ranger; military accommodation is no place for a little girl."

It wasn't a place for *any* child, male or female, I thought, thinking of my little ones. Of the strange life they'd had before the gas took even that. "So she—and the people looking after her—were living in one of the refuges set up after the war?"

"*Everyone* was living in refuges in the years immediately after the war." His voice was grim. "The humans did as good a job of destroying our camps and adobes as we did their cities."

I hadn't really thought about that, but then, my time during the war had been split between the constantly moving ranger camps and the bunkers. I really hadn't seen much of the destruction—not until many years after the war had ended, anyway.

"The farmhouse is a prime example of the twisted mess a rift can make of matter, so how come you, Nuri, and Penny escaped it basically intact? How did Sal and his partners?"

"Luck?" Another smile appeared, but once again faded as he glanced at me. "The truth is, no one is really sure. Luck *does* play a part, but we also suspect it has something to do with the type of rift you're hit by, and what else is in the immediate vicinity. You've more hope of surviving if you're in a clearing or a field rather than a forest or near anything man-made. And you can't be touching anyone."

"I guess that makes sense." I'd seen what had happened to wildlife who'd sheltered under trees and rocks at the approach of a rift, and it hadn't been pretty. "Is the rift the reason you're in Chaos with Nuri rather than living with your kin in the mountains?"

He nodded. "Initially, it was simply a matter of expediency—it was a means of protecting each other's back at a time when the world feared our presence."

Because it was believed survivors would attract the rifts. "And now?"

"We're a good team, the money is brilliant, and I'm using the skills I was born with." He glanced at me, eyebrow raised. "Can you honestly see me as a farmer?"

I studied him for several seconds through slightly narrowed eyes. "About as much as I could see me being one."

He laughed. It was a sound so natural, so relaxed, and so very real that it pulled at something deep inside me. I glanced out the window, fighting the tears that weirdly prickled my eyes. It wasn't as if I'd never heard a laugh like that before; I had, many a time. It had been part of my training to make shifters feel secure enough around me that they'd unwind and de-stress, but this was the first time it had happened without the barrier of being someone else. For the first time ever, I was simply me.

And he wasn't afraid of that, despite the history he'd had with déchet.

It was scary and wonderful all at the same time.

"How long will it actually take us to get back to the bunker?" I said, after a while.

He glanced at the clock on the instrument panel. "We should be there just before five."

It was just past three thirty now, so we really were taking the long way home. I yawned hugely, then waved a hand. "Sorry."

"Why don't you try to get some sleep?" Jonas said. "I'll wake you if anything happens."

"You sure? An extra pair of eyes might be useful given who's out there, trying to find us."

"Given the extra pair of eyes are struggling to remain open, the point is rather mute. Sleep, Tiger. You may not get another chance for a while."

I raised an eyebrow. "Is that Nuri's intuition speaking or yours?"

"I don't have intuition. I just have my training."

"So how did you come to the conclusion I wouldn't be getting much in the way of sleep in the near future?"

"Simple." The glance he cast my way heated my soul and yet could have meant anything. "You're going back to Charles. And if you were in *my* bed, sleep sure as hell wouldn't be on the agenda."

My heart began beating a whole lot faster. "Meaning

you've decided what you'd do if I indicated I was receptive to an approach?"

"Receptive to an approach?" Amusement flitted across his expression. "Such a mundane way of describing something I suspect will be anything but."

"You, Ranger, have an annoying tendency to avoid direct questions."

I couldn't help the edge creeping into my tone and his amusement got stronger.

"It's undoubtedly a result of hanging around a witch too long. As to the question—it remains a battle between the brain and the loins."

"Then stop throwing suggestive comments my way, because it's not helping."

"Then decide what you want, Tiger, so that we can both move on, one way or another."

"I wish it were that easy."

"It *is* that easy."

"No, it's not." Not for someone like me. I might have been created with the gift of thought and free will, but I wasn't entirely sure I was given the courage to go after something I *truly* wanted. Not after all these years. Because it wasn't just about sex, but rather emotion, and a connection. And maybe that was something Jonas could never offer, but until I took the risk and explored what might lie between us, I would never know.

"From the very beginnings of time itself," he said, "enemies have become friends, and friends have become lovers. It is not beyond the realm of possibility, even if history and experiences might be against it. Against us."

And they certainly *were* against us.

I wearily scrubbed a hand across my eyes. Why was it so much easier to decide to go to war against the vampires and the people who were in league with them than it was to accept the advances of one man?

"Jonas, I—"

He held up a hand to silence me. For several minutes he didn't say anything, but tension rolled from him, the feel of it so thick it made it difficult to breathe.

He swore and flattened his foot. The solar vehicle immediately leapt forward, the trees around us quickly becoming a blur as our speed grew.

"Is it the rangers?" I twisted around to look behind us, but there was nothing in the sky and nothing on the ground. Just trees and dust.

"No. Worse." The look he briefly cast my way was grim. "Rift."

I swore, even as fear leapt into my heart. I scanned the countryside again but still couldn't see anything out of the ordinary. "Are you sure?"

It was a stupid question, because I already knew the answer. Thanks to the fact that he'd already survived one rift, he was now sensitive to their presence. But part of me was hoping he'd say no.

That part didn't get the answer it wanted. In fact, he didn't even answer. He just kept his attention on the road.

"This thing should be able to outrun it, shouldn't it?"

"I don't know. It's fast, but the rift is moving at almost double our speed."

And we were in the middle of a damn forest. Rhea help us . . .

The trees seemed to go on and on, an endless sea of green. I had no idea how close the rift was, and no desire to ask. Some things were better not to know—and it wasn't as if I could do anything about it if it *was* close. All I could do was hope that the rift changed course and went on to destroy something else. That it left us alone and alive.

Even if the gathering tension and fear emanating from the man beside me suggested it was a rather forlorn hope.

With an abruptness that was startling, the forest gave way to vast emptiness. Something within me relaxed, if only slightly. At least we had a chance—a very minor chance—of surviving the rift in one piece and untainted by trees and rocks if it did hit.

The vehicle seemed to increase its pace in the open air— no surprise, given the sun was no longer being filtered through the canopy of the trees. I twisted around and studied the fast-disappearing forest fringe.

And saw the rift touch down.

It ripped up the road as it barreled toward us, a tornado of unseen energy that was twisting, unraveling, and remaking everything it touched before tossing it aside.

"Jonas—"

"I know."

I stared at the alien force behind us in growing horror, my heart racing so fast it felt like it was about to tear out of my chest. And maybe it was, because tendrils of the rift's energy were now whipping around us. The vehicle was shuddering under the force of them, and my skin stung and shivered and bled.

"We can't outrun this, Jonas."

He glanced in the mirror and swore. "You're right. We can't."

With that, he slammed on the brakes and flipped the doors open. "Run. Get as far away from this vehicle and the road as you can."

I was out and sprinting before he'd even finished. Energy

was fiercer out in the open; became a storm that was dust and destruction and nigh on impossible to run against. The empty landscape disappeared and all I could feel, all I could hear, was the roar of the rift approaching.

A hand grabbed mine and held tight. "Faster," Jonas yelled, almost yanking me off my feet. "You have to go *faster.*"

"I can't!" I was already at top speed. There was nothing more to give, nothing more I could do. "Shift shapes and leave me, Jonas. One of us needs to get out of here."

"A ranger never leaves a man behind," he snapped. "Now fucking *move.*"

I somehow found the strength to increase my speed. But only incrementally and that wasn't enough. My lungs were burning, my legs felt like lead, and the storm was so close it felt like fragments of my body were tearing away.

We raced on, speeding across the unseen landscape even as time and the rift now seemed to be crawling. Just for a minute the force of it waned and hope surged. Maybe Rhea had taken pity on us; maybe we *would* escape.

Then Jonas swore, his grip left mine, and the rift hit us and tore us both apart.

CHAPTER 11

Everything seemed to end. Everything except pain and consciousness. There was no sense of movement in this rift. It held no light, no sound, no life, even though it moved through a world that contained all those things. It was suffocating and deadly, and alien in a way I couldn't even begin to understand. It tore me apart and examined every particle and every facet of my being, as if each tiny piece of me needed to be fully understood before it was discarded. It was almost as if the rift was in some way sentient, though how that was possible when it was energy and magic rather than life I had no idea.

On and on it went, endless and unforgiving. But somewhere in the midst of it all, stubbornness flared. I'd been torn apart once already in my lifetime, though the source had been chemical rather than a force from another world. If I could survive the melting of flesh and muscle, I could survive this.

Death, some distant part of me thought, *you are once again rejected.*

And in a single moment of serendipity, that thought had no sooner crossed my mind than the force of the rift abandoned me and I was spat out whole and breathing into sweet sunshine.

I didn't move. I couldn't move. I simply lay there, sucking air into still-burning lungs as I stared up at blue skies and thanked Rhea—and every other god that might be listening—for the miracle of survival. And not *just* survival, because I could feel my fingers, my toes, and though every bit of me in between seemed to be nothing but a mass of agony, everything still seemed to be where it was supposed to be. I hadn't become some twisted, unrecognizable remnant of what I'd once been.

I was *alive.* And that meant I could return to my little ones, just as I'd promised.

Of course, to do *that,* I first had to uncover where the hell I now was. There was nothing but silence around me. There were no birdcalls, no familiar scents, no sense of life . . .

Oh Rhea, Jonas . . .

I tried to speak, to call out, but my throat was raw and no sound came out. I tried to move, to turn my head and look around, but my body was still a mass of quivering, aching jelly and refused to obey my commands. Had I been wrong? Had I come through in one piece but little more than an inert lump of flesh? Panic surged and a scream of denial tore up my throat. And though it came out as little more than a squeak, it broke through the fear and forced me to get a grip on my emotions. If I could squeak, I would eventually be able to talk. And I would probably be able to move, too. All I had to do was keep control and *heal.*

I closed my eyes and concentrated on regulating my

breathing. On fighting the panic and ignoring the burning in my lungs that suggested I wasn't getting enough air into my body. But the simple act of breathing in and out in a calm, orderly manner had never seemed so damn hard.

Eventually, though, the pain and weakness began to subside as the peace of the healing state descended. It was a state I remained in for hours—long enough that by the time I emerged, the heat of the day had left the air and dusk was spreading pink fingers across the darkening sky.

I took a deep, shuddery breath and sat upright. The sudden movement had my head spinning, which meant that although my body no longer felt like it had been pushed through a meat grinder, I was a long way from being fully healed. But it didn't matter; nothing did, except finding Jonas.

The plain stretched before me, a vast and empty space. There was no forest, no road, nothing to indicate where I'd landed. I twisted around and again saw nothing but emptiness. Rhea help me, he couldn't be dead. Surely the goddess would not be so cruel as to tease me with possibilities and then snatch them away . . .

In the distance far to my left I spotted an unmoving brown lump. Hope flared, even though I knew it might be nothing more than a rock twisted into a humanlike shape by the rift's force.

I pushed upright and scrambled toward it. The nearer I got, the clearer it became it was no rock.

I dropped to my knees beside him and felt for a pulse. It was there—rapid and thready, but there. Relief surged, a force so fierce that a sob escaped. I leaned my forehead against his arm and battled the sting of tears. Against all the odds, we'd both survived and in one piece . . . I stirred at the thought and began checking him for wounds, breaks, or any other sign that the rift had done something extreme to his body. But there didn't appear to be anything untoward. Nothing visible, anyway.

"Isn't that typical?" His voice was little more than a harsh whisper, but never had I heard a sweeter sound. He moved fractionally and his gaze met mine, the vivid green depths filled with relief and something else. Something I couldn't really name but that had my pulse racing. "A pretty woman decides to caress me and I'm unconscious for the majority of it."

Hopefully, that majority had included the few minutes of tears. I sat back on my heels and smiled. "Yeah, well, you might have slapped my hand away if you'd been awake."

"Doubtful." He drew in a breath, then released it slowly. I could almost see the strength flooding back into his body. "What's the damage?"

"You can't tell?"

He shook his head. "Everything is aching, although I feel a damn sight better than I did at this point last time. It took days before any of us could fully function. We were just lucky there'd been no predators in the vicinity to take advantage of our weakened state."

"If there had been, their DNA might have mingled with yours, and you would have come through as something entirely different."

"I know. Help me up."

I raised an eyebrow and didn't move. "Wouldn't it be better if you rested a little bit longer?"

"Probably." The smile that twisted his lips held little in the way of amusement. "But night is almost on us and I have no intention of being caught out in the open. The solar vehicle has to be around here somewhere—we should find it."

"Why? If the rift did a number on it, then it's not going to be of much use."

"Perhaps, but we might be able to retrieve some weapons or at least some rations from it."

"That's a pretty big 'might.'"

"So was surviving the rift."

"Good point." I rose, straddled his legs, then wrapped my hands around his and hauled him upright. It was an effort that left me shaking. Full strength, it seemed, really was a long way off.

His grip tightened briefly against mine, though he didn't appear to be battling for balance. I flared my nostrils and drew in the rich, wild scent of him, trying to find any hint of change. Trying to find some trace of *me*. He, Nuri, and Penny had become forever linked after they survived a rift, so it was possible the same had happened to us.

"We won't know what's been done to us," he said, obviously guessing my thoughts. "Not for days or maybe even weeks."

"Is that how long it took you and Nuri to discover you were telepathically linked?"

"Well, no, because I was barely awake when she told me to stop the mental cussing and start thinking."

A smile teased my lips. "Given that I can't hear any cussing, it seems likely we're *not* linked."

"Possibly." He half shrugged, then winced. "I was hoping to get a little of your healing magic, though, because right now I need it."

I frowned. "You just have to shift to cat form to heal, don't you?"

"That's presuming I still can—and I'm too damn weak right now to try it. But given my DNA has been diluted a second time, there's no guarantee I will be able to." He raised a hand and gently brushed my cheek. His fingers came away damp. "Were you crying over me, Tiger?"

Yes. "And why would you think that?"

"Because I've seen you near death after battling wraiths, relieved and bloody after surviving impossible odds against the vampires, and furious after being shot. Never once, on any of those occasions, were there tears. So why now?"

I hesitated, tempted to lie. But the rift—and the fear that he might not have survived—had made me realize just how much I wanted to explore what might lie between us, even if nothing lasting and real came out of it. But my throat seemed to close over at the thought of telling him that and my heart was trying to leap out of my chest again.

"And what if they *were* for you?"

It was softly said, but we were standing so close he couldn't help hearing it.

"Then I would ask just what they meant."

My gaze searched his. Looking for what, I wasn't sure. Certainly, he seemed to be keeping himself under very tight control. Only the pheromones that swirled around us in a dance that was both desire and something stronger— something deeper—gave any hint as to what might be going on within him.

"If you want honesty—"

"And I certainly do."

"Then the fact is, I really *don't* know. I'm trained in the art of seduction and assassination, and well versed in keeping my emotions under tight control. And yet, with you, that is nigh on impossible."

"*That's* a feeling I know very well." He cupped my cheek, his touch gentle. Warm. "There are so many reasons why you and I are completely wrong."

My lips twisted. "Are you trying to talk yourself *out* of the situation?"

"I've been trying to do *that* since I first met you. It hasn't helped. I can no more ignore your presence than I can forget to breathe."

He spoke with a certainty I'd yet to find. I knew what I wanted, but did I really have the courage to pursue it? To risk the heart my creators and history had been so sure didn't exist? "And what of Nuri? And Branna? Won't it cause problems within your group?"

"With Branna, undoubtedly. But I can deal with him."

I hoped so, because Branna's wish to wipe me out might well spill over to Jonas if he wasn't very careful.

"Forget about what others might think or do," he continued. "Forget about history and what we both are. None of it matters in the wake of the promise that lies between us. It is both impossible and undeniable, and it deserves to be explored, even if it is destined to do nothing more than flare bright and die quickly."

It was the dying quickly—being left alone with nothing but the ashes of emotion—that had me so worried. I could survive chemicals and rifts, vampires and wraiths, but I wasn't so certain I could survive having my heart broken.

But it wasn't in me to give in to fear and walk away, either.

I swallowed heavily, then somehow said, "I agree."

Instead of replying, he leaned forward and brushed his lips across mine. It was a kiss unlike anything I'd ever experienced before. It was so soft, so gentle, and altogether too fleeting, yet it ran with heat and passion. But there was something else, something indefinable—a whisper, a promise— that both scared me and thrilled me.

"Now we just need the time to explore," he said eventually. "But that time is not now."

His lips remained tantalizingly close, and part of me wanted to do nothing more than ignore the sense in his words and kiss him again. But we had children to rescue and a mad scheme to stop. We couldn't waste the time we had left on pleasure, no matter how much either of us might wish otherwise—not that either of us was physically *capable* of acting on anything as strong as desire right now. "Let's just hope both of us survive long enough to explore."

"Indeed," he said, then released me and stepped back. "We need to get back to the museum ASAP."

I took a deep breath to calm thwarted anticipation and looked around. "Do you have any idea where we are?"

"We're about fifteen kilometers north of where we were when the rift hit us." He must have caught my surprise, because he smiled and pointed upward. "The stars always guide at night."

"So the road is . . . ?"

"This way."

He began to walk, and I fell in step beside him. Silence reigned. I wasn't sure what to say. Wasn't sure anything *needed* to be said. Dusk disappeared into night, and the stars became brighter in the skies. It seemed to take forever for the flat emptiness of the horizon to give way to the promise of trees and rising mountains. A stirring wind brought with it the smell of eucalypt and pine, and the ground around us grew rockier.

I frowned. "Are you sure this is where we left the vehicle? I can't remember these rocks."

"That's because the rocks are the remains of the road." He paused for a second, his gaze scanning the area. "Ah, here we go."

He strode on. I followed and eventually spotted the vehicle—though the mass of twisted metal and rock no longer resembled anything that could remotely be called that.

I stopped a couple of meters away and watched him inspect the craft. He eventually retrieved a gun, two small flashlights, and the backpack; everything seemed to be in original condition, although how that was even possible I had no idea. He checked both flashlights; the bright blue-white light that flared out from them made me blink. These weren't ordinary flashlights, but ones designed as a counter to vampires. He switched them off and tossed one to me. Once he'd checked the gun, he tucked it and the other flashlight into a coverall pocket, then opened the backpack. His expression suggested whatever he'd been hoping to find inside wasn't there—something he confirmed by tossing it back into the twisted remains.

I slipped the flashlight into one of the accessory pockets on my pants. We had no use for it right now, but who knew what we'd come across before we made it back to the bunker? "What now?"

I really didn't fancy spending the rest of the night walking toward Central, but neither did I want to spend it here. Vampires might be scarce in the open plains, but they weren't our biggest concern right now. Humanity as a whole might fear darkness, but that fear wouldn't stop the rangers. If Sal's partners were desperate enough—and if they had strong enough connections—they could order the search to continue through the night. The rangers would obey, because that was what all good soldiers did.

And the ranger division had been—and probably still was—the best of the best.

"Now we make ourselves as comfortable as possible and wait for the cavalry to turn up." He reached into the mess of metal and tugged free what once had been the back of a seat, but was now an elongated, five-foot-wide strip of lightly padded metal. He dumped it on the ground, then sat down and patted the space beside him. "Come along. I won't bite."

I snorted and sat down, my shoulder lightly brushing his. "Does that mean you're still in contact with Nuri tele-pathically?"

He nodded. "I doubt she'll be able to convince anyone inside Chaos to come rescue us, but Jarren and his crew wouldn't have gotten back to base yet, so he's a possibility."

"So he's not night-blind like the rest of humanity?"

"No, he's an outlier like me. I'm guessing that's part of the reason he followed my footsteps into the mercenary business—he was well aware good money could be made by those not afraid of the dark."

"Then he isn't based in the Broken Mountains with the rest of your kin?"

"No. His unit runs out of New Port."

I raised my eyebrows. "Would this be the same New Port that suffered a major malfunction fifteen years ago that voided all RFID information?"

"The same." A smile ghosted his lips. "But we seriously had nothing to do with that. We've just taken full advantage of it ever since."

"So your grandson runs the unit there now?"

"Yes." He yawned hugely. "I guess it's my turn to say sorry, it's not the company."

"Give me the gun."

I held out a hand and he raised an eyebrow even as he obeyed.

"Why? Are you going to shoot the tiredness out of me?"

"I might have been tempted in the past, but right now?

No. Although I do claim the right to change my mind." I flashed him a grin as I checked the gun, then placed it beside me. "Get some sleep. I'll keep watch."

"Fine. But wake me the minute you see or hear anything."

I'd half expected him to argue, but it wasn't really surprising that he didn't. Rangers were nothing if not practical, and right now I was the stronger of the two of us.

Which wasn't really saying much.

He crossed his arms, leaned back against the vehicle, and was very quickly asleep. I drew my legs up and hugged them close to my chest, and battled to remain awake and aware as time ticked slowly by. It was well after midnight—something I guessed by the position of the moon—when I heard the rumble of an approaching vehicle.

I nudged Jonas lightly, then picked up the gun and rose. Far in the distance, coming from the direction of the forest we could barely see, was a solitary light.

"That's not a ranger vehicle." Jonas rose and stood beside me.

"How can you tell?"

"Sound of the engine. It's an old ATV, not one of the winged division's transports."

"So it's probably your grandson?"

"I can't think of anyone else who'd have a reason to be out in the middle of nowhere at night." He paused. "But keep the gun handy, just in case."

"Oh, I am, trust me."

"Unimaginably, I do." His gaze met mine, amusement crinkling the corners of his eyes. "Who'd have thought that a week or so ago?"

"Certainly not me." My voice was dry. "I sure hope he thought to load some food on board. I'm starving."

"It's common practice to keep extra rations on board, so that shouldn't be a problem."

Trail rations weren't exactly what I'd been hoping for, but they were better than nothing. "Isn't it rare for one telepath to be able to link with another over such a distance?"

"Yes. And while Jarren's a strong telepath, he's not that strong. Nuri uses the power of the earth to amplify her ability, and it allows her to connect to any telepath she wishes, wherever they are."

"Is that part of the reason you two can communicate no matter what the distance between you?"

He nodded. "Although I can't use the earth's energy as a weapon, as she can, and my telepathic abilities are somewhat restricted. I can't connect with Jarren, for instance, but I can with Ela."

"What about Penny?"

He frowned. "I can't directly converse, but I can receive images and impressions."

"Is that why you're so sure she needs to be near you to keep whatever was done to her at bay?"

A smile ghosted his lips. "No, that comes from sheer pigheadedness. Penny is *my* responsibility, and I will not renege on that until there is absolutely no other choice. We haven't reached that point yet."

And never would, I suspected. "What did Nuri gain out of the exchange?"

"The senses of a cat."

"But not the ability to change?"

"No." His gaze met mine. "It'll be interesting to see what—if any—fallout there is from our being caught together."

The ATV was now near enough that its headlights pinned us in brightness. Jonas didn't seem worried, so I tried not to be.

"Does that mean that some people escape rifts *without* alteration?"

He hesitated. "Only in that, because they were alone when the rift caught them, their DNA and blood are the same. But everyone who survives those things is forever altered."

"So how were Branna and Ela affected?"

"I didn't know Branna before the rift, so I can't really say. But it screwed him up mentally—"

I snorted. "You're telling me it did."

"And Ela," he continued, ignoring me, "came through with sharpened senses and telepathy."

I blinked. "The rift *gave* her telepathy?"

He nodded. "Nuri's theory is it was a latent skill the rift brought out."

I frowned. "When I was in our rift, I got the weird impression it was almost sentient. You don't think these alterations are deliberate, do you?"

"Why would a sentient force from another world want us enhanced in any way?" He strode forward as the ATV began to slow down. "And why would they kill the majority of those caught if they intended to help?"

"Given that we don't even know why some rifts are doorways while others are not, that's a question I really can't answer." I trailed after him. The internal vehicle lights came on, revealing that it was indeed his grandson at the wheel of the ATV. I made the gun safe and clipped it onto my pants. "I'm just telling you what I felt."

He grunted as the front and rear passenger doors opened. "I'll pass the information on to Nuri. In the meantime, let's get the hell out of here just in case the rift decides to double back."

He helped me into the ATV, then climbed into the front.

As the doors closed and the big vehicle began to pick up speed again, Jarren said, "There are a couple of ration packs and some water in the foot well behind my seat. Best I could do on short notice, I'm afraid."

As I leaned over to grab the packs, Jonas said, "Nuri told you what happened?"

"Yeah." Jarren's voice held a note of incredulousness. "Surviving a rift once is damn lucky, but twice? Rhea sure as hell loves you, because that's considered nigh on impossible."

"Obviously not, given that he's still here." I handed one of the ration packs to Jonas and opened the second one. Trail mix and beef jerky, just as I'd feared.

Jarren flashed me a grin via the rearview mirror. "Very true. You both okay?"

"We're alive." Jonas half shrugged as he tore open the beef jerky packet. "As to whether we're okay, only time will tell. You able to take us all the way in?"

"Nuri told me to dump you on the far side of the museum, just before the collapsed area. She said someone appears to be keeping an eye on the museum and that we needed to be careful."

"Meaning someone suspects that you taking the caretaker job at the museum was a little out of the ordinary." I poured some trail mix into my hand. "It's also going to make it damn difficult for us to get back in there."

"She said to wait until dawn. We're not going to get there much before five, so you won't have to hang around in the forest for too long."

"Says the person who's not going to hang about in the darkness for long," I muttered as I scooped another mouthful of trail mix.

"I can't. But I've got a couple of rifles in the rear you can have." Jarren's gaze met mine through the mirror. "Jonas will keep you safe enough—"

"Oh, she's not afraid of the dark," Jonas interrupted, voice dry. "And she's certainly not afraid of either vampires or wraiths."

"And that's where you're wrong," I said. "I'm terrified of them both."

"Yeah," he said. "That's why you went into a den of vamps alone—"

"I wasn't alone. The ghosts were with me."

"That," he said, "is hardly the point."

"Ghosts? What ghosts?" Jarren said, his gaze swinging between the two of us.

"Ghosts of the dead," Jonas said. "She can converse with them."

"Not a talent that would be that useful in this day and age, I'd imagine," Jarren said.

"And that," Jonas said heavily, "is where you would be very wrong. Can this thing go any faster?"

Jarren's amused expression suggested he was well aware *that* particular line of questioning was now well and truly out-of-bounds. "Why don't we find out?"

The ATV didn't exactly leap forward, but over the next couple of minutes it gradually picked up speed. I finished the trail mix, then started in on the beef jerky. It was even tougher than the stuff I had at the bunker, but it at least stopped my stomach from complaining too loudly. As the dark landscape continued to slip by, I leaned back, closed my eyes, and in very little time was fast asleep.

It was the lack of noise that woke me. I sat upright, blinking the sleep away as I looked around. Night still held sway, but the ATV had slowed, and was now moving silently through trees rather than vast, empty fields. Light shone in the distance, a glow so bright it chased the stars from the sky.

Central.

We were nearly home. Relief flooded me. I'd come so close to never getting back here. To leaving my little ones alone . . .

Cat, Bear, I'm back. Safe and whole, I wanted to add, but didn't. There was little point in alarming them with what might have been. It was better if they simply didn't know.

Jarren halted the ATV and flicked a switch. As the doors silently opened, he twisted around in his seat and said, "Right, I can't risk going any farther. The rifles are in the rear storage. Take what you want. And if you need any help, with anything else, you know where to find me."

"We do. And thanks." Jonas gripped his grandson's arm for a moment, then climbed out and walked around the back of the vehicle. I echoed Jonas's thanks, then jumped out and stepped back as the doors closed. Jonas reappeared and tossed me a rifle and some ammunition. I slung the former over my shoulder and clipped the ammunition to my pants. And felt safer for the weight of them. I might not be soldier-trained, but I'd certainly grown used to having weapons at hand over the years since the war—at least when I ventured out at night, anyway.

As the big vehicle began a slow-sweeping turn through the trees, my two little ghosts found me, bombarding me with images of everything that had happened since we left. Apparently, Nuri had been using the earth magic to do a little rock rearranging, and while she hadn't totally uncovered the hidden escape tunnel, she had exposed the beginnings of it.

"Why would Nuri . . ." The question faded as I glanced at Jonas. His eyes were narrowed and his expression was a mix of concentration and amusement. "What's wrong?"

"I can hear them."

I blinked. "The ghosts?"

Cat and Bear reacted to this bit of news by dancing joyously around his head. He half raised a hand, as if to swat them away, then stopped.

"And it sure as hell is going to take some getting used to." He paused. "Are they always this . . . rambunctious?"

"Only when they're excited. They're children, remember?"

"Something I hadn't really appreciated until now." His concentration grew for a minute, and then Cat and Bear laughed.

"What?" I said, not entirely sure I liked being left out of the conversation like this.

He said it was nice to meet us, Cat said. *But could we tone it down because we're giving him a headache.*

"You'll get used to it." Then I blinked. I'd heard Cat *clearly,* and her energy hadn't been touching me. *Bear? Say something but stay back.*

You sometimes give the strangest orders. He paused and his happy amusement ran like quicksilver through my thoughts. *This is a nice development.*

It was indeed. I switched my attention back to Jonas. "How clearly can you hear them?"

"It's not like you and me conversing, or even telepathy. It's more a muted, muddied stream. If I concentrate, it clears enough for me to understand it."

"It might intensify with time."

"And it might just remain an incoherent buzz in the back

of my mind." He touched a hand to my spine and briefly directed me to the left. "How on earth do you cope with the noise, given that there's . . . how many children in the bunker?"

"One hundred and five. But they don't all talk at the same time." I paused, my amusement growing. "Most of the time, anyway."

"And what about the déchet soldiers in the bunker?"

"They don't talk to me at all." My amusement died. "It is likely you'll be able to hear them, though whether they'd feel inclined to converse with someone they consider an enemy is another question."

"Something I have no problem with." His expression bore remnants of the cold distrust he'd cast my way when we first met. "Just because I trust you doesn't meant I've changed my opinion overall on déchet."

Meaning you dislike us? Because we're déchet, too, remember?

Bear's question came across like a shout, making me wince slightly even though I knew he was doing it to help Jonas hear him better—and he succeeded, if the apologetic expression that momentarily crossed Jonas's face was anything to go by.

"No," he said. "I don't hate you. I was simply talking about those who fought in the war. That war killed a lot of my kind."

Your people killed all *of our kind,* Cat countered. *All except Tiger. Yet we do not hold that against you.*

"And I," Jonas murmured, "have been firmly chastised. Are you sure these little ones of yours are actually children?"

The two ghosts laughed and danced around the both of us. *It is so good,* Bear said, *to be able to talk to another.*

I raised an eyebrow, my amusement growing. *Meaning you were getting sick of talking to me?*

No, but he's male.

Meaning Jonas had better learn the art of switching off the constant mental chatter sooner rather than later, because Bear was obviously going to make full use of having a man to talk to.

"I'm gathering," Jonas said, voice wry, "that you three are having a conversation involving me?"

I glanced at him. "You can't hear it?"

"No. But just heard Cat's giddy laughter, so I'm figuring either you or Bear said something she found highly amusing."

I ducked under a tree branch, veered to the left slightly, and stepped onto the remains of an old path that would lead us to a rear section of the museum. There was no accessible entrance into the museum from that area—Central had made sure there was only one way in and out of the place when they decided to transform the remnants of bunker's day-to-day operational center into the museum, but we would at least be out of the immediate sight of anyone who might be watching in Central. Whether we'd be out of sight of the vampires was a different question, but given I couldn't smell any hint of them in the slight breeze sweeping up the hill, it was probable they weren't in the immediate vicinity.

"Bear was just telling me he was happy to finally have an adult male to talk to."

"Oh."

"Yeah." I grinned. "Be prepared for nonstop chatter until the novelty wears off."

"Or I learn to filter them. Nuri might be able to help with that." He glanced at me. "I wonder what you've gained out of the DNA exchange."

I shrugged. "My connection with them has strengthened, but so far, that appears to be it. And you said yourself some people come through without any physical change."

"I said those who went in alone did. There's always repercussions for those caught with others. Your Sal is a perfect example."

True. I rubbed my arms against a sudden chill. Whether it was apprehension of a situation I could neither control nor change, or something else entirely, I couldn't say.

But the wind that whispered up from the museum suddenly seemed filled with darkness and threat, even though the night was silent and there was no scent of vampire or wraith riding the breeze.

"Why would Nuri be moving the pile of rubble in the museum?"

Jonas raised his eyebrows at the abrupt change of topic. "Is she?"

"So the ghosts say." I studied him. "She seems to be looking for something—something I suspect might be the second entrance into the bunker. Why would she be doing that?"

"I don't know. We can ask her when we get there—"

"You can ask her now, can't you?"

"Yes. But why is this suddenly so important?"

"Sal's partners might currently believe I'm buried, and maybe even dead." I scrubbed a hand through my hair, loosening some of the dirt matting it. "But if they also suspect I'm linked to you—and it seems they do if they're keeping an eye on Chaos—then trying to open the old stairs might just tell them I'm alive."

"That's an unlikely event. No one has come near the museum since the monitoring system was set up."

"Which doesn't mean they can't or won't." Especially

now that we'd successfully snatched two more kids from them. "That bunker is not only my home, Jonas, it's the resting place of everyone who was killed there—déchet *and* human. It deserves the same sort of respect that humans accord their cemeteries."

"Cemeteries are no longer used. It's now considered a waste of land."

"Which is *not* the point." I frowned. "What is done with the dead, then?"

"The bodies are cremated, the ashes treated, and then used for fertilizer and soil improvement. It's a law that emerged from the war and the vast numbers of dead on both sides." He paused. "Nuri said she has no intention of fully exposing the tunnel. She is just attempting to make it easier for you to get in and out."

"Then tell her to work on the south-side exit. That's the one I use the most."

He hesitated, then smiled. "She said you're an ungrateful wench."

"I'm just protecting my home. She'd do exactly the same thing if Central or Chaos was—"

I stopped as that sense of darkness—of wrongness—suddenly sharpened. I flared my nostrils, drawing the night air deeper into my lungs to sort through the various scents, trying to find the source of whatever it was I was sensing.

"What's wrong?" Jonas stopped beside me, a rifle held at the ready.

"I don't know."

I swung around. The glow from Central's lights rose like a dome high above it, stealing the night from the sky. But the growing sense of unease wasn't coming from the city . . . My gaze went left to the ramshackle, barely lit cluster of metal that clung to Central's curtain wall. "Ask Nuri if there's anything going on in Chaos, because I have this really weird feeling—"

I didn't finish. Because, right at that moment, the screaming began.

Chaos was under attack.

CHAPTER 12

Jonas bolted forward, moving through the trees so fast he was almost a blur. I followed, desperately trying to keep up even as the noise and confusion from Chaos grew and sharpened.

"Jonas," I yelled, raising an arm to protect my face from the branches that whipped past, "ask Nuri to punch a hole through the earth at the top end of the sunken tunnel area."

"Why?" The reply was curt.

"Because if I can get into the bunker, I can call the ghosts—"

"No ghosts," he bit back. "Not in Chaos."

"Why in Rhea not?" I leapt over a log but slipped on the leaf matter beyond it and wrenched a leg muscle. I cursed loudly but ran on.

"Because in a city filled with shifters and outcasts, déchet ghosts might not be able to resist the impulse to extract a little vengeance."

He was pulling ahead of me now. I cursed again and reached for more speed. "If they wanted vengeance, they would have taken it against you and the others when we attacked the vampire nest."

"By the time we'd arrived, their energy was well and truly depleted. That would not be the case here."

"But—"

"No ghosts!"

And with that, his form became fluid, moving from human to that of a black panther—one with faint, almost tigerlike white stripes. Another result of our merging, obviously, and one that made me wonder if I might now be able to take tiger form. While the DNA of a white tiger had been used in my creation, I'd never been designed to shift into that form, for whatever reason.

It was possible that the mixing of our DNA now meant that I could—but it wasn't something I was about to explore at this very moment. My first body shift had been something of a harrowing experience, and it had left me weak for days. Given that I was already at low tide when it came to strength, risking an attempt into a new—and unfamiliar—form wouldn't be the brightest of moves.

But it wasn't like I didn't have another option. I sucked in the night as I ran and drew it deep into my lungs. The vampire within me rose at its touch, and in very little time my flesh had become little more than dark matter. I zoomed forward, Cat and Bear at my side. While I normally would have sent them back to the safety of the bunker, I had a bad feeling the vampires in Chaos were only interested in one thing—Penny.

Jonas might have said no ghosts, but he'd meant the soldiers, not my little ones. And I certainly had no intention of making a rearguard attack on the vampires—Nuri and Jonas could take care of that. My goal was Penny herself. The bastards weren't going to reclaim her if I could help it—and protecting *her* was certainly something Cat and Bear could help with.

We caught up with Jonas just as he was leaping the muddy trickle of water that was the Barra River, and a low, annoyed snarl chased after us as we continued on. Up ahead, the sounds of fighting and gunshots now mingled with the screams, and the bottom levels of Chaos were ablaze—with fire rather than lights. But fire was a tenuous light—it cast some areas into fierce brightness and others into shadow—and unless they set the whole place on fire, it would not be enough to stop the vampires.

I raced through the entrance and swept up through the nearest air vent to the next level. People were everywhere, some dead, some not, some armed and fighting, and some simply bleeding. There were women and children among the dead and injured, and rage filled me. Not at the vampires, but at those who had ordered them here. *They* were responsible for this destruction, and by Rhea, one way or another, they would damn well pay for it.

We continued on to the next level. The sounds of gunshots and fighting grew sharper. Vampires lay among the dead, but their bodies smoldered rather than burned, even though the light from the nearby fires touched their forms.

Unease stirred, but I thrust it aside. The hows and whys behind their flesh remaining whole despite the touch of light could be worried about later. Right now I had one objective— beating the bastards to Penny.

I continued rising through the various air vents. The higher I got, the more prevalent regular lighting became, and the more it began to tear at my shadowed form. I made it to the fifth level before the shadows completely unraveled and

I became myself again. As I landed in a half crouch on the spindly metal bridge that spanned the width of the vent, Bear screamed a warning. I grabbed the rifle from behind my back, swung around, and saw three vampires coming at me.

And the light wasn't burning them. Wasn't stopping them.

Rhea help us, I thought, even as I fired. Two went down in a fountain of blood and gore, but the third hit me and sent me tumbling backward. I shoved the rifle sideways into his mouth to stop him from biting me, but his razor-sharp fingernails raked my side, drawing blood. Then energy surged as my two little ghosts tore him from me. As he hit the side of a container on the far side of the bridge and slithered down, I sighted and fired, spreading his brains across the grimy metal wall. I scrambled upright and ran forward.

"Bear, find me the nearest ladder onto the sixth level."

As he raced away, I ran across the rest of the bridge and entered the more shadowed laneway. Movement, this to my left. I flipped the rifle and swung it hard, then rapidly checked the blow. *A woman with a child, not a vampire.*

She grabbed a fistful of shirt, her grip fierce, as if she feared I'd shake her loose and move on. It made me wonder who had done so.

"Please," she said, her eyes wide and glimmering with unshed tears. "Help us. *Please.*"

Urgency was beating through my brain, telling me that I needed to get to Penny, that if I didn't, we'd lose her. But I couldn't leave this woman here, scared, alone, and unprotected. Especially *not* when she was holding a baby.

I studied the nearby containers for someplace safe. Cat screamed a warning. I wrenched my arm free from the woman's grip, then turned and fired. A vampire went down, half his leg gone. I finished him off and reloaded the weapon.

"This way," I said to the woman, voice tight.

She didn't argue. She just fell in step behind me, keeping so close she tripped over my feet several times. Up ahead, light filtered out from underneath the door of a solid-looking container. It was brighter than the light that flooded much of this level, and might offer a little more safety. I stopped and tested the handle; it was locked. I raised a fist and bashed on the door. The sound echoed faintly, and after a second, footsteps shuffled toward us. "Who is it?"

"I'm a mercenary," I said. "I have a woman and child here with me. You need to open up."

There was a moment's hesitation; then the locks were undone, bolts were slid aside, and the door opened a crack. An elderly man peered at us both for a second, then fully opened the door. "Come in, come in, quickly."

I stepped to one side and allowed the woman to pass. "Have you got any weapons?" I asked the old man.

He shook his head. "All we have is the generator and the light."

"Then keep the damn light as bright as you can, for as long as you can." I unclipped the gun we'd retrieved from the remains of the solar vehicle and handed it to him. "And keep this close."

He checked that the weapon was fully loaded, then tucked it into the front of his pants. "You're not coming in?"

"No. I have vampires to fight."

"Then keep safe, and may Rhea bless you."

It was a blessing I would undoubtedly need. As the old man shut and locked the door, I spun and ran on.

Bear returned. *There's a ladder twenty meters away, but vampires and men are fighting all around it.*

"Is that the closest ladder?"

Yes. There is one farther on, but it's also blocked by men and vampires.

I frowned. "How light is it up ahead?"

It is no different from here.

Meaning it was regular lighting rather than UV. And normally, that would have been enough to stop vampires, but something had very definitely changed in the last few days.

I leapt over several bodies but couldn't entirely avoid the large pool of blood that was spreading across the grimy metal walkway. It splattered across my legs, its coppery yet oddly sweet smell filling my nostrils. Sharpened senses, one part of my brain noted, even as I said, "How many vamps are we talking about?"

"Three. There are eight mercenaries trying to stop them."

I frowned. Those odds *should* have worked in the mercs' favor, especially given that the vampires' one major advantage—the ability to shadow and allow bullets to pass through them without causing any sort of harm—*should* have been nullified by the light. By all rights, the mercenaries should have been all over them.

So why weren't they? What in Rhea was going on? Were Sal's partners further along the immunity path than we'd thought? I really, *really* hoped that wasn't true—that this immunity applied only to firelight and non-UV lights. We'd be in a whole world of trouble if it also applied to UVs.

There was only one way to find out. As the sound of fighting grew closer and fiercer, I pulled the flashlight from the accessory pocket in my pants and switched it on. The clean blue-white light not only illuminated the shadows hunkering beyond the containers that lined this metal pathway, but spotlighted the fierce cluster of men and vampires up ahead.

Vampires screamed as the light hit them and almost

instantly, all three were little more than ash raining down on the blood and gore staining the bottom of the ladder.

One of the men—a fierce-looking black man with a platted beard longer than my arm—swung around. "What the fuck is going on? Do you know? Because these bastards aren't here for blood."

"No, they're not." I slithered to a stop and pointed up the ladder. "I need to get up there, and I need you and the others on this level to stop any more of them getting up there for as long as you can."

"A fucking hard request, given that these bastards seem immune to our lights."

"But not all light, as this flashlight proved. UVs still stop them."

"Not something we have much of here in Chaos." He stepped to one side and motioned to the ladder. "Go. We'll do our best."

"Thanks." I tucked the flashlight back into my pocket, then gripped the first rung and hastily began to climb. *Bear, could you scout ahead and see if you can locate Penny? She should be in Nuri's bar somewhere.*

Nuri might have said she was keeping her isolated, but I doubted, given Jonas's determination to keep her close and his belief that it was only their presence that was keeping her grounded, that she'd be too far away from their main base of power.

Up ahead, shadows danced against a backdrop of light. Men and vampires, fighting. *Cat, you want to check the exit? Make sure it's safe?*

She surged upward but didn't immediately report back. I slowed as I neared the top of the ladder, fear beginning to slide through me. *Cat? You okay?*

She immediately returned, her amusement and excitement high. *The ladder is now safe.*

A series of images flashed through my mind: Cat had tossed the two vampires who'd been waiting near the ladder's exit into the middle of another six, scattering them all and allowing the mercenaries who'd been fighting them to shoot the lot. I couldn't help grinning. "Good work, Cat."

She preened at that, but nevertheless raced ahead of me to make a final check and give the all-clear. I quickly climbed out, felt the metal walkway underneath me vibrating, and glanced right. The mercenaries were racing toward me. As I rolled out of their way, a bell began to peal loudly. It was coming from the middle portion of this level—which was exactly where Nuri's was. I scrambled upright and ran after the men.

They ran straight into more vamps.

As screams and gunshots began to echo, I grabbed the flashlight again and hit the switch. Its light bloomed, eradicating the nearest vampires and causing those behind the men to burst into flame. As the mercenaries finished the vamps off, I swung left into Run Turk Alley and raced toward Nuri's. There were no men lounging about this time, no legs to avoid or trip over. There were bodies—both men and vampire—but only a couple. Maybe, just maybe, they hadn't found Penny yet.

But even as that thought crossed my mind, I knew it was a forlorn one.

Nuri's came into view. The claxon ringing of the bell was coming from its interior, as was the sound of fighting. I thrust the door open but didn't immediately race in.

Safe, Bear said.

I bolted through the bar. It was empty, but it bore signs of the fight I could hear ahead—tables were upturned, chairs were smashed, and the torso of a vampire lay draped over the bar. Where his legs were I had no idea. Nor did I care.

I ducked through the second doorway and saw Branna running backward, firing his rifle at the three vampires in the room. There were another two on the floor, their bodies torn apart.

I raised the flashlight. Almost instantly the vampires became puddles of ash. Branna stopped and blinked; then his gaze rose and he saw me. Rage—blind, unthinking rage—crossed his face and he raised the gun again.

"Bear," I screamed, even as I flung myself sideways. A gunshot rang out; the bullet whistled past my butt as I slid along the greasy, bloody floor. Then there was a grunt, and the sound of something hitting the floor hard. I pushed upright. Branna was out to it, and a chair leg was hovering threateningly over him.

"Thanks, Bear." His energy danced around me, the chair leg briefly threatening to club me before he got it under control again. "Can you show me where Penny is? And, Cat, can you keep an eye on Branna? If he wakes, let me know."

You don't want me to knock him out again?

The question held a disappointed edge. I couldn't help smiling. "If he wakes up angry, feel free."

She zoomed off, and another chair leg was soon hovering over Branna's prone form. If he did wake up anytime soon, he wasn't likely to remain that way for long. Not if Cat had anything to say about it.

I followed Bear out of the room and into the walkway beyond. A short set of stairs later, and we were in an area I knew. I'd woken up in this area twice previously—once in a room that had been designed to hold vampires, and once in a basic but comfortable sleeping area.

I wasn't entirely surprised when Bear led me to the former rather than the latter.

I tested the door handle. It was locked. "Penny?" I said. "You there? You okay?"

"Yes." The answer was short, almost sharp, and even though it was Penny's voice, there was something within it that made my skin crawl.

The claxon alarm suddenly cut off. Awareness surged; there were vampires in the bar. How they'd gotten past the mercenaries guarding the entrance of this lane I had no idea, but if I didn't do something—didn't get Penny out of here— I'd soon be knee-deep in them.

Cat, there's vampires headed your way. Be careful. Aloud, I added, "Penny, the vamps are attacking Chaos in an effort to retrieve you. You're not safe here."

"I'm not safe anywhere." She paused. "I can feel them. Despite Nuri's spells, I can feel them in my head."

My gut churned. This *wasn't* a good development. I briefly closed my eyes, not sure whether it was better to make a stand here or get her out and run.

The choice was taken out of my hands as Cat yelled a warning and the vampires attacked. Two of them flowed up the stairs as one, a mass of stinking, snarling desperation. I raised both the flashlight and my rifle, firing one-handed even as their flesh exploded into flame. There was answering retort from behind them, and a second later the flashlight exploded in my hand, almost taking several fingers with it. As blood began spurting from the wounds, two more vampires appeared. One of them was holding a gun.

An *armed* vampire; it was almost too ludicrous to believe.

Bear, grab that thing. I flung myself sideways as the vampire fired another shot. It pinged against the container behind me, sending shards of metal flying into my face and hair. I cursed, but nevertheless twisted around and returned fire. I got one of them. Bear snatched the weapon from the other, who either didn't care or didn't notice. He just kept on running.

I raised the rifle again and pressed the trigger. This time, nothing happened. Out of ammo. With no time to reload, I simply flipped the rifle around and raised it above my head.

But the vampire wasn't after me. Instead, he flung himself, as hard as he could, at the door barring Penny's sanctuary. It was a sturdy metal thing, and the vampire's weight made little more than a dent. Bear tossed me the vampire's rifle. In one smooth motion, I caught it and fired. The force of the shot not only pushed me backward, but punched a hole through the vampire *and* the door behind it.

I blinked and momentarily glanced down at the weapon. Obviously, I was damn lucky to have a hand left, let alone all my fingers still attached.

Then the importance of the hole registered.

"Penny," I screamed. "Are you okay?"

Silence was my only reply, and my heart just about stopped. *Please, Rhea, don't let her be dead.*

Cat zoomed up from the back room. *The vampires and the men are fighting near Nuri's. I'm not sure the men will hold them.*

How many vampires?

Only four. But the lane is too narrow to allow much fighting room.

Because these lanes had never been designed for fighting. No one had ever expected the vampires to reach *this* far into Chaos.

And certainly no one had expected them to find immunity to ordinary lights.

Branna?

Got hit again.

Good. But it was absently said. My attention was on the container opposite, on the hole that revealed the brightness of the UVs that lit the room beyond. The scent of blood was thick and rich in the air, but its source was both the blood pouring from my hand and the gore of the vampire I'd blown apart. "Penny?"

"I'm here." Her voice was faint but didn't seem to be distressed in any way.

"Are you okay?"

"Yes."

Again, her tone was distant. I frowned and glanced toward the stairs at the faintest whisper of sound. No vampires appeared, but they couldn't be far away.

Should I run? Or make a stand? Adrenaline was probably the only thing keeping me upright at the moment, but I knew it couldn't last. Not given the bloody state of my hand and the rips down my side. In many ways, getting Penny out of here had been a forlorn hope to begin with, but given the number of vampires and their sudden immunity to light, it had become nigh on impossible.

Realistically, the only chance I really had of keeping her out of their hands was by joining her in that room. The UVs would at least crisp any vampire that took one step into the room, and I could shoot any that managed two.

"Penny, I need you to open the door."

"Can't," she said. "Nuri has the keys."

Of course she did. I took a deep breath to calm the urgency beating through my brain. "Cat, Bear, can you combine forces and get that thing open?"

Energy surged, and a heartbeat later the door banged back against the hinges. A tide of weariness washed through our link. They were both nearing the end of their strength and needed to rest. *Come in with me,* I said. *The lights will keep us all safe.*

It would be better—

Bear, I interrupted gently, *if the vampires find a way to cut the power to this room, then we're all in a world of trouble. We need to conserve our strength.*

He didn't argue. He just followed me in. I glanced around quickly and saw Penny in the corner. There was a smashed chair beside her and she was holding one of its legs in front of her like a baton.

"It'll be okay, Penny. Nuri and Jonas are on the way, and the mercenaries are winning the battle against the vampires."

"I know."

Her voice was even more distant, and despite the odd trembling in her bottom lip, there was no emotion in her face and little life in her eyes. I frowned but swung around and studied the door. When the ghosts had forced it open, they also busted the lock. I could close it but that was about it. Not that it really mattered. Vampires were rail thin, and the hole I'd blasted in the middle of the door was large enough for one of them to squeeze through.

"Right," I said as I turned toward Penny again, "if we just hunker down in—"

The rest of the words were cut off as the ghosts screamed a warning. I reacted, but far too slowly. Something smashed into the side of my head and sent me spinning to the floor. I hit hard and the air left my lungs in a huge whoosh. For too many seconds, I hovered on the brink of unconsciousness, battling a stomach that threatened to jump up my throat even as tears of pain—and maybe even blood—coursed down my face.

Voices echoed. One calm, remote, the other two filled

with confusion and fear. Then footsteps. Not coming closer, but moving away. Out of the room, down the walkway.

"Cat? Bear?" I somehow croaked. "What happened?"

Penny attacked you, Cat said, even as Bear added, *She said she'd order the vampires to kill you if we didn't let her go.*

Order the vampires . . . Three simple words that were going to provide a whole world of pain to Jonas. Whatever had been done to her, whatever changes had been made to her DNA, those words made it obvious she was now connected to either the vampires or those who controlled them. Maybe even both.

But if she was connected to Sal's partners, why hadn't they ordered her to finish me off?

Was it simply a matter of them needing Penny more than they wanted me dead?

"Where is she?"

She runs, Bear said. *Do you want me to follow her?*

I hesitated. Given that Penny was in thrall to either the vamps or Sal's partners, it could become very dangerous if they became aware of his presence. Which they very well might, thanks to the fact that Penny, as a seeker, could see ghosts. But I couldn't just let her disappear, either.

"Yes," I croaked. "But keep your distance, Bear. If you think she might have spotted you, run."

Will do. As he raced off, Cat said, *What can I do?*

"Warn me if the vampires come into the room. I need to heal."

Her energy left me. I didn't move for several minutes and certainly couldn't concentrate. My head ached, my body ached, my damn hand was throbbing, and my stomach just wanted up and out. But after what seemed like ages, I somehow dragged myself closer to the wall and pushed up into a sitting position.

It was an effort that left me panting and dizzy. But I closed my eyes and forced myself to relax, to ignore the pain and the hurt, and concentrate on breathing. Eventually, I was able to slip into the healing state, but it felt like a tenuous thing—something I could lose at any moment.

Nuri comes. Cat hesitated. *Jonas is with her.*

Not what I needed right now, especially when the healing had barely begun and my strength levels were still dangerously low. But I forced myself back to consciousness and tried to open my eyes. I couldn't, so I raised my good hand and discovered there was something crusting them together. Blood, no doubt. I gently rubbed it away, then opened my eyes and glanced down at my damaged hand. Ugly pink scars ran the length of both my thumb and index finger, and only half an inch of skin had stopped the two cuts from joining in the middle of my palm. I'd come so close to losing a portion of my hand altogether . . . I flexed my fingers and moved my thumb, relaxing a little when both responded. I'd been lucky. Again.

Nuri swept into the room, all anger and fury. The force of her energy was so great it felt like I was being hit by lightning, and a gasp escaped. She reined it in the moment she saw me. "What the fuck happened? Where's Penny?"

I didn't immediately answer, instead waiting until Jonas stepped into the room. There was a long cut above his eye and another down the length of his calf, but neither was currently bleeding. His gaze met mine; there was no emotion in his face and nothing but ice in his eyes.

"Answer the question, Tiger." His voice was flat, tight.

"She's gone—"

"Obviously," he snapped, "but where?"

"At a guess, wherever the hell the vampires want her to go."

"What in Rhea is *that* supposed to—"

"Jonas, enough." Nuri knelt beside me and grabbed my hand. She ran her fingers along the vivid scars, and then her gaze rose to mine. "What happened here?"

She wasn't referring to the scars.

"Penny happened." I didn't look at Jonas. I didn't dare. "I was intending to get her out of Chaos before the vampires found her, but I was too late."

"Then the vampires—"

"Jonas, shut the fuck up and just *listen*." Nuri's voice was sharp.

Jonas's fury swept over us, sharp and acidic. But he didn't say anything; he simply crossed his arms and glared. And even though I knew his anger stemmed more from his fear for Penny than anything I'd done, it nevertheless sent a shiver down my spine.

"They were already in the bar when I arrived. I cindered the ones Branna was battling, but the bastard turned around and tried to shoot me."

"Which explains why he is currently sprawled unconscious on the floor. Your ghosts took him out."

I nodded. "Bear told me Penny was up here, but more vampires hit us and others were on their way. I decided our best bet was staying in this room, under the protection of the UVs, and hope like hell the vamps didn't find a way to cut the power."

"None of which explains why you're here and Penny's not," Jonas said.

Nuri cast him an exasperated glance but didn't say anything. My gaze rose to his. "She told me she could hear them. That they were in her head."

"The vampires?" Nuri asked.

"She didn't say. It could have been. Or it could have been Sal's partners. I suspect they're the ones behind this attack."

"As I suspect they're behind the sudden rash of vampire immunity to light." Nuri frowned. "I'm guessing from that statement—and the nasty gash on your head—that Penny attacked when you entered the room."

I nodded. "I'm sorry, Jonas. I tried—"

He made a sharp "enough" motion with his hand. "I know. It's just—"

He cut the rest of the sentence off as Nuri glanced at him again, but I nevertheless knew what he'd been about to say— that he'd sworn an oath to his dead sister to protect Penny, and he kept on failing. A similar sentiment echoed through me. I'd sworn to never let another child suffer, and I was failing in that endeavor every bit as badly with Penny as I had with my ghosts.

"Do you have any idea where she went when she left here?" Nuri asked.

"No, but I sent Bear after her. He'll report back once he knows—"

"We are *not* waiting," Jonas growled. "We all know where they're headed—for Carleen and the false rifts. It's their only possible chance of escaping with her."

"You can't be sure of that, Jonas," Nuri said.

"The vampires were in retreat to the *south-side* exit, not the north, by the time we got up here," Jonas said. "So it's either Carleen or the vampire den we raided, and I doubt it's the latter unless it's the vampires who control her and *not* Sal's partners."

"I do not think—"

"Right now I don't *care* what you think. I'm going after my niece." His glare snapped to me. "Are you coming?"

"Yes." I pulled my hand from Nuri's and pushed myself upright. Dizzy weakness washed through me, and I briefly closed my eyes, fighting it.

"For fuck's sake, Jonas, the woman's almost dead on her feet. She needs time—"

"We haven't *got* time." His gaze swept me. "She'd say if she was incapable."

Nuri snorted. "Shows just how much you know, Ranger." She grabbed my hand, and energy bit at my skin, chasing away some of the tiredness. But she released me altogether too soon. "That's all I can do for now, so go. And be careful."

I nodded, picked up the rifle, and headed out. Jonas was already halfway down the walkway. I collected the second rifle, then followed as quickly as I was able, trying to ignore the stink of the dead as my stomach continued to churn.

Branna was just waking when we arrived in the downstairs living area. "What the fuck happened?" he said, and then his gaze met mine. *"You."*

"Yeah," I said. "And that's two times you've tried to kill me now. Try it a third time, and I'll return the favor."

"Only if you see me before I see—"

"Branna, behave." Jonas's tone was curt. "And get some weapons. The vamps have Penny."

I glanced sharply at Jonas as Branna scrambled upright and reached for his weapons, but the ranger studiously ignored me and kept on walking. *Cat, keep an eye on Branna for me. If he so much as twitches the wrong way, hit him.*

Her anticipation spun through me as she raced off to grab the chair leg she'd abandoned earlier. Obviously, she, like me, didn't believe Branna would be able to restrain his hatred for all that long.

I followed Jonas out through the bar and into the lane

beyond. The bodies of vampires lay everywhere, but if any mercenaries had died here, then their remains had already been moved. Beyond Chaos, night had given way to sunrise. I could feel it, even if I couldn't yet see it. And sunrise was deadly to vampires, unless that, too, had changed. But I doubted it—not given that UV light still stopped them.

So either they'd taken Penny to the den situated in one of the few drainage tunnels that hadn't been filled in when Central was rebuilt, or someone was meeting them. I suspected the latter, but until Bear returned, we wouldn't know.

As we moved down Chaos's levels, the number of dead and wounded grew, until the noise and the smell made my heart weep. So many people had either lost their lives or been seriously injured, and for what? For a dream of domination that would not only destroy the world as we knew it, but erase everyone within it.

I couldn't understand what Sal and his partners really thought they'd gain by such destruction. Surely they couldn't be foolish enough to believe that the wraiths would allow them to live any longer than their usefulness lasted? Wraiths came to this world to hunt and destroy. We were prey to them, nothing more, just as we were simply a food source to the vampires.

How would giving control of our world to either be of any benefit to Sal's partners?

But I guessed I hadn't been caught in a rift with a wraith, as they had. Nor had I been driven so close to death in a vampire attack that whatever infections they carried forced a mutation, and made me a dhampir—which was the reason behind Sal and his partners' ability to communicate with the vampires and wraiths.

Maybe both those events had changed the way the three of them viewed their relationship with our world. Maybe they no longer even saw themselves as part of this world. While I might have thought that Sal's contempt for humans had stemmed what had happened to déchet after the war, maybe its source was a rather more alien view of beings they saw as weaker.

Beings that needed to be erased.

I shivered and rubbed my arms as we wove our way through the grimy, chaotic ground level and out into sunshine. But it didn't make me feel any better. Didn't chase the coldness from my skin or my heart.

Jonas stopped and knelt, brushing his fingers lightly against the soil. I waited behind him, all too aware that Branna was behind me.

That he was watching. Waiting.

And while Jonas's presence was obviously enough to curtail his almost instinctive need to kill me, it could not and would not erase it.

I clenched my fingers and fought the urge to reach for one of the rifles strapped across my back. It was the sort of action that might just cause the attack I was trying to avoid.

"They split up." Jonas rose and glanced back, his gaze remote. "The main pack ran for the old drainage outlets. Four others headed for the park."

"And Penny?"

"I don't know. I can't find her footprints anywhere, and the scent of blood and death coming from Chaos is erasing everything else."

"Meaning they're probably carrying her."

"Yes. Our best bet is to split up. Branna, follow the tracks to the outlet and see if you can find any sign of her. Don't go into the den, though. We'll track the other four."

As Branna grunted and left, Jonas's gaze swept me,

assessing. "They've got a good half-hour head start. We need to run—will that be a problem?"

Yes. But that wasn't going to stop me. "I'll keep up."

He nodded and led the way forward, setting a pace that, at any other time, would have been easy for me to keep. I bit my lip and concentrated on putting one foot in front of the other and not falling behind.

We crossed the Barra River and ran up the valley to the rail yards. Pods were pulling into the station in readiness for the day, but Central's drawbridge hadn't yet come down.

We'd just passed the museum and were approaching the main road when Bear returned. Jonas stopped, obviously sensing his approach.

"Where did they take her, Bear?" His tone was terse.

Bear's energy touched mine. *They were met in the forest by a man in an ATV. Penny was transferred into the vehicle and taken on to Carleen. They went into a false rift.*

My stomach sank. I was in no state to traverse a rift. It would, without doubt, kill me.

"Tiger," Jonas snapped. "What has happened?"

"You didn't hear Bear?"

"Not this time. I suspect it was deliberate."

It was, Bear said. *He is very angry right now.*

But not at you. Not even at me. "The vampires were met by an ATV in the park. Penny was transferred and taken into Carleen. They went into a rift."

"Then we—"

"There is no *we* when it comes to traversing the false rift, Jonas." My voice was soft but determined. "And I haven't the strength to even try right now."

"But maybe I now *can*. I can hear the ghosts. Maybe that means I can enter the rifts as well."

"Do you really want to risk your life—and Penny's—on a maybe?"

"For Rhea's sake, I cannot stand here and do nothing!"

I understood his urgency—his desperation—but it was nevertheless frustrating that he was thinking with his heart rather than his head.

But then, if the situation had been reversed, had it been one of my little ones in trouble, I guessed I'd be reacting the same way.

"Fine. Let's go to Carleen. If you can see the false rift, you can then decide whether you'll step into it. But I won't."

His gaze narrowed slightly, but all he said was "Fair enough."

With that, he swung around and moved on, this time at a pace I didn't struggle with. It took just over an hour to reach Carleen. I paused on the broken wall that surrounded the city, my gaze sweeping the immediate surrounds. Nothing appeared to have changed since I was last here, but the air was thick with tension and angst. It stung my skin and demanded my attention.

But the last thing I needed was another problem. I studiously ignored that angst and the ghosts behind it, and followed Jonas into Carleen, weaving my way through the luminous weeds and broken remnants of life and buildings as we headed up the long hill that led to the main plaza.

"Bear, which false rift did they use?"

One on the far side of the hill.

Jonas must have heard that reply, because he moved off the road again, picking his way through the rubble and dust as he skirted the edges of the plaza. He obviously didn't want to risk getting too close to the wall of magic Sal's partners had raised to protect the false rift still sitting within the plaza's broken heart. After witnessing what that damn wall was capable of, I certainly had no objection.

It took us twenty minutes to reach the other side of the hill. The desolation here was almost complete—beyond the remnants of the road, there was just dust, weeds, and the sharpening demand for attention from the ghosts. It bit at my consciousness, insisting that I stop, that I acknowledge and talk to them.

Which I couldn't do. Not when I was so weak. It would kill me as surely as the false rift would. *Cat,* I said. *Could you explain to the Carleen ghosts that I'm barely functioning right now and that I can't talk to them? Then ask them what the problem is.*

She was silent for several seconds, then said, *They want you to know that the one who raised the wall and created the rift that resides in the plaza has set traps there for you. You should not enter that place if you wish to remain alive.*

And I certainly did. *What about the rift Penny was just taken through?*

Brief silence, then, *Nothing has been done to it yet. They have just altered those you have already gone through.*

Meaning, perhaps, that they were hoping I wasn't aware of the others. Or maybe it was simply a matter of not yet having the time to protect them. *Can you ask them to keep an eye on the other rifts for me? And let me know if any changes are made to them?*

They will.

Which at least meant it was one thing I didn't have to worry about. *Thank them for me.*

They said you can thank them by destroying the rifts and the wall that washes its darkness across their bones.

I frowned. *But Nuri shifted the rift away from their bones.*

Yes, but it hasn't helped. They said that while the false rifts have not changed in size, their energy output seems to be growing. It's fouling the air and the earth in ever-increasing circles.

Which wasn't surprising, given that while the false rifts had been created in *this* world, the knowledge and the magic had come from another. It was also precisely what Nuri had feared might happen. *Tell them we're trying.*

They said to try harder.

I snorted. It was *that* sort of thinking—a failure to see problems beyond their own boundaries—that had led to the war in the first place.

As we neared the bottom of the hill, energy began to lash at my skin. Up ahead, slightly to the right of the road, an odd, circular patch of darkness began to appear in an area that was nothing but sunshine and dust. *Rift.* Or rather, the wall of gelatinous shadows that protected one.

And Jonas wasn't reacting to it.

If he couldn't see the wall, then the likelihood of him being able to traverse the false rift within it was low. But I didn't say anything, simply waiting and watching as we continued down the last section of the hill, getting closer and closer to that black patch.

Eventually, I stopped and said, "Jonas, the rift is near enough to touch."

He swung around, his gaze sweeping the landscape before meeting mine. Frustration and anger burned the air, as fierce as the nearby shadows were foul.

"I can't see it."

"Obviously."

"Why in Rhea can't something go *right* for a damn change?" He flexed his fingers, but the anger continued to

radiate from him. "How long will it take you to regain
enough energy to go in there?"

"I'm not entirely sure that would be a wise move—"

"So we stand around out here and do nothing? That's not
going to happen, Tiger. You *have* to go in after them."

"Or what?" I snapped. "You'll make me? Have Nuri
threaten my little ones again?"

"No, of course not." He thrust a hand through his short
hair, frustration obvious. "But you're the only one who can
go through this thing, and that means you're Penny's only
chance. I need you to do this, Tiger. Please."

Despite my annoyance over his insistence, a smile tugged
at my lips. "A ranger pleading with a déchet for help. Who'd
have thought such a thing would be possible one hundred
years ago?"

"Certainly not me." Amusement briefly lit his eyes, but
faded all too quickly. "Your answer?"

"Fine, I'll go in," I said, even as every part of me said it
was a bad idea. "But not now. I need to get back to Central
and Winter Halo."

He frowned. "Doing so would be a dangerous ploy, given
that we snatched the children from them."

"We rescued another two, but there's still seven out there
somewhere." Eight, if we included the now-missing Penny.
"Besides, Sharran is due back at work tonight, and if she
doesn't appear they might just jump to the right conclu-
sions."

"We could simply send *her* back in. There is no need for
you to be there now."

"If we did that, we'd gain no knowledge as to what the
hell is going on in those upper levels." Besides, the last thing
I wanted was to put Sharran's life in danger, which it would

be if she were promoted. At least I had a fighting chance of escaping the drugs and the dissection; she did not.

"Rath Winter is no fool—it's highly likely he'll suspect you've infiltrated that place. Especially now."

"He undoubtedly will, but it's doubtful he'll suspect Sharran, as she hasn't yet been promoted to the upper floors."

He studied me for a moment, then said, "There's something you're not telling me."

I hesitated. "They have Sal's body."

"And this is a problem because . . . ?"

"Because Sal was one of the rare grays—a déchet whose DNA was mixed with that of a salamander. Only five of them ever survived; understanding *why* might just give his partners the information they need to successfully merge human or shifter DNA with wraith. I have to get in there and destroy his remains before that happens."

And, if I could, destroy the labs, free the women waiting in the holding cells, and release those on the dissection tables to death.

It was a tall order, and one I might not achieve. But I had to at least try.

Jonas didn't immediately say anything, but an odd buzzing began in the back of my mind. I frowned and tried to pin down its source. I caught a word—*chance*—and realized I was hearing—or *almost* hearing—the telepathic conversation between Jonas and Nuri. Or *his* side of it, at least.

Then the buzzing stopped and Jonas said, "Fine. I don't agree that it's the best course of action right now, but it would seem I'm outvoted."

"And does your disagreement stem from the danger, or from the fact that you'd rather I gain strength and then follow Penny and her captors into the false rift?"

"I won't deny I'd rather you do the latter, but to suggest

that overshadows my concerns about you going back into Winter Halo belittles both them *and* me."

He swung around and headed across the emptiness, his long, angry strides stirring up a thick cloud of dust. The slight breeze caught it, spinning it into circular patterns, until it seemed he was being followed by a multitude of dust devils.

Why was I destined to always say the wrong thing around this man? It was decidedly odd, especially when my success as a lure very much depended on always knowing what— and what not—to say. But maybe men were easier to understand when they were little more than targets whom I might or might not be attracted to.

I followed him at a slower pace. After a while, he stopped and waited for me to catch up, then remained by my side as we silently left Carleen and moved back into the forest separating it from Central.

When we finally neared the rail station, he said, "Remember, none of us can help you once you're inside Winter Halo."

"I know, but I have the ghosts."

"Even ghosts have their limitations. Just be careful, and report in when you're able."

There was something in his tone that had me wondering if Nuri had said anything specific about things going wrong in Winter Halo. But surely she wouldn't have agreed it was necessary for me to return to that place if she, in any way, suspected I might not get out alive? Not given her declaration that if I didn't rescue the children, no one would.

Or was that no longer true?

The future wasn't a fixed item; it was constantly being altered by the decisions and actions we made. It was more than possible that, after recent events, I no longer played a major part in finding those kids. It was even possible that they might now never be found.

But even if the future *had* altered, and one or even both of those possibilities were true, it wouldn't stop me. And it certainly *wouldn't* stop Nuri from using me. She might have professed a liking for me, but she'd also shown a steely determination to do whatever it took to get the job done. And if that meant risking the lives of her soldiers, then risk them she would.

As Jonas disappeared into the bright sunshine, I stepped back into the shadows and sat cross-legged on the ground underneath a somewhat battle-scarred old oak. I needed to be wearing Sharran's form when I went into Winter Halo, but there was no possibility of body-shifting until I least gained some strength back.

"Cat, can you go back to the museum and get the pack with my change of clothes in it? Bear, could you keep watch?"

As Cat zoomed off and Bear began to prowl around the area, I closed my eyes and called to the healing state. It took a while, but I eventually slipped into it. The sun had well and truly begun its descent into nightfall by the time I climbed back out. I stretched carefully, and was relieved when there was no responding pain. The scars on my hand hadn't fully disappeared, but would be easy enough to conceal when I body-shifted.

I resumed Sharran's shape, then stripped off the remains of my clothes and scrubbed the dried blood from my skin as best I could. After donning fresh clothes, I threw the pack over my shoulder, then, as several pods pulled into the station, quickly joined the throng rushing toward the drawbridge and the safety it offered against the oncoming night.

Once I neared Sharran's apartment, I pulled a sun shield around my body and climbed back in through the window. As Bear and Cat did a quick scoot around to check out what my neighbors had been up to during the day, I grabbed a shower and half wished I was back at my other alter ego's apartment, where there was more water than air in the mix.

After donning one of Sharran's tunics, I grabbed the pack she usually carried, stuffed a few protein bars into it, then headed out, the two ghosts happily updating me on who was doing what within the building. There were no such things as secrets when there were ghosts around—not that the people within Sharran's building appeared to have much in the way of secrets.

As I approached Winter Halo's main entrance, the security guards once again stepped forward, forcing me to halt.

The older of the two produced a scanner and, after I'd run my left wrist across it, checked the screen and nodded. At first glance, nothing appeared to have changed in the foyer since our rescue of the two children. But as I threw my pack into the plastic tub to be scanned, I noted there were a lot more guards in the section past the secondary scanner, and all of them were heavily armed. I walked through the scanner, collected my bag, then threw it over my shoulder and headed toward the elevator. Two guards immediately stepped forward, blocking my way and forcing me to stop. Cat and Bear pressed close, their energy fiery against my skin, ready to attack the guards and protect me. *It's okay. This is all part of the plan.* I hoped.

"Sharran Westar?" one of the guards said, voice brusque.

I didn't have to fake the sudden rush of trepidation. Despite my assurances to the ghosts, I was well aware this might be the first signal that I was in deep trouble. "Yes. Why?"

"You need to come with us. Now."

"But why? What's wrong?"

"Nothing. Just follow me, please."

He swung around and marched toward the elevator. After a brief hesitation, I followed. Neither of these two was armed and surely they would be if they suspected I was anyone other than Sharran.

But that didn't stop the tension curling through me. Didn't stop the hope that Rhea *hadn't* abandoned me. That my plans to destroy Sal's body weren't over before they'd even begun.

I guess I'd know soon enough.

CHAPTER 13

"What's going on?" I repeated as the elevator doors closed behind the three of us. "What have I done?"

"Nothing," the first man said. "You're being promoted."

Relief stirred, but it didn't ease the tension. If anything, it did the exact opposite. One part of our plan had worked; now I just had to hope I was taken to the same floor as the rest of the women *and* that I could actively do something once I was up there.

"If I'm being promoted, why the escort? I can't remember it happening when any of the other ladies were moved into positions upstairs."

"No," the guard said. "But new security procedures have been enacted overnight."

Because of our raid, perhaps? But even so, it was odd that an employee who'd been working here for a while—someone whom they intended to dissect—would come under the umbrella of any security upgrade. Were they simply ensuring that there were no mistakes, and that I went precisely where I was supposed to go?

Or did they, perhaps, suspect I wasn't Sharran?

The elevator doors opened and I was marched into the personnel department. The older woman who'd tended to me after the attack looked up as we entered, and something close to sympathy crossed her face. It quickly disappeared as she gathered up a scanner, then rose and walked toward us.

"You're feeling better, I hope?" She stopped on the other side of the counter and started flicking through the scanner's screens.

"Yes, thanks."

"Good, good." Her voice was absent. "I'm sure these gentlemen have informed you that you're being promoted. I just need you to sign off from your current position and then they'll take you upstairs."

"I don't suppose you know why this is happening?" It was a question Sharran probably would have asked. "I mean, I've haven't been here as long as some of the other guards."

"I'm afraid I just process the orders, dear. Sign here, please." She pointed to a line, then handed me the screen.

Just for a moment, I froze. I had no idea what Sharran's signature looked like. I'd never thought it would be necessary to learn.

"Hurry up," one of the guards growled. "We ain't got all day."

I hastily scrawled Sharran's name, and must have got close enough to the real thing, because the screen beeped in approval. The woman grunted and gave me a smile that held little in the way of sincerity. "Good luck with the new position."

You're going to need it. She might not have said those words, but they seemed to hover in the air between us. It made me wonder how much she knew about the events on the upper floor, or if it was simply awareness that those who ventured up there were never seen again.

I was led back into the elevator. As the doors began to close, one of the guards ran his RFID chip over the security scanner, then growled, "Twenty-nine."

That's the floor where they're dissecting people, Cat said.

Yes. I watched the floor numbers flash by and tried to keep a lid on the tension twisting my stomach into knots.

I do not think it would be a good idea for you to get dissected, Bear said.

I couldn't help the slight smile that tugged my lips. *With that, I wholeheartedly agree.*

Then what is the plan?

I don't know yet, Bear. We'll have to play it by ear once we're up there.

Which was a dangerous ploy, but our only option right now. I could probably take the two guards out, but I doubted I'd get much farther than this elevator; there were cameras in the ceiling, and undoubtedly men or women behind them, watching our every move. This place would become my tomb the minute we reached the twenty-ninth floor.

The elevator came to a smooth halt and the doors silently opened. The hallway beyond was bright and sterile, and the air devoid of any scents or sounds. There were no signs on the pristine walls, nothing to indicate where we were or what might be going on beyond the corridor's walls. I knew, but only because my ghosts had previously investigated.

But there was also absolutely no place to go beyond the door at the far end. It reminded me of the races livestock were herded into before they were either transported or killed.

The first guard stepped out of the elevator, but I didn't

immediately follow. Not until the second guard gave me a light nudge.

"What is this place?" My tone was hushed but seemed extraordinarily loud in the calm, cool hallway. "I thought we were going to another personnel section?"

"We have to go through processing first," the man behind me said. "I'm afraid everyone has to be screened and sanitized before proceeding into the main work areas."

Our footsteps echoed as we walked down the hall, a sound as sharp as my pulse rate. "Sanitized? What does that involve?"

"Nothing more than stripping, going through a purification chamber, and getting an injection."

Which would undoubtedly render me unconscious. I clenched my fists against the sudden urge to knock these two out and run. Running would be pointless. Besides, I had to keep playing the game until I was alone; only then could I risk tracking down Sal's body. Though how I was going to destroy it, I wasn't entirely sure.

The front guard paused, ran his RFID chip across the scanner to the left of the door, and then, when it opened, continued on. The next corridor was shorter, and this time the murmur of conversation could be heard.

We entered a small room that held little more than a desk and a chair. The tall, dusky-skinned woman who'd been standing near the desk swung around as we entered, affording me a brief glimpse of male features before the comm unit went dark. The face wasn't one I recognized, and relief shot through me. I'd half expected it to be Rath Winter. That it *wasn't* hopefully meant they didn't suspect Sharran to be anything more than another test subject; Winter would hardly lead me into the heart of his organization accompanied only by two unarmed men if in any way he suspected otherwise.

The woman gave me a wide, friendly smile. I guess it was supposed to put me at ease, but it did the opposite.

"Sharran, so glad you made it here." She stuck out her hand. "Janice Harvey. I'll be your coordinator until you're fully settled in."

I somewhat reluctantly shook her hand. Her grip was firm, but not overly so. "No one's actually told me what the new job entails. I was just escorted up here."

"Ah yes, sorry about that, but there's been a few problems and we've had to employ strict security conditions for the immediate future. No one goes anywhere without an escort."

"So that's what I'm going to be doing? Escorting and guarding people."

"Of course." She flashed a smile that seemed totally genuine but had the hairs along the back of my neck rising. "Now, if you'll just come this way?"

She's as fake as the guise you're wearing, Cat commented as I followed the woman. *Are you sure you don't want us to cause a little mayhem?*

Not yet. We'll save it for later.

You may be unconscious later, Bear pointed out.

In which case, I'll need you to keep me safe while I recover from whatever drug they give me.

Presuming I could recover, of course. After that incident in the tenth-floor foyer, it was entirely possible I'd be affected as badly as everyone else.

The next room held the purification chamber and a comfortable-looking chair. The woman stopped and looked past me. "Gentlemen, please wait outside. Sharran, can you strip? You can place your clothes in the small chute behind you. We'll get them sanitized and then return them to you."

Or not, as was more likely the case, given what they were doing to everyone they brought up here. I undressed, then tossed the tunic into the chute. The air in the room was cool, and goose bumps prickled my skin. I rubbed my arms lightly as the woman activated the chamber.

"Right." The fake smile flashed again as a soft hissing began inside the chamber. "Just step inside so we can clear your flesh of any contaminants—"

"I did have a shower before I came to work today." I knew it didn't matter in highly sensitive areas such as labs, but Sharran might not have.

Janice gave me a condescending sort of smile. "Yes, dear, but we have to be totally sure you didn't pick anything up between your house and here. Even the smallest amount of contaminant in a sterile lab could ruin billions of dollars of research."

I planned to do a *whole* lot more than simply ruin their research, but I could hardly say that. I lowered my head slightly so that my hair hid my expression and walked into the chamber. Once the doors at either end had closed, jets of warm, slightly antiseptic-smelling steam hit my flesh. I drew in a clean breath of air, then held it as the slightly noxious gas reached face level. The jets continued to stream air on and around my body; then fans kicked in and the gas—and presumably any contaminants—was sucked out again. The door directly in front of me opened, so I stepped out and released the breath I'd been holding.

Janice flashed me another of those insincere smiles. "Now, if you'll just sit on the chair, I can give you the injection and you can be on your way."

I sat as requested and half smiled when I realized the cushion was heated. Nothing like a final piece of comfort for those you were intending to dissect.

As Janice moved across to the sterilizer, I said, *Cat, can you tell me the name of the drug she's about to use?*

Cat followed the woman and after a moment said, *It says Oxy45.*

Which was a synthetic opioid drug similar to morphine, but a thousand times stronger. In its purest form, as little as one drop could kill someone in a matter of minutes, but Oxy45 was mixed with several other drugs that countered the worst of its effects, rendering people unconscious within minutes without causing severe respiratory depression.

It was also an older drug, which meant there was a good chance that I'd either be immune to it or, at the very least, be able to erase it from my system.

I held out my arm and watched as Janice brought up a vein, then injected me. It felt like ice. I frowned and instantly began the process that would drop me into the healing state, but kept enough awareness to be able to move for at least a few more minutes.

"Right," she said, withdrawing the needle and spraying a sealer over the entry point. "That might initially feel a bit weird, but it won't last. Just sit there for a few minutes so we can be sure there's no side effects."

She glanced at her watch as she moved back to the sterilizer. The ice continued to slide through my veins, but there didn't seem to be any immediate effect. I certainly wasn't slipping into unconsciousness, although that didn't mean the drug *wouldn't* affect me. It might just mean it was going to take a bit longer. *Cat, Bear, I'm going to close my eyes and chase the drug from my system. I'll need you to be my eyes. Bring me back if anything untoward happens.*

Like the threat of dissection? Bear asked, amused.

Definitely wake me before that. I love you both, but I'm not ready to join you in the afterlife just yet.

Good, Cat said. *Because it'd be boring if you were one of us.*

You've obviously forgotten the past hundred years. It's only in the last couple of weeks that things have gotten exciting.

Yes. Her mental tones were wistful. *I will miss them all when they leave.*

So will I. So much so that I didn't even want to think about it. Jonas might have said he wanted to pursue the attraction, but that didn't mean he intended to stick around once he *had* done so. Cats were not by nature monogamous, even if those who lived in the cities tended to stick by the same one or two mates. But *that*, I suspected, was more due to the lack of choice than any real desire to remain faithful to one person.

Not that I *wanted* monogamy so much as company that was real rather than ghostly.

I closed my eyes and dropped fully into the healing state. I could still hear, though, even if I couldn't see. Not that it meant all that much; if Janice Harvey was moving about, then she was quieter than a ghost. Time seemed to stretch as I chased down the drug in my veins and carefully erased its coldness and its effects from my system.

"Righto, gentlemen," Harvey eventually said. "You can come retrieve your prize."

Had I not been in the trancelike healing state, the sudden sound of her voice in the void of silence would have made me jump. I pushed myself back to consciousness but kept my eyes firmly closed and my body loose. Relaxed.

One of the men snorted. "She's hardly a prize. She's all skin and damn bone."

"But skin and bone that might well hold the remaining key. Dump her in cell six. I'll inform lab two she's in. And no playing, remember?"

"I've got better taste than this."

Hands grabbed me, their grip bruising as they hauled me upright. With little ceremony, I was dragged out of the room.

Bear? Where are we going?

His energy whipped through me, creating the light connection that allowed me to see through his eyes. We continued on down the shorter corridor. The door at the end opened as we approached, revealing a T-intersection. Bear surged through the doorway and stopped in the middle of the T. To the left and the right were dozens of doors; each one, I suspected, would lead into a small laboratory.

The dissection rooms are situated on the other side of the building, Cat said. *That is where Sal is.*

And the holding cells?

To the right.

There were six in total. All of them were opened. All of them were empty.

Do you want to find out what's happened to the women, Cat? I knew deep down that they'd probably be in the dissection rooms, but part of me couldn't help hoping I was wrong. That they were simply undergoing a final check of some sort, and were safe and whole. Saving them might not be a priority, but I would if I could. Having them in the cells rather than on tables gave them a better chance. But if they were on the tables . . .

I shut the thought off, not wanting to think about it. Not yet.

The two men took me into the end cell on the left and dumped me facedown onto the single bunk. One adjusted my position so that I was in no danger of suffocating, then followed the other man out the door.

As the sound of their footsteps faded, I said, *Bear, spin slowly around so I can see what's in the room.*

He obeyed. It was little more than a two-by-two-meter

square that was barely big enough for the bed. There was nothing else in the room except for the camera perched squarely in one corner, aimed right at the bed. I couldn't do anything until that was taken care of.

I can short-circuit it, Bear suggested.

Good idea. But start with the other cells first. We don't want suspicions raised.

As he broke our connection, then raced off, Cat returned. *The women are in the dissection rooms.* Her mental tones were solemn. *They are being connected to the machines that will keep their flesh alive.*

So they're still alive?

At this point, yes.

Which meant if I wanted *any* hope of stopping the procedure and giving them a chance, I would have to act quickly.

Bear returned and sparks flew as the camera short-circuited. A few seconds later came the sound of running steps.

Guards, Bear supplied helpfully. *They're checking all the rooms.*

The heavy steps came closer and then someone who smelled faintly of garlic came into the room. "This one's out, too," he said, voice loud. "Why the hell would all six go out like that?"

"How the fuck would I know?" came the reply from the next room. "Do I look like a technician to you?"

"No, you look like a dick, but I won't hold that against you."

"Asshole," was the good-natured reply. "For that, you can report back to Tech Support."

Garlic Man snorted. "I can't see how it even matters. They're all comatose, so it's not like they can actually do anything."

"We're being paid good money to watch the near dead, so quit the grumbling and go report to the tech heads."

Garlic Man continued to grumble as he left the room. I opened my eyes and sat up. To get into the more secure areas I was going to have to either take out the guards or shut down the power for the entire floor. The former was definitely the easier option—one that would give me at least *some* time before anyone suspected something was wrong. How I was going to get out once someone *did* was another matter entirely—and a question I couldn't yet answer.

One thing was certain—Sharran could never come back here. She didn't deserve to end up on a dissection table—or worse—for agreeing to help us.

I sucked in the power of the lights and created a sun shield, then hurried down the hall after the guards, who were still good-naturedly ribbing each other. Obviously, they, like the scientists, saw absolutely nothing wrong in any of the experiments being conducted in this place.

It made me wonder if there was any hope for humanity as a whole, because nothing seemed to have been learned from the mistakes of the past. The déchet program had been the result of experiments such as the ones that were happening on this floor, and while I owed my existence to them, they were definitely something that should have been left in the dust of the past, right alongside the bones of all déchet.

Bear, can you go back to the doctor's lab and grab a knife and the sealant for me?

He raced away again and Cat pressed closer, her energy biting at my skin. *We are nearing the dissection laboratories.*

I know. The faint scent of blood rode the otherwise sterile air.

We should help the ones who lie open, even if it makes them ghosts.

Right now our priority has to be getting rid of Sal's body. If we have the time afterward, then we can do something.

We could short-circuit everything. That will stop the machines that keep them alive.

And drain you both. We can't help everyone, Cat. In a war, sacrifices have to made.

We are not at war.

Not yet. But the principles still apply. I sent her a mental hug, and wished I could do it for real. *I want to help these women as much as you, but it may yet come down to a choice of saving them or getting out of here.*

And we need to get out of here to save the children. She was silent for a moment, then said, *I'd feel bad about not helping them.*

So would I, Cat. So would I.

The two men swung into a room on the left. I hurried up and snuck in behind them. Inside, there was a long desk filled with an array of light screens, a huge, rather sturdy-looking metal cabinet, and a third guard.

Think you can take him out, Cat?

Yes.

The determination in her voice had a smile tugging at my lips. As the door behind us began to close, the third man turned and said, "Well? What's the problem?"

"Fucked if I know," Garlic Man's companion said. "It's a job for the tech assholes, not me. Jim's about to give them a call."

"Since when did that become my job? You're the one getting paid the supervisory money, not me."

Now, Cat, I said, then stepped closer, raised a fist, and punched Garlic Man as hard as I could. As he went down,

I swung and booted his companion in the balls. His breath left in a wheeze and—as he instinctively clutched himself and doubled over—I hit him again. He fell treelike across the prone form of the first guard. A grunt had me turning quickly; the third man toppled from his chair, an assault rifle hovering—butt first—a foot or so above him.

"Good work, Cat."

She preened. I stepped past her and opened the unlocked cabinet. It was filled with weapons, and by all rights should have been locked. The guards had obviously suspected the worst when Bear shorted the six cameras, and had simply grabbed their guns and headed out without relocking it. Which was good news for me; if things went wrong—and they more than likely would once I started destroying things—then at least I had an arsenal to use.

Once I released the sun shield, I patted the men down, relieving them of their weapons, then hit the door switch and partially opened it again. Bear might be able to slip through solid matter, but anything he was carrying wouldn't.

As I waited for him to return, I sat down at the desk and studied the various light screens. There were more guards situated inside what I presumed were the main labs, given their size and the number of people within them, but none in any of the dissection rooms—including the one that held Sal's body. Janice Harvey wasn't in the purification room and didn't seem to be anywhere else on the floor. The two guards who'd escorted me up here were also missing.

Unease stirred, but I shoved it aside. I could deal with them if and when I came across them. Right now I needed to find a way out, and then I needed to go finish what I'd started at Old Stan's.

I keyed in a search for floor plans, and after a second or two they popped up on the nearest screen. This level was basically broken into three squares—the inner, smallest being the elevator foyer, the second being a series of large labs, and the third being smaller labs and rooms such as the cells and the dissection laboratories that ran around the exterior walls. One main corridor ran around the entire floor, and the corridor that led from the elevators appeared to be the only way in and out.

I frowned and made the image larger. There had to be fire escapes somewhere—it was illegal to build without them. After another couple of minutes, I found one tucked into a corner of a lab near the lobby, but I couldn't see where it was accessed.

I can check, Cat suggested.

"Please."

She returned the rifle to the cabinet, then headed out just as Bear was coming in. He plunked a plastic bag in front of me. Inside was not only the sealer and scalpel I'd asked for, but a syringe and the Oxy45.

Thought the latter might be useful, he said.

"You thought right."

I quickly injected the three men, then began stripping the uniform from the man closest to my size. While I was incapable of taking on a male form, I could certainly alter my features and make everything appear a bit manlier.

With that done, I grabbed the scalpel and cut his RFID chip out of his arm. Blood pulsed over both his companions and the floor, an indication that I'd probably nicked a vein. Whether he'd bleed out or not I didn't know, and to be honest, I didn't really care.

I cleaned off the chip and then, using the sealant, secured it to my palm. It probably wouldn't last as long as the false skin Jonas had used, but it didn't really need to. Once I'd altered both my features and my scent enough that a causal glance might mistake me as male, I changed clothes.

Eww, Cat said, when she returned. *That form is not your finest.*

I smiled. "The fire escape?"

Locked but otherwise not blocked off.

Locks could be shot off, but did I want to be trapped in such a small space?

Did I have any other choice?

Not really. Not unless I totally shut down all power to this place, and I could only do that by studying the electrical plans and finding the isolation switches. That would take time, and time was something I might not have a whole lot of right now. Not if Janice's comment about notifying lab 2 that I was prepped and ready meant they would be coming to fetch me sooner rather than later.

I ran my stolen RFID chip over the scanner, ordered up the main security control screen, and systematically shut down all the cameras on this floor. I couldn't afford to have them active when I began destroying things, because I had no idea if they streamed anywhere else other than this floor. Shutting them all down might well result in alarms being raised, but the guards had made an initial report about the camera fault in the cells, so they might just think this was an extension of that.

I pushed away from the console and walked back over to the weapons cabinet. I slung several assault rifles over my shoulder, clipped a couple of smaller guns onto the hooks at my waist, then pocketed as much ammo as I could carry. Then I hit the button to fully open the door and strode purposefully down the hall. Several white-coated men passed me, but none paid me any attention. I followed the corridor around to the other side of the building, slowing only when I approached the lab that held Sal's body.

I took a deep breath, steeling myself against Rhea knows what, then ran the stolen RFID chip over the scanner and entered the lab.

He was lying on a table in the middle of the room, his body barely visible thanks to all the machines that were keeping his flesh viable. But I could see his face even though his skull lay open and his brain was exposed. The ugly mask of hatred—the very last expression he'd managed before the Sueño I'd used on him robbed him of life—was still frozen on his face.

I ignored the stubborn remnant of remorse within me despite knowing I'd had no other choice but to kill, and moved closer. The metallic click of the pump that had replaced his heart filled the silence and sent unease shivering down my spine.

Aside from the pump in his chest cavity, there was a dialysis machine as well as a myriad of other bits of equipment monitoring his various life signs. Although life was a misnomer in this case, because this *wasn't* life, only flesh being kept alive. His spirit—his consciousness—had long departed.

I continued on past the table and studied the rest of the lab, looking for some means of destroying his remains. Cutting the power wasn't really enough; I had to make sure there was absolutely nothing of him left that they could use to further their macabre plans. Which meant I had two options; either I needed to find a powerful acid that would destroy every scrap of flesh, muscle, and bone, or I'd have to create a chemical reaction that would have the same sort of effect. Given that there were plenty of chemicals in most labs, surely I'd be able to find something to use.

After a moment, I spotted a secure cabinet and walked across. Inside were half a dozen or so chemicals in heavy containers, all of them bearing warnings about toxicity and handling. I had no idea what any of them did, but several had "acid" as part of their name, so I grabbed them as well as the pair of heavy-duty gloves hanging inside the doors and walked back across.

And felt it.

A stirring of energy across the far side of the room.

I stopped. *Cat? Bear? Are you both okay?*

They assured me that they were and then Cat added, *But there is a ghost here.*

The unease I'd felt when I first stepped into this room leapt back into focus. Given the number of women who must have been killed on this floor over the years Sal and his partners were dissecting and experimenting, there were plenty of reasons for ghosts to be here.

Plenty of reasons *not* to be afraid of them.

But *this* ghost was in the same room as the body of a man I'd murdered. And I really, *really* didn't want it to be *him.*

Can you see it? Maybe even talk to it?

It hides its form, Cat said. *I'm not sure it's aware of our presence. It seems solely focused on what you're doing.*

The tension within me ratcheted another notch. *Keep it that way, but warn me if it moves.*

As their agreement ran through my mind, I pulled on the heavy gloves, then carefully undid the lids and lifted the first container.

But as I started to pour its contents over Sal's body, the ghosts screamed a warning and the container was ripped from my hands. It flew across the room, spilling liquid all over the floor before skidding across a table and smashing into several glass vials.

Then, on the other side of Sal's body, a figure began to form.

It wasn't the ghostly form of any of the women who'd died here.

It was, as I'd feared, Sal himself.

CHAPTER 14

He looked so real it was tempting to reach out and touch him. To once again feel the heat of life in the man I'd once considered my closest—and probably only—friend.

But while *he* was real, his solidity was little more than an illusion. The newly dead tended to cling to the shape they'd worn in life, but over time, that necessity generally faded. Eventually, he'd become as insubstantial as any of the ghosts who inhabited my bunker.

His energy touched me, creating a link between us. It was an oddly gentle—almost tentative—caress, and yet there was nothing gentle or tentative about his expression or the steely, cold glitter in his eyes.

He knew who I was. Despite the fact that I'd changed my appearance, he knew me. But then, he always had.

How did you survive the poison I administered?

"I was able to get an antidote before it could take full effect."

My Sal would have known the lie. But this one—the one who was a product of a rift and who contained the memories and the DNA of three others—seemed to remember very little about the war and our time together.

"Was it you who stole the two children yesterday?"

I raised an eyebrow. "You could hardly call it stealing; it was more a retrieval."

Amusement touched his beautiful features, but there was something behind it that sent all sorts of warnings skidding through my mind. Sal had never been the type to stand around and chat. That meant he was doing so for a reason.

It was then I remembered that the rift hadn't only merged their DNA, but created a mind link between them all—and there was no reason to presume that link had ended on his death.

Cat, Bear, you want to go watch the elevators and the stairwell? I've a bad feeling he might have called reinforcements.

As they raced off, Sal said, *So why come back here? Why risk your life like that?*

My smile held very little in the way of humor. "Why do you think I'm here?"

To erase my flesh so that it cannot be used.

"Glad to see that death hasn't affected your intelligence."

An odd sound caught my attention and I looked past him. Whatever had been in the vials the container had smashed through was causing a reaction—one that had white-yellow smoke curling toward the ceiling.

Was it strong enough to cause an explosion? There were certainly plenty of substances in laboratories that *could*, but—as far as I was aware—it was generally the noxious vapors generated when two incompatible substances were mixed that were the main problem. Some of those gases *were* flammable, but I had no idea whether there had to be an ignition source for that to happen. There were no open flames in this laboratory, nothing that I could use to start a fire with.

Except, maybe, the machines that were keeping Sal's body alive.

If the gases were strong enough—flammable enough— then maybe all I needed was a spark. Even an exposed wire might be enough.

I flexed my fingers and returned my gaze to Sal. New ghosts generally weren't in full control of their abilities, nor were they overly strong. He might have wrenched the container from my hand, but that, combined with his insistence on appearing solid, would weaken him.

If I was fast enough, I might just be able to do what I'd come here to do.

"You always were a little idealistic," he said. "It was your downfall in the past, and I'm afraid it will be your downfall now."

"They've got to catch me first, Sal."

"It would be one against hundreds, and you are a lure, not a fighter." The smile that tugged his lips didn't erase the cold calculation from his eyes.

My muscles were wound so tight my body was practically humming. I placed my hands on the table and leaned forward, as if I were trying to get closer to him. "I will die before I let those men or your partners take me alive."

"Good," he said. "It will save us the effort of killing you. But rest assured we will dispose of your body in an appropriate manner—after we've dissected every part of you, of course, and gathered every scrap of information we might need."

Two elevators filled with guards just arrived, Bear said. *They're running toward you.*

Meaning my time had just run out.

"Sorry, Sal." I shifted my grip on the table. "But that's not happening, either."

I kicked the second bottle of acid and, as its contents spilled across the floor, heaved the table up and over. Wires and IVs tore from both his body and several of the machines, while other machines toppled over, hitting the floor with a resounding crash. As the table landed with Sal face-first in the liquid, I grabbed a gun and fired at the nearest machines. Sparks flew; then, with a huge whoosh, fire erupted.

Bitch! Sal's voice was filled with anger. Energy surged, but it wasn't aimed at me. The table holding his body shifted several feet to the left, but it didn't stop either the fire or the liquid from consuming his flesh. His ghostly body wavered, fading in and out of existence. He was close to his limits, but that didn't mean anything. He'd never had much respect for limits when he was alive—I doubted that had changed in death.

The guards are in the main corridor, Bear warned.

As fire alarms began to shriek and sprinklers dropped from the ceiling, I leapt over the table and ran through the fire and the water—not toward the door, but rather the other table. Thick smoke was still issuing from the chemical mix that was now dripping onto the floor, but there were still unbroken vials on the table and they were my next target. *Cat, is the fire escape clear?*

So far, yes.

I skidded under the table, then rose and braced it against my back. With a grunt of effort, I straightened, flipping the table onto its side. Glass vials and various other apparatus smashed to the floor, their contents quickly mingling with the fluids already there. There was a flash of light and then a huge *whoomp*, and I was blasted several feet backward. I hit the wall with a grunt and slithered to the floor, my breath a rasp, my throat burning, and my clothes on fire. I swore and scrambled, on hands and knees, under the nearest sprinkler, letting the water douse the flames even as I became aware of the heat in my feet. I twisted around; the soles of my shoes were melting.

The acid.

I swore, but resisted the urge to rip them off and go barefoot. Right now there was an ocean of chemicals between me and the door, and what was left of these boots was all I had between my feet and said chemicals.

The guards are nearing the lab, Bear warned. *You need to get out. Now.*

I pushed upright and ran for the door. Caught a flash of movement out of the corner of my eye and ducked instinctively. The chair that would have sent me sprawling hit the wall behind me instead and clattered to the floor in several pieces.

I spun, raised a gun, and fired at the ghost trying to stop me. He reacted as he would have had he still been flesh—he flung himself to one side, and the bullets hit several machines instead. Sparks flew, reigniting the smoke, creating a wave of liquid heat that roared toward me.

I swore again and lunged at the door, waving my hand across the scanner, then all but rolling into the corridor. The wave chased me out, boiling the air around me and making it difficult to breathe. Hands grabbed my arms and pulled me clear.

Guards, not ghosts.

I twisted, kicking one in the face before lunging around and biting the other. He swore and released me. As I fell backward, I raised the gun and fired. The two men went down as one, their brains splattering across the wall behind them.

More figures loomed beyond the smoke and fire. I unleashed several more shots and the guards split, some going into the labs on the left, the others to those on the right. I rolled upright and bolted in the opposite direction.

My feet were truly on fire now, but I couldn't stop. Bullets were pinging off the walls around me, several of them cutting through my stolen uniform and tearing into flesh. Pain was beginning to bloom everywhere, but I ignored it and kept running. I had to reach that fire escape to have any hope of getting out of here.

Bear, is the way clear up ahead?

His energy zoomed past me and then, after a moment, the image of two guards flashed into my mind. They were around the corner, standing between me and the lab that held the fire escape, their weapons at the ready.

A bullet ripped through my thigh and I stumbled, my fingers brushing the floor as I battled to keep upright. I grabbed a second gun, then twisted around and unleashed a barrage of bullets. When both guns were empty, I clipped them onto the belt hooks and pulled one of the assault rifles free.

Bear, create a noise behind the men ahead.

I pressed back against the wall, keeping an eye on the corridor behind me as I listened for Bear. There was a soft clatter, and then something round and metallic rolled toward me. Grenade. Or maybe a smoke bomb. I shot it. The thing exploded, firing sharp shards into the air that thudded into the metal walls and tore into my left calf; a heartbeat later, there was a second explosion down at the other end.

Bear's diversion.

I ducked around the corner, raised the rifle, and fired repeatedly. The man facing me went down, blood pouring from a shattered right hand and a gut wound. The other man twisted around and returned fire. I was out in the open and had no protection. Bullets thudded into my thigh and my arm. My legs went out from underneath me, and my knees hit the floor.

This was it. I wasn't going to escape.

A fire ax appeared out of nowhere and smashed across the guard's head. Blood flew as he fell sideways, his finger still on the trigger and the bullets tearing a path up the nearby wall and onto the ceiling.

The weapon was wrenched from his grasp and flung sideways, and then Bear was next to me. *Up, up,* he said, his energy on my arm, trying to lift me. *The guards are coming.*

I can't—

Try, he growled, tugging at me again.

I took a deep breath, then, somehow, managed to climb to my feet. But there was a roaring in my ears and I wasn't sure if it was the sound of the approaching security forces or the pounding of my blood as it poured from my many wounds.

I staggered forward. As I neared the guards, I heard a voice scream, "Alive, I want her alive!"

Then something smashed into my back and sent me sprawling. Energy surged, a dangerous force my two little ghosts were gathering in an effort to defend me.

Don't, I somehow said as the shadows of unconsciousness threatened. *Wait. They want me alive, so there's still a chance of escape.*

But what—

I didn't hear the rest of Bear's question.

The shadows claimed me and I knew no more.

CHAPTER 15

Waking was a slow and painful process. Not only because my body was a maze of heated agony, but also because someone was systematically slapping my face.

We can fix that, Bear said. *Just give the word.*

Not until I'm sure I can move. Where am I?

In Rath Winter's office, Cat said. *He's the one slapping you.*

"Why isn't she waking?"

The voice was deep, dark, and male. Rath Winter, I knew, simply because I'd heard his voice before, after he'd rung Sal when I was staying with him.

"You're damn lucky she's even alive, given the number of bullet wounds littering her body." The second speaker was also familiar—it was Janice Harvey. "Just be thankful for small mercies, and give the drugs time to work."

"We may not *have* time. We have to presume what we're doing here is—or soon will be—common knowledge."

"You've notified the authorities that there's been a chemical spill and that the hazmat team is dealing with it." This speaker's voice was warm, smoky, and unfamiliar. "It buys us a couple of hours, at least."

Winter grunted. "Unless that fucking witch uses her family connections to force the issue."

"Which I can counter if delay is necessary."

Winter slapped me again. My face stung and it was all I could do to remain still. To have any hope of getting free and out of here, I had to at least be able to walk. And that meant I needed to heal. Whether that was possible given Winter's determination to force me awake was another matter entirely.

I tried to concentrate, to ignore the pain in my body, the heat in my feet, the restricting tightness of the rope that bound my arms behind my back, but no matter how hard I tried, I simply couldn't fall into the trancelike state that was necessary for healing.

My face stung with the force of another blow. I swore silently. Healed or not, I was going to get out of here. But not before I killed the bastard hitting me.

"How much fucking longer is this going to take?" Winter said.

"Going by the vital signs, she's waking, so not long."

Meaning I was not only tied but hooked up to monitoring machines.

Via an IV in your wrists and monitors on your chest and temples, Cat said.

None of which I could feel right now. But they wouldn't provide much in the way of impediment once my hands were free. *Who else is in the room?*

Winter, Harvey, and the two guards who escorted you up to the twenty-ninth floor, Bear said. *There's also two guards on the other side of the door.*

And plenty more between the ground floor and us. To get out I was going to need more than luck, especially in my current condition.

What about the other woman I heard?

She's watching via a comm unit.

Of course she was. It was too much to hope that all my targets would be nearby. They weren't that stupid.

And Sal?

Still downstairs, with his body.

Which was something of a surprise. While new ghosts did tend to stick close to their remains in the weeks or even months after their death, I'd expected Sal to want revenge deeply enough to be here, watching. *Does that mean the acid and the fire didn't consume his flesh?*

It is mostly destroyed, Cat replied. *Just feet, skull, and a few fingers remain.*

Which might still give them enough to work with if this place wasn't shut down. *Are the guards here armed?*

Yes.

What happened to my weapons?

They threw them on the table along with your clothes.

So I'm naked? Not that it really mattered. Nudity and I were old companions.

Yes—and in your own skin.

No surprise there. With my energy levels so low, my body would have instinctively reverted to preserve strength. *Entry and exit points?*

Aside from the main doors, there are exits to the right and the left.

Fire escapes?

No. They lead to the rooms that hold the false rifts.

Someplace I did *not* want to go. Not in this condition. *What about the wounds?*

You healed your back, calf, and thigh when you were unconscious, Cat said. *But there are many more wounds on your torso that still bleed.*

That wasn't entirely surprising, given how many times I'd been hit by bullets and metal shards, but how in Rhea had my body even healed the three worst wounds? I had to be in the healing state, not an unconscious one, for that to happen. *Is it possible for one of you to untie my hands without anyone noticing?*

There was a slight hesitation, and then Bear said, *If you wake and talk to them, their attention will be on you rather than on what might be happening behind you.*

Keep an eye on the guards, then, Cat. Warn Bear if they look our way.

Will do.

I groaned softly, let my neck roll back and my eyes flutter open.

"Finally," Winter muttered.

He stood in front of me, a thin-faced man with shadowed skin, magnetic blue eyes, and a ragged, ugly scar that ran down the side of his face from his temple to his jaw. I'd seen scars like that before, on the remains of those who'd been unfortunate enough to come across a wraith. Winter had been the closest to the wraith when he and the others encountered it in the rift, and the fact that he'd survived was testament to his strength and his courage. It was also a warning that I should not underestimate him.

I looked past him. Harvey was standing slightly to his left, watching the various monitors.

I blinked, swallowed, then said, "Who the hell are you?"

My voice was little more than a rasp of air, the question almost inaudible. Winter raised an eyebrow and glanced at Harvey. She adjusted a dial; cold liquid raced into my veins and the chill sent shivers through my body. I had no idea what it was, but my heart began beating faster and I suddenly felt stronger. How long that feeling would last I had no idea, but I suspected I better make use of it while I could.

Bear, untie the ropes. Cat, go over to the table with the guns. If the guards move, unleash hell.

My pleasure.

I lifted my gaze and met Winter's. He smiled; it was the sort of expression a cat gave its prey a second before it devoured it.

"I'm surprised you haven't guessed."

Energy began tugging at the bindings on my wrists. "Oh, I know you're one of Sal's partners. I just don't know who or what you were before you killed Rath Winter and stole his life."

He raised an eyebrow. "*That* is not important. What did you do with the two children you stole from us?"

I echoed his expression, mocking him. "*That* hardly matters, given you won't ever get your hands on them again." I switched my gaze to Harvey. "Why are you helping these people? What do you gain out of giving the vampires light immunity?"

"I get the satisfaction of seeing the shifters annihilated," she said. "I get to see them torn apart, as my kin were torn apart in the war."

I frowned. "You're not old enough to have been alive in the war."

"No, but my grandparents were war survivors. The things they saw . . . It changed them."

Embittered them, from the sound of it, and they'd passed it on to their children and grandchildren. "The vampires won't just kill shifters. They'll destroy us all."

"Not us. We have a deal with them."

Almost there, Bear said.

I glanced at Winter. "How in hell did you get her to swallow *that* sort of bullshit? Because you and I know once the light no longer stops them, the vampires will run amok."

He smiled. Chills skidded down my spine. There was nothing pleasant about that look. Nothing human about the light in his eyes.

"It's not difficult when it's the truth." He lunged forward, wrapped his fingers around my neck, and shoved his face close to mine. His breath, filled with dead things, washed across my face. "Where are the children?"

"I don't know." It came out as a wheeze. "We were met by mercenaries out on the old City Road, and they were taken away."

The bastard's grip tightened. "Who took them away?"

"I don't know. Nuri doesn't exactly share information like that with someone like me." My hands were beginning to tingle as the ties binding them loosened and blood rushed back into my fingers.

Nearly done. There was weariness in Bear's mental tones. I'd pushed them to their limits today, and it made my heart want to weep. Especially given that it wasn't over yet.

Winter stared at me, his gaze boring into mine, as if trying to unearth the secrets from my brain. After a moment, he snorted and released me. "No, I guess she wouldn't. Especially when she's got shifters on her staff. It's a wonder you're still alive."

"She needs me." *Cat,* I added silently. *Get ready to toss me one of the assault rifles.*

"Give her the truth drug." Winter turned and walked across to the huge desk that dominated the other side of the room.

Undone, Bear said.

Cat, get ready. I waited until Harvey's concentration was on the monitors rather than me, then ripped the IVs from my arm and threw myself sideways. I was out of the chair and rolling away from it even before it hit the floor. As Winter twisted around, Cat tossed me the rifle. I plucked it from the air, flipped it around, and unleashed at the guards. As they went down, the doors opened and two more men spilled into the room. I shot them as well, then jackknifed around and aimed at Winter. But he'd already disappeared behind the rather old-fashioned but solid-looking wooden desk. A second later, an alarm sounded, its shriek so loud it hurt my ears.

"Help is on its way," Winter shouted. "There's no escape for you, Tiger. This time, you *will* die."

"Like *fuck* I will."

I tore the remaining monitors from my chest and temples and sat up. I couldn't see Winter, but Harvey was cowering behind one of the monitors, her expression terrified.

"Please," she said. "I can help you . . ."

"Like you helped the children? Like you helped those women being dissected on the tables?" She didn't reply, which only increased my fury. "How can you justify what is happening here? How can you even *sleep* at night, knowing what is being done to those women, let alone to the *children*?"

"They are shifters—"

"They are *children*," I yelled, and, without a second thought, shot her.

As she fell lifeless to the floor, I grabbed the chair and used it as a brace as I forced my battered body upright. It hurt. Everything *hurt*. But that wasn't going to stop me from confronting the man cowering behind the desk. Nothing would, not even the guards who were undoubtedly on their way thanks to that damn alarm.

The effort of standing left me light-headed. I sucked in several large gulps of air, then hobbled toward the desk. My two little ghosts joined me, their energy tingling across my skin, offering moral support but not strength. They were too close to exhaustion themselves.

And, Rhea help us all, I still needed their help.

Cat, I said, my gaze not wavering from the desk and the man still hiding behind it. *Go to the foyer and let me know when the reinforcements get here. Bear, close the doors and then see if you can find some way to short them out.*

As they raced off, I raised the rifle and shot at the desk. The bullet thudded into the wood, sending deadly splinters flying but doing little else. As I drew closer, I realized why. The desk might look like valuable wood, but underneath its skin lay metal—and not just any metal but, from the look of it, armored plating. No wonder the bastard was hiding behind it. I took a step sideways, and saw that the foot well area had been totally sealed. Winter obviously had every intention of sitting inside his safe little box until reinforcements got here.

"Well, well, well," a sultry, smoky voice said. "Sal was right. You *are* extremely resourceful."

My gaze jerked up to the light screen on the desk. The speaker was the dark-skinned woman I'd followed into the rift at Carleen—the one that had led to Government House. As my gaze met the green of hers, that odd sense of familiarity ran through me again. "I know you."

"No surprise, given you followed me into the rift," she said. "How did you manage that?"

"Magic." I limped around the desk, studying the bolts

holding it in place. There were only two—one at either side rather than at each of the corners—but they were sturdy and undoubtedly drilled deep into the concrete.

"Give up the children, Tiger, and we might just let you live."

"I've seen your version of living in the labs downstairs," I replied. "Thanks, but no, thanks."

Guards are here, Cat said. *Ten in each elevator.*

Bear?

Almost—he paused—*sealed.*

I limped to the nearest bolt, aimed the assault rifle, and fired repeatedly. Dust and concrete flew, becoming a cloud thick enough to make me cough. By the time the clip had run out, a deep trench had been dug around the bolt. Bear carried over more ammo; I reloaded and continued.

The men are outside the door, Cat warned. *They are attempting to break in.*

It'll take them a while to do that. If Winter—or whoever he truly was—had fortified his desk, I was pretty sure he would have done the same to the doors.

I kept firing at the concrete, until the ends of the bolts were finally revealed. I repeated the process on the other side, using every scrap of ammo I had, then pulled the two anchoring bolts free and tossed them to one side.

"You can shoot all you want, but it won't do you any good," Winter said into the silence. "This cabinet is fully sealed and impregnable."

"Maybe," I said. "And maybe not."

I limped over to the two dead guards, picked up their weapons, then limped back. The woman was still watching me, her expression amused; condescending. It made me wish I could reach into the light screen and throttle her.

"I do not understand what you hope to achieve here," she

said. "You're trapped and you *will* die. You know it, I know it."

"What I know," I said, "is that the person currently known as Rath Winter is about to die. And when I've done that, I'm coming after you. And *that's* a promise."

I raised the handgun and shot the control box sitting on the top of the desk. The light screen flickered, then died. I clipped the weapon to my belt, then pressed my hands against one end of the desk and heaved with all my might. The desk slid several feet forward, but the effort left my head swimming. I sucked in a breath and pushed again. Another few feet forward.

Inside his metal fortress, Winter squawked, "What the fuck are you doing?"

"You said the desk was impregnable," I replied, with another push. Something tore in my calf and warmth began to pulse down my leg. I ignored it. "But I'm figuring it's not immune to the laws of gravity or a thirty-floor drop."

Bear joined me at the end of the desk, and together we moved it another few feet forward.

"You can't have taken out the windows. They're bulletproof."

"You keep thinking that, if it makes you feel any better."

We shifted the desk again, but this time little more than a few inches. I let my head drop and sucked in air. My body was trembling with fatigue. I was soaked with blood and sweat, and almost out of time.

I was trapped in this office as Winter was in his box.

A sharp, almost metallic whine bit into the silence. *They're using a drill on the locks,* Cat said. *They said it will take ten minutes.*

Which meant I had half of that to finish my task here and figure a way out.

But how?

If Winter held his nerve and stayed in his box, then everything I'd done here—everything I'd gone through—was for naught. Fury rose and I shoved at the desk violently.

As I did, Bear screamed, *Duck!*

I obeyed without question. The windows lining Winter's office exploded inward, showering the room with a deadly rain of glass. When it stopped, I carefully peered around the edge of the desk.

All that remained of the windows immediately in front of the desk were the broken remnants of the frames that had once held them. I guess the windows weren't bulletproof after all.

I glanced beyond them and saw—standing on the rooftop of the building opposite and holding the biggest damn gun I'd ever seen—Jonas.

And he was waving.

Bear, go see what he wants. I heaved the desk again. This time, it slid right to the very edge. A few feet more and we'd all find out how well metal boxes could fly.

The guards are almost through, Cat warned. *You have a few minutes, if that.*

I braced myself for one more effort, but before I could do anything, the back of the desk opened and the rat threw himself out of his hole.

I grabbed my weapon and fired, but my hands were shaking so badly I got everything except Winter. He rolled to his feet and sprinted away. I kept firing; the bullets nipped at his heels but did no damage.

Jonas says run, Bear said.

I glanced across at the other building, saw Jonas raise what looked like a bazooka, and bolted, with every scrap of speed I could muster, for the nearest side door—one on the opposite side of the room from Winter.

The guards are through, Cat screamed. *Run faster!*

I couldn't. There was nothing left in the tank now. The main doors were kicked open and men flowed into the room. There was no time for finesse now; I launched myself at the side door, twisted around, and hit it feetfirst. A scream of pain tore up my throat, but the door slammed back hard and I was through. As I hit the ground and rolled to the side, there was a huge *whoomp* behind me, and the office literally exploded. I threw my hands over my head, my ears ringing as heat and concrete and Rhea only knows what else punched through the air. As silence and dust began to fall around me, I crawled back to the wall and peered around the door. All I could see were shattered remnants, be they building or men.

Cat, where's Winter?

Wait. Then. *Crawling toward the other rift.*

For Rhea's sake, why wouldn't the bastard just *die*? Then the rest of her sentence impacted and I became aware of the sting of energy across my skin. I slowly turned. Sitting in the middle of the long, wide room was the biggest damn rift I'd ever seen. This time there was no inky wall of darkness to hide its presence, and its gelatinous, gently spinning surface ran with ragged thrusts of foul-looking lightning. It felt dark, dangerous, and I couldn't help wondering if this was one rift I was better off leaving alone.

But *that* was a question for another day.

I sucked in a breath and then, using the wall as a brace, pushed upright. My head swam and my knees buckled. I swore and concentrated on remaining upright. On remaining conscious.

"Tiger?"

Jonas's voice. I waved a hand; I didn't dare do anything more, lest I topple.

Footsteps approached and then he appeared, an angel dressed in full corps battle gear. He lifted his visor. His expression was grim, his eyes hard. "You're a mess."

"But a mess that's alive, thanks to you." My voice came out scratchy. Hoarse. I swallowed heavily, but it didn't seem to help the aching dryness in my throat. "Why are you here?"

"Because I knew you were in trouble."

"You knew? Not Nuri?"

"Call it a shared realization. And no, I will not explain that right now." Amusement glimmered briefly in his eyes. I wondered if he'd caught the half-formed thought, or whether he simply knew me well enough to guess. "Corps are evacuating the building, and despite the uniform I've borrowed, we aren't out of the woods yet. Let's get out of here."

"We can't—"

"Tiger—" Exasperation filled his voice. "We have only a small window of confusion in which to make—"

"Winter's alive," I cut in. "And heading for a rift."

Something entered his eyes. Something that was as dark as the rift in the room and just as deadly. "That," he said softly, "cannot be allowed."

"No." I pushed myself away from the wall. "Let's go."

"You are in no state—"

"Ranger, just stop arguing and do as I ask for once."

"If all déchet had been as stubborn as you, we might have lost the war." He shouldered his weapon, then shoved an arm around my body to support me as we headed into the broken remains of Winter's office.

"Stubbornness is born out of emotion and having

something to care about," I replied. "Most déchet had neither of those."

"Or you just got more than your fair share of it," he muttered.

I smiled, then caught sight of the jet pack sitting on top of Winter's desk. "How did you get that? I thought they were rarer than hen's teeth."

"They are these days, but I've been a mercenary for a very long time." He skirted around a huge chunk of ceiling concrete. "There isn't much I *can't* get my hands on."

Hurry, Cat said. *Winter is near the rift. It spins.*

Jonas must have heard her, because he cursed, swung me fully into his arms, and ran. We all but flew across the rest of the office and through the open doorway into the next room. This was a replica of the one on the other side, but the rift here was slightly smaller. Winter was midway down the room, dragging his body toward the slowly spinning rift, leaving in his wake a bloody trail. Both his feet had been blown off.

Jonas deposited me against the nearest wall, then strode forward, grabbed Winter by his calves, and dragged him back.

Winter screamed and fought, kicking and punching, to little effect. Jonas simply dragged him back to me, then planted a heavy boot on the back of Winter's neck, mashing his face into the carpet. Winter continued to scream, but the sound was muffled and accompanied by odd gurgling sounds.

Jonas's gaze rose to mine. "Do you want the honor?"

I sucked in a deep breath, then slowly shook my head. "You do it."

For Penny, and for all the other children. I didn't say

those words, but I didn't need to. He heard them anyway. I saw it in his eyes.

He flipped his rifle from over his shoulder, aimed, and fired.

Rath Winter's head exploded and his body stilled.

The bastard was finally dead.

Relief swept me, a tide so strong my knees buckled and I fell sideways. Jonas swore and lunged forward, somehow managing to catch me before I hit the bloody floor.

"Now we get you out of here." His voice was grim. "Corps are on their way up. We can't be found here—they had orders not to enter this floor."

Orders given by the woman with the smoky voice and leaf green eyes, no doubt.

"If the jet pack can't be traced back to you, leave it," I said. "Take me down to twenty-nine instead."

He took off his coat and wrapped it around my body, then swung me into his arms again and strode back into the office. "What's down there?"

"Dissections." I rested the side of my face against his chest and listened to the steady beat of his heart. It was an oddly soothing sound. "And women who can still be saved."

I hoped.

"There's only one woman I care about saving right now." His voice was grim. "You need urgent medical attention—"

"I can heal myself, but they can't. Please, Jonas. It'll be our way out. Bear, show him."

After several moments, Jonas swore. He shifted his grip on me, then punched the elevator call button and said in a gruff voice that wasn't his own, "This is four-five. I've reached the twenty-ninth floor. I need medical teams in hazmat suits up here immediately. I'm bringing one badly

injured woman down, but there are at least six others needing urgent attention."

I didn't hear the response. Jonas was obviously wearing
an earpiece. The elevator door opened, and he stepped inside
and pressed the ground-floor button before waving what
looked like a plastic card across the scanner. The doors
closed and the elevator quickly began to descend.

But not as quickly as the darkness descending on me.
But this time it was okay. I was safe. My two little ghosts
were safe. Jonas would get us all out of here, and I would
recover.

I *had* to recover.

I had a promise to keep.

DON'T MISS THE FIRST NOVEL
IN KERI ARTHUR'S SOULS OF FIRE SERIES,

FIREBORN

NOW AVAILABLE FROM SIGNET SELECT

All of us dream.
Some of us even have pleasant dreams.

My dreams might have been few and far between, but they were never, ever pleasant. But worse than that, they always came true.

Over the course of my many lifetimes, I'd tried to interfere, to alter fate's path and prevent the death I'd seen, but I'd learned the hard way that there were often serious consequences for both the victim and myself.

Which was why the flesh down my spine was twisted and marred. I'd pulled a kid from a burning car, saving her life but leaving us both disfigured. Fire may be mine to control and devour, but there'd been too many witnesses and I'd dared not use my powers. It had taken me months to heal, and I'd sworn—yet again—to stop interfering and simply let fate take her natural course. But here I was, out on the streets in the cold, dead hours of the night, trying to keep warm as I waited in the shadows for the man who was slated to die this night.

Because he wasn't just *a* man. He was the man I'd once loved.

I shifted my weight from one foot to the other and tried to keep warm in the confines of the abandoned factory's doorway. Why anyone would even come out by choice on a night like this was beyond me. Melbourne was a great city, but her winters could be hell, and right now it was cold enough to freeze the balls off a mutt—not that there were any mutts about at this particular hour. They apparently had more sense.

The breeze whisked around the parts of my face not protected by my scarf, freezing my skin and making it feel like I was breathing ice.

Of course, I *did* have other ways to keep warm. I was a phoenix—a spirit born from the ashes of flame—and fire was both my heritage and my soul. But even if I couldn't sense anyone close by, I was reluctant to flame. Vampires and werewolves might have outed themselves during the peak of Hollywood's love affair with all things paranormal, but the rest of us preferred to remain hidden. Humanity on the whole might have taken the existence of weres and vamps better than any of us had expected, but there were still far too many who believed nonhumans provided an unacceptable risk to their existence. Even on crappy nights like this, it wasn't unusual to have hunting parties roaming the streets, looking for easy paranormal targets. While my kind rarely provided any sort of threat, I wasn't human, and that made me as much a target for their hate as vamps and weres.

Even the man who'd once claimed to love me was not immune to such hate.

Pain stirred, distant and ghostly, but never, ever forgotten, no matter how hard I tried. Samuel Turner had made it all too clear what he thought of my "type." Five years might have passed, but I doubted time would have changed his view that the only good monster was a dead one.

And yet here I was, attempting to save his stupid ass.

The roar of a car engine rode across the silence. For a moment the dream raised its head, and I saw again the flashes of metal out of the car window, the red-cloaked faces, the blood and brain matter dripping down brick as Sam's lifeless body slumped to the wet pavement. My stomach heaved and I closed my eyes, sucking in air and fighting the feeling of inevitability.

Death would *not* claim his soul tonight.

I wouldn't let her.

Against the distant roar of that engine came the sound of steady steps from the left of the intersection up ahead. He was walking toward the corner and the death that awaited him there.

I stepped out of the shadows. The glow of the streetlights did little to break up the night, leaving the surrounding buildings to darkness and imagination. The ever-growing rumble of the car approaching from the right didn't quite drown out the steady sound of footsteps, but perhaps it only seemed that way because I was so attuned to it. To what was about to happen.

I walked forward, avoiding the puddles of light and keeping to the darker shadows. The air was thick with the growing sense of doom and the rising ice of hell.

Death waited on the other side of the street, her dark rags billowing and her face impassive.

The growling of the car's engine swept closer. Lights

broke across the darkness, the twin beams of brightness spotlighting the graffiti that colored an otherwise bleak and unforgiving cityscape.

This area of Brooklyn was Melbourne's dirty little secret, one definitely *not* mentioned in the flashy advertising that hailed the city as the "it" holiday destination. It was a mix of heavy industrial and run-down tenements, and it housed the underbelly of society—the dregs, the forgotten, the dangerous. Over the past few years, it had become so bad that the wise avoided it and the newspapers had given up reporting about it. Hell, even the cops feared to tread the streets alone here. These days they did little more than patrol the perimeter in a vague attempt to stop the violence from spilling over into neighboring areas.

So why the hell was Sam right here in the middle of Brooklyn's dark heart?

I had no idea and, right now, with Death so close, it hardly mattered.

I neared the fatal intersection and time slowed to a crawl. A deadly, dangerous crawl.

The Commodore's black nose eased into the intersection from the right. Windows slid down smoothly, and the long black barrels of the rifles I'd seen in my dream appeared. Behind them, half-hidden in the darkness of the car's interior, red hoods billowed.

Be fast, my inner voice whispered, *or die.*

Death stepped forward, eager to claim her soul. I took a deep, shuddering breath and flexed my fingers.

Sam appeared past the end of the building and stepped toward the place of his death. The air recoiled as the bullets were fired. There was no sound. *Silencers.*

I lunged forward, grabbed his arm, and yanked him hard enough sideways to unbalance us both. Something sliced across my upper arm, and pain flared as I hit the pavement. My breath whooshed loudly from my lungs, but it didn't cover the sound of the unworldly scream of anger. Knowing what was coming, I desperately twisted around, flames erupting from my fingertips. They met the sweeping, icy scythe of Death, melting it before it could reach my flesh. Then they melted *her*, sending her back to the frigid realms of hell.

The car screeched to a halt farther down the street, the sound echoing sharply across the darkness. I scrambled to my feet. The danger wasn't over yet. He could still die, and we needed to get out of here—*fast*. I spun, only to find myself facing a gun.

"What the—" Blue eyes met mine and recognition flashed. "Red! What the *fuck* are you doing here?"

There was no warmth in his voice, despite the use of my nickname.

"In case it has escaped your notice," I snapped, trying to concentrate on the danger and the need to be gone rather than on how good he damn well looked, "someone just tried to blow your brains out—although it *is* debatable whether you actually have brains. Now move, because they haven't finished yet."

He opened his mouth, as ready as ever to argue, then glanced past me. The weapon shifted fractionally, and he pulled the trigger. As the bullet burned past my ear, I twisted around. A red-cloaked body lay on the ground five feet away, the hood no longer covering his features. His face was gaunt, emaciated, and there was a thick black scar on his right cheek that ended in a hook. It looked like Death's scythe.

The footsteps coming toward us at rapid speed said there were another four to deal with. Sam's hand clamped my wrist; then he was pulling me forward.

"We won't outrun them," I said, even as we tried to do just that.

"I know." Sam's voice was grim. Dark.

Sexy.

I batted the thought away and risked another glance over my shoulder. They'd rounded the corner and were now so close I could see their gaunt features, their scars, and the red of their eyes.

Fear shuddered through me. Whatever these things were, they *weren't* human.

"We need somewhere to hide." I scanned the buildings around us somewhat desperately. Broken windows, shattered brickwork, and rot abounded. Nothing offered the sort of fortress we so desperately needed right now.

"I *know*." He yanked me to the right, just about pulling my arm out of the socket in the process. We pounded down a small lane that smelled of piss and decay, our footsteps echoing across the night. It was a sound that spoke of desperation.

The red cloaks were quiet. Eerily quiet.

A metal door appeared out of the shadows. Sam paused long enough to fling it open, then thrust me inside and followed, slamming the door shut and then shoving home several thick bolts.

Just in time.

Something hit the other side of the door, the force of it enough to dent the metal and make me jump back in fright. Fire flicked across my fingertips, an instinctive reaction I quickly doused as Sam turned around.

"*That* won't help." His voice was grim, but it still held echoes of the distaste that had dominated his tone all those years ago. "We need to get upstairs. *Now*," he added, as the door shuddered under another impact.

He brushed past me and disappeared into the gloom of the cavernous building. I unraveled the scarf from around my face and hastily followed. "What the hell are those things? And why do they want to kill you?"

"Long story." He reached a grimy set of stairs and took them two at a time. The metal groaned under his weight, but the sound was smothered by another hit to the door. This time, something broke.

"Hurry," he added rather unnecessarily.

I galloped after him, my feet barely even hitting the metal. We ran down a corridor, stirring the dust that clung to everything until the air was thick and difficult to breathe. From downstairs came a metallic crash—the door coming off its hinges and smashing to the concrete.

They were in. They were coming.

Fear leapt up my throat, and this time the flames that danced across my fingertips would not be quenched. The red-gold flickers lit the darkness, lending the decay and dirt that surrounded us an odd sort of warmth.

Sam went through another doorway and hit a switch on the way through. Light flooded the space, revealing a long, rectangular room. In the left corner, as far away from the door as possible, was a rudimentary living area. Hanging from the ceiling on thick metal cables was a ring of lights that bathed the space in surreal violet light.

"Don't tell me you live here," I said as I followed Sam across the room.

He snorted. "No. This is merely a safe house. One of five we have in this area."

The problems in this area were obviously far worse than anyone was admitting if cops now needed safe houses. Or maybe it was simply a development linked to the appearance of the red cloaks. Certainly I hadn't come across anything like them before, and I'd been around for centuries. "Will the UV lighting stop those things?"

He glanced at me. "You can see that?"

"Yes." I said it tartly, my gaze on his, searching for the distaste and the hate. Seeing neither. "I'm not human, remember?"

He grunted and looked away. Hurt stirred again, the embers refusing to die, even five years down the track.

"UV stops them." He paused, then added, "Most of the time."

"Oh, that's a comfort," I muttered, the flames across my fingers dousing as I thrust a hand through my hair. "What the hell are they, then? Vampires? They're the only nonhumans I can think of affected by UV."

And they certainly hadn't *looked* like vampires. Most vamps tended to look and act human, except for the necessity to drink blood and avoid sunlight. None that I'd met had red eyes or weird scars on their cheeks—not even the psycho ones who killed for the pure pleasure of it.

"They're a type of vampire."

He pulled out a rack filled with crossbows, shotguns, and machine pistols from under the bed, then waved a hand toward it, silently offering me one of the weapons. I hesitated, then shook my head. I had my own weapon, and it was more powerful than any bullet.

"You'll regret it."

But he shrugged and began to load shells into a pump-action shotgun. There was little other sound. The red cloaks might be on their way up, but they remained eerily quiet.

I rubbed my arms, felt the sticky warmth, and glanced down. The red cloak's bullet had done little more than wing me, but it bled profusely. If they *were* a type of vampire, then the wound—or rather the blood—would call to them.

"That blood might call to more than just those red cloaks," he added, obviously noticing my actions. "There're some bandages in the drawer of the table holding the coffeepot. Use them."

I walked over to the drawer. "I doubt there's anything worse than those red cloaks out on the streets at the moment."

He glanced at me, expression unreadable. "Then you'd be wrong."

I frowned, but opened the drawer and found a tube of antiseptic along with the bandages. As medical kits went, it was pretty basic, but I guess it was better than nothing. I applied both, then moved to stand in the middle of the UV circle, close enough to Sam that his aftershave—a rich mix of woody, earthy scents and musk—teased my nostrils and stirred memories to life. I thrust them away and crossed my arms.

"How can these things be a type of vampire?" I asked, voice a little sharper than necessary. "Either you are or you aren't. There's not really an in-between state, unless you're in the process of turning from human to vamp."

And those things in the cloaks were neither dead *nor* turning.

"It's a long story," he said. "And one I'd rather not go into right now."

"Then at least tell me what they're called."

"We've nicknamed them red cloaks. What they call themselves is anyone's guess." His shoulder brushed mine as he turned, and a tremor ran down my body. I hadn't felt this man's touch for five years, but my senses remembered it. Remembered the joy it had once given me.

"So why are they after you?"

His short, sharp laugh sent a shiver down my spine. It

was the sound of a man who'd seen too much, been through too much, and it made me wonder just what the hell had happened to him in the last five years.

"They hunt me because I've vowed to kill as many of the bastards as I can."

The chance to ask any more questions was temporarily cut off as the red cloaks ran through the door. They were so damn fast that they were halfway across the room before Sam could even get a shot off. I took a step back, my fingers aflame, the yellow-white light flaring oddly against the violet.

The front one ran at Sam with outstretched fingers, revealing nails that were grotesque talons ready to rip and tear. The red cloak hit the UV light, and instantly his skin began to blacken and burn. The stench was horrific, clogging the air and making my stomach churn, but he didn't seem to notice, let alone care. He just kept on running.

The others were close behind.

Sam fired. The bullet hit the center of the first red cloak's forehead, and the back of his head exploded, spraying those behind him with flesh and bone and brain matter.

He fell. The others leapt over him, their skin aflame and not caring one damn bit.

Which was obviously why Sam had said my own flame wouldn't help.

He fired again. Another red cloak went down. He tried to fire a third time, but the creature was too close, too fast. It battered him aside and kept on running.

It wanted *me*, not Sam. As I'd feared, the blood was calling to them.

I backpedaled fast, raised my hands, and released my fire. A maelstrom of heat rose before me, hitting the creature hard, briefly halting his progress and adding to the flames already consuming him.

My backside hit wood. The table. As the creature pushed through the flames, I scrambled over the top of it, then thrust it into the creature's gut. He screamed, the sound one of frustration rather than pain, and clawed at the air, trying to strike me with arms that dripped flames and flesh onto the surface of the table.

The *wooden* table.

As another shot boomed across the stinking, burning darkness, I lunged for the nearest table leg. I gripped it tight, then heaved with all my might. I might be only five foot four, but I wasn't human and I had a whole lot of strength behind me. The leg sheared free—and just in time.

The creature leapt at me. I twisted around and swung the leg with all my might. It smashed into the creature's head, caving in his side and battering him back across the table.

A final gunshot rang out, and the rest of the creature's head went spraying across the darkness. His body hit the concrete with a splat and slid past the glow of the UV, burning brightly in the deeper shadows crowding the room beyond.

I scrambled upright and held the leg at the ready. But there were no more fiery forms left to fight. We were safe.

For several seconds I did nothing more than stare at the remnants still being consumed by the UV's fire. The rank, bitter smell turned my stomach, and the air was thick with the smoke of them. Soon there was little left other than ash, and even that broke down into nothingness.

I lowered my hands and turned my gaze to the man I'd come here to rescue. "What the hell is going on here, Sam?"

He put the safety on the gun, then tossed it on the bed and stalked toward me. "Did they bite you? Scratch you?"

I frowned. "No—"

He grabbed my arms, his skin so cool against mine. It hadn't always been that way. Once, his flesh had matched mine for heat and urgency, especially when we were making love— I stopped the thought in its tracks. It never paid to live in the past. I knew that from long experience.

"Are you sure?" He turned my hands over and then grabbed my face with his oh-so-cool fingers, turning it one way and then another. There was concern in the blue of his eyes. Fear, even.

For *me*.

It made that stupid part of me deep inside want to dance, and *that* annoyed me even more than his nonanswers.

"I'm fine." I jerked away from his touch and stepped back. "But you really need to tell me what the hell is going on here."

He snorted and spun away, walking across to the coffeemaker. He poured two cups without asking, then walked back and handed the chip-free one to me.

"This, I'm afraid, has become the epicenter of hell on earth." His voice was as grim as his expression.

"Which is about as far from an answer as you can get," I snapped, then took a sip of coffee. I hated coffee— especially when it was thick and bitter—and he knew that. But he didn't seem to care and, right then, neither did I. I just needed something warm to ease the growing chill from my flesh. The immediate danger to Sam might be over, but there was still something *very* wrong. With this situation, and with this man. "What the hell were those things if not vampires?"

He studied me for a moment, his expression closed. "Officially they're known as the red plague but, as I said, we call them red cloaks. They're humans infected by a virus nicknamed Crimson Death. It can be transmitted via a scratch or a bite."

"So if they wound you, you become just like them?"

A bleak darkness I didn't understand stirred through the depths of his blue eyes. "If you're human or vampire, yes."

I frowned. "Why just humans and vampires? Why not other races?"

"It may *yet* affect other races. There are some shifters who seem to be immune as long as they change shape immediately after being wounded, but this doesn't hold true in all cases. More than that?" He shrugged. "The virus is too new to be really certain of anything."

Which certainly explained why he'd examined me so quickly for wounds. Although given I could take fire form and literally burn away any drug or virus in my system, it was doubtful *this* virus would have any effect.

"So you've been assigned to some sort of task force to hunt down and kill these things?"

Again he shrugged. "Something like that."

Annoyance swirled, but I shoved it back down. It wouldn't get me anywhere—he'd always been something of a closed shop when it came to his work as a detective. I guess that was one thing that *hadn't* changed. "Is this virus a natural development or a lab-born one?"

"Lab born."

"Who in their right mind would want to create this sort of virus?"

"They didn't mean to create it. It's a by-product of sorts." He took a sip of his coffee, his gaze still on mine. There was little in it to give away what he was thinking, but it oddly reminded me of the look vampires got when they were holding themselves under tight control. He added, "They were actually trying to pin down the enzymes that turn human flesh into vampire and make them immortal."

"Why the hell would anyone want to be immortal? Or near immortal? It sucks. Just ask the vampires."

A smile, brief and bitter, twisted his features. "Human-kind has a long history in chasing immortality. I doubt the testimony of vampires—many of whom are unbelievably rich thanks to that near immortality—would convince them otherwise."

"More fool them," I muttered. Living forever had its drawbacks. As did rebirth, which was basically what vampires went through to become near immortal. But then, humans rarely considered the side effects when they chased a dream.

I took another drink of coffee and shuddered at the tarlike aftertaste. How long had this stuff been brewing? I walked across to the small sink and dumped the remainder of it down the drain, then turned to face him again. "How did this virus get loose? This sort of research would have been top secret, and that usually comes with strict operational conditions."

"It did. Does. Unfortunately, one scientist decided to test a promising serum on himself after what appeared to be successful trials on lab rats. No one realized what he'd done until *after* he went crazy and, by that time, the genie was out of the bottle."

And on the streets, obviously. "How come there's been no public warning about this? Surely people have a right to know—"

"Yeah, great idea," he cut in harshly. "Warn the general population a virus that turns people into insane, vampirelike beings has been unleashed. Can you imagine the hysteria that would cause?"

And I guess it wouldn't do a whole lot of good to the image of actual vampires, either. It would also, no doubt, lead to an influx of recruits to the many gangs dedicated to wiping the stain of nonhumanity from Earth.

I studied him for a moment. For all the information he was giving me, I had an odd sense that he wasn't telling me everything. "The red cloaks who were chasing you acted as one, and with a purpose. That speaks of a hive-type mentality rather than insanity to me."

He shrugged. "The virus doesn't *always* lead to insanity, and not everyone who is infected actually survives. Those who do, do so with varying degrees of change and sanity."

I frowned. "How widespread is this virus? Because if tonight is any example, there's more than just a *few* surviving it."

"About sixty percent of those infected die. So far, the virus is mostly confined to this area. We suspect there's about one hundred or so cloaks."

Which to me sounded like a serious outbreak. It also explained the patrols around this area. They weren't keeping the peace—they were keeping people *out* and the red cloaks *in*. "And everyone who survives the virus is infectious?"

"Yes."

It was just one word, but it was said with such bitterness and anger that my eyebrows rose. "Did someone close to you get infected? Is that why you swore to hunt them all down?"

He smiled, but it wasn't a pleasant thing to behold. Far from it. "You could say that. Remember my brother?"

I remembered him, all right—he wasn't only the first child his mom had been able to carry to full term after a long series of miscarriages, but the firstborn *son*. And, as such, had never really been denied anything. He'd grown up accustomed to getting what he wanted, and I'd barely even begun my relationship with Sam when he'd decided what he wanted was *me*. He certainly hadn't been happy about being rejected. Sam, as far as I knew, was not aware that his older brother had tried to seduce me, although there had been a definite cooling in their relationship afterward.

"Of course I remember Luke—but what has he got to do with anything?"

"He was one of the first victims of a red cloak attack in Brooklyn."

If he'd been living in Brooklyn, it could only mean he'd truly immersed himself in the life of criminality he'd been dabbling with when I'd known him.

"Oh god. I'm sorry, Sam. Is he okay? Did he survive?" I half reached out to touch his arm, then stilled the motion when I saw the bitter anger in his expression. It was aimed at himself rather than at me, and it all but screamed comfort was *not* something he wanted right now.

"Luke survived the virus, but his sanity didn't." The fury in Sam's eyes grew, but it was entwined with guilt and a deeper, darker emotion I couldn't define. But it was one that scared the hell out of me. "I was the one who took him down, Red."

No wonder he seemed surrounded by a haze of darkness and dangerous emotion—he'd been forced to shoot his own damn *brother*. "Sam, I'm sorry."

This time I *did* touch his arm, but he shook it off violently. "Don't be. He's far better off dead than—" He cut the rest of the sentence off and half shrugged. Like it didn't matter, when it obviously did.

"When did all this happen?"

"A little over a year ago."

And he'd changed greatly in that year, I thought, though I suspected the cause was far more than just the stress of Luke's death. "How the hell could something like this be kept a secret for so damn long?"

"Trust me, you wouldn't want to know."

A chill went through me. It wasn't so much the words, but the way he said them and the flatness in his eyes. I had no doubt those words were a warning of death, but even so, I couldn't help saying, "And what, exactly, does that mean?"

"It means you tell no one about tonight, or it could have disastrous consequences. For you and for them."

And there it was, I thought bitterly. Fate's kick in the gut. When would I ever learn to stop interfering with the natural course of events?

Sam stalked over to the bed, placing the shotgun in its slot and then picking up a regulation .40-caliber Glock semi-auto pistol—a partner to the one he already carried. "We need to get out of here."

"But I want to know—"

I stopped as his gaze pinned me and, with sudden, sad clarity, I realized there was very little left of the man I'd known in those rich blue depths. Only shadows and bitterness. I might have saved him tonight, but the reality was I'd been about twelve months too late. This was nothing more than a replica. He might look the same, he might smell the same, but he held none of the fierce joy of life that had once called to me like flame to a moth. This man's world had become one of ashes and darkness, and it was not a place where I wanted to linger.

"Let's go," he said.

"Don't bother, Sam."

He briefly looked confused. It was the second real expression I'd seen—the first being that moment of surprise when he'd realized who'd saved him. "What do you mean?"

I walked across to him. Ashes or not, he still resembled the man I'd never get over—not in this lifetime, anyway—and it was hard not to lean into him. Hard not to give in to the desire to kiss him good-bye, just one more time.

"I'm one of them, remember?" Bitterness crept into my voice. "One of the monsters. And I'm more than capable of looking after myself."

He snorted softly, the sound harsh. "Not in this damn area, and maybe not against the—"

"I got in here without harm," I cut in, voice as cold as his, "and I'll damn well get out the same way."

"Fine." He stepped aside and waved me forward with the barrel of the gun. "Be my guest."

I looked at him for a moment longer, then walked toward the door. But as I neared it, I hesitated and turned around. "I don't know what has happened to you, Sam Turner, but I'm mighty glad you're no longer in my life."

And with that lie lingering in the air, I left him to his bitterness and shadows and went home.